"How ma[ny]... been in?"

"Depends on what you consider a relationship."

"Have you ever been with someone you thought would go the distance?" Like Deet.

Travis's long silence revealed there must have been.

She moved her head to see his profile. He had long blond lashes and his blue-gold eyes glowed in the dim light.

"Have you?" he countered.

He didn't want to talk about the woman who'd surely meant enough for him to go the distance, but for some reason hadn't worked out.

"I've had a few relationships," she said. "None where I fell madly in love, though."

His gaze moved from her eyes to her mouth and back again. She let her head relax a little more against him, bringing her mouth closer to his. A few seconds later, he closed the distance between them and kissed her. Her heart surged with excitement and responding desire. Heat erupted out of nowhere.

A loud ripping noise broke them apart. The freight train was in the cottage. The roof above them broke apart with a sickening sound and sailed away. Rain and debris poured down upon them. Raeleen screamed.

JENNIFER MOREY

Two-time 2009 RITA® Award nominee and a Golden Quill winner for Best First Book for *The Secret Soldier,* Jennifer Morey writes contemporary romance and romance suspense. Project manager du jour, she works for the space systems segment of a satellite imagery and information company. She lives in sunny Denver, Colorado. She can be reached through her website, www.jennifermorey.com, and on Facebook.

JENNIFER MOREY

Seducing the Colonel's Daughter

HARLEQUIN®

entertain, enrich, inspire™

Recycling programs
for this product may
not exist in your area.

ISBN-13: 978-0-373-27788-9

SEDUCING THE COLONEL'S DAUGHTER

Copyright © 2012 by Jennifer Morey

THE SECRET SOLDIER

Copyright © 2008 by Jennifer Morey

www.Harlequin.com

Printed in U.S.A.

CONTENTS

Dear Reader,

It's been a while since Travis Todd has been on a mission. He's overdue, don't you think? He was shot protecting Haley Engen in *Unmasking the Mercenary,* but now he's back and fully recovered—just in time to rescue popular food-network show host Raeleen Randall.

Big, intimidating and looking for the right woman, Travis has met his match in Raeleen…if he can seduce her into forgetting her rule about men who work for her father, the secret colonel who backs Tactical Executive Security—the infamous counterterror organization that is All McQueen's Men. Will Travis be able to convince her there's more to him than being one of TES's most daring secret solders? Read on and find out!

Thank you, dear readers, for requesting Travis's story. Here it is! Get cozy and enjoy.

Jennie

Seducing the
Colonel's Daughter

For my mother, Joan Morey.

February 11, 1937–July 8, 1997.

Chapter 1

One of the heavy wooden double doors slid shut as Raeleen Randall stepped out of the restaurant in a daze. Incredulous. Humiliated. Appalled. Mad as hell. All did a good job of summing up how she felt right now. Strangely missing from that mix was…hurt. Grappling with why had her in a tailspin. Why wasn't her heart breaking into pieces? Numbly, she started toward her rental car, vaguely aware of the scattering of clouds gathering amidst a mid-September Caribbean day.

Dietrich Artz was married. Deet. The man she'd been traveling to Anguilla to see every month for the past year had seemed perfect for her. Never crowding her. Never bossing her around. He didn't remind her of her father. He was a nice guy. Accommodating…or so she'd thought. Oh, he'd been accommodating, all right—to meet his own selfish needs. The man she'd thought might work out enough to actually marry was…already married.

Why wasn't her chest constricting with the emotional wreckage of pain that surely ought to accompany such a betrayal? Was it her busy schedule? As the host of a popular Dining Network show, she was very busy. The long-distance relationship suited her hectic life. Or had it? Deet had been undemanding, a quality that had drawn her to him and kept her coming back. Had her preoccupation with *Pop's Place* dulled the intensity of her emotional investment? After finding out he was married, she wasn't going to miss him. Was that because he'd lied to her, or was it just that she didn't *feel* enough for him to care?

Seeing that she'd passed her car and was almost to the end of the empty parking lot now, Raeleen stopped and turned around, a slight breeze ruffling her shoulder-length blond hair. The restaurant was closed, but Deet was going to make her breakfast before her flight home. Instead, she'd met his wife.

Where had she gone wrong? When had she lost sight of her needs? When had her needs taken a backseat to her fun, fast-paced career with *Pop's Place?* And above all, why did she think she had to settle for undemanding? Her show was demanding. Why shouldn't her needs from a man be equally demanding?

She could argue that maintaining a long-distance relationship with someone who lived on an island was demanding enough, but it was his distance that she'd liked. And that's what bothered her. Was she afraid of commitment? Her? Dining Network star. Cheeseburger addict. Daughter of the almighty Colonel Roth. It baffled her to consider the possibility.

Walking between her car and the minivan parked one space over, she dug into her purse for the keys.

If there were any lesson to be learned here, it was that things had to change. *She* had to change. No more men until she knew what she wanted. Really knew. Because clearly she didn't.

Where were those blasted keys!

Digging harder, she finally pulled them from her purse, just as the side door of the minivan slid open. Who would be at Artz Eatery on a day that it was closed? Too distracted to ponder that for long, she fumbled for the key fob and pressed the button to unlock the door. Just as she did that, a man appeared next to her. The person who'd just gotten out of the minivan. He was average in height, with light brown hair and brown eyes that seemed full of crazed energy.

Alarm made her pay more attention. Was he a fan?

Just when she was going to ask him what he wanted, he lifted his hand and stabbed her arm with a needle. A needle?

Raeleen screamed and dropped her purse as she twisted away. He let go of the needle and reached for her. She threw the keys at his face and yanked the half-empty needle out of her arm. Staring down at it, her vision blurred and she began to feel woozy.

Oh, my God! What had he injected into her, and why?

Horrified, she threw the needle over the top of the rental car. Catching her off guard, the man grabbed her other arm and roughly pivoted her, bringing her back against him. He wrapped his arms around her then, trapping her as he forced her toward the open door of the minivan. Screaming her fear, weaker this time—like in a bad dream—she fought him, dug her feet in resistance and tried to wiggle free of his arms, but whatever drug he'd given her made her too sluggish. Everything her father had taught her was useless now. Releasing her arms, he pushed her hard. She tripped over the edge of the open doorframe, falling into the minivan. As she tried to regain her balance, he lifted her by the waist and propelled her all the way inside. She fell onto the backseat. Kicking her legs, she was only able to graze him a couple of times before he slid the door shut.

She propped herself up, her head spinning madly. Fighting all-out panic, she saw the man come around to the driver's side and get in. What the hell was going on? Who was he, and why was he kidnapping her? Was he a rapist? An unstable fan? More frightened than ever, she fought to sit up. Her arms felt like Jell-O. What had he given her? Was she dying?

The minivan began to move. Raeleen thought she'd lose consciousness but didn't. The man probably had intended for that to happen. Luckily, she'd stopped him from administering the entire dose. She didn't know how much time had passed before the minivan stopped, but she didn't think it was long. Anguilla wasn't a big island. Maybe it had been long enough. The drug's intensity didn't seem quite as strong.

The door slid open.

Raeleen let the man pull her to a sitting position and then wrap his arm around her waist to help her outside.

"Who are you?" she asked.

When he didn't reply, she wondered if he hadn't understood her. She thought she'd spoken clearly but couldn't be sure. He leaned her against the minivan to close the door. She moved toward the rear, hip and hands on the vehicle to keep herself upright. The drug still lingered.

He took hold of her arm and steered her forward.

"Why are you doing this?"

He remained focused on the direction in which he guided her.

She took in her topsy-turvy surroundings. There was a house and a lighthouse, the sea whitecapping beyond. There were no other buildings visible from here. She looked toward the angry sea again and recalled the weather forecast.

A hurricane was headed this way. She was supposed to be off the island before it hit.

"Why are you doing this?" she repeated more urgently, her head clearing a little more.

"Nothing will happen to you if your lover does what we ask."

"Deet?" What did Dietrich have to do with this?

She had to get away.

Yanking free of his grasp, she did her best to pivot and run. The ground bounced wildly. She stumbled and fell, landing hard on her knees and forearms.

"Ouch!" Rolling onto her back, she slapped his reaching hands.

He grabbed her and hauled her to her feet. She drove her knee into his stomach.

Grunting, he took hold of both her wrists. She kicked his leg. Kicked again, and that time he dodged her. Finally, he whirled her around and wrenched both hands up behind her back until her arms hurt.

"Hey!" she yelled indignantly, wiggling her shoulders and trying to loosen the strain.

Ignoring her, he forced her toward the lighthouse, shoving her when she resisted.

"What are you doing?" She wished her head wasn't so fuzzy.

Another shove hurt her arms.

"Watch it!" she yelled.

"Keep moving."

She had to make him listen to her. "Whatever you're planning to do, you're going to regret it. My father will send men for me. If you hurt me at all, they'll track you down and kill you." She slurred a little, but at least she could talk now. The effect of the drug might be wearing off. He hadn't been able to give her the full dose. Maybe that would work in her favor.

When that didn't elicit a response from him, she persisted. "You don't know my father. He's a colonel. And not just any colonel. He runs a secret military operation." She twisted her neck to see him. "No one knows it exists, but it's very powerful. My father is a very powerful man. You're in a lot of trouble if you don't listen to me."

He looked straight ahead and didn't acknowledge her.

"The men he hires are special-forces types. SEAL. Delta. CIA. Some of them are even ex-mercenaries."

Now his gaze lowered to meet hers.

"Yeah. That's right. Mercenaries. I'd think twice about whatever you're planning to do. Let me go now and I'll make sure nothing happens to you."

"Shut up." Shoving her toward the door of the lighthouse, he made her trip and sent pain shooting through her still-bound arms as she righted herself.

Panic welled up in her. He didn't believe her. Who would? Sometimes even she thought her father was a figment of her imagination.

Holding both her wrists with one of his hands, he opened the lighthouse door.

"My cameraman is expecting me at the airport." She tried to tug her wrists from his hand. "What do you think he's going to do when I don't show up?" When she'd hired him she'd given him explicit instructions if anything happened to her. "He's going to call my father. And then my father is going to call someone very dangerous. Someone with the resources to come get me...and take care of you."

"I said shut up!"

He forced her through the door and up the first flight of winding stairs. If it weren't for the pain in her arms, she'd fight harder.

"Let me go and we can forget about this. I'll tell my father that I'm okay." While she detested Tactical Executive Services for stealing him from her, she never disputed that what he did stood for a good cause. And TES was very powerful. Best if this man understood he'd be better off if one of its secret men weren't unleashed.

She tripped on the stairs and he held her upright. "If you don't believe me, do an internet search on the name Cullen McQueen." He'd read about Cullen rescuing Sabine, now his wife, and nothing more, but it would be enough. "That's who's going to send men here after my father hears that I'm missing." She was probably revealing too much, but she was really scared. She had to make him understand what he was in for if he continued down whatever path he'd laid for himself.

"If you don't shut up now, I'll kill you."

And then there'd be no point in sending anyone to rescue her, would there? "You're a dead man, either way." Her father would definitely have him killed if he murdered her. There would be nowhere he could hide.

They reached another door, this one open.

"I'm a dead man if I don't do this."

Releasing her wrists, he pushed her hard. She stumbled through the doorway and fell, sprawling onto the wood floor as she heard the door close behind her.

Raeleen scrambled to her feet and went to the door, gripping the handle. Locked from the outside.

"You better listen to me, you stinking pig! My father will hunt you down like the hog you are and kill you! You think I'm making this up? You wait and see!"

All she heard were his fading footsteps as he descended the stairs.

"Let me go!" she screamed.

Only silence followed.

* * *

Travis Todd stepped out of the jet near Roaring Creek, Colorado. Cullen McQueen had called and asked to meet there. The short notice and Cullen's urgency told him this would be a special mission. He'd worked for Cullen ever since the agency's inception. He was accustomed to calls like that, the ones that had him dropping what he was doing and flying to this private airstrip. The woman he was going to take out to lunch hadn't been all that happy when he'd called to cancel. He wouldn't be surprised if she told him she was no longer interested after he finished this assignment, whatever it was.

All he knew was some woman had disappeared in Anguilla and he had to find her. It wouldn't be the first time he'd been asked to extract someone. That was the reason Cullen had called him. He was experienced and more than ready for action.

Seeing Cullen get out of a big, black SUV with dark tinted windows, Travis walked over to him and shook his hand. "Got yourself a new SUV, huh?"

"Yeah, my daughter is getting popular in town. I need the room to cart all the kids around."

Picturing a man like Cullen carting kids to birthday parties was as amusing as it was awe-inspiring. If he could do it, so could Travis. The right woman hadn't come along yet, that's all.

"How is Sabine?" he asked.

Cullen's daring rescue of his wife from Afghanistan was legendary among TES operatives.

"Good. Bookstore is staying afloat, and she's talking about having another kid."

"You're a lucky man." The women Travis encountered either shied away from his towering frame or needed more time from him. He was a big man like Cullen, but Cullen had the advantage of working right here in Roaring Creek, across the street from his wife's bookstore. Travis couldn't see himself staying so stationary all the time. He needed a woman who felt the same. Someone strong and independent, but no one he met on assignment. A mission had to be just that. A mission. Nothing drove that home for him more than his last one.

"Sometimes I wonder. Sabine can be quite a handful at times."

The best kind of woman. "You were pretty vague on the phone." Enough small talk. "Why am I taking a vacation to Anguilla?"

"The missing woman is Colonel Roth's daughter. Colonel Roth is my boss. And that's classified."

Travis had to take a second to dissect Cullen's declaration, a loaded one at that. Everyone who worked for TES knew Cullen had high-ranking government officials backing his organization. Cullen never spoke of them. He never spoke of the man he frequently met, and he kept those meetings—and the identity of the man—a closely guarded secret. One Travis had discovered long ago and kept to himself. Now the very colonel who made TES possible had tasked Cullen to rescue his daughter.

He glanced around at the chilly mountain landscape, finding Cullen's version of a secure place to disclose classified information amusing.

Nothing like a little pressure. What if the woman were already dead? "What's her name?"

Cullen handed him a sealed folder. "Everything you need is in here."

Travis took it from him.

"I don't think I have to tell you how important this assignment is."

Fantastic. "I'll find her." Dead or alive, he'd find her.

"I know I can count on you. I'd have removed you from another assignment to send you. You're the only one I want down there."

"I'm flattered, especially after what happened with Haley." Haley Engen was another operative that Cullen had frequently partnered him with because he knew Travis would keep her safe. She had enough trauma in her past, and Cullen hadn't wanted any more harm to come to her. Travis had a background full of rescue experience, except things with Haley hadn't gone all that well.

"You would have been shot on that mission with or without Haley."

When he and Haley had been followed and the tires of their Jeep were shot out, he'd spun the vehicle so that the driver's side would take the bullets. Had he been alone, he wouldn't have done that. He would have been able to take out the attackers. He'd done his job. He'd protected Haley. And he'd do it again if he had to. But there was a big difference between rescuing a package and having her for a partner. He'd thought of Haley as a package. That had been his mistake. It's what had distracted him enough to miss being followed until it was too late.

"You've done more extractions than anyone else, and you have a zero failure rate," Cullen went on. "You're the best man for the job."

Travis wondered if that was more of a handicap than an attribute. There was a reason he'd gotten this good. One he didn't talk about.

"You sure you're back to full health?" Cullen asked.

"I've told you more than once that I am. I've been ready to get back into it for months now."

"You needed refresher training."

Cullen had insisted he train like a new operative. He had run him through a program that had him stronger than he was before he was shot. But that was Cullen. He cared more about the welfare of his men than he did about the importance of an assignment.

"If she's alive, I'll bring her back," Travis said, and he watched as Cullen read his meaning.

"I'd sure hate to have to tell Colonel Roth that his daughter is dead."

He didn't doubt that. "Like I said. If she's alive…"

Cullen smiled wryly and looked toward a waiting plane on the airstrip. "That'll get you where you need to be by late afternoon or dinnertime. You have a car and hotel reservations for the next three nights. Odie set it all up."

"Of course she did." Odelia Frank was TES's number-one intel officer. She'd finally broken down and married Jag Benney, an ex-Delta man like Cullen and the type of man she'd vowed to never end up with again after the death of her first husband, who'd also been an operative. If TES wasn't such a secret organization, a soap opera could be written about its personnel. Travis wanted no part of that script.

Just when he was going to ask about gear, Cullen said, "Everything you need is on board. And you've got clearance when you get there, so take whatever you think will be necessary."

That would save him a lot of time. "Tell Odie thanks for me."

"You don't have to thank her. She knows who Roth is, remember?"

Right. And now he did. Nothing like a little pressure. Giving Cullen a salute, he turned and headed for the plane and saw a stewardess waiting at the top of the stairs. One thing Odie was good at was making his job as easy as possible. Logistics rarely got in the way.

"Contact me as soon as you know something," Cullen called after him.

"Will do," he answered over his shoulder.

"Oh, and just so you know, there's a hurricane on its way to Anguilla."

Incredulous, Travis stopped at the bottom of the stairs and faced Cullen.

"Helga," Cullen said with an cynical grin. "You might not make it out before she hits. Odie said the airport will probably close before the night is over."

Fantastic. "Thanks for the warning."

"Should only be a Category 3, maybe 4."

"Is that all?"

Cullen held up his hand and turned for his vehicle.

Climbing the stairs, Travis nodded to the woman there. She went about closing the door and he took a seat.

He pulled out a folder from the envelope Cullen had given him. The first thing he saw was a picture of a stunning woman. After choking on a sip of water and noticing the stewardess look back at him, he looked again at the photo.

She was standing on a deck at the top of three shallow steps leading to the lush landscape of a yard, her hand curled around a post. Blooming clematis tangled over a lattice rail. Thick blond hair fell wispy around her face to her shoulders, and sparkling blue eyes smiled at whoever had taken the shot. She had a wide, toothy smile that showcased her beauty. Tall and leggy, she wore a black sundress that came to the top of her drool-worthy thighs, and the dress had a scooped neckline where subtle cleavage teased.

He placed the photo facedown on the open folder and read the report on the next page. Host for the hit show *Pop's Place,* she featured family restaurants passed down from generation to generation. She had a public job, which struck him as odd given her supersecret father's ties to TES. He imagined that must be an issue from time to time.

She lived in New York City. Not married. No kids. Traveled to Anguilla a lot, this time to shoot an episode. She had a cottage on the island, so she hadn't stayed at the same hotel as her crew. She was having an affair with a restaurateur. Dietrich Artz, or "Deet" as she called him, owner of Artz Eatery. Landon, her cameraman, said she'd called early this morning to let him know she was going to have breakfast with Deet at his restaurant before meeting him at the airport. Now she wasn't answering her phone.

Odie had included a quick and brief background report on Deet, complete with photos of him and his wife and brother-in-law. Married...

He wondered if Raeleen knew that.

Her name was Vivian. She had parents and a brother on the island. Deet's parents were deceased. He and Vivian had no kids. Deet had taken over the restaurant when his father developed cancer. His mother had died of breast cancer a few years earlier. Artz Eatery had been in business for twenty years.

No motive from what he could see, yet. Odie's handwritten note said she was still gathering financial information. If there was a motive, they'd probably find it there. The last of the details in the report included Raeleen's address and home phone, cell and passport numbers.

He turned over the photo of Raeleen and stared at the picture again. Figures, his first assignment after recovering would involve a successful, beautiful woman. The irony killed him. The last woman to captivate him like that was his partner on his previous assignment. This one was none other than Colonel Roth's daughter. She probably didn't have a vulnerable bone in her amazing body. He'd go in, get her and bring her home. Mission accomplished. Nothing would deter him from that.

* * *

Travis drove his rental past Artz Eatery. The small parking lot was empty except for one car. Turning into an alley that ran alongside the building, he parked near a loading dock in the back. There were two more cars back here.

Reaching over to his duffel bag on the passenger seat, he lifted out his Mark 23 and tucked it behind him in the waist of his jeans. Getting out of the car, he made sure his short-sleeved dark blue shirt hung over the weapon. He noticed the lack of activity in the area and remembered Hurricane Helga was on the way. Looking up at the sky, he saw that the clouds were growing much heavier. A strong breeze lifted his dark blond hair. He didn't have much time before the storm reached land.

Going to the back door, Travis tested the knob and found it unlocked. Opening the door, he listened and heard nothing. All clear. He entered the kitchen.

Two rows of stainless-steel counters filled the cramped space. Pots and pans hung above ovens and ranges along the adjacent wall. Only a few lights were on. He moved to the entrance of the dining area, cracking open one of the double swinging doors. The room was quiet and still. With the overcast sky and sparse lighting, it was dim.

The doors swung closed as he walked forward. Old stools lined a bar to the left. Bottles packed glass shelving, and beer taps jutted out in the center of the bar. Four bistro tables with fake pink flowers were partially hidden by a half wall.

In the dining room, chairs were placed up on the tables... all but one. There, two chairs were on the floor, tipped on their sides. And among them, two feet. A woman. He hurried over, fearing he'd discover the colonel's daughter. But as he got closer, it was clear that this woman wasn't Raeleen. He knelt beside her. Seeing her face now, he recognized her as Deet's wife from the report Odie had put together. While questions began firing away in his head, he felt for a pulse.

Nothing. But her skin was still warm.

Whoever had killed her could still be here. Travis stood, scanning the empty restaurant.

Hearing a sound in the kitchen, he quietly pulled the slide back on his pistol, ready to fire now. He went to the double swinging doors and pushed one open. Seeing nothing, he entered, moving in a circle with his pistol aimed.

A man sprang up from behind the far row of stainless-steel counters and Travis ran after him. The man reached the back door. Travis pushed it shut and punched the man's kidney. He yelped and slid in pain to the floor, leaning against the door.

Travis straddled him and aimed the pistol at his head.

"Don't shoot!" the man pleaded, holding up one hand as if to ward off a bullet.

That's when Travis recognized him from the file on Raeleen.

"You're John Rey, Vivian's brother."

The man stared up at him with intensifying fear. "Who are you?"

Crouching, Travis patted the man's pants, checking for a weapon. Finding none, he let John push himself up to stand against the door. But he wasn't ready to let him try to sneak outside.

"Give me your car keys, and go stand over there." Travis gestured toward the counters.

John dug into his front pocket, where Travis had felt the keys, and handed them over. He moved to the nearest counter.

"What do you want?" John asked. "Are you the one who killed my sister?"

So, he'd only just arrived like him. He must have hidden in the kitchen.

"I'm looking for Raeleen Randall. Do you know where she is?"

With the mention of Raeleen, John's eyes popped wide with a fresh wave of fear.

Travis stepped closer, intending to intimidate the man. It wasn't hard. John whimpered and cringed away, easily overpowered. Too easily. This was no professional. Had Vivian's killer kidnapped Raeleen? Surely it couldn't have been this man. And yet, he clearly knew something.

"Where is she?" Travis demanded.

"I'm not the one you want." John's voice quivered.

"Where is she?" he repeated.

"D-did her father send you? S-she told me about her father. Look, we can make a deal."

Travis went still. "If she told you about her father, I might have to kill you." He wouldn't, but the scare tactic seemed to be working.

"No! Please." John had trouble catching his breath. "I—I thought she was lying." He leaned backward as though trying to get away, putting his hands on the edge of the counter. "Please…I—I had no choice."

No choice in what? Kidnapping Raeleen? Then who had killed Vivian? And why? "Where is she? I won't ask you again." Travis put the gun against John's forehead.

"Please, mister. They killed my sister.…" He began to sob. "My sister…" He turned his head, trying to escape the gun.

"Who?"

The man only sobbed wretchedly.

"Who killed your sister, and where is Raeleen?" He was done messing around. He needed answers. Now.

"I—"

Just as the man began to compose himself and Travis was sure he'd become a fountain of information, a sound he knew too well interrupted. Silenced gunfire. John slumped against him. Travis took his weight, dropping the keys and dragging John quickly behind the protection of the industrial kitchen counter. He lowered John down to the floor just as another bullet pinged.

John was having trouble breathing, this time not from fear. He reached for Travis, his eyes large with disbelief and horror.

"Hang on," Travis told him. "Just hang on."

Remaining crouched, he moved past John to the edge of the counter and peered around the corner of the metal cabinet, gun ready. The double doors swung shut and he heard chairs toppling. He emerged from cover, jogging to the kitchen entry. There, he pushed one of the doors open to check the dining area.

The front door swung open and a shadowy figure slipped outside. Travis followed, peering out into the darkening night. Whoever had shot the dead woman's brother jumped into a car that was already screeching away from where it had been parked in the street. Two. Three. Four men.

Travis stepped outside and aimed for the rear right tire. Return fire ruined his aim, forcing him to duck behind a huge planter outside the front entry. The car vanished down the street. Cursing, Travis checked for witnesses before going back into the restaurant. Not seeing any, he locked the front door behind him and hurried into the kitchen.

Behind the counter, he knelt beside John Rey. His eyes were open and blood ran down one side of his mouth as he struggled to breathe. Blood pooled underneath and around him. Too much blood.

Travis cursed and reached for his cell phone to ask Odie

to call the local police. He couldn't do it himself. He didn't have time to answer their questions. He had to find Raeleen.

John lifted his hand weakly and stopped him. He muttered something unintelligible.

Travis leaned closer. "One more time, buddy."

He gurgled something that sounded like "Nighthawk."

"What was that?" Nighthawk? What did it mean?

John's eyes rolled and a final breath left him. Silence filled the kitchen.

Travis felt for a pulse. There was none. He'd seen death enough times to know when it was useless to try to revive someone. Regretfully, he closed the man's eyes. Whatever John Rey had gotten himself into, he wasn't the bad guy. Neither was his sister. Was Deet? Travis hadn't gotten a good enough look at the men inside the car that had sped away. John had kidnapped his brother-in-law's lover for a reason. Raeleen was leverage for something. Why or how, Travis couldn't begin to guess.

Looking away from John's dead face, his gaze landed on the car keys, where he'd dropped them on the floor. A charm hung from the ring. A lighthouse.

Lighthouse, not Nighthawk. John had tried to tell him something.

Chapter 2

The sound of heavy boot steps made Raeleen stop pacing the small confines of the lighthouse service room. Who could it be? Was it that man again? She didn't think so. He was small and wouldn't make that much noise. She probably wouldn't have even heard him over the wind. She searched for any type of weapon. There was nothing more than a few essentials—dry food, bottled water, a portable toilet. Her kidnapper had obviously planned to leave her here through the hurricane.

She'd tried to kick the door down and yelled for help, but to no avail. The horrible sounds outside strung her nerves into a tight live wire. Black clouds had disappeared with the setting sun, and the storm had gathered intensity. With each beam of rotating light from the lantern room above, she got a glimpse of the angry sea. Talk about unsettling.

The boot steps stopped on the other side of the door. Her

heart thumped madly. She went to the portable toilet, removed the empty plastic bag and folded the frame.

Seconds later, the door was kicked in. Raeleen jumped and backed up until the wall stopped her, lifting the toilet frame above her head, ready to strike.

The biggest man she'd ever seen entered, pistol drawn. From gigantic black boots, up the trunks of his thighs, to a thick, muscular torso and hulking arms, he was a spectacle. Tall and imposing. His dark blond hair was windblown, and his blue eyes met hers with unflinching alertness, a gold hint in them intriguing her.

"I'm here to bring you home," he announced. "My name is Travis Todd. Your father sent me."

Heaving a sigh of relief, she lowered her arms and dropped the toilet frame. "It's about time you got here."

He cocked his head, looking from the toilet frame to her face.

"Let's get out of here." She walked toward him. "Being locked in this lighthouse was pure torture with a hurricane on the way."

Stepping over splintered wood, she felt him take hold of her hand, bringing her to a halt.

"I can see the resemblance to your father, but I'll go first."

She wasn't anything like her father. Why was he saying that?

Before she could complain, he passed her on his way out the door, checking the stairway with his gun raised. She doubted her captor would still be here, but she allowed him the precaution and followed him down the stairs.

Outside, wind and pelting rain were much stronger than they had seemed from inside the lighthouse, and she stumbled against its force. Travis took hold of her hand again and pulled her toward a Jeep parked in the sopping-wet gravel driveway. Hearing the terrible roar of the sea crashing violently against the shore, she glanced back to see the churning mass eerily illuminated by the lighthouse.

"Oh, my God." She didn't even hear her own astonished murmur.

"We have to get farther inland," Travis shouted through wind and rain.

A small branch hit her head and she shrieked.

The rumble of another huge wave smashed the shoreline, this time reaching the lighthouse wall. An enormous spray of seawater exploded around it, and she felt a few stinging drops on her face. Something flew through the air. A piece of wood? It crashed through the lighthouse window.

"Oh, my God." She was just in there!

Travis gave her a tug and she ran the rest of the way to the Jeep. He opened the passenger door and cradled her effortlessly in his arms to dump her onto the seat. Slamming the door shut, he ran around to the other side and got in. Revving the engine, he jerked the vehicle into Drive and spun into a half circle, racing down the driveway and fishtailing onto the main road.

Raeleen grabbed hold of the door handle and watched leaves and branches and other unidentifiable objects fly across the beam of headlights. A section of someone's fence tumbled onto the road.

Travis swore as he swerved around it. "We aren't going to make it to town."

"No kidding." She white-knuckled the door handle.

He drove faster, dodging debris without slowing. He had to compensate for the force of the wind, manhandling the steering wheel. He must have had a lot of experience with this type of driving, she thought.

Another road came into view and she got an idea. Her cottage was one of the highest places on the island.

"Turn up here!" She pointed to the road.

His only response was to set his brow and mouth tersely. He slowed at the road and surveyed where it led first. She didn't have to tell him this was as good as any place on the island. They needed high ground.

He made the turn and sped up the Jeep. "What's here?"

"My cottage." This was the back way.

A huge tree branch fell in front of them. Another smaller one hit the roof of the Jeep. Raeleen screamed and put her free hand on the dash as Travis drove off the road to avoid the branch. Sparks from electric lines sprinkled the road as they passed.

Travis swore again, racing along the road, swerving to avoid more branches. He slid off into some mud and fish-tailed back onto the road. Raeleen hadn't let go of the door handle and braced her hand on the dash again.

"How much farther?" he shouted.

"Not far. The houses are just ahead. At the top of the hill."

Just then yet another branch came sailing out of the darkness. Travis braked and swerved to avoid it. Raeleen's seat belt kept her body from flying to the roof of the Jeep as he drove off the road. He narrowly missed a precariously leaning tree. They were thick through here, and he wasn't as lucky the next time. The Jeep crashed into the thick circumference of a palm tree and stalled. A blur of whipping branches and vegetation was obscured by sheets of rain in the headlights.

Travis tried to restart the Jeep, but only the headlights dimmed. The Jeep wouldn't start.

"We have to walk," he announced.

"Don't you mean run?"

"Run." He climbed out of the Jeep.

Raeleen got out on her side and fought the wind as she climbed toward the road. Travis was already there, a duffel bag looped over his massive shoulder. He took her hand and started jogging. Her boots splashed into the soggy ground.

"You're going the wrong way!" she yelled over the din of wind and whipping vegetation.

"I saw lights this way!"

"My cottage isn't that way!"

"It has to be!"

Glancing back, she couldn't see the road and couldn't remember if it curved in the direction he was headed.

A leafy branch swatted her shoulder and cheek. "Ouch!" She tripped and fell onto her hands and knees.

Travis lifted her by the waist as if she were a sack of dog food and righted her on her feet. A sudden gust of wind almost knocked her down again.

"Come on!" Travis grabbed her hand and ran.

At a fallen tree, he turned, quick and smooth, to lift her over it ahead of him. Then he grabbed her hand again and resumed running.

Buildings came into sight. Recognizing her cottage, she pointed. "It's that one!"

She'd chosen it for its partial view of the ocean. Like the other cottages along the street, all the windows were boarded. Her neighbor helped her with things like that. He helped her with all her maintenance issues.

Travis kept her hand and they reached her backyard. "I don't have my key!"

Without responding, he hauled her along the side of the cottage. At the front door, he crouched over his duffel bag and straightened with a key. Her key? How had he…?

He opened the door and she rushed in behind him. Water dripped to the floor from her hair and clothes, and her skin was drenched.

The walls vibrated from the wind, but it was quieter than being outside. After allowing some time to catch her breath, she turned. Travis stood facing her, holding his bag, listening to the wind slam against her cottage and probably mentally assessing the construction.

Typical of someone her father would send. What she hadn't expected was for him to be hot. She pictured men her father employed to have pocked skin, no hair and Neanderthal bodies. She drank this one in. His straight nose was proportioned with his strong jaw and cheekbones, his otherwise smooth skin peppered with manly stubble. He had a soft and kissable mouth. His wet hair stuck out in places and still managed to look sexy, and those fearless blue-gold eyes were almost hard to meet. Stunning and magnetizing, they glowed with indomitable sureness. Besides his size, he was an intimidating man. Which was why she should not find him the least bit attractive.

"The first room on the right is yours," she said, so disconcerted that the storm had drifted to the background for a few seconds. "There's a bathroom across the hall."

His head lowered from examining the ceiling. "We won't be sleeping in separate rooms tonight."

Because of the hurricane. "I meant so you can change into dry clothes.... Do you have any?"

Without answering, he went down the hall.

She couldn't help feeling a little petulant. While she knew her father would send the best—and were it not for Travis, she'd still be in her lighthouse prison—she hated what men like him represented. They were the fathers of children who grew up in their absence. Functioning dysfunctional families. Like those of alcoholics. Her father's addiction was government and military, and the power he had in manipulating the politics that came with them. She'd rather steer clear of men like that. She'd admit she had some commitment issues as a result of her upbringing. It wasn't easy finding a manly man who could handle her busy lifestyle and whose ego didn't need to wear the pants more than she did.

She'd thought Deet might be that man. But she'd already established that she lacked the proper insight in that regard. Was her insight lacking again with Travis?

Fresh from a quick shower—who knew how long they'd have fresh water, let alone electricity—Raeleen emerged into her living room. Ordinarily, the cozy interior relaxed her. But the steady creaking of the cottage's walls and the growl of wind changed all that.

What she wouldn't give for the mainland and a big, juicy double cheeseburger.

Travis sat on her dark red sofa. He glanced up from checking the blade of a big knife, those incredible eyes of his roaming down and then back up her body. The unmistakable interest made her a little uncomfortable. She wore jeans and hiking boots and a plain white scoop-neck cotton shirt. He'd dressed similarly in a dark T-shirt and jeans. He'd put his boots back on, she saw. They must be waterproof. Of course, why wouldn't they be?

Walking around the white, rectangular table with a lamp and some books along the back of the sofa, she went into the kitchen to find something to eat. There was nothing that interested her. Nothing that could be kept in a cabinet for months interested her, especially when she was craving a cheeseburger.

Returning to the living room, she sat on the chair across from her coffee table and noticed her purse.

"My purse." She'd dropped it outside her rental car when she'd been abducted. She recalled the key he'd used to open the door.

Travis put the knife away and leaned back against the

sofa while his gaze roamed over her. "I found it at Artz Eatery. Inside your rental."

The way Travis looked at her was distracting. More than his orders hovered there. She cooled her warming reaction.

Lifting her purse from the table, she dug into it for her cell phone. No service. Not that she expected there to be. Travis had put her keys back in there, and she also found her passport. Her kidnapper must have put her purse inside the car. Odd that he hadn't taken anything. All her money and credit cards were in her wallet.

"I returned your rental and just left the keys on the driver's seat," he said. "I'd rather not have the police connect you to the murders until we know what this is all about."

"Good thinking. And thanks." She held up her purse. "This saves me a lot of trouble. You, too, since I couldn't leave the country without a passport."

"I'd have found a way."

Of course he would have. He worked for TES. She withheld a cynical retort and instead admired his bulging biceps and chest muscles. "How did you find me, anyway?" Her purse couldn't have led him to her.

"When I arrived at Artz Eatery, Dietrich Artz's wife and her brother were there. She was already dead. He was killed while I was there."

Instant questions bombarded her along with a good dose of shock. "What? What happened?" She put her purse aside. "How do you know about Deet? Was he there, too? Why was his wife's brother there? How do you know it was him?" And then she realized this was one of her father's soldiers. Travis had probably known everything about her before he landed in Anguilla.

"I went to the restaurant looking for you." Travis leaned back. "When I arrived, I found Vivian lying on the floor. She was dead, but her brother wasn't. He must have arrived just before me. The back door was open and the killer was still there. He fired at both of us. Vivian's brother was shot. I chased the killer, but he got away. A car with three more men was waiting in the street."

He'd arrived right in the middle of it all. "Who were the men?"

"I didn't get a clear view. Deet, as you call him, wasn't inside the restaurant, but he could have been in the car."

She struggled to digest it all. Deet...? "Didn't you see the car before you entered the restaurant?"

"It wasn't there when I arrived. They must have seen me, though."

"That still doesn't explain how you found me."

"Vivian's brother told me you were in a lighthouse. The report I was given had information about a house on the coast that Deet and his wife owned. There was a lighthouse there."

Deet had mentioned the house but not the lighthouse. It was his second home. "Very clever. Thorough." She expected nothing less. A moment or two more of thought and she backtracked to something he'd said. "You think Deet killed his wife?"

"It's a possibility."

Deet didn't seem like the type to her. "If he killed his wife, why was I kidnapped?"

"It was Deet's brother-in-law who kidnapped you. John Rey. He and his sister must have been working together."

Deet's wife had arranged her kidnapping? Why?

"Did you know Deet was married?" Travis asked.

Was he more interested in her morals than the reason two people had been killed? She supposed someone who'd seen a lot of death would be immune to it, but...

"No," she finally answered. "Deet was going to make me breakfast before my flight home. His wife was waiting for us at the restaurant." She grew angry with herself all over again for not seeing through his duplicity. "She introduced herself."

"How did she find out about you?"

"I didn't ask. I left as soon as she told me she was his wife."

Something hit the plywood that covered the window off the dining area, startling her and causing Travis to look around the room. The lights flickered as they had several times now but didn't go out. After the strong gust receded to a steadier wind, Raeleen relaxed her stiff grip on the chair's armrests and noticed Travis looking at her as though she were more than the package he had to deliver to her father. She found herself returning the uncontrolled interest.

Then Travis cleared his throat, an uncharacteristically awkward sound coming from a man like him. "The element of surprise worked in Vivian's favor."

While his declaration steered them back to their conversation, it also explained why he'd asked her those questions. "I was definitely surprised Deet was married. And I was even more surprised to be kidnapped."

"It must have had her desired impact on Deet, too."

"Yes, I suppose so." She let go of the armrests to put her hands on her knees. "But why did John and Vivian kidnap me?"

"Deet must have something they wanted," Travis said. "Or they tried to stop him from doing something they didn't want him to do."

"Why would he kill his wife and brother-in-law before he knew where I was?"

"Don't forget there were four men in the vehicle I saw."

More than just Deet was involved, whether Deet was in the vehicle or not.

"I was locked in the lighthouse for hours. If Deet's wife

was just murdered when you found her, how could Deet have done it? The restaurant was closed."

"It may have taken time to meet her with whatever she demanded in return for your release."

Ah, yes. That made sense. He had it all figured out. And the men in the car had provided assistance. What did Deet have that they wanted…and would kill to get? Deet must be willing or his wife wouldn't have arranged to kidnap Raeleen to stop him.

"I'm waiting on a financial report from Odie, but I'll bet she'll find Deet's restaurant is in trouble," Travis said.

"Odie?" Why was he asking someone else to look into it?

"You don't know who Odelia Frank is?"

"No. And maybe I don't want to know." She was probably another one of her dad's pet soldiers.

A loud bang against the side of her cottage gave her a jolt. Expecting something to penetrate the wall, she shot to her feet and glanced around as the sound of a freight train rumbled outside the cottage. She could feel the vibration in her chest, feel the pressure changing in the house. Instinct brought her over to the sofa where Travis sat. He opened his arm for her and she sat beside him without thinking.

"It's getting really bad out there." Talking helped keep panic at bay.

Saying nothing, he moved his arm around her shoulder, his hand coming to rest there, sending streams of sunlit awareness through her core. All the while, he was oblivious, his gaze moving over the walls and ceiling as though he could see through them. Then those eyes returned to hers.

"It's probably time to prepare for the worst."

He sounded so matter-of-fact. "Don't try too hard to be a ray of hope."

"I'm not Poseidon."

No, he just worked for her father's secret organization. As much as she despised that, she hoped it was enough to get them through the storm.

Travis rummaged through Raeleen's refrigerator while she paced the living room. It was impatience more than fear. The way she'd fearlessly held up the frame of a portable toilet seat kind of sealed his impression of her as Colonel Roth's daughter. Training had cured him of impatience. Fear wouldn't do anything to help him survive, so he never succumbed to it. Raeleen just hadn't learned that yet.

They needed to prepare for the worst. Food, water, a solid place to go if the walls started to fall down.

Finding nothing in the refrigerator, he moved on to the pantry and had better luck there. Putting some crackers and chips into a box on the kitchen counter, he noticed Raeleen had entered the kitchen. No more pacing. Good. She could be proactive with him.

"Go get some blankets and pillows and put them in the bathroom," he told her.

Her brow lifted ever so slightly at his take-charge tone.

"Not the master bath. The one across from your guest room," he added. "It's in the middle of the house."

"I know where it is."

Were it not for the storm, he'd spend some time exploring what made her so testy with people who gave orders. "I only meant it would be safer there."

With a huff, she headed for the hall closet and began pulling out blankets. He tried to ignore her prone butt, and the reminder it gave him of his hand on her shoulder...so close to those fantastic breasts.

He set the box down on the bathroom floor. "Do you have a battery-operated radio? We both have cell phones, but service will probably be patchy or nonexistent."

"No radio."

"Do you have an extra flashlight?"

"I think so."

"Good. Go get it."

"You remind me of my father," she snapped.

And that was a bad thing? "Flashlight?"

"Are you always this bossy?"

"Would you rather tell me what to do?" He had a good idea that she would. She was telling him he was like her father when she was the one with the resemblance. Minus the attitude. Travis had never met Colonel Roth, but a man like that had to be in control of his ego. So maybe his daughter was different....

A hard gust of wind slammed against the cottage, rumbling and creaking the roof and walls. A near-continuous hailing of debris banged against the siding and windows now. Something tangled with the patio railing off the kitchen. Sounds came from everywhere, above the garage, the corner of the kitchen, bedrooms.

Travis saw Raeleen walk back into the living room. A violent crash came from a neighbor's house. There may as well have been ten freight trains roaring by. The television wavered between a clear picture and disturbance, the image of a weatherman gesturing toward a huge swirling red mass over the Caribbean.

Yep, things were about to get real interesting.

The lights flickered, went out and came back on. Standing at the threshold of the hallway, he watched her frightened eyes and the soldier in him began to take over.

"Stay calm. We'll make it through," he said.

A loud crash in the garage made her jump. Something had gone through the roof.

"Oh, my God."

The lights and television flickered again, this time going out.

"Bathroom. Now."

She started toward him—not arguing, amazingly enough. The door to the garage banged open and wind and rain came roaring in.

Shrieking, she threw herself against him. He lifted her and turned, taking her into the bathroom and depositing her in the tub, easily and gently.

"Stay here."

Leaving her standing stiffly in the dark with freight trains swirling everywhere, he went back into the living room, shut the door to the garage and dragged the sofa in front of it. Then he grabbed his duffel bag, got out the flashlight and returned to the bathroom, all the while wondering if he was going to have to take Raeleen from this cottage to find more secure shelter.

Closing the bathroom door behind him, he put down his bag and rested the flashlight on top.

Raeleen got out of the tub and sat on the toilet seat, putting her head in her hands. He wished he could reassure her. The waiting would be the worst. How long would the storm last? All night, at least.

Travis stepped into the tub and sat on the blankets. "Come here."

When she looked at him, he patted the blanket between his legs. The tub was a good sized one that had a Jacuzzi and enough room for the two of them. She left her perch on the toilet and climbed into the tub, sitting down and leaning back against him. He wrapped his arms around her and rested his head on the wall behind him, glad the hurricane would deter his baser instincts. She let her head fall back onto his shoulder and threatened that rationale.

"Do you have a girlfriend?" she asked.

He lifted his head off the wall. What an odd question at a time like this.

"I'm not asking because...you know...I'm interested or anything," she said. "It's just...talking helps."

He relaxed again, keeping his senses tuned into the storm at the same time. "I met a woman last week. I was going to take her out for a lunch date when I got the call to come and get you. I doubt she'll be interested in seeing me when I get back."

"Why do you think that?"

"When I called to cancel, she didn't sound very happy. I already know she was skeptical about my job." She hadn't liked that he was called away so abruptly, part of his profession.

"What did you tell her you did for a living?"

"The standard. I'm a security consultant." He couldn't tell them the truth.

"So, she knew you weren't telling her much."

He lowered his head, his mouth close to her ear. "It happens a lot."

"Is that why you never married?"

Was she really asking him all this just to calm her nerves? "I'm in no rush for that. I just haven't met the right woman. If it's right, it'll happen on its own."

Sometimes he wished that would be sooner than later. Not that he regretted his choices. Doing what he did for TES gave him a sense of purpose, one that had deep-seated meaning to him, meaning that he never discussed.

"Would you change professions to settle down with someone?" she asked after a while.

"I shouldn't have to. I like what I do. The energy. The cause. The unpredictable schedule. I hope the woman I fall for can understand and appreciate that."

"I know what you mean."

He'd read about her show. "It must have taken a lot of hard work to get where you are."

He felt her head nod.

"You're busy a lot."

"Yes."

"On the road a lot."

"You have no idea."

"Actually, I do."

Her head tipped up and she looked at his face, his eyes. He wished she wouldn't do that. Didn't she know he was trained to put things like a hurricane on the back burner if it meant his survival?

"Why do you do it, then?"

Aware of her one-sided opinion, he countered, "Why do you?"

"You want a woman who's never home?" she shot back defensively.

"No. I want a woman who's independent. Strong. Her own *thinker*. Not insecure."

"What about kids? A family?"

This was a heated topic for her. Did she even realize that? Suddenly, her ignorance to Deet's marital status became clear to him. But he'd go along with this for a bit longer.

"I'm fine with that," he answered neutrally.

"But you'd never be home."

He leaned his head back, almost grinning. "I'd be home enough."

"According to whom?"

Sass and attitude radiated from her. He loved it. "The woman I marry won't have an issue with that."

"Don't you think that's asking a lot?"

He lifted his head again, meeting her fiery eyes. "I'd be there enough."

Watching her register his innuendo, he cautioned himself not to flirt too well.

"How many relationships have you been in?"

Was that a challenge? "Is this working to take your mind off the hurricane?"

Instantly, her tension vanished and she smiled. And with a little bit of a laugh, she said, "Yes."

Whatever darkness that had stoked her emotions was defused, softened with humor. He loved that, too.

"Depends on what you consider a relationship." This was too good not to keep going.

"More than dating. You actually took the time to get to know them for a year or two."

"Not many of those. A couple."

"Have you ever been with someone you thought would go the distance?"

Now, there was a question he didn't feel like answering. She moved her head to see his profile in his silence.

"Have you?" he countered.

"I've had a few relationships," she said. "None where I fell madly in love, though."

The letdown of Deet's deceit must have made that a reality. "Not even Deet?"

"He fit my schedule."

Sarcastic response. "That's what you look for?"

"That and someone who doesn't remind me of my father."

He chuckled. She really had a hang-up about men because of her father. "You want a man who sticks around and yet you get involved with the ones who don't." Interesting.

She remained quiet for a time. "I was beginning to think Deet and I had a future. I would have moved to Anguilla. But then I met his wife. That ruined it for me."

"It would for me, too." Fidelity was something he looked

for in women. He needed to be with someone he could trust.
That wasn't easy to find.

"Has it ever happened to you?" Raeleen asked.

This was getting too personal. "I've had women leave me
for other men, yeah, sure." It was bound to happen.

"Men who have stationary jobs?"

"An executive, a dentist and a Critter Central manager."

"A pet-store manager? How did that happen?"

"She had a dog."

Now it was her turn to laugh. "It's not often things pro-
gress beyond dating for me. Most men want a woman who's
more available than I am. I don't spend enough time with
them to fall in love."

"Sounds familiar."

They stopped talking as it became obvious that he was
thinking the same as her. They both had jobs that kept them
busy. She claimed she didn't want a man like her father, and
he claimed he'd be around enough if he ever had a family.
Were they both deluding themselves? Even more disturbing, he wouldn't have to lie to her about his job. She already knew all about where he worked. Disturbing...and
yet...intoxicating.

She tipped her head back to look up at him. Warmth kept
the storm in the realm of really loud white noise. He took
in her eyes and mouth and wanted to kiss her.

Allowing his training to keep the storm at bay for just
a few moments longer, he moved his head down. Her eyes
met his for seconds longer before he closed the distance.
Passion flared. Fireworks spread. Like the storm tearing
the landscape beyond the walls, desire ravaged him. How,
he couldn't fathom.

Why her?

A loud ripping noise broke them apart. The freight train
was in the cottage. The roof above them broke apart with a

sickening sound and sailed away. Rain and debris poured down upon them. Raeleen screamed. Wind created a suction. The bathroom door crashed in on them.

Travis turned his upper body to protect her from flying wood. Then he stood, stepping out of the tub and grabbing his bag. After shoving the flashlight inside, he slung the bag over his shoulder so that it hung across his back. Taking her hand, he hauled her out of the tub and then the bathroom.

Unidentified objects pelted them. Her cottage was being torn to shreds!

Travis led her through what once had been her living room. The walls were demolished. The garage was no longer there. Water was everywhere.

Jumping over mangled furniture and pieces of the house, he lifted her over one obstacle after another. Then he took her hand again and ran out into the driveway. Away from what was left of the structure of her cottage, the wind pushed Raeleen off her feet. Travis righted her, but he had to fight the force of it himself.

Leaves, debris and rain spat down on them, the finer grains like a compressed air sander. He could barely recognize the street.

Wind pushed Raeleen against him. She didn't weigh enough for the force of it. She lost hold of his iron grip and fell, tumbling across the street in the strong wind. He went after her, using his bulk to fight the pressure. Just when he nearly reached her, she was knocked off her feet again, rolling onto a grassy surface, bumping into fallen debris. Digging her knees into the ground and crouching low, she tried once more to stand. As soon as she started to rise, she was knocked over again.

Travis reached her and went down onto his hands and knees, caging her so that she'd stay put.

He put his mouth right next to her ear. "Hold on to me. I'm going to stand."

"Okay!" she yelled above the supernatural din.

He slowly inched his way up. She hugged his leg and crawled up his body, the wind at his back. While Raeleen clung to him for dear life, he scanned their surroundings and saw the neighbor's cottage still in one piece. It was made of stone. Anchoring her to him with his arm, he moved forward, keeping his back to the wind.

They made it to the side of the cottage. In the back, the wind wasn't as strong. Travis checked a garage door. It was locked. He moved on to a small window. A bathroom window. He put her back against the stone of the cottage.

"Grab hold of the bush!" he yelled.

She sat down and turned her face away from thrashing branches, grabbing twines and wrapping them around her arm. The wind rocked her, tugged her toward the abyss of the backyard.

Travis worried she'd be swept away again. Working quickly, he used a broken piece of fencing to bash the plywood covering the window. He hammered the side until the nails loosened, then pried the plywood free. Picking up the wood again, he broke the window and cleared the glass.

He bent for Raeleen, his body wavering in the brutal wind. Grabbing hold of her, he lifted her up to the window sill. She fought her way over and inside, falling onto the bathroom floor and bumping her head on the toilet.

"Ah!" She scooted back just before Travis followed, landing partially on top of her.

Their breathing joined the hissing wind and missiles of unidentified objects outside the broken window.

"Come on." He got to his feet and went out of the bathroom.

Raeleen followed, shutting the bathroom door. Leaning her back against it, she caught her breath. The hall was pitch-black.

"Hello?" Travis called.

No one answered. The house was vacant. He lowered his duffel and unzipped it, removing the flashlight.

"I don't want to die," Raeleen breathed, obviously scared.

Turning the flashlight on, he illuminated her face without blinding her and stepped closer. Brushing his damp fingers across her cheek, he said, "You won't."

She blinked once as though believing him for a split second.

Flashing the beam of light up and down the hall, he was relieved to see this cottage was holding together well. The sounds were more muffled. The interior was very similar to Raeleen's, except the bathroom was right off the living room and it wasn't as nicely appointed as hers, with older furnishings and outdated colors.

Travis checked all the doors and windows and began to feel better that they'd be okay until morning. He found a hammer in the garage and went to the backyard, wind, rain and debris swirling. Quickly boarding up the broken window, he hurried back to the garage, seeing Raeleen waiting for him. Dropping the hammer onto a workbench, he picked up the flashlight he'd left there and followed her inside.

She stood in the middle of the room, turning in circles, listening to the storm.

"You're going to be okay," he said.

She stopped moving. "How do you know that? You said you weren't Poseidon."

"You don't need Poseidon. You only need me."

As he hoped, her attitude shifted into high gear. She folded her arms and narrowed her eyes. "I don't *need* you."

"No? Not even when you were tumbling across the ground in the wind?"

"That isn't fair."

"Do what I tell you and you'll make it just fine."

"Or what? You'll send me tumbling again?"

He fought a grin. "Not exactly."

She observed him shrewdly, the storm nearly forgotten. "You're using your military brawn to control the situation."

Military brawn. So it was the military streak he had in him that she didn't like. Her father was all military and therefore she despised all men who resembled that.

"I plan on surviving this storm," he told her. "Stay with me and you will, too. You can be the boss when we get back to the States."

"When we get back to the States, I'll never see you again."

For a moment he regretted that, and then he remembered his mission. He'd bring her back to her father. It didn't matter what else happened on the way. If Raeleen meant to ignore the obvious chemistry that was brewing between them, he'd let her.

"The invitation is open in case you change your mind," he teased, anyway.

Chapter 3

A muffled gust of wind rushed against the cottage. Though not as violent as previous torpedoes, the sound crept into Raeleen's dream. The same way noise woke her, the absence of it did now. No more creaking and banging. No more freight trains roaring by. She ran her hand up her bumpy mattress. Mattress? It took her a moment longer to remember she was on a sofa. Underneath her, Travis moved in response. She moaned, vaguely aware of her breasts smashed against him.

It was dark. Travis must have turned off the flashlight. Her hip rested between his legs. She could feel the walls of his thighs on each side of her. She lifted her head and grunted with the aches that came to life everywhere in her body. Travis still slept. One of his arms was bent and supported his neck and head, muscles tight and sculpted. His other arm draped over her lower back. His body felt hard and big and strong against her smaller, softer curves.

His eyes blinked open then and she came face-to-face with their awaking intensity. Even in the darkness she could see their blue color, close to the color of hers, except she knew that in the light there were hints of gold in his.

"The wind is dying down," he said.

His raspy voice brought her attention to his mouth. "Yes." They'd survived.

She looked back into his eyes and saw him responding to waking with her like this. Drawn to him, she rolled onto her stomach and inched higher up his chest. Her pelvis dragged along his, over the hard ridge in his jeans. Still enveloped in a sleepy daze made sultry by lying on top of him, she didn't let any further thought ruin the lovely glow building in her.

Moving his arm from behind his head, Travis cupped her cheek and traced her lips with his thumb. She watched his eyes smolder and knew hers were doing the same. Instant flames. He slid his hand into her hair, curving his palm over the back of her head. Then he pulled her down and pressed her mouth to his.

Raeleen sucked a breath of air with the shock of the touch, so sudden. Giving her no time to recover, he angled his head and she fell with him into deeper intimacy. Tingles radiated through her and made her yearn for more. All reason fled.

He kept kissing her, slow and searching. The sound of their breathing broke the quiet. He moved his hand down her body, and now both hands slid to her rear. Pressing her harder against him, he deepened the kiss, sending shivers of sensation rippling through her. He groaned into her mouth and slid his lips from hers. She kissed the corner of his mouth, seeking more of this unexpected passion. An animal part of her knew it would be good, and temptation clamored for satisfaction. Rising up, she was about to remove her top when her mind awakened from the dregs of sleep.

He worked for TES! He was the epitome of everything she strove to avoid in a man. How could she want him this much?

She propped herself up with her hands on his chest. His eyes were hot with desire, causing a flash of the same reaction in her. "What the hell?" She climbed up off the sofa, fishing around for the flashlight. Finding it, she turned it on and saw him stand up, too.

"Sorry, I thought you…" He let the sentence trail off.

She had, but…

"It was just…waking up like that…"

She held up her hand. "You don't have to explain. I get it." Men had morning erections. They'd survived a really bad storm. Nothing to worry about. Right?

She went to the front door. It was still overcast and breezy outside, but the hurricane had abated considerably. Destruction was everywhere. Across the street, her cottage was in ruins. Her heart fell with anguish. They'd have been killed if they'd have stayed there. A few of the other cottages on that side of the street were in similar shape. Not only that, but they were flooded with water.

Travis appeared beside her.

She started to move again, stopping at the edge of her yard. The extent of the damage was nearly incomprehensible. Although many of her memories of this place would involve Deet, her cottage had meant something to her. She'd never owned an island retreat. A cottage with an ocean view had grown into her prized possession, a symbol of all her hard work and success. Now she looked upon a ravaged shell of a once-treasured sanctuary and just felt empty.

Only three walls remained standing. Dirt and debris filled the open spaces, making what once had been nearly unrecognizable.

Tears rushed into her eyes, and she struggled to stop the

tide of emotion. She had insurance. She could rebuild. But it would never be the same.

The irony was inescapable. She'd bought the cottage when she'd begun her relationship with Deet. Now it only mirrored the destruction of her personal life. Gone was the enchantment.

Travis hadn't bothered Raeleen when she'd stared at her demolished cottage, thick blond hair waving in the breeze above her shoulders. Beautiful. Sad. A picture worth documenting. Maybe not to her, but he'd seen how much losing her cottage meant. He couldn't tell if she hurt more from the symbolism of her lover's deceit or from the loss of precious property, but seeing the damage couldn't have been easy. Memories and loss all melding into one.

He walked beside her toward The Valley, maneuvering around debris as they followed the street. Now that the storm was no longer a threat, he was acutely aware of Raeleen. Kissing her had been explosive. Just as he'd suspected, she was different than Haley. There was nothing fragile about Raeleen. It surprised him how much he liked that about her. How long had he been looking for a woman like her? Long enough. Just his luck, she had an aversion to military men, men who worked for her father. She'd already made it clear she wasn't interested in him. No point in lining himself up for heartache.

Brief affairs had never bothered him before now. He'd always enjoyed women, whether on assignment or off duty. As long as they had mutual desires, brief was exciting, and he was always open to more meaningful relationships. If it was right, he'd know it, and until now he'd never felt that way. Why did it have to be the colonel's daughter?

"Why do you dislike your father so much?" The question came with his frustration.

Her head jerked to see him. "I don't dislike him. I love my father."

"Do you?" She had a strange way of showing it.

"He was just never around when I was a kid."

"But he is now?"

"He…" She didn't finish.

No, he was still never around. He could read the answer in her body language the same as if she'd spoken to him. She rarely ever saw her father. And that made her mad as hell. "How often do you see him?"

"Why are you asking me all these questions about my father?" she shot back.

He ignored her defensiveness because it only confirmed what he already knew. "You keep reminding me that I'm just like him."

"I see him on holidays," she relented, turning forward.

She had a really great profile, blond hair bobbing as she walked, graceful slope of her nose, soft skin. "What about your mother?"

"I see her, too."

"So they're still married?"

She eyed him as though wondering where he was going with this. He was a little leery about it, too, but he was curious.

"She must have loved him enough to let him do what his passion called him to do," he said.

He watched her catch his carefully placed barb, blinking fast a couple of times and averting her gaze. She'd accused him of being like her father when it was she who bore the resemblance. Travis's only affiliation was through his work. She not only pushed away men who tried to control her, she was just as driven as her father in her career. She had passion for what she did, something she condemned in Travis, even though she didn't see the correlation. Yes, they both wanted partners who accepted and loved them despite their demanding lifestyles, but for Raeleen, a man's lifestyle could never be military. Or so she'd managed to convince herself.

Travis wasn't going to be the one to enlighten her. He had a mission to do. That had to come first. Especially now that he knew where he stood with her.

Stepping over a fallen tree, he reached to help Raeleen. She swatted his hand away and stepped over it herself.

He watched her butt move as she marched ahead of him, enjoying the view.

A Jeep emerged over a hill in the littered landscape. It weaved slowly around obstacles on and off the narrow paved road. The vehicle wasn't marked. Travis adjusted his duffel so his gun was more accessible.

The Jeep stopped next to them. Three men were inside.

"We are volunteers with Anguilla's Disaster Management," one of the men said in a rolling island accent. "Are you all right?"

"We could use a ride into town," Travis said, slipping his hand away from the side pouch on his duffel.

"Are there others you have seen?" the driver asked.

"We haven't seen anyone," Travis said.

"We will check to be sure." The man pointed behind him. "There is another Jeep. They will take you."

"When will the airport open?" Raeleen asked. "Do you know?"

Travis wasn't sure if she'd asked to know how soon she could be on a flight home and away from him or if she wanted to know how much time she had to track down Deet.

"They have had damage to the radio tower. It will be a few days before the repairs are complete," the man answered.

Travis could probably find an undamaged boat to sail

to another island with an operating airport, but something made him decide not to, and he was afraid that something was Raeleen. The sooner he brought her home, the sooner he'd never see her again. He couldn't tame the desire to crack her shallow opinion of him. He'd bring her home, but not before he tested her resolve a bit more. He'd just have to be careful not to get too attached.

As they neared the second Jeep, a third approached. He stopped. Raeleen grunted when she walked right into him.

"Hey," she complained, moving around his side to stand next to him. Then she saw the third Jeep. The driver was visible from here.

"Is that who I think it is?" he asked.

"Deet," she breathed.

Together they watched him stare back at them. Travis didn't miss how he stared the longest at him. Why had he come here the morning after the hurricane?

Deet began to turn the Jeep he was driving around. Had he come here searching for Raeleen? He could have gone to the lighthouse first. What was the urgency?

Raeleen started forward and Travis grabbed her arm to stop her.

She tugged at the restraint. "Let go!"

"He's already driving away."

She tugged harder. "We need to talk to him!"

The Jeep that would take them to the hotel stopped beside them.

"Let's go." Once she was home and safely out of the way, he'd have a moment or two with Deet. Without her.

Reluctantly, she climbed into the Jeep.

"The first thing I want is a cheeseburger."

Wearing new clothes purchased from a street vendor monopolizing on the aftermath of the storm, Raeleen walked next to Travis into the hotel. The Valley hadn't suffered much damage. Vegetation seemed to be the worst hit. Hotel workers busily clipped bushes and trees and pruned flowering plants that had lost their petals. Even the main roads were clear already.

"Cheeseburger, yes. Deet, no." Travis stepped up to the check-in counter. "Reservation for Todd."

Both his first and second command abraded her like being washed over coral. "I need a room, too."

"One is all we need." Travis sent her a warning look while the hotel clerk's eyes shifted back and forth between them.

"I want two."

"One. I'm paying." He handed the woman his card, but she didn't take it yet.

"I can pay for my own room."

Agitated, Travis turned from the counter to face her. "I can't protect you if you're separated from me by a cement wall."

"Get an adjoining room."

"I am sorry, we have no availability. Only single rooms with two queen beds," the clerk said.

"Then two rooms." Raeleen began to dig into her purse. Travis's big hand clamped around her wrist. She looked up at his stern expression, unbending.

"I'm not trying to boss you around."

"I barely know you. We should have separate rooms."

"You woke up on top of me this morning. I think you can manage a separate bed."

Raeleen slid her gaze to see the clerk's smothered amusement.

Still facing her, he once again extended his card to the clerk, who took it and processed the room.

The ding of her cell phone told her that service was back up. She found it in her purse and faltered. It was a text from Deet.

Can you meet me at the Valley Grill? We need to talk.

Yes, she texted back.

Come alone.

The Valley Grill was a public place and it was the middle of the day. It was also right up the street from here. If she could sneak away...

"I'll bet they'll have a cheeseburger," he said, finished getting the room.

She followed his forefinger to the hotel restaurant. "You have no imagination." She started toward there.

"It's a cheeseburger."

"In a hotel restaurant." She played along with him, but as soon as she could break away, she would.

Reaching the restaurant, she spotted the restrooms near the front.

"Two?"

"Yes," Travis answered the hostess.

She began to lead them.

"I'll be right there," Raeleen said. "I need to use the bathroom." She pointed lazily to the facilities.

Travis saw them and spent a second too long contemplating her and then nodded. Did he suspect she was about to bolt?

She turned and walked to the bathrooms, certain he was watching her. After going around the corner, she inched her way back to peer into the dining area. He was looking at a menu.

She hurried from the restaurant and ran out the front door. Still jogging down the street, she slowed as she ap-

proached the Valley Grill. It was a newly renovated building designed with gingerbread-house style.

Deet sat on the open patio. Seeing her, he stood. As she
approached the table, he moved toward her.

Raeleen stopped. She felt completely different about him
now, and if he tried to touch her, she might throw up.

He stopped, too, looking wary of how she'd react to him.
"I'm glad you made it through the storm all right."

"Why was I kidnapped, Deet?" She wasn't in the mood
for small talk.

He started to pull out a chair for her when something
out on the sidewalk caught his attention. "I asked you to
come alone."

"I did…" Twisting her neck, she saw Travis striding toward them on the sidewalk, brow low and shadowing angry
eyes. He reached the edge of the patio.

Turning to Deet, she saw that he was gone. She caught
sight of him running to the back of the patio and a gravel
parking area where he'd left a motorcycle.

Raeleen ran after him. "Wait! It's okay!" She reached the
parking area but Deet had already fired up his motorcycle
and sprayed gravel as he raced away.

"Deet!" She jumped up and down waving.

There was no way she could catch him on foot. Crestfallen, she turned to go back to the patio and bumped into
Travis. His brow creased between his fiery blue eyes. Not
happy with her. Not at all.

"Don't ever do that again."

Taking offense to his drill-sergeant command, she retorted, "Or what?"

"Or I'll cuff you to something stationary in the room and
feed you hotel food until we can leave the island."

Oh…the torture…

The smell of grilled food made its way to the parking
area. Her stomach growled.

"I was this close to finding out why I was kidnapped." She held her thumb and forefinger a fraction of an inch apart, right in front of his nose.

"Bring me along next time."

"Apparently he won't talk with you around. He ran off when he saw you." She gave his big body an up and down. "I can't say I blame him."

"You either bring me or you don't go."

There he went again. "Don't be such a commando." Brushing past him, she returned to the table Deet had gotten and sat down.

Travis joined her, sitting across from her. "I take it we're eating here instead."

"This is better than your choice." She lifted one of two menus that were already on the table and had her cheeseburger picked out an instant later.

Leaning back in her chair, she removed her cell phone and sent Deet a text.

You don't have to worry. You can talk to Travis, too.

Travis yanked her phone from her, read her message and then entered one of his own.

"Hey." She grabbed for her phone but couldn't wrestle it from him.

Finally, he let her have it back and she read what he'd sent.

Come near her again and I'll kill you.

"Great. That's just great. Superb. Wonderful. Now he'll never talk to me and I'll never know why I was drugged and kidnapped and forced to endure a hurricane with Mr. Mission First over here."

"What can I get you?" the waiter asked with an impish grin.

"A knuckle sandwich for him. I'll have your triple-decker."

The waiter wrote the order.

"I'll have a triple-decker, too," Travis said.

"There really is a knuckle sandwich on the menu," Raeleen said after the waiter left.

"Running off like that isn't very smart, Raeleen."

"It's the middle of the day and there are people everywhere." She glanced around at the sparse patio and even sparser sidewalks and recalled the vacant parking lot where she'd been kidnapped. It had been daylight then.

"Don't do it again. I mean it." Sitting back, dwarfing the table and chair, he had a commanding presence. Commanding presence never worked on her. He might intimidate most people when he talked like that, but not her.

"Fine. Let's go see him at his house after lunch," she said.

"No."

"Excuse me? Then I'm going alone."

"Go ahead and try."

While she envisioned being handcuffed and fed hotel food, the waiter returned with waters.

"He can tell us what we need to know," she said, trying to reason with him after the waiter left.

"He can tell me, *after* I get you home."

Oh, no. Was he really going to stick to that? "It might be too late by then."

"He sought you out. It can wait."

"Not if you keep scaring him away."

Travis leaned forward, bringing his handsome face closer to hers. "He tells you to come alone and you do it?"

"You're being overprotective."

His eyes hardened and he leaned back again. "I'm taking you home, and that's final."

Chapter 4

Habib Maalouf saw Lucian LeFevre walk into his Monrovia, Liberia, market and was happy for the sparse appearance of customers this morning. Lucian always dressed well and was one of the few clients Habib trusted. While he didn't believe Lucian's claims that he purchased diamonds only to fund his interest in art, Habib didn't mind doing business with him. He didn't care what the man did with them when he left. He only was grateful he wasn't tied to Hezbollah or other terrorist-labeled groups. Habib had lost too much from men of that sort to feel at ease doing business with them.

"Mr. Maalouf, and how might you be today?" Lucian asked in his rich, deep voice. He kept his thinning brown hair trimmed short, and his starched white shirt peeked out from the suit jacket, tucked into dark gray slacks. He wore a tie as well, managing to still look cool on this warm September day.

"I am well. Thank you. And you?"

"Very well." He glanced around.

"There is no one," Habib assured him. "Not such a good day that way, I'm afraid."

"Ah." Lucian smiled. "Then I have something for you that will improve it." He pulled out an envelope from an inside pocket of his jacket. "This is the usual deposit."

Habib took the money from him and slipped it beneath the counter. He kept the shelves along the front of the market stocked high so as to hide transactions such as this. In Monrovia he didn't have much to fear from authorities, but one could not be too careful.

"What is it you need from me? I did not expect you to return so soon." From what Habib had learned so far, Lucian bought and sold diamonds to support his growing black-market art sales. Lucian frequently shared details of his activities with Habib, particularly those that gave him pleasure. That was mainly due to their common bond. Both dealt in illicit business.

"I have a very special piece of art I am trying to purchase. The seller is a bit shy, however, so I fear I will have to be very persuasive. More persuasive than I have been. This is a deal I will have to take care of in person, it seems."

"You sent someone to make an offer and the buyer declined?"

Lucian inclined his head in affirmation. "It was a generous offer. But he is shy, as I have said, and rather attached to the piece. He also does not want his identity known. Lucky for him, I can understand his predicament."

Which was why he intended to offer more. "Then you are in a hurry, I presume?"

The smile that still remained renewed its energy on Lucian's mid-thirties face. "That is why I am so fond of doing business with you, Mr. Maalouf. I am never disappointed."

"It's business such as yours that feeds my family." He

glanced around the market. "This brings me a bare minimum here in Monrovia, but it falls far short of keeping us comfortable."

"Then we do each other equal service. How soon can you bring me double of what I previously ordered?"

Double...so much. "How soon do you have a need for it?"

"I would be most appreciative if I could arrange for my pilot to fly me to Anguilla by this evening. I realize this is not much notice for such a transaction, however, and can make allowances."

Habib began to worry. He couldn't get that much in such a short time. Lucian would have to come back. "If this is a special work of art to you, then it is special to me, as well. If you give me one hour, I can have half for you today, but I am afraid I will need a few days for the other half." He kept an inventory of diamonds in a locked safe, but not for the amount Lucian had requested.

Habib feared half wouldn't be enough. Lucian's heavy sigh made him nervous.

"Very well. I shall return in a few days for the balance."

"What is this special piece of art that awaits you in Anguilla?" Habib had little interest in Lucian's black-market activities, but Lucian was one of his best clients. He had to keep him happy.

"A rare painting." Excitement lit up Lucian's entire face. "I have been searching for this particular piece for many months. It is very valuable. Stolen from a Jewish art collector during World War II."

"Stolen, you say?"

"Yes, by a Nazi collaborator. But what's even more spectacular is the story that goes along with the theft."

Habib felt himself lean closer. Not only had he managed to keep his client happy, this was fascinating.

Lucian hesitated. "Maybe I shouldn't even be telling yo
this."

"I have little interest in art, Mr. LeFevre. So if you are
concerned I may try and outbid you, rest assured, I will not
It is your business here in my market that I most value."

Lucian's smile changed. "My apologies, Mr. Maalouf.
meant only to protect you from further hardship."

Catching his meaning, Habib was grateful for his cautio
and also alerted to the danger of his interest in the paint
ing he sought.

"I have not forgotten the sorrows you have suffered, my
friend," he added.

With the allusion to his wife, Habib lowered his head, un
able to meet Lucian's gaze with the fresh and powerful grie
that always consumed him when talk of his beautiful and
loving wife arose. Their five children were motherless now

"I am so sorry. I did not mean to—"

Habib lifted his head and right hand to stop his clien
from continuing. "No. Your sympathies are most appreci
ated."

"Your business is most appreciated by me."

"It is my pleasure, sir."

Lucian regarded him with more trust floating from his
not-so-handsome face than was probably wise. Habib held
no alliance with any man. Not after his love had been taken
from him. Not after his life had been torn apart by terrorists

Lucian's only redeeming quality was that he was an ar
dealer, not a terrorist. But what he didn't understand wa
that Habib sold these blood diamonds because he had to.

"This painting," Lucian finally said, entirely too pleased
with himself, "belonged to a Jewish woman whose lover wa
murdered by her husband. Upon her death, the painting wa
passed to her son, a Jewish man who married a woman who

also had an affair with a German businessman who supported Hitler's ideology."

Habib found himself leaning in again.

"This German was in love with the Jew's wife. But when he professed his devotion, she rejected him and chose to stay with her husband. The German became a Nazi collaborator and eventually stormed into the couple's house and took the painting, but not before killing the woman."

Habib straightened. "He murdered her?"

"Yes, and then he fled Germany with the painting before the war's end. No one could find him."

Until...

"You're saying that you..."

Lucian's smile beamed brilliant rays of pride. "I have found his descendants...in Anguilla."

"How? That is quite simply fascinating, Mr. LeFevre."

"Now you know why I love collecting art."

"Not any art, sir."

"No. Not any art. My art is untraceable. That is why it sells so well in my market."

A black market...

Habib did not want to know any more.

"What do you mean I should go back to California?" Jada Manoah asked the art dealer she'd been working with for several months now. "You know how long I've been looking for that painting." She stood in the salon of his eighty-foot yacht, refusing to accept that she'd come here for nothing.

Rorey Evertszen turned from the double glass doors leading to the aft deck as he'd done a few other times since she'd come to see him. "I told you. Someone else has discovered it. Another dealer less than reputable. I've gotten several phone calls from him with offers to buy it. When

I tell him I already have a buyer, he insists that he's the buyer now."

She tucked her long brown hair behind one ear and tapped her small purse against her red sundress. "Are you saying you're going to sell it to him instead?"

"I'm saying I want to get away from here for a while. I want you to get away from here for a while."

"Do you think he'll give up if we do?"

Rorey sighed with exasperation. "I don't know."

He was really afraid. And she might lose the painting because of this dealer.

The television played a documentary on whales and was annoyingly loud. She wished he'd turn it off. "You know what this painting means to me."

"Yes, Jada, I do. But these people are dangerous."

"Who are they? How did they know to call you?" Just her luck. Someone had found her painting. Why did they have to get in her way now? She was so close....

"Word must have gotten around when I was looking for a buyer." Rorey twisted his upper body and looked toward the doors again.

"We can still arrange a meeting with him. As soon as the deal is done, the dealer will leave you alone."

He scoffed. "You have no idea what you're saying. I'm not arranging anything. I'm sailing to Yost van Dyke this evening. The only reason I stopped here today is to warn you."

It was close to six now. She was supposed to have the painting by three this afternoon. She wasn't leaving without it.

Rorey didn't get it. And she was growing tired of playing this docile part. "Go ahead to Yost van Dyke. I'll handle this myself from here. Just tell me who the owner is and where he lives."

"He doesn't want his identity revealed."

He'd stuck to that nauseatingly well. As many times as she'd tried, he'd refused to divulge the seller's name. She could understand why. Art collectors and museum curators all over the world would rush for the chance to possess *The Portrait of Sarah*. And the current owner was likely related to the Nazi who stole it.

"Things have changed. I want the painting before the other dealer gets it. Tell me who the owner is."

"It isn't safe, Jada. You have no idea what you'd be facing if I told you and you got the painting. This dealer will do anything to have it."

"So will I." That was the part he didn't get.

He looked at her with new dawning.

Voices on the aft deck made them both look toward the sliding glass doors. She caught sight of three men. Jada's pulse quickened with apprehension.

"It's him. Go out the side door. Hurry," Rorey said. "Don't get caught."

"What about you?"

"Just go." He pushed her toward the hall along the galley.

If a black-market dealer was coming to see him, he should run with her. But he'd made his decision, and Jada wasn't going to waste any time. She ran to the side door and paused, hearing the sliding door open. She cracked the door ajar. A man with a gun approached along the deck, looking toward the upper deck. She was trapped.

Shutting the door, she searched for a place to hide.

"Mr. LeFevre," she heard Rorey say. The narrow hall offered a scant view of the salon. Leaning just a bit toward the room, she saw Rorey's back and another man beside him holding a gun.

"My apologies for this unannounced visit," an accented voice said. She couldn't see this man. He sounded French.

"I told you I already had a buyer. I can't sell you the painting."

"Circumstances have changed since our last conversation. Since just this evening, in fact."

Seeing Rorey back up toward the hall, she spotted a closet in the opening that led into the galley. She'd seen Rorey use it when she'd first arrived. Upper-level shelving securely held cans and other non-refrigerated food, but the lower half was reserved for bulkier items that Rorey hadn't utilized. There was enough room for her to crouch inside. She pulled the door with her fingers under the bottom edge, not shutting it all the way out of fear that she'd be heard. Now she was glad Rorey hadn't turned off the television.

"I don't have the painting," Rorey said.

"I am well aware of that. Your hesitation has cost me not only time but opportunity. I wasted an entire trip to West Africa and had to arrive here by boat due to the airport being closed from the storm. I am at the end of my patience."

Rorey didn't respond. They were still in the salon, but close to the galley.

"Where is Dietrich Artz?" the Frenchman demanded.

"You know his name?"

The man who possessed the painting. Jada had his name now.

"Where is he?" the Frenchman said again.

"Have you checked his restaurant?"

"Do not play games with me, Mr. Evertszen. As I have informed you, my patience wears thin."

"I don't know where Deet is. I haven't seen him since before the storm."

A storm she'd weathered in a nice, comfortable hotel. All for the same painting this...this...criminal was after. She wouldn't have traveled at such a time if not for the painting. Now some stupid Frenchman was here asking for it. She should have acted sooner. She should have insisted Rorey rush the sale.

Shuffling alerted her to things turning physical.

"I swear I don't know where Deet is. I just sailed back to Anguilla today. A hurricane and boats don't mix too well."

"Then you are of no further use to me."

"Wait."

"Kill him."

A muffled shot preceded a grunt from Rorey. And then she heard his body fall to the floor. She covered her mouth. Had the man with the Frenchman shot Rorey? Was he dead? She didn't hear him moving.

The Frenchman was willing to kill for the painting....

Footsteps made her feel faint. She needed more air but didn't dare take deeper breaths.

"All clear," another Frenchman said. The third man, the one she'd seen on the deck.

"We go now."

Jada waited for several more minutes before she felt safe to leave the closet. Her knees ached and her limbs trembled as she emerged. Only the loud television broke the stillness, eerie, deadly.

Crawling because she didn't think her legs would support her, she went to Rorey. Blood pooled under his body. His eyes were closed. She checked for a pulse. Nothing.

What should she do?

She couldn't talk to the police. The police would want to know what had happened. The painting would be revealed. It would be in the news. She couldn't allow anyone to know she was here.

Standing up, she went into the galley and tore some paper towels off the roll and began wiping everywhere she'd touched. Then, leaving out the side door, she looked around. No one was on the yacht next to Rorey's. She left off the aft deck, passing a yacht with people laughing around a table, drinking wine. They didn't notice her.

It was all she could do to walk normally down the dock to her rental car.

By the time the taxi stopped in front of her hotel, Jada was calmer. She'd managed to get herself back on track. She had a reason for doing what she was doing. A purpose.

She alighted from the taxi and entered the hotel lobby.

Ever since she'd learned the story of the painting, she couldn't forget it. She began collecting similar pieces, pieces that were stolen by Nazis, and returning them to their rightful owners. The injustice of the thefts fueled her. She'd developed a reputation, and when asked why she did it, she simply replied, "I'm Jewish."

Eventually, she ran across an amateur art collector who'd gone to Anguilla on vacation and had a conversation with a man who lived there who claimed to own *The Portrait of Sarah*. The art collector couldn't recall the man's name, but he'd given her enough, a location. She'd kept her excitement hidden and feigned ignorance. The amateur art collector hadn't known the value of the painting, only thought the history was interesting. And Jada hadn't enlightened him. After searching for an art dealer who could help her while keeping her identity anonymous, Rorey had contacted her. She'd been so close. And now this.

The lounge of a hotel restaurant caught her eye. Realizing she'd stopped in the middle of the lobby, she wondered what she'd do next. Try to find Dietrich Artz? Fly home in the morning?

She'd come too far to go home now. Even Rorey's murder wasn't going to stop her. But she had to remain anonymous. Deet, as he seemed to be called, didn't know her.

The black-market art dealer didn't know her. She had to keep it that way.

Needing some time to think, she went into the lounge and sat at the bar.

"Iced tea," she said. "And I'll take a menu."

Glancing down the length of the bar, a man sitting with two others at a table gave her a shocking jolt of recognition. It was the man who'd held a gun on Rorey. Beside him another man looked right at her.

The Frenchman.

Did he know who she was? He couldn't. None of them had seen her. Still, fear chased through her until she managed to control it.

He tipped his glass of wine toward her and sipped, a look in his eyes she didn't misinterpret. He liked what he saw.

After a moment of indecision, she smiled. This could work in her favor. It was risky, but the payoff would be worth it.

He spoke to his friends and stood. Tall, lean, with thinning medium-brown hair and unremarkable brown eyes, he wasn't a handsome man by her standards, but he had an aura about him. Power. Intelligence. And a passion for her painting. He dressed expensively, wearing an impeccable black suit. She felt herself responding to his confident approach. There was something intoxicating about that. About his power. She didn't have to fear him if he took an interest in her.

He reached her and said in a strong voice that matched his energy, "Lucian LeFevre." He held out his hand.

She swiveled on the barstool and gave him her hand, unprepared for her unexpected attraction to such a man. "Jada Manoah."

Lifting her hand, he kissed the tops of her fingers. "You are very beautiful, Ms. Manoah."

Maybe it was his accent. "Jada."

He smiled seductively, a man full of himself and his prowess with women who captivated him. "You may call me Lucian."

"Lucian."

"Would you care to join me for dinner?"

"I'd like that very much." Finding that she meant it more than she should, she paid no heed as he took her tea and led her to his table. With a nod, the two with him got up and left.

He ordered for himself and Jada when a waiter appeared.

"What brings you to Anguilla?" Sitting back in his chair, he absorbed her, took in her face with leisurely thoroughness, not hiding his masculine interest. She was safe for now.

She decided right then not to lie. If she could use him to get her painting, she would. "A painting."

More of that satisfaction flooded his eyes. "A painting? Here?"

"It's called *The Portrait of Sarah*." She put her arms on the table and leaned toward him, returning his look with a sultry one of her own. His gaze flitted to her cleavage. "It's extremely valuable."

"What a coincidence. I came here for the same reason."

She smiled. Genuinely. Big, bright and full of the excitement that charged her blood. They'd both essentially admitted that they each knew what the other was after.

The waiter appeared, refilling Jada's tea.

"Send our meals to my room," Lucian instructed. Then he stood and held out his hand. "Come. We have much to discuss."

She put her hand in his and he led her to the elevators. Standing beside him, feeling his anticipatory gaze travel all over her body, she felt apprehension rear up. He made her respond in a way that put her at odds with her purpose. She would use him to get the painting, and yet she responded to his attraction.

Opening his room door, he let her in ahead of him. It was a large suite with a view of the ocean.

She walked to the windows, savoring the sunset. She wasn't afraid of Lucian. In a way, he was a lot like her. Nothing would stand in his way of acquiring the painting. It kind of excited her, meeting someone with the same passion.

He came up behind her, reached around and tipped her chin up. "Why do you want *The Portrait of Sarah?*"

"I'm Jewish."

Grinning shrewdly, he looked down at her lips. "You've an interest in stolen Nazi art?"

"I have for years. And *The Portrait of Sarah* was stolen from a Jew. That makes it Jewish art, I believe."

His lustful gaze met hers and she wasn't sure he believed her. "The painting will be mine."

"Then I'll help you get it."

"And let me keep it?"

"Could I take it from you if I tried?"

He chuckled.

He didn't think she could. "I didn't come up here to manipulate you."

"No?"

She arched her head to bring her mouth closer to his. "No."

"Why did you come here?" He slid his hands up her torso to cover her breasts.

Electrified sparks of passion inundated her. Her response to his touch spun her mind into confusion. Why was she reacting so strongly to him?

"You want the painting," he said.

"Yes." Passion made her thoughts fuzzy.

"What will you do to have it?" He stepped away from her, backing toward the wide opening that led to the bedroom.

She followed, knowing he was testing her. Her pulse quickened with apprehension and a peculiar kind of thrill. Would she do anything?

In the bedroom, he removed his suit jacket and tie and began to unbutton his dress shirt. She had no doubt of his intentions. She should admit her mistake and leave, but something kept her from doing so.

Was the painting worth doing this? One inner voice answered with a resounding yes, while another prodded her to turn and go.

If she had any chance of obtaining the painting, she'd have to go along with this.

He reached his hand to her, his eyes dark with lust.

She moved forward and put her hand in his. He pulled her to him, sliding his arms around her.

"I'm not doing this for the painting," she said, but it was a half-truth.

His brow rose in tantalizing doubt.

Stepping away from his arms, she pushed the straps of her red sundress off each shoulder. "Why do you want the painting so much?"

"I love history."

"That's too vague."

"I love the history of *The Portrait of Sarah*. I've loved it since the moment I learned of it. Two murders. The affair between a Nazi and a Jew. Stolen art…"

His reason stoked her passion hotter. He appreciated the painting as much as she. Oddly, that acted as an aphrodisiac.

She let her sundress drop to the floor at her feet.

He looked fully, dark, evil desire roaming all over her. She knew nothing about this man except his obsession with *The Portrait of Sarah*.

He took off his dress shirt and began unfastening his slacks.

Certainty swirled inside Jada. She'd have this man tonight. She'd enjoy every touch. Every stroke. But he was a fool if he underestimated her. No matter how rich and powerful he was, nothing would stand in her way. The painting was hers.

Chapter 5

Sitting across from Travis on the patio of the Yellow Umbrella, a hotel café that Travis had deliberately dragged her to, Raeleen ended the call she'd tried to make to Landon, her cameraman. She'd called him several times since cell service was restored. Something was wrong, and she was beginning to get very worried.

Travis glanced up at her as though wondering if she'd tried to call Deet, and then he resumed reading that damn newspaper as if she weren't even there. He was aware, though. She wasn't fooled by his show of utter calm. A stranger would think he was enjoying his vacation after surviving a hurricane. Just a handsome man sitting with his girlfriend on a lovely Caribbean morning. She hated how that appealed to her, especially since he refused to let her out of his sight and she'd already had repeated arguments in her head over why she was letting him control her. She was surprised he'd allowed her to go shopping for a small piece of luggage and some clothes to get her by.

Turning toward the street, sunlight sprayed down from a cloudless sky. No wind. Warm and beautiful.

Where was Landon? Travis told her he'd talked to him when he'd arrived on the island, and the travel coordinator at the Dining Network confirmed he hadn't flown home before the hurricane. The airport wasn't open yet. Landon had to be on the island, but why hadn't he tried to call her, and why wasn't he in his room? Had he been caught in the storm?

His absence and the ever-present unknown over Deet and her kidnapping had her on edge. Why had Deet driven to her cottage after the storm? Why had he tried to meet with her alone? She'd have gone to see him by now if Travis wasn't so adamant about not letting her out of his sight. He had his orders. And his orders were to bring her home. He was sticking to them ever since she ran off on him to meet Deet.

Travis turned a page of the newspaper, and she was once again drawn to him. His long eyelashes. The strong features of his face, jawbone, brow, cheeks. Firm lips. Manly hands that held the paper. He had clean, trimmed fingernails. He was well-groomed, but nothing could soften his rugged exterior.

She refused to acknowledge that that had anything to do with why she was listening to him and not trying again to sneak out and meet Deet. Besides, he did have a point about the wisdom of meeting him alone.

"Still not answering?" Travis asked without looking up from his paper. The man had an annoying ability to appear unruffled in the most dire situations.

"No."

He put down the paper. Having seen how worried she was getting, genuine concern seemed to sober him. He put cash on the table to close out their tab and stood.

"Come on. We'll go look for him."

Raeleen stood and walked with him out into the lobby.

Her cell phone rang. Stopping, she pulled it out of her purse. Seeing Landon's name in the display, she shut her eyes in relief and sighed as she answered. "Landon, it's about time you called. Where are you?"

"Ms. Randall?" an unfamiliar voice said.

Her short-lived relief altered to apprehension. "Y-yes?"

"I am a nurse at Princess Alexandra Hospital. Mr. Morgan asked me to call you. He is all right, but he will be spending another day or two here. He has been beaten rather badly."

"Beaten?" She looked at Travis, who could follow just fine.

"He asks that you come see him."

"Tell him we'll be right there." Raeleen ended the call and hurried to the front of the hotel to flag a cab.

With Travis searching their surroundings, Raeleen entered the hospital ahead of him. White walls with barely anything on them engulfed the beige information desk.

"May I help you?" the woman sitting there asked.

"I'm looking for Landon Morgan."

The woman searched on her computer and gave them the room.

Raeleen and Travis navigated the hallways and took an elevator to the second floor.

Finding the room, Raeleen entered and stifled a gasp, shock jolting her when she saw his condition. His head was bandaged, his leg in traction, and his face was so swollen she couldn't recognize him. Too shaken to say anything, she allowed Travis to go in ahead of her. He took her hand, and she stood beside him at the bed.

Landon didn't open his eyes. He probably couldn't, they were so swollen.

"Landon?" she said.

He stirred, but barely.

"It's Raeleen and Travis."

His mouth moved, quivered, and he struggled to breathe.

Raeleen looked toward the door and then at Travis. "Should he be having visitors?"

Landon's weak grasp on her wrist brought her turning back to him. One of his eyes quivered like his mouth as he fought to keep it open a sliver. She felt helpless for him.

"Landon. Oh, my God." Tears burned her eyes. "Who did this to you?"

"Th-they kn-know." He swallowed and his breathing grew unsteady. His eye closed.

"Stop trying to talk." She turned back to Travis. "Go tell them he needs attention. He needs to be moved. He needs to be in the United States!"

Travis only barely acknowledged her. He stepped closer to the bed, a man with a purpose. He leaned down on the opposite side, bringing his face close to Landon's.

"What do they know?"

Was he heartless? "Landon needs better medical attention than this. Look at him!" She had to point with her left hand since Landon still gripped her right one weakly. "We have to get him out of here."

Landon squeezed her hand. "Roth."

Roth. Her father.

"Whoever beat you knows my father?" As the implications of that settled, she looked up at Travis. He straightened with fierce eyes.

"Who did this to you?" Travis repeated her earlier question.

Landon slowly rolled his head from side to side. His attacker hadn't revealed his identity. But it had to be whoever was behind Vivian's and John's murders.

"He was beaten for information on you," Travis said.

"Deet's wife arranged to have you kidnapped, and whoever killed her wanted to learn what made you so important."

She was important because she had been Deet's lover. Vivian had tried to use her against him, but all of that paled in comparison to the discovery that she was Colonel Roth's daughter. She was now a viable threat. She, and even more significant, the man who'd been sent to rescue her.

"I'm…sorry," Landon choked. "They made me…"

"Don't apologize." She felt ill. She'd told John about her father and that he'd send someone for her, but he must not have revealed that to anyone. Landon had been forced to instead. It would almost be better if John had been the one to talk. Then she wouldn't be looking at Landon beaten so badly. She felt ill.

"I'm so sorry, Landon." However he'd discovered her father was a colonel who operated his own military organization, it was her fault. She must have gotten careless.

"R-Raeleen." Landon's chest rose and fell with stress. "I'm the one…who's s-sorry. I…heard you…talking to him once. You…were angry…" He breathed raggedly.

"It isn't your fault." She was angry with her father a lot. It wasn't surprising that she'd said more than she should over the phone. One tear then another and a third fell out of her eyes. She leaned over him, making sure he understood. "It's okay, Landon. I'm just so happy you're alive." She touched his cheek, careful not to hurt him. "I never liked what my dad did for a living, anyway."

He caught her joke because he laughed, but it cost him. He groaned in pain over and over again.

Raeleen cringed and wished there was something she could do to help him. "We're going to get you out of here. We'll make sure you get the best treatment."

Landon writhed a little longer and then his one eye blinked and he nodded.

"What are the people who did this to you after?" Travis asked.

A new resolve radiated from him. Raeleen marveled over it while Landon rolled his head to look at Travis. "A...painting." He breathed through his pain. "I...I don't...remember anything else."

All of Travis's energy zeroed in on her. "Where does Deet live?"

He was going to take her there? All that take-charge dominance would normally set her off, but she found it incredibly sexy now.

Raeleen followed Travis out the front of the hospital. He didn't stop walking until he spotted a cab and waved it to the curb. Seeing Landon beaten had lit a fire in him. He'd called Odie and told her to arrange to have Landon transported back to New York as soon as the airport was open. Now he was taking her along with him to hunt down Deet. She was thrilled.

Vivian's and John's murders were one thing, but the moment an innocent was hurt, he'd switched into retaliation mode. This was the soldier that carried out dangerous TES missions. She should not enjoy the spectacle. This was something her father would do. It's what kept him away from home so much. And because of Landon, she unabashedly cheered him on.

Travis turned to her in the cab. "You'll do exactly as I say when we get there."

She cocked her head at him. He was going to start with that again? What made him so overprotective, anyway? The more she thought about it, the more certain she became that there was a reason.

"I'd take you back to the hotel, but I can't be sure you'll

be safe there," he said, cementing her conjecture. "You probably wouldn't stay there, anyway."

"I'm not a do-as-you're-told kind of girl," she said, testing him. It wasn't as though it was a lie. She didn't like to take orders.

"No kidding."

Is that what bothered him? He was afraid she wouldn't do what he told her, that he would lose control of the situation and something would go terribly wrong? That could happen on any mission, so why was this one different?

"I'm not as fragile as you think, Travis."

"I don't think you're fragile." He observed her entire body as though affirming his statement. "You're anything but fragile."

"Then why do you always treat me like something will happen to me if I don't do exactly as you say?" Why did he have to be in such rigid control?

"I'm trained for this. You aren't."

It had to be more than that. "It's like you're afraid of failing or something."

"Nothing's going to happen to you, because I won't let it."

That wasn't good enough. "Have you ever failed on a mission before?"

He stared at her. "Why are you asking me that now?"

"Because now is the right time." She'd hit on something. His reaction told her so. Something had happened to make him paranoid about protecting women he encountered on assignments. It wasn't that he lacked confidence, he just put extra energy into it, as though he had to make extra sure nothing went wrong.

"Pull over here," he told the driver.

"Have you?" She got out of the car and walked beside him down the sidewalk. She wasn't going to let this drop.

In his usual fashion, he surveyed their surroundings. "Not with TES."

She believed that. His vigilance was on overdrive. "But you have...before that?"

He just kept walking, his long strides gobbling up the concrete, moving with agility that belied his size. Deet's house wasn't far from here. Up the street to the right, just outside downtown and close to his restaurant. His primary residence.

"What happened?" There was something buried deep inside him that needed to come out. Otherwise, he'd always have this problem, and some day it might backfire on him. Just as she was sure he feared, he'd become too preoccupied with overprotecting his "package" and something would go wrong.

He didn't respond.

A couple passed, the woman pointing to a clothing shop like she'd discovered gold, probably one of few that were open this soon after the hurricane. Cars were beginning to fill the streets.

"Something must have happened," she said, to no avail.

He wasn't going to talk about it. And that only worked to convince her all the more that he needed to face it or it would eventually come back to haunt him.

They turned the corner and Deet's house came into view, forcing her to table the topic for now. His yard was in shambles but his house fared pretty well, like all the other houses here. All along the street, neighbors worked in their yards. Where had he gone during the storm?

She followed Travis to the front door. He knocked and continued his scrutiny of their surroundings.

When no one came to the door, he tried the handle. The door opened. Slipping inside and to the left of the door, she saw him pull out his gun, out of sight from the neighbors.

He gestured for her to follow, and she stepped inside. While Travis closed the door, she took in the destruction. It hadn't been caused by the hurricane. Pictures were on the floor, pillows and cushions off the sofa and chair, rugs covering the tiled floors were overturned. Books had been wiped off a white shelf that ran the length of one wall behind the sofa.

"Someone's already been here," she said.

He pressed a finger to his lips. "Shh." And then, putting his face close to hers, he added in a low voice, "You wait here."

"But—"

His brow lifted and his head dipped as though challenging her to argue.

"Okay," she whispered, resisting the spark of affection that came over her. He might be overprotective, but he was also very capable.

He angled his head in doubt.

"I will," she assured him.

With one last look, he walked with his gun raised through the living room, disappearing up a stairway.

Raeleen surveyed the living room and peered into the kitchen, which was in similar disarray. Other than a bathroom, there were no other rooms down here.

Listening for Travis, she heard no sound and began to wonder what was taking so long. Was he all right?

She took a step toward the stairs and then stopped. He'd asked her to stay here. No, he'd ordered her.

That suddenly nettled her.

What if he needed her right now and his overprotectiveness was getting in the way? She climbed the stairs. At the top, she looked up to see glimpses of blue sky through a tangle of tree branches. A tree had caused the roof to partially collapse. The bathroom was destroyed and part of one bedroom. She went down the hall to that room. At the doorway, she faced Travis's gun. So much for needing her...

His face changed from a soldier's readiness to a scowl of frustration. "I told you to wait."

"I'm not a dog. And you're way too overprotective." She looked around the room. "Did you find anything?"

"No."

"Deet didn't kill his wife, did he?" Someone had gone through his house looking for the painting Landon had told them about.

"It's hard to say. His wife kidnapped you."

"But someone ransacked his house." And that someone had beaten Landon. Had they also killed Vivian and her brother? "What kind of painting does Deet have?"

"A dangerous one. Come on, let's get out of here."

Sitting at a hotel bar beside Raeleen, Travis tried to focus on the soccer game on TV. She had on a pair of white shorts that showcased her long legs, torturing him. Last night they'd gotten word that the airport would open in the morning. They had a flight out at 8:00 a.m. Deet was nowhere to be found, and neither were the men after the painting. He was beginning to doubt Deet had killed his wife and brother-in-law. He also didn't think he intended for anyone else to. That left two possibilities. Either Vivian and her brother had worked a deal with the killers, or Deet had and the deal had somehow gone bad. If Deet had made the deal, his wife had tried to stop him by kidnapping Raeleen. If Vivian and her brother had done it, they'd kidnapped Raeleen to force Deet to hand over the painting. If he'd refused...

"Thanks for arranging to transport Landon home."

Travis turned to Raeleen. "You can thank Odie. She did it all." She'd called him just before he'd come to the hotel bar.

"I don't see why we have to go back now, though."

They'd already argued about this. She wanted to stay and track Deet down. He planned to get her home where she belonged.

"You're safer there." He turned back to the soccer game on the overhead bar television, waiting for another argument. Instead of dreading it, he actually welcomed it.

He met a lot of women through online sites and in public places, but few captivated him as much as Raeleen. This was just like Haley, except he wasn't afraid to hurt Raeleen. She wasn't afraid of him, either, and that was the best part. She felt like his equal. Another reason to get her home. She might break his heart if he wasn't careful.

"I'm safe with you, aren't I?"

He turned to her soft, sweet eyes and the alluring curve shaping her glossy lips. Her effect on him dulled the sense that she was baiting him. "Yes."

"Then why can't we stay and find Deet together?"

Together. "This is getting too dangerous." It wasn't only Deet involved.

Recalling how she'd probed for what had happened to make him so overprotective—just as Haley had—he realized where this was going.

"I'm beginning to understand you pretty well, Travis Todd." She almost sounded smug.

"Starting to see me for the man I am instead of stereotyping?" he teased, hoping she'd stop. He didn't want to talk about why he was so protective of women.

"I see you for the man you are."

"I doubt that." He wasn't the kind of man who'd neglect his kids or try to control the woman he was with, both things she'd attributed to her father.

"I don't think you do."

He wasn't talking about what made him a TES operative

anymore. "You can't even see who you are. How could you see me any deeper?"

"We were talking about you, not me."

Not anymore. "You've closed yourself off to the truth."

She plopped her elbow on the bar and twisted to face him more, totally confrontational, and totally appealing to him. "What truth?"

"You're just like your father." He waited for the fallout from that to come down on him, watching her beautiful blue eyes fire daggers.

"I am nothing like my father." She paused between each word for emphasis, which only made him remember her attitude when she thought he was giving her orders during the hurricane.

"No?" At least he'd stopped her from digging into his personal affairs again.

"No!"

Her defiance confirmed he was right. "You're obsessed with your job and don't like to be bossed around."

"I don't run a secret military organization. I'm the host of a TV program."

"Yes, and now I know why."

Defensiveness bubbled and boiled under her hold on its eruption. He found it entirely too adorable. She held back what he was sure would have been a spectacular comeback.

"Do you really think choosing a profession that's nothing like your father's makes you different than him?" he asked. "You're as busy as he is."

With jerky movements, she swirled on the barstool and faced forward, looking up at the television without watching the game. He took her in, sitting there fuming. He'd gotten her thinking, though.

"I don't mean that as an insult. It's refreshing." *She* was refreshing. Too much so. He could get in trouble with her.

After taking a moment to assimilate that, she gazed slowly down his body, all the way to his big black boots resting on the platform at the base of the bar, before it traveled back up. Her anger faded in lieu of her new interest. "It's refreshing that I'm as busy as my dad?"

"It's refreshing that you're as *strong* as your dad."

As his meaning took shape, the fiery light in her eyes simmered to a warm glow. "You aren't used to that in women?"

"I haven't met many women like that."

"Do you meet a lot on assignments?"

"I meet them." And had relations with them, but none of them lasted.

"You probably meet a lot of them. Do you like that?"

"When it works, yes. I don't seek it out." He had relations but didn't have to. He was a patient man. He could wait for the right one. And it was disturbing that he felt the possibility building with Raeleen.

The soccer game became a diversion again. He wasn't sure this opening of hearts was such a great idea for them. Her antimilitary stance made it that way. That and her probing.

"What was that woman you stood up before coming to Anguilla like?"

"I didn't stand her up." Was this her strategy to get him to talk about what she was really after?

"Oh, okay, you called her. But you still stood her up in the name of your job. What was she like?"

"Nice. Sophisticated. Smart. Reserved."

"Reserved?"

Figures, she'd catch on to that word. He continued to watch the soccer game, although nothing registered. Raeleen consumed every synapse in his brain.

"The, 'I'm not going to sleep with you too soon,' reserved, or the, 'You terrify me,' reserved?" Raeleen asked.

He deliberately ignored her.

"Did she do what you told her to do?" she persisted.

"I didn't tell her what to do."

"She was just…what…intimidated by you?"

It was time to aim the cannon on her now. "Was Deet intimidated by you?"

She looked up at the television.

Priceless. "He was. Not intimidated. Accommodating."

"Which is why you conveniently didn't know he was married."

He saw her catch his meaning, and her mask of indifference melted with affront. "He lied to me."

"I don't think you cared that he was married."

Her mouth dropped open and then she closed it, unable to dispute what he said. She hadn't cared; moreover, she wasn't hurt by the betrayal. And the reason was that Deet hadn't interfered with her busy schedule.

They were both looking for people who didn't interfere with their work. Would Raeleen try to change him if they fell in love? Would she require that he be there for her whenever her schedule allowed? He could never live that way. Besides, she refused to give any military man a chance. He was a military man, albeit in secret. And that wouldn't change. He wouldn't change for anything.

"If you ever get over your neglect issue with your dad, let me know," he said.

"If you ever quit working for my father, let *me* know."

He drank the rest of his water and put the glass down, letting the conversation end there. She was too stubborn, and certain things about his past were off-limits.

"Why do you work for him, anyway?"

He should have expected her not to let that go. "I come from a long line of military men."

Raeleen's head angled as she studied him. "So it was just a natural progression?"

"Put the drink on the room," he told the bartender. Then to Raeleen, "Let's go." Sitting at this bar only invited conversation. He needed to get her mind on other things. If only those other things didn't center on getting her naked.

"Why can't you tell me?"

"We've talked enough. Let's go up to the room."

"And do what? Talk more?"

Would she continue to fish for answers he refused to give? There would be nowhere he could go to escape her. Whether here or in the room, she'd keep digging into his past.

She must have registered his emotion, because her tactic softened. Putting her drink down, she regarded him with new understanding.

"It wasn't just a natural progression," she said. "Was it?"

He could tell by the way she spoke that she didn't expect him to reply. She hadn't really asked a question. She'd voiced her thoughts aloud. He'd expected her to keep pressuring him, and instead, she'd eased off.

Just then, he caught sight of a dark-haired man in a wrinkle-free cream-colored dress shirt watching them from a table just beyond the bar. How long had he been sitting there? Awhile, it appeared, with two bottles of beer on the table, one of them probably empty. The cash on the table told Travis he'd be ready to get up and leave without having to close out a tab.

Travis inwardly swore. He couldn't believe he hadn't noticed him until now.

He moved to the bar. "On second thought, I'll wait for you to finish your drink."

Raeleen looked up at him in surprise.

Covertly checking the man at the end of the bar, he saw him doing the same, only now he was more alert. While Travis had been preoccupied with Raeleen, he'd felt at ease watching. Now that Travis had seen him, that comfort zone had changed.

Damn. This man was a professional. Whoever was after that painting knew who Travis worked for. It would be foolish to send anyone less capable to tail him. The man was about six feet tall and muscular. Short, cropped dark hair. Dark eyes. Mustache. He looked Cuban.

As Travis let him know he was onto him, the man drank some beer and put the bottle down. A waiter came to the table and Travis shook his head. How had he found them at the hotel?

"What are you looking at?" Raeleen followed his gaze and saw the man. "Who is that?"

The man got up and walked toward the exit.

"Wait here."

"What? No…" She stood from the stool and bumped against him. Soft breasts mashed to his chest and feminine hands spread over his shoulders. Her face tipped up as their gazes collided.

Meanwhile, the man he'd seen was getting away.

Pushing her a step back, Travis watched him leave the bar.

"Wait for me here." It was imperative that she listen to him.

"No. I'm going with you." Her head bobbed to the side so she could see around him. "We should hurry."

He took her by her shoulders and gave her a gentle jerk. "Raeleen, I need you to wait here for me. It's public and you'll be safe. Don't go to the room. Don't leave the hotel. Just stay right here."

"Stop overprotecting me."

She kept saying that, and he refused to budge. She thought she understood but she didn't. Regardless of who her father was, she wasn't trained for this. If he was being overprotective, then she'd just have to deal with it. "You aren't listening to me."

She planted a defiant hand on her hip. "I think it's safer if I stay with you. You think I'm not and that's your mistake, Travis."

Swearing, he strode through the bar and entered the lobby. There, he stopped to search for the man. Had he left the hotel or was he staying here?

Raeleen stood beside him. "Where did he go?"

Ignoring her, Travis left the hotel and searched for signs of the man out on the street. He was nowhere.

And why would he be? Travis had wasted too much time arguing with Raeleen.

Just as he was about to start swearing some more, he heard tires squealing and looked in time to see the man driving down the street.

Chapter 6

Having no choice other than to take Raeleen with him, Travis quickly searched around and spotted a taxi cab driver removing luggage from the trunk of his vehicle.

"Get into that cab." Now he was ordering her. And she better do what he said.

She did. She headed for the cab with him. As the driver closed the trunk and took cash from two disheveled passengers who'd likely been displaced from the hurricane, Raeleen hurried to the passenger's side. Travis slipped behind the wheel as Raeleen took a seat beside him. They both closed their doors and Travis drove off. Under the lights of the hotel entrance, the taxi driver raised a fistful of cash, shouting something.

Seconds later, Travis spotted the taillights of the car ahead. It drove without a hurry along the highway. The driver hadn't seen them. He probably thought Travis wouldn't follow. After his delay because of Raeleen, he could see why. If he had chased him out of the hotel, he'd have more reason to hurry. But arguing with Raeleen had actually worked in their favor.

Disguised in the cab, they followed for a couple of miles before the car turned off the road toward an inn. Travis drove in after him. Seeing the other man park, he pulled to a stop just past the front entrance.

"Don't get out yet," he told Raeleen.

"Actually, I was thinking about introducing myself."

Her smart remark made him chuckle despite the fact that she'd done it because she thought he was being overprotective again.

She watched in the side mirror and he watched in the rearview mirror as the man walked from his car to the entrance, glancing from one side to the other. He didn't notice them in the cab. A cab in front of an inn wasn't unusual.

"Let's go."

She stepped out of the car with him.

Ever aware of her as he headed for the front of the inn, Travis steeled himself to the task at hand. If anything went wrong, he'd get Raeleen out of there and deal with the man who'd been spying on them later.

The inn was quiet. A house converted into a bed-and-breakfast, its entry featured a couch and two tables. Archways to the left and right led to a dining room and a parlor. Straight back was the kitchen through two swinging half doors. He heard someone working back there.

Pointing to the stairs and seeing Raeleen nod, he climbed them. At the top he stopped to check the hall. With Raeleen behind him, he paused at each door to listen. At the second door, he heard a television.

"Are you going to kick the door down?" she whispered.

"Do you want me to kick the door down?"

Seeing that he was teasing her, she cocked her head at

him and then knocked on the door. There was no peephole or he'd have stopped her.

An old man answered, his face turning perplexed. "You don't look like room service."

"Sorry, wrong door." Travis guided Raeleen away, hearing the door close.

At the last room, he heard a man's voice talking. Testing the knob, finding it locked, he glanced over at Raeleen. She watched with big, round, crystal-clear blue eyes. Fearless eyes. She wanted questions answered just like he.

The door opened a crack and a familiar face appeared. The man from the hotel bar tried to shut it. Travis put a booted foot in the opening and pushed with one hand.

The man stumbled backward as Travis entered and reached behind him to stop Raeleen from entering with him. He hoped she'd get the message. And do what he wanted.

Advancing on the man, Travis saw in his peripheral vision that Raeleen entered the room and closed the door. Frustrated by that, he took in details at the same time. The king-size bed opposite the door with tables on each side. Two chairs in front of a window to his left. A television centered with the bed and next to the door, and a desk next to it with a pistol by the lamp. The man hadn't expected visitors.

Travis maneuvered so that the man's back was to the bed and his was to the pistol. The man watched him and didn't seem concerned he had no gun. Travis hadn't drawn his yet. No fear. He was a trained fighter.

"Who sent you?" Travis asked.

The man didn't alter his stance, only backed between the bed and the chairs as Travis moved toward him. At one of the bedside tables, the man lifted a lamp and yanked the cord from the wall. Then he lunged toward Travis.

The man threw the lamp and Travis blocked its well-aimed trajectory. A second later, he had to block the man's swinging fists and kicking feet. He finally answered with two well-placed chops and a stomp against the man's ankle. The man went low, his hands on the floor and his legs scissoring for a kick. He struck Travis and almost took him off his feet. He flipped his tall frame and landed behind the man, then slammed his foot against his back. The man crashed against the television and would have gone for his gun if Travis hadn't been ready. He grabbed the man and threw him to the side, away from the gun and close to the door and Raeleen, who sidled deeper into the room, approaching the gun.

She better not even think about picking up that gun. The man collided with him and he went down. Travis cursed at his own distraction. Cursed again for Raeleen causing it. The man punched him and tried again, but Travis rammed his palm against his chin, jerking the man's head backward. Raeleen appeared above them, the lamp raised in her hands, Amazon woman in sexy shorts. She hadn't gone for the gun. Instead, she beaned the man on the back of his head. The man fell off Travis and jumped to his feet to go after Raeleen.

Rage filled him that the man would dare to try. He sprang to his feet and kicked him in the kidney, sending him sailing sideways toward the two chairs and the window. Raeleen moved out of the way as he corrected his fall. Travis went after him, but the man kept running and crashed through the window.

Raeleen joined Travis there. He could barely make out the man struggling to get out of a beat-up Dumpster. Glancing at Raeleen, wishing she'd listen if he told her to wait for him, Travis ran through the door. He heard her behind him in the hallway. They passed the old man who stood in the hall gaping at them. As they ran downstairs, a man wearing an apron appeared at the base, no doubt responding to all the noise. Travis pushed him aside and ran with Raeleen behind him toward the front door.

"Hey!" the man yelled.

"Sorry!" Raeleen called as she followed Travis through the door. "We're sorry."

Outside, the man who'd jumped into the Dumpster was at his car, grabbing the door handle.

Just as Travis was about to reach him, he abandoned the locked car door and ran toward the neighboring building, a house similar to the inn but smaller. Travis gained on him as they reached a strip mall with kiosks scattered about. People worked to clean up what the winds had torn apart.

Ahead, the man pushed a woman with her arms full of rumpled clothes. She dropped her burden and Travis caught her before she fell. Letting her go, he saw the man duck into a small clothing store. He heard a man yell, "We are closed!"

Raeleen was ahead of him now, running into the kiosk.

Travis swore and ran after her. Inside, he saw Raeleen duck from a blow the man intended for her while the shop owner spoke rapidly in indiscernible English, waving his hands in a futile attempt to stop the destruction of his meager possessions. Raeleen dodged more kicks and swinging hands from the man who attacked her.

Her ability surprised him as much as he was relieved. She was okay. She wouldn't be able to fight the man much longer, though. She'd be no match for him. Travis grabbed the man's wrist and punched his nose. The man yelped and twisted free. When he ran, Travis let him go. He didn't like how glad he was that Raeleen could fight. What if she was hurt?

Raeleen pivoted to follow, but Travis stopped her with his arm around her waist, bringing her against him and forcing her to look up at him. Damn, he could feel himself falling for her more.

"What are you doing?"

"We're going back to the hotel, and in the morning, I'm taking you home." It had been a bad idea to go after the man. He shouldn't have gone to Deet's house with her, either.

"Travis, we can catch him. You can make him tell us who's behind all of this."

"I don't want you involved anymore. It's too dangerous." He took in her alert blue eyes and messy blond hair and was too aware of her soft curves against him. If he didn't end this now, he might pay for it later. With his heart.

"We can't leave now. That man was watching us. Let's go. He's getting away!"

"Then let him." Travis wrapped his other arm around her.

Her hands were on his chest, and she began to notice the heat building between them. Her gaze lifted and a different kind of alertness radiated in them.

The kiosk owner appeared beside them. "You go now!"

Travis used the interruption and took Raeleen's hand to lead her out of the kiosk. Out into the night, he walked with her toward their hotel, staying on the busy street and searching for another cab. The stolen one would be discovered soon, if it hadn't already. The inn owner had surely called the police.

"I can't believe you're just going to let him get away."

"I'm not. I'll handle this after you're safely back home." He'd find the painting. Then anyone after it would come to him.

"Safely back home," she muttered. "You need to let go of whatever happened to make you so paranoid."

She could call him overprotective until the next ice age proved global warming was just another spike in geological history. He was getting her out of here. Then she was her father's problem. He wouldn't have to worry about her and she wouldn't be around to tempt him. He kept his reasons to himself. He couldn't tell her that he was taking her to her father any more than he could tell her how much he wanted her.

Back in the room, Raeleen turned on the television while Travis went over to the window, scanning the street and everywhere else. She still couldn't believe he'd allowed that man to get away. She could see how he'd want to protect her. It was dangerous chasing that man. Normally she wasn't afraid of defending herself, but she'd been afraid of him. It had been a while since she'd practiced martial arts. She'd veered away from it after the disenchantment with her father had settled in.

But that's not all that was at play with Travis. Something deep was going on there, and she meant to unravel the cause.

Travis moved to the foot of one of the queen beds and unfastened his belt, slipping it free and dumping it into the duffel bag.

She moved to the foot of her own bed, where her suitcase lay open. "Why are you so anxious to get rid of me?" It wasn't the question she wanted to ask, but it was a good start.

"I don't want to get rid of you. I'm just keeping you safe, that's all." He pulled out his gun from the waist of his jeans and checked its ammo.

"Mission accomplished."

He lowered his gun. "It's more than that."

Sensing he meant it, she moved toward him. Without asking aloud, she waited for him to explain.

"I don't want anything to happen to you."

She couldn't refute that, but there was something else driving him. And it had nothing to do with this insane attraction between them.

Going to the table between the beds, he put his gun there.
End of discussion.

That's when she realized that he believed his protection
of her wasn't overdone. While it hadn't been tonight, most
of the time it was.

"Who was she?" It had to be a woman.

He turned to face her.

"The woman who made you so overprotective."

"Haley always called me that," he said, noncommittal.

"Haley?" Just as she thought. A woman.

"Why are you asking me so many personal questions?
I thought you had a distaste for men who worked for your
father. I'm starting to get a different impression."

Wow, he was really good at turning things back onto her.
And then she chided herself for allowing her guard to go
down. Instinct had led her to probe for what lay in his heart.
Instinct had made her feel that they were growing closer,
that this sexual magnetism might have some merit. When in
truth they were strangers who didn't belong together. And
Travis had just reminded her of that.

"Sorry, I...I shouldn't have asked." Turning away, she
rummaged for the long T-shirt she always slept in, an old,
soft thing that she'd never be able to replace when it was
too torn to wear.

"Haley Engen."

Going still with the unexpected sound of Travis's voice,
she dropped her T-shirt and gave him her full attention.

He moved closer to her now. "She was an operative, a
communications specialist for TES. We were on assignment
in Monrovia, doing surveillance on a diamond merchant,
when our cover was blown. We were ambushed by the merchant's client. I was shot and a mercenary saved Haley. He
was after the client. Later on, he and Haley ended up catching the man."

"He was a mercenary?"

"Yes, but not the kind you might expect. He affiliated his private military company with TES. If it hadn't been for him, I wouldn't be alive right now."

"Do you resent that?"

"Not at all. I'm grateful he showed up when he did. After I was shot, I couldn't protect Haley anymore. He finished the job."

It had been a job to him, protecting Haley. That sort of explained his hang-up. If he was busy protecting a woman, especially one he was attracted to, he was less focused on the mission. Except, Travis was always focused on the mission. He was capable of carrying it through with or without a woman to protect. Didn't he see that about himself?

There had to be more. "Would you have been shot if Haley hadn't been with you?"

"No."

He was sure of it. "But you were because you were protecting her."

"Yes." What about this woman was so different? He'd protected Raeleen just fine, and she wasn't even a TES operative.

"Before joining TES, Haley was captured in Iraq," Travis explained, obviously reading her unspoken questions. "Insurgents brutally beat and raped her. It's what led her to work for TES. She wanted to fight terrorists. But her experience had more of an effect on her than she liked to admit."

She'd convinced herself she was stronger than she was and it had nearly gotten Travis killed. At least, that was his version.

"I admire her courage," Raeleen said. "Not many women could do that. Come back from an experience like that and join an organization like TES."

"She's an incredible woman." His affection spread all

over his face, softening his eyes and lifting his mouth, the creases in his skin sealing the message.

He clearly had feelings for this woman, but they weren't together.

"Was she afraid of you?" she asked.

"Very, at first. But then we became friends after working together so much."

And then she wasn't afraid anymore. "You loved her?"

He blinked, closing out the affection. "I wouldn't say that. I was too protective of her."

At least he recognized that much. "And you don't think you're too protective of me?"

"I wasn't too protective of Haley when I was shot."

In other words, it was either him or her. He'd saved her and risked his life doing it. That made sense, but something was still missing in Raeleen's mind. "Then why didn't you have a relationship with her?" She was sure he would have had he not felt the need to protect her. Why had he felt so obligated, so driven, to do that? "Did you lose someone before her?"

"I think we've had enough heart-to-heart for one night." He pulled off his shirt and twisted his impressive torso to toss it to the floor in front of his bed.

She was momentarily sidetracked with the sight of his bare chest. If it hadn't been for that, she'd have fretted over pinning his hang-up.

"I'm not Haley." She took a single step closer to that bare chest. All that smooth skin over hard muscle...

"No. You're not."

"Am I like the woman you lost?" Although she didn't want to ask that question, it was the only explanation that would make him the way he was. He hadn't lost Haley. She was only part of the equation. But he must have lost someone. Someone very close to him.

"Yes. You ask too many questions."

She looked down at his chest and then back into his magnificent blue-gold eyes. "Did you love her?"

He saw where her gaze had gone, where it kept going, and glanced down the front of her tucked-in sparkly gray and dark pink T-shirt. "Yes."

Whoever the woman was, he had her tucked deep, deep down inside, and the emotional wreckage was the black coal that fueled his purpose. It was also what made him so overprotective with women in danger. But it wasn't enough to stop her from touching him.

"Who was she?" She had to know. She couldn't avoid it.

Instead of answering, he slid one hand around her waist and firmly pulled her against him. An instant later, he raked his other hand through her hair, gripping and drawing her head back. She was too startled to react to anything but the tantalizing sexual sparks shooting everywhere.

He kissed her, igniting the sparks into an incredible blaze. She heard her own moan and slid her hands up his bare chest, loving the feel of him. He was just as smooth and hard as she imagined.

"Travis," she whispered against his warm mouth, running her hands up to the back of his neck.

He kissed her again, harder this time, crushing, needy.

Somewhere through the fog of desire lingered the realization that he'd started this to avoid answering her questions. He'd kissed her to shut her up. But once he'd started, the reason changed. Now he kissed her with the same intent she had. Their passion was more powerful than she could have anticipated.

He tugged the hem of her T-shirt out of her shorts. Raeleen stepped back to pull it over her head and felt Travis's fingers unfastening the clasp of her bra. Heat scorched her. She wanted this so badly. She wanted him. Her bra slackened, releasing her breasts. She let it fall to the floor and the intoxication continued when his hands held her soft flesh.

She watched his face, how his lashes lowered over eyes that were riveted on her breasts. She lifted her hand and touched his face, tracing her fingers over his brow line, to his cheekbone, then his lips.

Taking her hand into his grasp, he put her finger into his mouth and sucked. She had to catch her breath as her pulse quickened with excitement. She couldn't wait for him to be inside her.

He kissed her again, this time much sweeter, taking his time. She glided her hand from the side of his face, down his chest, over his abdomen and finally sank her fingers into the waist of his jeans. He put his hands on her butt.

"These shorts have been driving me wild all day," he said just above her mouth.

She smiled. "Good."

"But now I want you to take them off."

The sound of his voice and the burning look in his eyes made her tremble with humming desire.

"You have such sexy legs." He stoked her fires hotter. He moved back and began to unbutton his jeans, all his glorious muscles working as he unzipped them.

Raeleen watched him, aroused to throbbing need.

"Take off your shorts."

Registering what he said, she unbuttoned her shorts, seeing his jeans go down with his boxers to expose his erection.

Travis finished first and came to her as she kicked off her shorts and underwear. She'd never seen a man more endowed than him. On his way to her, he dragged her suitcase one-handed off the bed. It landed between the two beds, some of her clothes spilling out. She didn't care. All that mattered was him.

At the foot of her bed, his arms drew her against him and he kissed her. Their naked bodies pressing together swarmed her senses. Her breasts mashed against his chest. His erection lay rigid on her lower abdomen. He put his hands on her butt and ground her against him.

Raeleen moaned and climbed up onto him as if he were a tree trunk. He lowered her onto the bed, easily sliding her up to the pillows.

She opened her legs, impatient. But he had other ideas.

He kissed her endlessly and ran his hands down her body, toying with her breasts and tasting her nipples.

"Travis." She couldn't wait any longer. She arched her hips upward so that his hardness slid against her wetness.

Travis groaned, deep and gruff. Instead of putting himself inside her, he moved down her body, making her jerk with sensation as his knowing mouth kissed her ribs and the center of her belly.

He went lower.

"No." She tried to coax him back up. "You're going to make me—"

His tongue found her aroused clitoris, performing expert circles.

"Travis!" she cried out.

"Yes." His tongue delved into her, stimulating just the right spot and electrifying her unbearably. She came with pulsing intensity, vaguely aware of her loud yell.

She heard him cursing with sexual wildness as she floated back to coherency. Pushing her knees wide, he used his thumbs to arouse her again. She couldn't stand it. Gripping his hair, she tugged.

He worked his magic a bit longer, nearly making her come for a second time. Then blessedly he moved over her. She held her legs wide as the tip of him entered her. He stretched her wet flesh. Tight. Soft. Hard.

He slid in farther, achingly slow, until he sank all the way in. He drew back and slid back in. She felt every inch of him.

Suddenly he stopped, holding himself inside her, his face contorted with ecstasy. He was on the edge, but he held off to wait for her.

Raeleen reached her hands above her head, bracing herself against the wood headboard. Travis propped himself up on his hands push-up style and began moving again.

Mind-numbing sensation paralyzed her. Travis thrust harder and she cried out. He relentlessly continued, finding the spot that sent her rushing into oblivion.

He groaned with her release and moved faster, jerking her body with each penetration, prolonging her orgasm. No... stimulating another one. A deeper one.

"Travis," she breathed, so hot she thought she'd go out of her mind.

"Yes. Say my name again."

"Travis," she all but worshipped.

He groaned again, pumping deep, and reached his finale.

Her heart throbbed, and she couldn't catch her breath. "Wow." She could barely speak.

Travis lay on top of her, spent like her, softening inside her but still pulsing.

At last he rolled off her and they lay side by side as reality descended. She'd just had the most unbelievable sex she'd ever experienced. With Travis. A TES operative.

"You did that on purpose," she said.

Chapter 7

The next afternoon, Raeleen walked beside Travis after landing at Dulles International Airport. TES's private plane had gotten them here, and now she assumed she'd go into the airport and take a commercial flight to New York. Seeing a waiting car ahead, she wondered if he was just going to get in and leave her behind without ado. She'd never see him again.

After angrily denying he'd seduced her on purpose, he'd rolled over and gone to sleep. Waking up this morning had been horribly awkward. She'd hardly slept, and he'd slept like a baby. That rattled her ire. She burgeoned with affront, and he'd made no attempt to rectify anything.

What grated on her was that he seemed perfectly fine with that. Totally unruffled by what had transpired. No man had ever hurt her. She'd always been the one in control. Why did it have to be Travis who managed to strip that from her? The graphic recaps of them on the hotel bed weren't a big help, either. She couldn't believe she'd had three orgasms. She'd never had that many.

"Did you make arrangements for me to fly to New York, or will I have to do that in the airport?" she asked tersely. Why he'd flown them into D.C. she didn't know. Up until now, she hadn't thought to find out where he was headed from here. Maybe D.C. was home for him.

"There are no arrangements, and you aren't making any. You're coming with me."

"What?" She stopped walking.

He reluctantly did the same, looking at her with leashed annoyance. "Your father wants to see you. I'm taking you to the D.C. TES office."

TES had an office here? He hadn't told her that!

A man who must work for TES passed them and put her luggage in the trunk of the black sedan. "Hey! That's my bag." She started walking toward the sedan.

Travis caught up to her and opened the back door of the car. "You can go home after I take you to your father."

"Don't you mean after you've completed your orders?" she retorted.

He remained unmoving. "Get in."

Didn't he care about last night at all? A terrible emotional weight fell upon on her. How could this be happening to her?

"Why did you kiss me if it wasn't on purpose?" she asked, more of an accusation.

"Just get in, Raeleen. After I take you to your father, you'll be rid of me."

"I don't want to be rid of you." Or did she? Suddenly, she was so confused.

"No?"

She'd been very resolute about her antimilitary rule. Would it be wise to change her mind now? Sticking to that rule made her feel safe. The way she felt with Travis just now didn't feel safe.

She needed safe.

"We had sex," she reasoned.

After studying her face in what had to be perplexity, he said, "What are you saying? That you want to start seeing me on a regular basis?"

She flinched, her head jerking back as the impact of that idea hit her. "I…"

The same anger that she saw last night and this morning toyed with his mouth and eyes. "Get in."

She did, but only because she was so confused. Did she want to see more of him? After they went to see her father, what then? She'd go her own way. It would be bad to get involved with him if she wasn't sure it was right for her.

"It was good sex," she said when he got into the seat beside her. The best she'd ever had.

"Glad to be of service. Anytime you want a repeat, just give me a call."

His sarcasm stung. Didn't he see that it had meant something to her? "I don't have your number."

More of that anger zeroed in on her. He pulled out his wallet and handed her a business card. Only his number was on it. She looked there and then up into the challenge in his eyes. Snatching the card, she stuffed it in her purse.

He looked perplexed again.

Would she call him? For more amazing sex? Maybe…

The driver sat in his seat and began to maneuver out of the airport.

"Can we stop for a cheeseburger on the way?" Eating would settle her stomach, and nothing would satisfy her more than her favorite.

"Sure."

"It can be a drive-through. In fact, sometimes those are the best. Greasy. Cheesy. Full of pickles and sauce..."

"I know just the place."

Was he wooing her now that she had his number?

Travis took her to the Burger Shack, in the middle of a tree-lined block of colorful three-story buildings with carriage-house charm. Long and narrow, the yellow, orange and green interior was well maintained and brightly lit. Seated across from Travis at a yellow-tiled table, she tried not to feel like this was their first date.

Raeleen picked up the juicy double cheeseburger, a couple of drips of grease assuring her it would rank among her favorites. No lettuce. No tomatoes. Just plenty of pickles, cheese, onions and a secret sauce. She took a big bite and savored the experience.

Travis pointed to the corner of his mouth, indicating she had something on hers. She licked it off, and his eyes smoldered briefly before his rigid control, back since sleeping with her, resumed and he ate some of his burger, an exact replica of hers. He wanted to see what she thought was a good burger.

"This is a little different than a hurricane," she said.

"Kind of hard to go to a burger joint during one, yeah."

She laughed a little. "Burger joints are my best shows."

"I'd have never guessed," he teased.

"The one that sticks out the most is this place called the Roadrunner Diner in Obetz, Ohio. It's right off a main highway and is run by the family matriarch—a seventy-five-year-old woman who shows no signs of retiring within the next decade. She keeps everyone in line, from her two daughters and four grandsons, to the wait staff and busboys. Her restaurant was awarded number one sixteen times by the health department."

"And the burgers?"

She rolled her eyes heavenward. "The bomb."

"The one I'll never forget is in Istanbul. A man and his wife run it. It's a small café that relies on tourism to survive, but it's not located anywhere mainstream. I only found out about it from a cabdriver. I like it there because it's clean and they always have fresh food, even though it sometimes is hard for them to keep it in their inventory. The menu is small, but every entrée is special. And yes, their burgers are good."

"You've been there more than once?"

"Tried every item on the menu." He ate a bite of his burger.

"I'll have to give them a call. One of my venues fell through at the last minute. Maybe they can accommodate me."

"I'm sure they would."

Not only did he complete dangerous, heroic missions on his travels, but he also met many different kinds of people, in many different economic situations. And he cared about them.

"You'll have to send me their information."

"I'll give it to your dad."

With the mention of her father, Raeleen's enchantment at being introduced to a new restaurant faded, and she finished in silence. She also fought a poignant disappointment that he'd contact her father and not her. He'd given her his card but hadn't asked for hers.

Why should that bother her, anyway? She had no intention of taking this further than it had already gone. She had already allowed it to go too far. Unless it was only for sex...

He paid for her dinner and let her leave the restaurant ahead of him.

Melancholy stole over her as she walked beside Travis,

looking for the sedan but not seeing it. Having sex with him had been a mistake on so many levels. It made walking away so much harder. Walking away should not be hard at all, and yet her heart was an opposing magnet to it.

Travis put his hand on her lower back. "Dad's is just ahead."

"Dad's?" No wonder the sedan wasn't here. Dad's was a bakery right up the street, the sedan in front of it.

She saw the sign from there, a brick storefront with a bright and cheery sign lit with a single word: *Dad's*. Her melancholy grew heavier. Her father was in there.

Travis held the door open for her. A bell jingled and the refurbished hardwood floor creaked as she stepped inside. Passing a handful of small, square tables with white runners and fresh carnations on them, she took in the iconic photos of D.C. in varying shades of sunlight and smelled fresh coffee wafting with the scents of baked bread and pastries.

The wall behind the L-shaped counter was full of tea and coffee machines, and a glass case featured the day's specials. What sounded like '50s jazz played at a moderate level, but just above that she heard voices coming from the kitchen. Then the swinging door leading there opened and her father appeared, followed by a man and a woman.

Seeing her father gave her a good dose of resentment, harbored resentment. She hadn't seen him since Christmas. A big man with graying hair that was thinning to expose more of his head, he looked like he'd lost some weight. His stomach was trimmer now.

"Raeleen," he said with a strong voice full of relief.

When he reached for her as though to embrace her, she avoided him, stepping aside and focusing on the attractive couple next to him.

"Hi, I'm Odie." The dark-haired, dark-eyed beauty smiled

and stuck out her hand. "This big bakery chef is my husband, Jag."

Raeleen shook her hand and then Jag's. His green eyes revealed no emotion, but the white apron with *Dad's* scrawled across his chest hinted to a personality. Along with her father, they formed a half circle in front of her and Travis.

"Great to meet you." Or not. More of her father's secret soldiers. She was surrounded by them.

"Travis." Odie checked him out. "You heal well."

"I only had more than two years."

"Cullen likes to be sure his team is healthy."

"I couldn't be healthier."

"Haley was glad to hear you're back to work. You know she and Rem are running a private military company now, don't you?"

"I heard, yes."

Raeleen watched for signs of feelings in Travis but couldn't tell if the news of Haley's life with another man bothered him. She didn't think it bothered him much, since she was pretty sure that wasn't the real reason he had trouble with women on assignments. Something deeper drove that, and she'd love to find out what that was. If only she would see him after tonight.

"You know about Haley, don't you, Raeleen?" Odie's leading tone suggested she did this a lot, fish for information.

"Travis told me a little about her."

"Did he now." She looked speculatively at Travis.

"Odie…" Jag warned. He must know his wife. It lent a touching note to people who'd seen a lot of violence in their work.

Finding herself connecting, Raeleen distanced herself, eyeing her father, who was busy assessing everyone.

"She worries about you," Odie said to Travis, ignoring her husband.

"That's Odie for you," Jag interrupted. "Always interested in everyone's personal lives."

Odie elbowed him. "You're lucky I was interested in yours."

Jag chuckled. "Don't I know it."

"Why does Haley worry about Travis?" Raeleen asked, well aware of her father's continued silence. He had a habit of holding back while others carried on a conversation. It gave him time to gather information before he dived into whatever point or purpose he had in mind. And now that point or purpose was centered on his daughter.

Odie's hesitation became obvious. She glanced between Travis and Raeleen as though she'd just confirmed a curiosity.

"Does she think I'll get shot again?" Travis joked.

Odie turned to him. "Far from it. She's afraid you'll never get married." Then she looked at Raeleen. "I'll have to reassure her."

"And I'll have to have a different discussion with Travis than I planned," her father finally said, indomitable eyes pointing at Travis.

Both he and Odie had noticed something in Travis and Raeleen. What had it been? Travis didn't seem to know, either. But then how close he stood to her materialized, and so did the way she'd asked about Haley.

"Raeleen has an aversion to TES operatives," Travis said.

Was he trying to say he and Raeleen weren't having a relationship? They weren't. He'd rescued her and they'd had sex. Did that constitute a relationship?

Odie laughed. "I don't believe it." Then she amended, "And then again, I do. Being the daughter of Colonel Roth and all."

"Odie had one of those with me," Jag said to Travis. "An aversion."

"I hope it's not contagious," Raeleen couldn't help quipping.

"Enough," her father interrupted. "We don't have time for that nonsense."

"Right. Because everything is always about work," Raeleen complained.

"We can talk more about your relationship with Travis if you prefer," her father replied. "Since there appears to be one." When no one commented, he moved to a table. "I want to know why my daughter's cameraman was beaten in Anguilla." He sat down and everyone else did the same, all five of them huddled around the small table, her father on one side of her, Travis on the other.

"Odie looked closer into Dietrich Artz's financial situation," Jag said, effectively steering the topic where it belonged. "He's about to lose his restaurant."

"Motive for wanting to sell valuable art," Travis said.

"Art?" Odie looked confused, something Raeleen was certain was a rare occurrence.

"Landon told us the people who beat him up were after a painting, but he couldn't tell us what kind," Raeleen explained. Travis hadn't told her father anything of what Landon had said. After telling Odie he'd been beaten, he'd said he'd brief them when they arrived in D.C. Only at the time, with her standing near while he spoke on his cell, he'd said when *he* arrived in D.C. The urgency of transporting Landon to a hospital in the States had taken precedence.

"Why was your cameraman involved?" her father asked.

Raeleen turned to him and hesitated. She'd always been careful about protecting his secrecy, even though she hated it. But this time she'd slipped up.

"They wanted to know why Raeleen had been kidnapped," Travis said for her. "What made her important enough to use for leverage."

"She was Deet's lover," Odie surmised.

"Yes, but if John and Vivian kidnapped her, why were they killed?" Travis asked.

"Maybe Deet was trying to sell the painting to whomever beat the cameraman up," Odie answered.

"And Vivian tried to stop him." Travis nodded with the plausibility of that.

"Deet is on the run. His house was ransacked," Raeleen reminded them all.

"Could Vivian have been the one trying to sell the painting?" Colonel Roth put in.

That didn't add up for Raeleen. "Why would the buyers kill her if she was trying to get them the painting?"

Travis frowned his agreement. "That's what has me stumped."

Across the table, Odie's eyes narrowed as she thought about it. "Maybe Vivian was the one who didn't want to sell. Deet has a failing restaurant and his marriage was ending. He wanted to sell, Vivian tried to stop him and the buyers killed her."

"Still doesn't explain why Deet's house was ransacked," Raeleen said, shaking her head.

The table went silent as everyone realized she was right.

"It also doesn't explain why Raeleen's cameraman was beaten," her father said. "They must have already known she was Deet's lover."

Raeleen glanced at Travis, uncomfortable with the direction this was headed. Her father's company could be in jeopardy if his connection to it were ever exposed.

"They knew I was sent to rescue her," Travis said. "And Landon knew things about you, things he heard Raeleen say."

Her father's gaze moved to her and she watched him process what that could mean. Then anger stormed into a black cloud around his eyes. "I've told you time and again not to argue with me on the phone!"

"Dad—"

"You know how damaging the press can be for me. Are you trying to ruin me?"

Now anger flared in her. Instant and sharp. "As usual it's all about you." She shoved her chair back as she stood, leaning over and pointing at his face. "You don't care about anything but your damn company!" She was so mad and upset. "You never cared about me!"

Lowering her hand, she straightened and noticed her audience. No one talked to Colonel Roth like that.

"You always say that, and it isn't true."

It irked her that he remained so calm, as if none of what she felt mattered. "Then prove it."

He pushed back his chair and stood to face her. "How? By exposing TES? That's the only thing that will make you happy, Raeleen. You'd rather put hundreds of people out of jobs than let me keep running the organization."

"There is such a thing as balance. I'm sorry Landon exposed you. I didn't know he overheard me on the phone with you. But if you spared two minutes of your time for me every once in a while, I wouldn't feel like yelling at you every chance I get, which ends up being not very many." She turned. "I'm leaving. I'm going home. While you all thrive on this kind of excitement, I don't. Thanks for sending Travis to come and get me."

"Raeleen, wait." Her father followed her, stopping her at the door.

She didn't want to look at him anymore, the father she didn't know as a father.

"How much did Landon tell them?"

With heavy resignation, she met his purposeful eyes. He'd stopped her to ask her about that, not about how his neglect hurt her. "Ask your pet soldier."

He didn't let her go. "Raeleen, you're my daughter. I know I don't spend the kind of time with you that you'd like, but that doesn't change the fact that I love you."

Empty words. Spoken so methodically. He would never change. "Landon told the men who beat him that you ran a secret counterterrorism organization and that Travis works for them. He didn't know the name, but he knew your name of the organization, and he knew you were the one behind it."

"A fact that should deter most people. And yet, you and Travis were followed at your hotel." He was all business. Forgotten was his daughter, who'd just yelled at him—again—for not being there for her. He could rescue her, oh yeah, but to be a father? What a disappointment.

"It might not deter a black-market art dealer," Travis said.

Around her father's shoulder, she saw Odie looking grave with her elbows on the table. Jag nodded.

"We don't know who's after the painting. We only know they feel untouchable enough not to run," Odie said. "That's not good."

"It has to be someone who's into art," Travis continued, and Raeleen agreed that a black-market dealer made the most sense. A private collector would probably be less likely to go to such extremes.

Travis still sat at the table, relaxed against the back of the chair with his hands on his thighs. His intrepid eyes shifted to her and the hint of angry emotion flashed. Remembering she'd called him a pet soldier, she understood why. Contrition weighed down her energy. She'd also nearly walked out of the bakery without so much as a goodbye.

Moving past her father, she stopped beside Travis's chair,

reluctant to do this in front of everyone but seeing no way around it. Not if she had any hope of getting out of here and away from her father. "Travis."

Stiffness answered her.

"Thank you for getting me out of that lighthouse."

"Just doing what any good pet would do."

"I didn't mean—"

"Don't make it worse, Raeleen."

"He's a big boy, he can handle it," Odie said.

"Stay out of this, honey," Jag told her.

Raeleen looked down into Travis's eyes, knowing she'd miss looking into them. But this was it. There was no need for him to stay with her. He'd brought her home. End of mission. He'd done what he'd promised to do. The rest was in TES's hands. Her father's hands.

"Goodbye." When he didn't say goodbye in return, she walked toward the door.

Her father stood in her way. She didn't feel like saying goodbye to him. To her amazement, he let her pass.

"See you at Christmas," she said. "If you're free."

He didn't respond, and that waved an invisible red flag. What was he thinking? That she'd see him sooner than that? She didn't believe it. Not for a minute.

"It's almost as if she's one of us."

Travis was getting tired of Odie's smart mouth. She'd picked up on the undercurrents between him and Raeleen. Everyone had. And it only reminded him of losing her when he'd never had her from the start. Dinner with her at the Burger Shack had felt…normal. Like he could share hundreds more of them with her. A lifetime of dinners and other everyday activities. Once again he'd found a woman he'd enjoy exploring and she turned out all wrong for him.

She'd try to change him. She'd never accept his profession, and he'd never be able to make her happy.

"Don't worry, she'll come around," Odie continued. "They all do."

Travis sent her an unappreciative look.

Roth moved away from the door after watching his daughter get her luggage from the driver of the sedan and then catch a cab.

She'd go back to the airport and then home to New York. Gone for good. Out of his life, and it had been so easy for her to walk away…after labeling him one of her father's pet soldiers. It told him more clearly than anything that she still thought of him that way. Negatively. He was no different than her father to her, a man she rarely saw, a man she wished she knew more than she did and felt never would. She loved her father but didn't get enough in return. She was afraid of having the same inadequacy with his pet soldiers.

"I need you to keep watching her."

Travis snapped to attention with what Roth had just said. "What? No." He shook his head. "My mission is finished. Send someone else."

"I'm sending you."

"She'll be mad as hell."

"What if she's followed?"

He hadn't thought of that. He was too busy thinking about how easy it had been for her to walk away.

"She was Deet's lover," Odie added.

They were right. Travis had no choice. To find the painting and catch the black-market art dealer behind all this, he'd have to stay close to Raeleen. She was the first person they'd go after if they couldn't find Deet before Travis did.

"Fantastic," he muttered.

Chapter 8

A long nap and then a glass of wine on her apartment balcony with the stereo on low. That's what Raeleen needed. De-gassing after the adventure she'd just had. So many thoughts cluttered her mind that she felt exhausted. All the way here everything that had happened since Travis broke down the lighthouse door replayed for her analysis. Waking on top of him after the hurricane. Sleeping with him. The Burger Shack. Warm longing filled her, the bittersweet ache of new love, and then angst and frustration, vacillating back and forth.

Opening her midtown Manhattan apartment door, she breathed in the smell of home. It was so good to finally be here. Shutting the door, she froze.

Furniture was overturned in her wide-open living room. Clothes littered the hardwood floor, trailing from her bedroom into the hallway. Pictures had been pulled from the walls. Her kitchen cabinets were open and some dishes were broken on the floor. Immediately on alert, she let go of her luggage and dug for her phone, ready to dial 911 if she needed to. She didn't hear anything. No one was lurking in her open, modern living room and kitchen. Heading toward the short hall, she passed her office. It had been torn apart like the rest of her apartment. The bathroom wasn't as bad, but her big bedroom was in shambles.

She put her phone on the dresser and went to the balcony off her room. The door was locked. No windows were broken. Back in the living room, the second balcony door was also locked. Her apartment was ten floors up. How had someone broken in? The doorman only worked days, so it was possible to get in the building undetected.

The door buzzer gave her a jolt. She pressed the intercom. "Yes?"

"There's a Mr. Deet Artz here to see you," the part-time doorman said.

Deet? What was he doing here in Manhattan?

Taking a chance, she told the doorman to let him in. Moments later, he appeared in view of her peephole, dark green eyes fearful and thick, black hair uncharacteristically messy. He usually kept it combed, but today it stuck out all over his head as though he'd raked his fingers through it after skipping a shower this morning. His head turned from one side to the other, as though fearing he'd be seen.

She opened her door.

"Raeleen." He sounded relieved. His long-sleeved light gray dress shirt was unbuttoned at the neck and had wrinkles all over it. His blue jeans had dirt stains on them. How long had he been wearing the same clothes?

Whatever his reason for being here, she didn't feel threatened. She didn't feel anything except the need to learn about the painting. Stepping aside, she gave him room to enter.

He checked the hall once more before his six-foot frame

passed her. Then, seeing the condition of her apartment, he stopped.

"They've been here." He ran his hand over his mouth as though agitated.

Raeleen closed the door and walked over to him. "Who?"

"That's not good. That means they know I'm here. They must have followed me." He seemed so frightened. This was a side of Deet she'd never seen. She'd only seen the part of him that met her at her cottage for a weekend here and there. Fun and light. Nothing serious. Certainly nothing dangerous.

"Who, Deet?" She had to get some answers out of him.

He recovered, controlling his fear and gearing his attention toward his purpose here. He put his hands on her shoulders. "I'm sorry about all of this, Raeleen. I'm sorry for everything. What you must be thinking…"

"Why did you come to my cottage after the hurricane?" she asked.

"I never meant to involve you in this."

She stepped back, out of reach of his hands. He wasn't going to tell her.

"I was going to divorce her."

That didn't matter to her. Even if he'd been single, their time together would have run its course. He was handsome enough, but there simply had not been a connection. Not the way she'd connected with Travis.

As soon as that materialized in her thoughts, she pushed it aside. "Deet—"

"I was. I swear it. I just didn't have time to tell you." Moving closer, he put his hands on her again. "I'm in love with you, Raeleen."

Smothered by the announcement, Raeleen stepped back again. He had to stop touching her. After being with Travis, it felt dirty. "You have to tell me about the painting."

"Please, Raeleen. Listen to me. I fell in love with you. I know you thought the long-distance relationship was working, but I missed you like crazy every time you left."

"You never told me you were married."

"I was going to divorce her." He let out a disgruntled breath. "I wanted to tell you, but I was afraid of scaring you away."

Scaring wasn't the word she'd use. "You were married. You should have never started anything with me. You should have told me you were married."

"Would you have been with me if I did?"

He had to ask? She didn't bother answering him. How unfair of him to keep that secret just so he could have her. She must have known he lacked integrity on a subconscious level, and that's what had kept her at a distance.

"Raeleen…" he pleaded.

"I don't love you, Deet. I never did."

He searched her eyes in denial. "You're just upset that I was married."

"Actually, I don't care that you are." Were. Vivian was dead. "There's a reason I preferred you on the island and me in New York. I didn't want anything serious with you." It had taken her too long to figure that out.

As exactly what he probably refused to accept settled in his mind, Deet said nothing.

"Tell me about the painting," she demanded. "Were you going to sell it to save Artz?"

"How do you know about my restaurant?" When she didn't explain, he filled in his own blanks. "It's that man I saw you with. Who is he?"

He was jealous. Was that why he'd turned around when he'd seen them after the storm? He couldn't face her with another man there? "That isn't important. The painting, Deet. I need to know about the painting."

"Your father sent him, didn't he?" He was still stuck on the other man who'd been with her. She'd told him about her father. Not about TES, but apparently it was enough.

"Travis is helping me," she answered vaguely.

Staring at her for endless seconds, he finally moved farther into her apartment, rubbing his hand over his jaw. Lowering his hand, he turned and stared at her again. "I need you to give me the painting, Raeleen. Don't ask questions. Just give it to me. They'll leave you alone as soon as you do."

"I don't have it."

"You do have it. I mailed it to you."

"You mailed it to me here?" Anger flared with incredulity. Not only had he lied to her about his marital status to satisfy his own selfish needs, he'd put her in danger by mailing her the painting. He'd used her. Again.

She looked around her apartment cynically. "Well, then I don't have it anymore." She wasn't about to tell him that her neighbor Marcy took care of her apartment when she traveled, which was a lot. That included getting her mail.

If Deet had sent her anything, Marcy would have it. In a flash, she worried that whoever had searched her apartment had discovered that and harmed Marcy. She needed to get rid of Deet. But first she needed him to tell her more.

Deet approached and put his hands on her shoulders again. "I have to have that painting."

She stepped out of his reach. "Why?"

"It's best if you don't know."

How could she make him tell her?

In the quiet pause, he looked over her body and spent some time absorbing her face, as though remembering their affair. Had it excited him to have an affair? Did sleeping with another woman give him perverse pleasure? Both women not knowing...

An ill feeling in the pit of her stomach expanded. That

was the only part that bothered her about his betrayal. The disgusting reality that he'd been sleeping with two women and she'd been one of them. The only thing she ever saw in him was his faraway address and lack of strings. She hadn't known him well, and now she was paying the price.

"I do love you, Raeleen."

That only made her sicker. "Did you kill your wife so that you could sell the painting?"

He blinked once. "No."

"Who did?"

"I don't blame you for not believing that I love you."

Why would he not let that go? "I do believe you. But I don't love you. Now, who killed Vivian, Deet? Start answering me."

"That man you were with must be good if your father sent him to find you. You're attracted to him, aren't you?"

"I'm getting tired of this—"

"Did you sleep with him?"

She nearly blanched with the suddenness of his question. "That's none of your business!"

"I can tell there's something going on between you. You're…different. I know you, Raeleen. You would never have backed away from my touch if there wasn't another man in the picture."

"You're married!"

"That doesn't matter. You wouldn't have backed away. I'm not saying you'd still want to be with me. You just have this…barrier now, and it isn't there because I kept the fact that I was married from you."

Really? She had a hands-off barrier after being with Travis? Like she was…his?

"All right, yes. I did sleep with him. And it was the best sex I've ever had in my life. Earth-shattering. Mind-blowing. Incomprehensible…completely incredible sex."

Maybe now he'd stop forcing his love on her. Love he'd developed while cheating on his wife and lying to her.

She achieved her desired result. His whole face turned to stone, going still in tense resentment. "Give me the painting, Raeleen."

"I told you, I don't have it."

"You have no idea what you're up against. Give it to me."

When she just stared at him, he began walking through her apartment, searching. After just a few seconds, he stopped, realizing it was futile. "Where is it?"

Footsteps brought them both turning. Travis stood inside her apartment, one hand on the doorknob, the other holding a gun at his side. How had he gotten into the building? His eyes shifted from Deet to her, and she had no doubt he'd heard what she'd said.

In that moment, Deet moved behind her. Pressing a gun to her temple, he locked his big, meaty arm around her upper torso.

"The painting. Now."

Undaunted, Travis moved forward. "Let her go and I won't kill you."

"All I want is the painting. Give it to me and I'll go."

"He said he mailed it to me," Raeleen explained to Travis.

"Who took care of your mail while you were away?" Deet asked.

"I always stop it before I travel," she lied.

He poked her with the gun, hard enough to make her wince and draw Travis one long stride closer. "It was mailed here. Someone in this building signed for it."

Did he know who? Anxiety soured her stomach.

Deet moved her as Travis neared, a face off that ended with Deet's back to the front door.

"You won't kill her," Travis said.

Raeleen tipped her head a little to see Deet. His gaze

met Travis's uncertainly. Travis had read him accurately. Deet was afraid. He was acting out of fear and desperation.

That didn't mean he wouldn't pull the trigger. "Deet..."

He looked down at her.

"What are you doing?"

With a low growl, he shoved her hard.

She stumbled against Travis as two gunshots went off. Deet was firing at them. Not feeling any bullets penetrate, she held on to Travis as he took them both to the floor, rolling so that she was underneath him, protecting her from gunfire, aiming his pistol back at the door. No one was there.

Travis looked down at her. "Are you all right?" He began checking her body, his face a contortion of worry.

"Yes. I'm fine! I'm fine!" She pushed off of him, coming to her senses. Deet was getting away!

He seemed to realize what his hesitation had cost them and sprang to his feet, hauling Raeleen up after him. They ran through the apartment door. Neighbors peeked out of their apartments.

The elevator doors were closed. The stairwell was empty. They rode the elevator down to the main level, but the lobby was void of Deet.

Seeing the doorman standing calmly outside the front door, Raeleen elbowed Travis and he slid his gun into the waist of his jeans before anyone noticed.

"Where is the painting?" he asked her.

She headed back for the elevator. "My neighbor's apartment. I haven't picked it up yet." She stepped into the elevator with him.

"The best sex you've ever had in your life, huh?"

She fought the heat that climbed up her neck. "He kept saying he loved me."

Travis chuckled. "That worked to sway him?"

"Yes, it did."

After a moment, he said, "It was the same for me."

Was he minimizing it, or did he mean it had been that good for him, too?

The elevator doors opened. People were out in the hallway, peering into her apartment and talking fast about the gunshots they'd heard.

"Raeleen, you're back!" Her neighbor Marcy approached. "Are you all right? Look at your apartment. No one heard a thing until those gunshots. These walls sure are thick."

"I'm fine, but I would really like my mail now."

Marcy looked confused. "Should we call the police?"

"I already did," her neighbor down the hall said.

"We need to hurry," Travis said.

And she agreed. No cops. Cops would lead to her father, and she'd already caused enough trouble for him as it was.

"Please, Marcy, can I have my mail?"

"S-sure." She eyed Travis's big form, wary of him, but at last she turned and went into her still-open apartment across the hall from Raeleen's. A moment later, she returned with a moderate stack of mail in one hand and a FedEx tube in the other.

Raeleen took the tube.

"Thanks." Travis steered her out of the apartment and would have guided her down the hall if she hadn't stopped to grab her luggage and shut her apartment door.

"The police will be here soon," Marcy said.

"Tell them it was a false alarm," Raeleen said, ignoring Marcy and the other neighbors' perplexed looks and exchanges.

"What about the rest of your mail?" Marcy held up the bundle.

The elevator doors opened. "I'll be back for it. Thank you, Marcy!"

Travis pushed her into the elevator and rolled her luggage in after him. The doors closed.

"What are you doing here, anyway?" she asked him.

"Your father—"

She held up her hand. "Don't tell me."

"Your father asked me to watch you," he said anyway.

"Wonderful."

If her father was still worried about her, why hadn't he brought her home with him? Why couldn't he invite his own daughter to stay with him for a while? Why put one of his men in charge of it? Because he was more concerned about exposing his damn company than her. His company came first. Always.

"He didn't know Deet would mail you the painting," Travis said in her silence. "But he wanted to be sure you were safe."

"So here you are. Under orders again." A giant hole expanded in her chest. Not only didn't her father love her the way a father should, but she had feelings for a man who was just like him.

"Look on the bright side: at least as a pet, I'll know my place this time."

His place was hardly that miniscule, but he wasn't telling her that to reassure her.

"I'm sorry I said it, okay?"

"I'm not."

He'd also heard her describe their sex. Not a relationship or the potential for one. Sex.

The elevator doors opened and Raeleen saw several policemen entering the building. Travis guided her out into the lobby, rolling her luggage.

One of the policemen saw them and approached. "Did you two hear any gunshots?"

"No. There were gunshots?" Travis answered, a fine performance.

"I suggest you either stay down here or leave the building until we're finished, then."

"What happened?"

"We don't know yet. Someone reported gunshots on the tenth floor."

"I hope everyone's okay," Raeleen interjected, earning a look from Travis.

Once again, he guided Raeleen with his hand on her back.

At his new rental car, he opened the back and put her luggage inside.

"Travis…" She didn't know how to say it. He wasn't sorry she'd called him a pet soldier, and something drove her to tell him he wasn't. Which went against everything she believed about men like him. He worked for her father's secret organization. He was the kind of man she'd always promised herself never to love.

But what if that thinking was what had led her to avoid marriage altogether?

"We need to get away from here."

She got into the car. "You aren't a pet soldier. I was only trying to hurt my father."

"No explanation necessary."

No, because he had a job to do and that didn't include seducing her. "Where are we going?"

"Somewhere we can look at that painting."

"Back to TES?" Dread filled her.

"No. I have a better idea."

Down in Lower Manhattan, Raeleen walked beside Travis along a cobblestone street and followed him into a small antiques store called Harry's. Not very original, but the building was old and full of charm. Painted yellow with white trim, it was long and narrow and a bell jingled when they entered. The dull wood floor creaked and old crystal chandeliers lit tall shelving cluttered with merchandise— everything from ancient stuffed animals to trunks of every size and dining sets.

A man sat behind a counter reading a paper and had looked up when the bell jingled. He seemed fixated on Travis. Slowly he stood and moved around the counter. A big man, his white hair was clipped brutally short, and for an older man he was in great shape.

"Travis Todd? Is that you?"

"Harry. How the hell have you been these last few years?"

The two shook hands. "Great. Still not missing military life, that's for sure." He glanced at Raeleen as though hesitant of what to say next.

"This is Raeleen Randall, Colonel Roth's daughter."

Now Harry would know he could talk freely, and Raeleen began to piece together how Travis knew him.

"Not by choice." She shook Harry's hand and he chuckled.

"I imagine being the daughter of a man like Roth wouldn't be easy."

"Sure it is. I just had to grow up faster than most kids." Because her father was never around to guide her, anyway, and her mother hadn't stepped in to take up the slack, either.

Travis's head turned to her and his eyes held mocking disagreement.

Did he think she hadn't grown up yet?

"And you probably didn't date much in your teens," Harry said, referring to the almighty Colonel Roth. What a domineering presence he must have been, Raeleen could almost hear him thinking. If only he knew...

She smiled congenially. Her father hadn't been around

enough to scare anyone away. Lucky for him, she developed a phobia of controlling men.

"When did you work for my father?" she asked.

"I retired ten years ago."

"Harry did private missions for your dad," Travis explained. "That was before he found Cullen and formed what is now TES."

"Is that how Cullen found you?" Raeleen asked.

"Cullen doesn't know Harry and I are friends."

"Oh, I bet he did. My father probably told him to send you."

Harry and Travis exchanged a startled look. Harry was the first to shake it off. "What matters is you're finally here. What brings you here? Are you on vacation? Somehow an excursion to the Statue of Liberty doesn't seem like your thing."

Travis chuckled. "Not on vacation. Raeleen stumbled upon a painting that someone is willing to kill to get. We need help figuring out what kind of painting it is. Is your wife still a museum curator?"

"No. Meena retired two years ago. We run this shop together now."

"Where is she?"

"At home, waiting for me." He grinned and there was no mistaking his love. At almost six, it must be nearing closing time.

"I guess that means you're joining us for dinner."

Meena, whose full name was Philomena, and Harry lived in an apartment right above the antiques shop. Harry had gotten a laugh over their reaction to that revelation. His wife was waiting for him upstairs.

Though in her early sixties like her husband, Meena wore her dark hair long, dyed to hide the gray, and was in amazing health for a woman her age. Her wrinkled face didn't change the evidence that in her youth she'd been a beautiful woman.

Raeleen entered the small apartment full of antiques. Decorated in clean color and sea-faring decor, the cozy apartment felt upscale despite its lack of square footage.

"Do you sail?" she asked as Meena and Harry led them into the living room.

"We have a small motor yacht," Meena said. "We fly to Florida every chance we get."

"The Caribbean is my favorite destination." Raeleen put the tube on the coffee table as she sat next to Travis on the sofa.

"Raeleen is the host of a Dining Network show," Travis said.

"I've seen that show!" Meena breathed her fascination. "That's terrific."

"I'm not sure it's as terrific as your home, and sailing... What a dream."

"Well, thank you. But we're no celebrity."

Raeleen admired anyone who could live simply even though they had a lot of money. And she could tell by the style of their apartment that they did have that. Fresh taupe walls and white trim, polished wood floors, the solid red leather sofa and multicolored striped chairs, a big-screen TV—all of it screamed money. She could see the Brooklyn Bridge through the huge, white-framed living room window that was coiffed with a sweeping sheer red scarf and dust-free white blinds.

"So, aside from knowing my father, how did you and Travis meet?" she asked Harry, who instantly shifted his gaze to Travis.

Meena didn't seem to notice the exchange. "Travis was on an extraction mission when my Harry met him."

How had their paths crossed? Raeleen turned from Travis to Harry, who reluctantly said, "His sister was in the army and ran into some trouble in Afghanistan."

Travis reached for the tube and opened one end. "We should take a look at this now.

"Saved his ass from doing something stupid," Harry continued, studying Travis. "Still don't like talking about it, do you?"

"Talking about the past doesn't change it."

His sister. It had been his sister that he'd lost.

"What happened?" she asked.

At first she didn't think he'd tell her. With Meena and Harry present, maybe he felt he had to.

"She was in a medical convoy when it was ambushed," Travis said. "No one could get in to save them in time. She died in a car bombing." He looked at her in resentment. She'd asked and now he was forced to sit there and participate in this conversation about a sister he couldn't save, the only mission he'd ever failed. Except no one could really call it a mission.

"She probably died instantly, but Travis here was hell-bent on going in to get her," Harry said. "Made it all the way to town before the insurgents sniffed him out."

"But my Harry was there on another mission." Meena beamed.

"I was working for Roth at the time," Harry said. "One of my last missions."

"Harry and his team got me out," Travis told Raeleen. "They killed the insurgents who'd captured me."

"Did they hurt you?"

"Every man has a reason for signing on with TES," Travis said instead of answering. "Mine was that."

He did what he did because of his sister, because she was

the one mission he'd failed, and he couldn't tolerate that. No wonder he hadn't failed since.

"My Harry was on his honeymoon with his first wife," Meena said. "A suicide bomber came into the restaurant where they were having breakfast."

"I lived. She didn't."

"I almost didn't get the man I love," Meena said, reaching over to cover his hand with hers on the armrest of his chair, which was close to hers by design, Raeleen surmised. "I didn't think he'd ever get over her."

"I just needed time, my love. If you hadn't been so patient with me, I might never have found love again."

She smiled with the effect of his words.

The warm, genuine moment showed Raeleen what she was missing by dating men like Deet. She could also equate the sentiment with something she'd felt with Travis. She turned to him. He was looking at her as though the same thought had touched him. They'd had a glimpse of that kind of love their last night on Anguilla.

Travis pulled out the painting.

Yes, enough of that. Ridiculous to be entertaining such sappy sentiments with a man like him. He probably had the same opinion about her. She was wrong for him and he was wrong for her.

"Oh, careful with that." Meena rose from her chair and hurried to one of the rooms down the hall, reappearing with gloves on her hands and four paperweights and a cloth.

Travis took the weights and gave her the rolled painting.

Raeleen cleared the table and helped spread the cloth. Meena rolled the painting out, placing weights on all corners.

There was nothing striking about the painting. A woman sat on a chair in front of a bedroom window, hands folded on her lap, looking at the painter with a slight curve to her mouth. Her dress indicated the early twentieth-century. Raeleen didn't recognize the work of art as anything famous. Meena retrieved a magnifying glass from her pocket and began studying the painting.

"I've never seen anything written about this one." She hovered over the signature. "Cyrus Dickenson." She straightened. "Hmm. There's something familiar about that name." She tapped the magnifying glass against her lip.

Then she went back into the office, and long moments passed. Raeleen was the first to venture there, Travis and Harry following.

"Here it is!" Meena exclaimed excitedly, sitting before a website opened to a page titled *The Portrait of Sarah.*

Raeleen leaned over her shoulder, Travis on the other side, and Harry behind her.

"This painting was done by a Jew before World War II. The woman was his mistress. His wife found out about them and killed him. She was tried and sent to prison, but Sarah still had the painting and passed it down to her son. During the war, the son's wife had an affair with a Nazi. It was a similar tale to his mother's. Sarah's son found out about the affair just about the time his wife decided she loved him and not her lover, the Nazi.

"The Nazi was a collaborator for Hitler. He raided the homes of Jews and stole their valuables. The day he showed up at Sarah's son's house, he planned to take more than valuables. He planned to take the woman, too. When she refused, he shot her and Sarah's son. The painting was never found."

Raeleen read for herself that the woman had written about the Nazi in a journal. His name was Armen Brauer.

"The painter of *The Portrait of Sarah* did a few other works that were lost during the war. His pieces are rare. The few that have been recovered have gone for millions."

Reading along with her, Raeleen discovered the paint-

ing Deet had was the most valuable of them all because of
its history.

"What happened to Armen Brauer?"

"He disappeared."

Raeleen straightened and looked over at Travis. "How did
Deet end up with a painting like that? He isn't even into art."

"He doesn't have to be if it was passed down to him."

"He is German...."

The value of the painting didn't surprise Travis, but it
did kick-start his foreboding. Harry was a good friend and
Meena was the love of Harry's life. He couldn't let anything
happen to them.

"We should go now," Travis said to Raeleen, who was
still immersed in the sensationalism surrounding the painting's history. "The longer we're here, the greater the danger
of dragging Harry and Meena into this."

"Give me a little credit," Harry said. "I'm old, but I can
still shoot a gun."

"Raeleen."

"Just a minute, Travis." She resumed her conversation
with Meena about Sarah. Where she lived. How she'd met
a married man. The murder...

"It's so unusual that a woman in that time committed
murder," Raeleen said.

"And for history to repeat itself in Sarah's son," Meena
added, drawing Harry back into it.

"Except his wife had an affair with a Nazi. She was Jewish."

Travis took in the scene of the three of them ensconced
in scandalous history, then walked out into the living room.
He rolled the painting back up, not caring about preserva-
tion. Now that they knew what it was, this would be the last

time he touched it. His main priority was getting away from here. Harry was like family to him.

"Did Sarah's son have any children?" he heard Raeleen ask. She was still in the office.

A good question. If they could find Sarah's descendants, they were the rightful owners of the painting.

"It doesn't say on this site," Meena answered.

"Maybe try another search." That came from Harry.

So, that's what happened to a man who retired from special forces. He lost his edge. Had he forgotten that TES could find what they were surfing the internet for? It was comical.

"This site might be good," Meena said.

"What did you say that guy's name was?" Harry asked. "The guy who sent you and Travis the painting?"

"Deet. Dietrich Artz."

"Yeah. Him. We need to do a background on him."

Relieved that Harry hadn't completely gone soft, Travis went to the door of the office to see all three gathered close to the computer, completely oblivious to him.

"Raeleen."

She glanced at him and then said, "Do a search on Cyrus Dickenson."

"This is a good genealogy site," Meena commented.

"Odie can do this a lot faster, you know."

"There's a lot of them." Raeleen sounded disappointed.

Taking out his cell, Travis called Odie.

She answered right away. "What have you got?"

"See what you can find on Dietrich Artz's ancestry. Did he have any Nazis in his bloodline?"

"Why ever do you ask?"

He told her about finding the painting, including what they'd learned about Sarah and her son.

"No wonder it's so popular. But why now?"

"No one discovered its whereabouts until now."

Their original assumptions were still pretty much on track. Deet had tried to sell the painting, and his wife had tried to stop him.

"Something must have gone wrong in the sale," Odie said.

"Why did Deet mail the painting to Raeleen? Did he change his mind, or is something else at play here?" Travis would go with something else at play.

"That's a good question." The one they needed answered. "Roth isn't going to be happy to hear about this."

"Tell him I'm with Raeleen 24-7 now. And see if you can track down Sarah's son. If he has any living descendants, I'm sure they'd like to know about the painting."

"Finally, something fun to look up. Okay, I'll get back to you…oh…"

Just as he'd suspected, she'd already found something.

"Nothing comes up on Deet's family."

"You mean he has no history?"

"No. He has solid history. His family has lived on that island since they migrated there from France. He isn't German. Well, not completely. His grandmother married a German, but only after moving to Anguilla. Checking her family…" A few seconds passed. The trio before the computer still struggled with the genealogy site.

"No Nazis in her family," Odie said.

How did she do that so fast? She must have access to dozens of databases and had gotten so much practice over the years that she not only knew where to look, but speed was her trademark. She probably had six screens in front of her, each one doing a different task for her. And her brain was quick enough to keep up.

"What about Deet's wife?" he asked.

"Checking now." He heard her fingers busily working

the keyboard. "Wait a minute. Let me check a few other sources." She typed away. "Nothing."

"Nothing?" Another solid background, or did she mean the opposite this time?

"I don't see anything on her grandfather."

"No history at all?"

"Vivian's maiden name was Rey, and according to these records, her grandfather died before arriving in Anguilla."

"That's sort of impossible." Odie was onto something, and he followed her train of thought. "Do we have a case of stolen identity?"

"His name wasn't Rey?"

"No, it was Armen Brauer. That's who had the affair with the Jewish owner of the painting." The trio in front of the computer had uncovered that.

"Then that's our Nazi collaborator."

That provided a twist to their original speculations, but didn't change the outcome much. The painting didn't belong to Deet. It was Vivian's.

"I'll look for the rightful owner of the painting. I'll have to go visit a friend of mine. Will you take a good picture of the painting and send it to me?"

"Yes. Coming right now."

With the three at the computer still unaware of him, he returned to the coffee table and spread the painting out once again. Taking a picture with his phone, he sent it to Odie. Then he rolled the painting up again, tucked it away into the tube and returned to the office.

"There has to be something on Deet's ancestry somewhere," Raeleen said.

Travis went to stand behind her. "It's not Deet's ancestry you should be looking for. It's his wife's."

At last he had their attention. Harry straightened and so

did Raeleen, her back bumping him with a little squeal as she pivoted to face him.

Meena stopped surfing and twisted to look up at him.

"Her grandfather was a German who stole someone's identity before moving to Anguilla. He was the Nazi collaborator who had an affair with Sarah's son's wife. Armen Brauer. He must have defected during the war, after she rejected him and he killed her."

Meena and Raeleen gaped at him.

But Harry just grinned. "I should have known better."

"Yes, you should have." Travis grinned back.

"How do you know all that?" Raeleen asked. "You were just…" She pointed toward the door. "And we haven't been…" She pointed to the computer.

Travis couldn't let this priceless moment go. She was flabbergasted that he'd learned what he had so quickly. "You should really give TES more credit, Raeleen. Your father, too. He's a brilliant man. Brave. Patriotic. And resourceful. You could learn a thing or two from him."

"Uh," she breathed with derisive disgust. "Stop it."

"We need to go."

Meena sagged with disappointment. "Are you sure you can't stay for dinner?"

"You might as well stay the night," Harry added. "An antiques shop makes great cover." When Travis hesitated, he gave him a hard pat on the back. "Stay."

"The painting is going to attract trouble, Harry."

"And I've never dealt with that before," Harry retorted. "Are you calling me old?"

Travis breathed a laugh. "No." Maybe one night would be okay. "We'll stay." Harry wasn't going to let him refuse, anyway.

"We only have the pullout in the living room, but it's

comfortable." Meena glanced between each of them. "And cozy."

"Travis is sleeping on the floor."

Like hell he was.

Chapter 9

Dinner was a delight and now the conversation was finally dying. Meena was a wonderful cook and an entertaining host, just like her husband. Raeleen finished her glass of wine, content to spend time with a couple she would love to keep as friends. Unfortunately, they were Travis's friends.

"I'll get the bed ready for you." Meena got up from the kitchen table where they'd all sat for hours.

"I'll help you." Raeleen stood up and followed her to a hall closet, where Meena pulled out several blankets and extra pillows.

Carrying them into the living room, Raeleen saw that Travis and Harry were involved in a low-voiced conversation.

"They're probably talking about past missions." Meena's pride rang through.

"Has it been that long since they've seen each other?"

"Travis makes his way here whenever he can. It's been

about three years since his last visit. He usually tries to come here at least once a year. But with him being shot and all, that slowed him down. It was a long recovery." She spread a sheet over the cushy mattress on the opened pullout couch.

"And now he's back at it." Marching straight into the line of fire, dominating adversaries. *Dominating* being the key word.

"You sound disapproving."

She spread the top sheet down, not feeling like getting into that. Her father dominated, demanded and disappeared into his work. She knew all too well what that was like and how those close to him suffered. Is that what Travis would bring her if she continued to fall for him?

"Travis was in the military when his sister was killed, did you know that?" Meena asked in her silence. "He was training for Delta."

Raeleen helped her put two blankets down onto the mattress, reserving some for Travis on the floor. "How nice."

Meena ignored her sarcasm. "He flew to Afghanistan after he found out her convoy had been attacked by terrorists. At the time, no one knew what had happened to his sister. When he got there, it didn't take long to discover a suicide bomber killed her and the other soldiers. Travis searched for the terrorists, but there were so many, and being American, it wasn't long before they turned on him. If it wasn't for my Harry, he wouldn't have been around to be shot in Monrovia. He still punishes himself for not being there to save her. Short of fighting the Taliban all by himself, there was nothing he could do. He can't seem to accept that. You saw how difficult it is for him to talk about."

Yes, she had. She struggled with sympathy that was too intimately tied to him. "How could he have predicted that she'd be killed in a car bombing?"

"He couldn't, but he would have been in Afghanistan if he

hadn't decided to join Delta. He wasn't in a position to save his sister. He wouldn't have been, anyway, but that helplessness tortures him. I think that's why he finally joined TES. There, he can go after as many tyrants as possible, and he can save the innocent from their murderous ways. And he has. Travis has a reputation for saving people who are kidnapped or captured in unstable countries. That's why he works for your father. He's one of the best."

"They all are. My father wouldn't want Cullen to recruit any other kind." Again her bitterness showed, and Meena took note of it.

"It's good what your father and his men do."

"Yes, it is."

Meena stopped making the bed with her. "Why so angry?"

"I grew up without a father. It's good what they do, but it's not good for their families."

Raeleen arranged the blankets for Travis on the floor, dropping a pillow there.

"My Harry was there for me. We had four kids together. He never missed a birthday, and I have never felt unloved."

Not liking the ray of hope that gave her, Raeleen sat on the newly made bed and Meena sat next to her.

"Your father is one man. Don't you think it's unfair to judge them all based on that?"

She looked over at Travis, who still leaned an elbow on the table and spoke quietly with Harry. "He has the same drive."

"Yes."

"And he's closed off in some ways. Like how he can never talk about his sister. And besides, he's already admitted that he's looking for a woman who won't make him stop working for TES. That tells me he'll put TES first."

"He has to put TES first when he's on a mission. He'd

be killed otherwise, but Travis isn't the kind of man who'd come home to his wife and neglect her. He's a lot like my Harry that way."

Unable to refute what she said, Raeleen continued to resist the warm enticement threatening her resolve. "Neither was my father. He loves my mother. Always has."

"Do you really believe he wasn't a good father?"

She lowered her head, not sure her father deserved such harsh judgment or if her aversion to anything remotely resembling love with Travis had brought it on. There had been a few times when her father had been home for special occasions. And he never missed Christmas, either.

"You love your father very much, I see."

"Of course I do."

"Any child would want her daddy to be around all the time. He wasn't around enough for you, because you love him so much. Don't waste any more time hanging on to that. Cherish the time you do get with him. That's how it was with my Harry. Now we're together all the time, and sometimes I wish he was still active in the military." She laughed. "For maybe two seconds."

Raeleen laughed with her. "You're lucky."

"Yes, and you will be, too."

Before Raeleen could argue, Meena rose and headed down the hall. "Come on, Harry, let these two get some sleep before that trouble Travis mentioned gets here."

Harry gave Travis what must be his trademark hard pat on his back and stood from the table. Telling Raeleen goodnight on the way, he and his wife closed their bedroom door.

Raeleen met Travis's gaze across the quiet room. He hadn't gotten up from the table. She broke the tense look first and went to get ready for bed.

Her guard was down because of her talk with Meena. Meena had made her realize that she truly did love her father. She loved him like she had when she was a child. He was her daddy. The most important man in her life. She didn't get to spend enough time with him. He didn't have the time to give. That's what hurt. And that hurt had turned to anger a long time ago.

Emerging from the bathroom in her night T-shirt, Raeleen saw Travis lying on top of the covers on the sofa bed. She stopped beside it. He'd taken his boots off, and his feet hung over the edge of the mattress. His hands were folded over his flat stomach, and his chest stretched his white T-shirt. He'd taken off the shirt he'd had on over it.

His eyes opened.

"You're supposed to sleep on the floor."

"Says who?"

Her. But he didn't take orders from anyone. He gave them.

Yanking the covers back, she pretended not to see the grin fighting for a chance to shine on his face and climbed onto the bed. Curling with her back to him, she pulled the covers over her. It would be a long time before she was able to sleep.

The interstate stretched before her tired eyes. She could no longer see her dad. They were supposed to meet somewhere. She couldn't remember where. If she lost him, she wouldn't be able to find him. But she was so tired. If she could just close her eyes for a few minutes that would help.

Seeing an exit ahead, she took it and began looking for a place to pull over. The road here was too narrow. Turning left onto another road that went beneath the highway, she saw a patch of dirt on the side of the road. She drove there, parked and closed her eyes.

When she opened them, she had no idea how much time had passed, and now she stood in a subway. Looking down, she noticed she didn't have her keys or anything. Where was her car?

She had to find her father.

To her right, a brick passageway led to some stairs. She could see daylight. If she went up there, maybe she could see where her father had gone. Stepping up them, she saw another train, this one open to the air.

She climbed aboard and looked all around for her father. She didn't understand how she'd gotten here. One minute she was sleeping in her car, and the next she was here.

The train began to move.

She couldn't get off. She didn't know where she was. Her father wouldn't be able to find her. She wouldn't be able to find him.

"Where am I?" she asked a man standing next to her.

"You're on a train going to the Square. We're all going shopping." He smiled and everyone around her was happy and looking forward to this excursion.

Shopping...

She didn't have her purse or her phone or her car keys. What was she going to do?

Panic set in. Why had her father driven ahead of her? Why had he left her behind? Was he even looking for her?

She was lost....

"Raeleen." Someone gently shook her shoulder.

Was it the man on the train? He seemed to be trying to change her focus to the sights around them.

"Raeleen."

Coherency settled upon her and she realized she'd just had a dream. A strange one that a dream expert would probably say meant she was having issues with her father. Not being able to catch up to him. Not knowing where she was or if he'd find her.

She looked over her shoulder and saw Travis up on one elbow.

"You were having a bad dream."

"I was dreaming about my father."

"Don't worry, you'll get that figured out eventually." His thumb caressed her shoulder through her T-shirt.

He meant her father. What a sweet thing to say. Despite her calling him a pet soldier, he still cared that she'd had a bad dream about her father.

"Meena said some things that must have gotten me thinking."

"What did she say?"

"That I should cherish the moments I have with him instead of being angry and resentful that I don't see him as often as I wish."

"Good advice."

"In the dream, he didn't wait for me and I couldn't find him."

"Maybe that means you should stop trying."

She'd given up trying to get her father's attention a long time ago. Now she resented him for that.

"It was just a dream." But the dream hung over her, dampening her spirit.

Travis was lying close to her, his body curved along her backside. Now there was a protrusion growing where it shouldn't.

"Travis…? You have a…"

"You're making me that way."

All she'd done was have a bad dream. Light from the kitchen dimly illuminated the living room. She could see enough of his eyes to gauge their warming in tune with her own.

At some point during the night, he'd removed his clothes

down to his boxers and gotten under the covers with her. He'd waited until she'd fallen asleep.

Her T-shirt had hiked up to her hips. The idea alone tossed caution aside and infused her with molten need.

With his elbow still on the bed, he hooked her head between his forearm and biceps and kissed her.

He slid his other hand down her hip, catching the waistband of her underwear and tugging them to her knees. Raeleen shimmied out of them and he pushed his underwear down enough to free his erection.

He kissed her again, rubbing his soft-skinned, bare hardness against her. Sliding his knee between her legs, the tip of him probed and sank into her.

Raeleen struggled to keep her breathing quiet, fearing they'd be heard. But it wasn't enough to stop this delicious stimulation. It was also good that she was on the Pill if this kept happening.

With his palm on her abdomen, he held her as he moved back and forth. In three of those mind-blowing strokes, he made her come, kissing her as she tried to stifle a sound.

Shoving the covers off them, he climbed on top of her.

"What if someone...?"

He spread her legs and plowed into her. The expensive sofa didn't even squeak. Meena was her new best friend.

Pushing her T-shirt up, he mouthed her breasts before resuming his thrusts, rising up by his arms. The wet friction stirred her to a new peak. She bit her lip with the second, stronger orgasm. Travis grunted and moved faster. With one final thrust, he collapsed onto her, his face beside hers. He kissed her softly on her cheek and then tenderly on her mouth. She ran her fingers up his back and down again, touching his butt before gliding over the firm muscles of his back once more.

"I wish you wouldn't have had that dream," he murmured.

He must be as confused as she. How good it was between them...

"We can't sleep in the same bed without this happening."

Harry and Meena's bedroom door opened. The sofa bed was out of sight, but if anyone walked down the hall they'd see them like this, her legs open and Travis between them, her shirt rumpled around her neck and her breasts mashed against Travis's chest, his bare butt, underwear around his ankles. The only thing left to the imagination was his penis still lodged inside her.

Travis pulled out of her and jerked the covers over them, curling beside her. Quickly adjusting her T-shirt, she rolled to her side so her back was to the room. The bathroom light switched on and then the door closed.

"Do you think they heard us?"

"No. You weren't that loud."

"You grunted."

"If they heard us, they wouldn't have come out into the hallway."

"Not until we finished..."

"Shh. Close your eyes."

She closed them as the toilet flushed. The water ran and then the door opened. Either Harry or Meena walked through the living room, clearly trying to be quiet.

The refrigerator opened and Harry or Meena poured something into a glass. The refrigerator closed and the person walked back through the living room.

When the bedroom door closed, Raeleen relaxed. That's when she realized whoever had gotten up had seen her lying with Travis this way, with his arm over her waist and her head tucked on his shoulder.

"It was Harry."

Harry had seen them sleeping like this.

The next morning, Travis pretended not to notice Raeleen emerge from the bathroom where she'd taken all the sheets from their bed to put them in the wash. Was she cleansing herself from the memory or concealing evidence?

Meena handed her a cup of steaming coffee. "You can sleep over anytime."

If only she knew the real reason Raeleen had washed the sheets. He'd like to know himself.

"I'm betting you will," Harry said from across the kitchen table.

Travis turned to him with a scowl. Was it something he saw in him or something in Raeleen that had him thinking they were a couple already? He didn't want to know.

"We should get going." He stood.

"Yeah," Raeleen agreed, putting the cup down on the table.

"Seriously, Travis." Meena approached him. "Don't let years go by before we see you again."

"Let us know when the wedding is," Harry cajoled.

Enough was enough. "There isn't going to be one." Raeleen and her annoying trouble with her father would see to that. Damn it. Why had he allowed them to have sex again? He may have thought he could do casual with her, but now he wasn't so sure. He couldn't remember ever feeling hotter for a woman, or if the sex had ever been better. It was like no other woman compared to her. What that meant worried him.

"Something on your mind?"

Travis looked at Harry. "Yeah, a painting that's going to attract killers." He shook Harry's hand. "I'll call you."

"Soon," Harry said, searching Travis's face. He knew

something was up. In a lower tone, he said, "She's a nice girl, Travis."

"A nice girl who's not into military men."

Harry glanced over at Raeleen, who was busy talking to Meena about her show. "That's not what I saw."

It was rare when Travis felt uncomfortable, but he did now. Harry hadn't seen them making love, but he'd seen the aftereffect of it. The way Travis had held her and the way she'd lain so close to him.

"Thank you both for everything." Raeleen hugged Meena and then moved to Harry.

"Don't thank us. You're always welcome here." He hugged her while Meena rose up on her toes to do the same with Travis.

He handed Raeleen the tube containing the painting, slung his duffel bag over his shoulder and then lifted her small luggage. Finally he had her outside in the bright New York morning. The tension in him began to ease. A little. He still had to deal with Raeleen.

"Harry heard us."

He looked at her. "No, he didn't. He saw the way I was holding you and now his retired, romantic ass is delusional."

He checked up and down the street. Deet was bound to be around somewhere. He'd seen him on the way to Harry and Meena's. If it had been anyone else, he wouldn't have agreed to stay the night here.

A white Ford Taurus was parked down the street and there was a man inside. Predictable. What kind of trouble had Deet gotten himself into? It was long past the time when he found out.

"Is that...?"

"Get in." He guided her to the passenger door with his hand on her lower back, scanning the street for anyone more dangerous than Deet. There was no one. Just as he planned. Good.

He got into the car.

"You knew he was here, didn't you?"

"He's a lousy tail." Travis turned the car around and drove along the cobblestone street, watching Deet follow in the rearview mirror.

"Is that why you wanted to leave last night? Do you think the people who are after the painting followed him?"

He didn't respond. After he was a safe distance from Harry and Meena's, he began to slow the car. He would have stopped, but Deet drew a gun and stuck it out his window.

He was going to shoot at them. A desperate man resorting to desperate measures.

"Get down!"

"Wh—"

Shattering safety glass made her duck as Travis sped the vehicle up and then slammed on the brakes. He had to stop him. Now.

Deet hit their rear end and then swerved, crashing into a parked car. Travis jumped out of the car, pistol aimed at Deet while he regained his equilibrium. Deet wasn't going anywhere now. Nowhere except with them. He strode toward the driver's door.

"Please, don't shoot!" Deet dropped his gun to the pavement and held his hands up so that Travis could see them.

"Get out." Travis picked up the gun and tucked it into his pants, glancing around as he opened the car door.

A man peered through the window of a flower shop, a cell phone to his ear. Seeing Travis, he moved out of sight. A car drove by, the driver not noticing anything. He had a few minutes at best before the police arrived.

Deet kept his hands up and Travis gave him a shove to get him moving toward the other car. He did as he was told.

Travis almost took pity on him. He was so far out of his league it was a miracle he'd survived this long without help.

At the other vehicle, Travis patted him down, checking for any other weapons. Finding none, he let him sit on the backseat.

Travis bent down to look in the car at him. "Try anything and you're a dead man."

"What are you going to do?"

"More than you can." Travis sat behind the wheel beneath Raeleen's wide-open gaze.

"What *are* you going to do?" she asked.

"Go somewhere we can talk." He drove down the street and turned a corner.

"You're making a mistake. You should give me the painting and forget it ever existed."

And leave Deet to handle a black-market art dealer all alone? Hardly. Travis ignored him as he drove into a small parking area underneath an overpass that ran along the water. It was just off the South Street Seaport, and the overpass provided good cover. The road wasn't heavily traveled at this hour of morning.

"What are you doing?" Raeleen asked as Travis opened the back door.

When Deet didn't get out, Travis grabbed his shirt and dragged him out. Deet found his footing and stood next to the car.

Raeleen rushed around the trunk and stood beside them, looking apprehensive.

"Tell us everything." Travis kept his pistol tucked into his jeans. He didn't think he'd need it.

Moistening his lips and then swallowing, Deet glanced at Raeleen uncertainly.

"It's the only way," she told him. "Tell us. Travis will be able to help."

Deet reached up to pinch the bridge of his nose. He'd probably lacked a lot of sleep over the past few days.

"They killed my wife and brother-in-law."

"Who?" Raeleen asked.

"Start from the beginning," Travis redirected him. He wanted the whole story. "Tell us everything."

Defeat weighed in his eyes before he nodded. "About a month ago, I found an art dealer who said he could sell Vivian's painting. Discretion was important. Vivian was against me selling it, but I could see no other way to save my restaurant. I had to do something. That restaurant has been in my family for generations."

"You were going to sell it without her consent?" Travis had to be sure.

"Yes, but this dealer promised anonymity. He told me he had a private buyer, one who'd keep the painting for herself and not reveal its history. I didn't love Vivian, but I respected her wish to protect her grandfather's name." He turned to Raeleen. "Just before you came to do your new show, my dealer began to get threatening phone calls. He said he'd pay me for the painting."

"And you refused," Raeleen said.

"When my dealer told him we already had a buyer, he said he was the only buyer we were going to deal with from then on. I didn't know what to do. Vivian would be devastated if her painting fell into the wrong hands and I knew nothing about this new buyer except that he seemed illegitimate. So I mailed the painting to you to be safe. I planned to come to the States with you, but Vivian was waiting for us…and then… Oh, God." He broke down into sobs, covering his face and leaning over a little. "This has gotten out of control. What I hoped would save my restaurant has turned into a run for my life. If I don't give this man the painting…"

"What is your dealer's name?" Raeleen asked.

"Rorey Evertszen."

"Have you spoken to him recently?" Travis asked.

Deet shook his head. "After the hurricane, he told me he was leaving Anguilla."

And then the new buyer had come after Deet. Travis wondered what had happened to the art dealer. Had he left Anguilla as he'd claimed?

"Who is the new buyer?" That was who must have killed Vivian and John.

"I don't know."

Travis cocked his head in disbelief. Surely he had to know. "Haven't you been in contact with them? How much did they offer you for the painting?"

"They offered my dealer more than his buyer was going to pay, but I refused, remember."

And now they were just going to kill him to get it. "Who are they? Who is the one who made the offer?"

"I swear I don't know. He never revealed his name, and Rorey never told me. Four men chased me once. They must have been hired by the man who calls me with threats."

When Travis took a menacing step toward him, Raeleen stopped him with her hand on his arm. "He's telling the truth. He doesn't know."

How could he not know? Why wouldn't his dealer tell him? Then Travis took in the man. He'd been on the run since his wife and brother-in-law had been killed.

"Did your dealer ever tell you the name of his private buyer?"

He shook his head. "He only said she was an art collector. Discretion was important."

"Fantastic." Once glance at Raeleen confirmed she believed him.

Deet was in a lot of danger. Lucky for him, he'd done the right thing by sending the painting to Raeleen.

He turned to Deet. "I suggest you go somewhere and hide until this is over. Stay away from Anguilla. Leave New York."

"They'll find me. They searched Raeleen's apartment. That means they know I sent her the painting. If they find me they're going to kill me."

"They definitely know where you are right now. And they'll know what happened to the painting. I'll make sure of that."

"But—"

"Give me your cell phone."

Perplexed, Deet did as he demanded.

Travis checked the phone and after a few minutes navigating through its programs, found evidence of the tracking software someone had installed.

He put the phone into his shirt pocket. "Now it's me they're going to find."

Chapter 10

Habib had finished inventorying his stock when he heard the front bell ring, signifying someone had entered his market. He took his clipboard with him, seeing Lucian LeFevre standing at the entrance, waiting. It had been a few days since he'd seen him. Putting the clipboard down on the front counter, he went to lock the front door and close the plastic blinds that were so hard to keep clean.

"Sorry I am late," Lucian said.

"Come, come." Habib did not care why he was late. He had the rest of his diamonds.

In the back of his market where a small room served as his dual-purpose office, Habib found a key on his key ring and unlocked his safe.

"Did you have any trouble?" Lucian asked.

That was another way of asking if anyone had grown suspicious of his impatient buyer. "No. All as usual." Since he'd severed his Hezbollah ties, he'd found another mine from which to purchase his rough diamonds. Word of mouth had spread of his business and he'd accumulated an assortment of buyers and dealers. Removing a metal box from the safe, he put it down on the computer table and began separating Lucian's purchase.

He enjoyed this part of his life. His market brought in an adequate income. With his wife gone, he had no one else here in Monrovia. Many times he considered selling his market and retiring, but Lebanon was not an area he considered good for retirement. Neither was Monrovia, but alas, these were his dilemmas, dilemmas that no longer mattered so much now that his wife was dead. He could return to Lebanon, but he still had enemies there. He was relatively safe here in Monrovia. Better that than having to look over his shoulder.

Flattening a piece of velvet on the table, he placed the dull chunks of rough that would soon be sparkling in jewelry. He showed Lucian, who inspected the pieces with a magnifying glass. When he straightened with a nod, Habib gathered the velvet and began to tie it with a ribbon. Lucian preferred to carry his rough in his pockets.

Handing Lucian the diamonds, he waited for payment. "Have you been able to locate your painting?" He'd rather not ask and only did to be courteous. Lucian had been so captivated by the painting the last time he'd been here.

As he expected, Lucian's face brightened with enthusiasm, but then something darkened it immediately thereafter. "Unfortunately, there has been a delay."

"The seller is still reluctant?"

"I have been unable to locate the seller, and his dealer refused to divulge this information."

"Do you mean the seller has disappeared?"

"I shouldn't bore you with the drama of it all." Lucian lifted his eyes with the trouble it gave him.

"I am quite interested. But if you are not comfortable discussing it with me…"

Lucian regarded him for a time. As Habib suspected, he could not resist talk of his precious painting.

"Until now, I have been most patient with this seller's need for discretion. My men would have persuaded him had it not been for his wife interfering. I would not have had to travel to Anguilla were it not for her."

"I don't understand. His wife is against the selling of this painting?"

"Her grandfather was the Nazi who stole it."

Intriguing. "Ah."

"And she kidnapped her husband's lover to stop him from selling."

"Drastic measures. I see why you call this a drama. What will you do?" Habib slid his gaze to the clock, hoping he'd be able to go home soon. His day was finished here.

"This woman who was kidnapped complicates matters."

"How so?"

"Her father is someone very powerful. A man I do not wish to learn my identity."

"Oh?" Habib could not help his interest.

"He controls a secret military operation for the United States government. The man he sent to rescue the woman who was kidnapped works for him. And now they have my painting."

Habib began to worry that Lucian would no longer have a need for the second half of his purchase. He'd paid him only a deposit so far. "This is serious, then." He was familiar with how these types of organizations operated.

"I will have my painting." Lucian's fist clenched at his side.

Habib hoped he would not forget to pay him for the diamonds that were now in his pocket. "What is this man's name? The one who rescued the girl?"

Lucian seemed suspicious that Habib wanted to know. Habib needed to be careful.

"I cannot recall." He reached into his jacket and retrieved his billfold. From inside, he pulled out a photograph, on the back of which he'd written a name, but Habib was transfixed by the photo of a large man walking beside a woman he didn't recognize. But the man he did recognize.

Very careful. Very careful, indeed...

Jada heard the hotel room door open. Lucian was finally back from his trip. He hadn't told her where he was going and had been gone for two days. Yesterday he'd asked her to meet him in New York. He'd booked a room at the Waldorf. Although she wasn't comfortable with how fast things had turned intimate with him, something about him made her okay with that. Not just the painting. The painting was the only reason she'd gone to his room with him that night in Anguilla. His passion had attracted her to do more.

Lucian walked toward her in the hotel suite, taking in her red dress with building lust. He stopped to just look at her.

It felt like they were meeting for the first time all over again. She was nervous. Uncertain. He'd killed Rorey. She was using him to get her painting. And there was this dark desire between them.

Before he'd left Anguilla on a business trip, they'd spent twenty-four hours having sex. After that first time, they'd had dinner and he'd taken her to bed again. She'd woken the next morning and they didn't leave the room. They hadn't even spoken much. Only silent communication passed between them. This inexplicable passion they had, both for the painting and for each other. They'd both simply accepted it.

At last he stepped close to her. "I'm glad you are here."

"Where else would I be?" She leaned against him, flattening her hands on his chest.

"If you had the painting?"

If she had the painting, she wouldn't be here. Or would she...? She wasn't sure anymore. The time in his hotel room had changed things.

"The painting will be yours."

Wicked satisfaction warmed his eyes before he stepped back and loosened his tie. Then he turned and walked over to the bar.

"We have a problem." He poured a scotch.

She loved how he said *we.* "What kind of a problem?"

He drank the scotch and faced her. "The painting is missing."

Missing? How long had he known this? "Dietrich doesn't have it?"

"He sent it to the woman his wife arranged to have kidnapped. She lives in New York."

So that was why Lucian had asked her to meet him here. He'd told her all about the kidnapping the morning after she'd gone to his room, one of the few things they'd talked about. Dietrich's lover. His wife and brother.

"Why is that a problem?" All he had to do was take it from her.

"The woman is a problem."

"Who is she?"

"That isn't important. What's important is she has help. A man is protecting her. Someone I hoped would not interfere once he freed her and brought her back to the United States."

Dietrich had sent her the painting and now she was involved, making this man involved. Jada walked over to him, moving to stand in front of him to run her hands over his chest. "Everything's going to work out." It had to. "You'll see."

"I'm starting to have my doubts."

"It isn't like you to fear another man."

"This man is a professional. Military, and not the traditional kind. He works for a counterterrorism organization. One that operates in secret. The man who runs it is the woman's father."

Jada felt chilled. This was not good news. "What organization?"

"That's all I was able to find out."

Which was why he was worried. She ran her hands up to his shoulders and tipped her head back, her mouth close to his. "No one can stop you now. You're too close. You'll do what you have to do and the painting will be yours." He had to. For her. This had to work.

Her encouragement worked to ease his tension. He slid his hands around her to grab her butt. "Yours, too, darling." He bent to kiss her.

The strangeness of seeing him after the hours they'd spent making love in his hotel room began to melt away. The chemistry they'd discovered renewed and exploded into something even more powerful. Jada craved him. She'd missed being away from him, from this.

He kept kissing her, both hands on her butt, kneading her against his hard-on.

"You have all you need to take the painting, baby. No one can stand in your way." She loved that about him. His danger. His ruthless determination.

Mumbling something passionate in French, he kissed her harder. She needed him to be at the top of his game right now. She'd do anything to see that he was.

Grasping the front of her skintight red dress in his hands, Lucian yanked, jerking her body as the material ripped. Her breasts sprang free.

"When you talk to me so, you drive me mad." He took

one of her nipples into his mouth and pulled her ruined dress down until it dropped to the floor.

Just get me that painting, she thought.

Chapter 11

After sending Deet off on one of TES's private planes a day after he'd tried to chase them, Travis walked beside Raeleen toward their rental car. They'd sent Deet to Kansas, where another TES operative was waiting.

So far there'd been no sign of anyone following them. Travis had made sure of it until Deet was on his way to somewhere safe. The man had done nothing but try to save his restaurant. He hadn't killed anyone. He hadn't stolen anything, not really. The painting was just as much his as it had been Vivian's. He'd even tried to find a private buyer, one who'd keep the painting and never let it out into the open market. He'd at least tried to satisfy his wife's wishes, even after having an affair. He didn't deserve to die for his infidelity and attempt to sell a painting that meant something to his wife.

Travis drove away from LaGuardia International Airport, heading back to the hotel where he'd left Deet's cell phone. He'd registered the room under a false name, using one of several passports he had. Raeleen sat quietly in the passenger seat. Since catching Deet, he hadn't been alone with her until now and felt the tension thicken.

"Now what are we going to do?" she asked.

"Wait until someone comes after the painting."

"That doesn't sound very reassuring."

"I'm not thrilled about it, either." But not because he was afraid of the black-market dealer.

By the way she jerked a glance at him, he knew she'd caught his real meaning.

"It won't be much longer," he said. "They may even already be at the hotel. And Odie had backup waiting there."

"Oh, well, good then. I'll be rid of you sooner than I expected."

Her snide remark came with a load of emotion. She didn't really feel that way. Their sexual encounters were bothering her as much as they were him. Last night had crawled a little too far into his heart.

"Yes, and you can go find yourself a nice, nonmilitary man that you can boss around. It's what you want, anyway." He couldn't stop his own emotion.

"At least I know what I'm looking for."

"You don't have a clue what you're looking for."

Yes, she did. She just didn't see it yet. "I haven't stopped anything from happening between us. That was all you."

His cell phone rang.

"Todd," he answered sharply.

"Ohh, somebody is grumpy today."

"Odie." Figures, she'd call right now.

"You're getting awfully popular," she said, thankfully not pressing him, but that was also a bad sign. She had something. Something big.

"Why is that?"

"You've got people calling you from Monrovia."

"Really." What was she talking about? "Who?" Any mention of Monrovia was a red flag.

"Do you remember Habib Maalouf?"

The name instantly resonated. "How could I ever forget? He was the market owner in Monrovia, the one Haley and I were watching." And then he was shot. "He called?"

Raeleen turned from her vigilance out the window.

"He called the main numbers of several units, and of course no one there could say they knew you. Finally someone got a message to Roth. I called Maalouf and kindly explained to him that no one by the name of Travis Todd exists, a claim the army will readily support."

Since he was a TES operative, and TES didn't exist. "What did Maalouf want?"

"He wouldn't say. He will only talk to you. You're the only one he trusts, probably because we helped him get out from under the thumbs of Hezbollah."

"Interesting." Why was he calling now? Any why him?

"Call him, then come to Dad's. Something else has come up that we need to discuss securely. I've got a plane waiting for you at LGA."

They'd just come from there. Travis began to look for a place to turn around. "On our way now."

Odie gave him Maalouf's number and they disconnected.

"What's wrong?" Raeleen asked.

"We're going to find out." He drove toward the airport. He wasn't in the mood to argue with her.

"Where? How?"

He didn't answer.

"Not *Dad's* again."

The double meaning triggered a grin in him. "Your dad won't be there."

She relaxed against the seat. "Who is Maalouf? Why were you and Haley watching him?"

"He was a diamond dealer with ties to Hezbollah in Monrovia, Liberia. Unwanted ties."

She seemed to digest that a moment. "Is that when you were shot?"

She was quick to piece it all together. "Yes. That's the mission that went sour and Rem D'Evereau intervened."

"The mercenary." She nodded slowly.

Travis pressed the speaker button on his cell and entered Maalouf's international number. Handing Raeleen the phone, she held it while the connection went through.

"Hello, this is Habib Maalouf." The voice was heavily accented, a little Middle Eastern and a little West African.

"I hear you've been trying to reach me."

A slight pause carried through as Habib registered who he must be.

"You are no doubt curious as to why."

"I'm wondering a lot of things." And he wasn't going to give anything away.

"This organization you work for is the reason you were in Monrovia that time, is it not? The reason Farid Abi Salloum and his son were captured?"

Did he need confirmation? Salloum had been a terrorist funneling money through West African diamond mines.

"We were sent there to gather intel, that's all." And that's all he'd tell him.

Another lengthy pause traveled the distance. "I have it from a reliable source that the woman you were sent to rescue is the daughter of the man who runs this organization. She is the daughter of a very powerful man."

Looking over at Raeleen, seeing apprehension flare in her, Travis replied calmly, "I don't know what you're talking about."

"I imagine that you do, Mr. Todd. There are not many men like you in the world. I am not mistaken."

How did Habib know about Raeleen's rescue? There could be only one way.

"You know about *The Portrait of Sarah*." The dealer hunting down the painting must have obtained a photo of Travis, and somehow Habib had recognized him.

He waited through Habib's stunned silence.

"Then you possess the painting," he finally said.

"Why are you dealing with someone who is willing to kill to have it?" Travis countered.

"I have a client. A man who frequently purchases diamonds from me."

So he was still selling diamonds. No longer to Hezbollah, but to the likes of a black-market art dealer.

"He's a friend of yours? This client?"

"No friend. It is business, you understand."

"Black-market business."

"Business, nonetheless. No one holds the heads of my family to force me. I choose my clients now. And there is one client you will be very interested in, because this client has a particular fascination with World War II artifacts. He especially covets paintings stolen from Jews. Nazi thieves stole the art for Hitler. Some of the art has been recovered, but there is much that has not."

"*The Portrait of Sarah* being one of them."

"Yes."

"Who is this client?"

"Lucian LeFevre. Many in the black-market art world know of him. He is a very wealthy man with a dangerous agenda. Not only does he dabble in the arts, but he buys diamonds to launder money for various terrorist groups."

"And you said you choose your clients."

"I was not aware of this until recently. My business is

vulnerable to that sort of controversy. It does not mean that I support what LeFevre is doing."

"Why are you telling me this?"

"LeFevre's talk of the painting unsettles me. As you have said, he will kill to have it. Your organization saved my life. When I saw a photo of you in LeFevre's possession, I could not believe our paths had crossed again. But I am also grateful. I mean only to repay a debt and to ensure that LeFevre causes me no trouble."

He'd been through enough with Hezbollah.

Raeleen watched Jag go to the front door of Dad's, turn the lock, switch off the Open sign and pull down the white roller blinds. They weren't open for dinner. She sat beside Travis at a table near one of the two windows in front. Across from them, Odie spread photos out and what looked like a spec sheet on Lucian LeFevre. She also had something on Rorey Evertszen.

"Lucian LeFevre," Odie began, pointing to a photo of him. "Four houses, one in the Cayman Islands, all of them mansions. He's established a name for himself. It wasn't hard to find someone to talk. Divorced twice. No children. Single for now. Definitely likes to do business. In addition to his diamond and drug dealing, he's a yacht broker and owns a charter company in Italy. Not much comes up on him about his interest in art, but my contact did say he frequents shows and galleries that feature World War II pieces."

"Seems harmless so far," Travis said, looking at the photos Odie had arranged on the table.

"You haven't let her get to the good part." Jag came to stand at the table, pulling the chair out beside his wife but not sitting.

Travis turned to Odie, who continued.

"When he locates a piece he likes, he makes an offer to

the owner, and if that owner doesn't sell, he simply steals the art. In a couple of cases, it's suspected that he's killed to possess them. The man has a real fetish for certain pieces. Artifacts that belonged to Jews who were gassed or to Nazis who were executed after the war and the family members who suffered as a result, things like that."

"*The Portrait of Sarah* is his kind of art," Travis said.

"Yes," Odie said. "And it explains why he'll stop at nothing to get it."

"Kill to get it," Raeleen added, finding the pictures of LeFevre eerie. Even in still shots he looked menacing. "He's done that before."

Odie nodded. "Our good pal Deet got himself in a fine little mess. He should have listened to his wife and not tried to sell."

Despite his lies and halfhearted regard for his wife, Raeleen did feel sorry for him. "I'm sure he didn't know what he was walking into."

"Obviously." Odie began putting photos and papers back into a file folder. "Now he's faced with a murdered wife and brother-in-law and losing his livelihood, the very thing he sought to preserve. The poor bastard."

What if they gave the painting back to him after LeFevre was caught? What would TES decide to do with it? As far as Raeleen was concerned, the painting belonged to Deet.

"LeFevre will go where the painting is," Travis said. "We should choose our battleground carefully."

Jag leaned down and slid the last photo to his wife's reaching hand. "Rorey isn't answering his phone."

Odie picked up the photo with an agreeing nod. "He could be dead for all we know." She put the photo into the folder with the others and closed it.

"Or running scared just like Deet is," Raeleen added.

"Then we have our battleground." Travis stood and

pushed in his chair. "I'll fly to Anguilla to check on him. LeFevre won't be far behind."

Of course, he'd say that. Raeleen was about to say something.

"Actually, you're both going." Odie stood and walked around the table to Travis, handing him the folder. "You and Raeleen."

Incredulous, Travis took the folder. "It's too dangerous. If she doesn't have to go, she should stay here. You two can watch over her."

Raeleen couldn't tell if he was being overprotective or not. It would be dangerous for her if she went with him, but it would be dangerous for her no matter where she went. Deet had mailed the painting to her.

"We're working another assignment." Jag put his arm around Odie when she came to stand beside him. "We don't have time."

"Then get someone else to watch her."

"No one else is available," Odie said.

"Hey." Raeleen was the last to stand up. "I'm not a twelve-year-old. I'm going with you, Travis. You don't have to find a babysitter for me." He was only resisting this because of his fear of failure. She wished she could make him see that.

"I didn't mean it like that." He met her gaze and then his eyes traveled down her body. "I don't want you getting hurt."

For intimate reasons, she guessed, by the way he'd just looked at her. She felt it all the way to her toes. Their early morning quickie had a potent effect on both of them.

"There's another reason why she needs to go with you." Raeleen turned with Travis toward Odie.

"It's the reason we needed you to come here," Jag said.

"Three men broke into Harry and Meena's home and tore it apart looking for the painting. They tried to rough them up a bit to get them to talk. 'Where is the painting? Where did Travis take Raeleen?' Those kind of questions."

Travis cursed a couple of choice words. "Are they all right?"

Concerned for her newest friends, Raeleen moved closer to Travis, putting her hand on his big shoulder.

"Of course. Harry got the upper hand and chased all three of them away after one of them hit his wife. He's not one to mess with, that Harry."

"Where are they now?" Raeleen asked.

"On their way to Cape Canaveral, where they'll be waiting for you two on their boat. The four of you are going to Anguilla. You'll be there by tomorrow night."

Raeleen looked up at Travis and exchanged a worried look with him.

"Harry was so mad that anyone dare harm his wife that he joined TES," Odie added.

"He's a sixty-year-old man!" Travis roared.

"A sixty-year-old man who's in fantastic shape. And he's a temporary employee. Not a full-timer."

"I don't believe this."

"Rorey lives on a yacht." Raeleen lowered her hand from Travis's shoulder, seeing Odie and Jag's logic now.

"Odie's arranged everything," Jag said. "Once you get to Sandy Ground, you'll be right where you need to be."

Close to Rorey.

"I'll be where I need to be. The other three are debatable," Travis protested.

Odie moved away from Jag. "Get out of yourself, Travis. She's Colonel Roth's daughter and Harry is no novice. They're not completely helpless."

"Let's go," he grumbled to Raeleen, taking her hand.

She waved goodbye to Odie and Jag and went outside with Travis.

"If anything happens to you, it will kill me, you know that, right?"

He still held her hand as they walked down the street toward the rental car.

"If anything happens to you, it will kill me, too."

He turned his head toward her as they walked, intimacy in his eyes the same as she was sure was in hers. Last night had brought them inexorably closer. She cared so much for him. Felt him getting closer to facing his sister's death and the way it influenced him in his work. She wanted to help him get there. But would doing so be a mistake?

He was a military man. M-i-l-i-t-a-r-y. She'd made herself a promise a long time ago to avoid men like him. Was it wise to forget?

Chapter 12

Arriving at the boat in time for dinner the following night, Raeleen had insisted on having her own cabin, and while Travis had agreed, he hadn't taken it well. She had to get her head straight regarding him. No more relationships that weren't good for her. She had to be sure. And she wasn't sure about Travis.

Meena sat beside Harry, who sipped an after-dinner decaf coffee and talked to Travis about what they'd do when they reached Anguilla.

"One of us needs to stay on the boat with the women while the other pays Rorey a visit on his boat," Travis said.

Of course, he'd say that. Mr. Protector at work again.

"You talk to Rorey. I'll watch the girls."

Meena leaned back against her chair, the boat rocking gently in a calm sea. Harry smiled his love and took Meena's hand in his, leaning back with her.

Raeleen refrained from commenting that she didn't think

Travis going alone was a very smart idea. She and Meena would be fine alone on the yacht, or all four of them should go. Rorey hadn't been answering his phone; there was no telling what they'd find when they went to see him.

Travis picked up another fishing lure from a box he'd been sifting through for an hour now. "We can stay in contact with radios."

He'd need a lot more than a radio.

"I don't think we have much to worry about. It will take a while for LeFevre to catch up to us."

That, at least, was a relief to Raeleen.

"I'm hoping we find him first."

She watched Travis fingering the fishing lure, smooth and sure, and with reverent appreciation. He was more relaxed than she'd ever seen him and she wondered why. Her attention wandered to his torso, his stomach and wide chest. Muscular shoulders. Blue-gold eyes that softly regarded her. She was what had him so relaxed.

She turned away, disconcerted by the instant ignition of desire that that gave her.

"I remember when I first met Harry," Meena began, increasing her discomfort because she must have noticed the way she and Travis were looking at each other. "He terrified me. I didn't think for one minute that we'd last past the first kiss."

"I couldn't stay away from her." Harry lifted his wife's hand and kissed the back of it.

"And I fell madly in love with him."

Losing his wife had to have been a hurdle, but if it was meant to be, it was meant to be.

Raeleen looked over at Travis, wondering if he was meant to be.

If she didn't have her predisposed notion of military men, how different would things be between them?

Bothered by her wavering thoughts, Raeleen stood up. "I'm going to go up to the bow."

She walked the narrow plank along the salon and pilot-house, putting her hands on the railing, wind lifting her shoulder-length blond hair.

Her relationship with Deet had made her realize she'd been choosing convenient men. Men who allowed her to avoid commitment. Was she afraid of commitment? Was she afraid she'd end up with someone who'd neglect her the way her father had? Maybe it wasn't only military men she avoided.

Depressed, she left the railing and found her way to a side door, needing to be alone for a while. She'd go down to her cabin and hopefully by morning she'd have figured herself out.

Unfortunately, Travis must have planned the same thing. She bumped into him when she reached the narrow deck, just as he reached for the door handle.

She jumped back.

"Sorry...I was..."

All the pent-up lust billowed. She didn't move, and neither did he.

"Harry and Meena went to their cabin."

She nodded. "I was just heading to mine."

He nodded, too, still relaxed the way he had been fingering the fishing lures, but now with sultry flames licking in his eyes. She'd enjoyed watching him fish earlier today. She enjoyed watching him no matter what he was doing.

When he stepped toward her, she didn't back away. The physical took over, and before she knew it he slid his arm along the back of her waist and had her pressed against the railing. Then his face was just above hers.

"I'm tired of fighting this," he murmured. "If it doesn't last, I don't care." And then he kissed her.

His words ran over and over in her head. But then his tongue caressed hers and pulled at her desire. His mouth moved with hers, perfectly matched. When he kissed her neck, she let her head fall back. The stars twinkled above.

He kissed her mouth again, his hands rubbing over her clothes, thumbing her nipples through her T-shirt, over her rear, between her legs. She ran her hands from his biceps to loop around his shoulders.

Kissing him was a dream.

He lifted her up and she felt his hardness. Almost wrapping her legs around him to make him fit better there, she heard his words filter through her head again.

If it doesn't last, I don't care....

There was a time when that would have been fine with her. If it didn't last, she didn't have to worry about ending up with someone who wouldn't be there for her. All her steadfast rules had been in place for a good reason, so she wouldn't end up with the wrong man. She'd rather be alone than give herself all the way to the wrong man.

Bringing her arms down, she pushed his chest.

He stopped kissing her and met her gaze.

"I care," she said.

Looking from her mouth to her eyes again, he assimilated her meaning. "Nothing lasts with you, Raeleen. I would think an arrangement like that would appeal to you."

Had he taken this strategy on purpose? Offering up a convenient affair to appeal to her? Did he hope to woo her into more? Trick her?

"I never get involved with anyone if I don't think it will last."

"But it never does."

"Especially if you've already decided it won't." She pushed him again, stepping back.

He hung his hands at his sides, but she sensed he was

ready to take her back into his arms. "Sex is good between us. Let's go with that."

It was good, but she was starting to want more from him, and that confused her. More with Travis went against all her beliefs. He represented everything she'd promised to avoid, in order to prevent a mistake.

"If you were Deet, I'd be happy to hear that."

"Don't talk about him now."

"I'm not saying I'd have sex with him. If you were any other boyfriend I've ever had, I'd be happy to hear that."

"But I work for your father."

Yes. And more and more she was beginning to think that that no longer mattered. Her heart was drawn to him. If she relented to the pull, would she line herself up for a future of unhappiness after she discovered her original assessment was accurate and he wouldn't be there for her? The powerful pull in her heart argued that he could be what she had been looking for all along. Which challenged her decision to avoid military men. What if avoidance was a way for her to avoid committing to one man instead?

When she didn't respond, he swung open the door and stormed inside. He thought she'd just rejected him. He didn't know that it was her confusion that caused her to step back, and she wasn't sure she should enlighten him.

Travis looked through binoculars as Harry navigated the yacht into Sandy Ground and the newly constructed marina. He spotted the sailboat called *Summer Storm* and shouted to Harry, who steered toward their slip rental, which happened to be close.

Helping Harry tie off to the deck, he headed for the stern to get off the yacht. Raeleen was waiting there, purse over her shoulder, movie star sunglasses on, dressed in a white sundress that drew his eyes to all her curves and those long, sexy legs.

He was still raw from last night. He wasn't angry, just frustrated with her. He could see her confusion and fought the urge to keep pushing her. The only thing stopping him was her resolve to steer clear of men who worked for her father. He didn't think wasting time on women who weren't certain about him was particularly bright. He could see her misconception, her mistake in assuming all men in her father's profession were the same. The woman he ended up with would accept him for himself, profession and all. He wouldn't have to feel like he had to change, to be someone he wasn't. Quit his job and find another to enable her phobia.

If only she'd wake up about her father. See him for the man he was instead of the one he wasn't, never there for her. Or not enough. Didn't she realize her father loved her?

And why had she decided to torture him by dressing like that? Damn, she was beautiful.

"We'll be watching from here," Harry called, his smile saying he knew what Travis was up against.

He turned to Raeleen. "Don't argue with me. Let's go."

With a smug look, she turned and walked onto the dock, hips swaying just enough, long legs tugging him to follow.

"Did you wear that on purpose?"

Her chin lifted in defiance.

"To make me pay more attention to that than arguing about whether or not you'd go with me today?" The tiny sapphire flirting with her cleavage captured him for a few strides. "Or are you trying to punish me for attempting to seduce you without strings?"

"You're a control freak."

How had she drawn that conclusion? She was the one who'd placed restrictions on the men she dated.

"Me?" he said leadingly.

"Overprotective. Haley was right. Does she know why you're like that?"

She was referring to what had happened with his sister, and he didn't feel like talking about that. "I'm not the one who stereotypes the people I will or won't date."

He couldn't see her eyes behind her glasses, but the pinched corners of her mouth were enough of an indication that her confusion had returned. She really was on the fence when it came to him.

One push…

"If it makes you feel any better, at least you made it this far avoiding military men. That's not a bad record."

She humphed. "Just my luck to run into one who'd actually think I would agree to a sex-only affair."

"Isn't that what you had with Deet?"

Incensed, she stopped walking. "No!"

He could tell by her sharp reaction that at least part of her acknowledged the truth. She may not have thought of it that way when she was seeing him, but that's how her relationship with him had ended up.

"How can you call a long-distance relationship anything other than casual?" he asked. "You flew to Anguilla to have sex with him, not marry him."

"He was already married."

Her defensiveness only proved his point. "A fact that you should have figured out a lot sooner than you did."

"Let's just find out what Rorey knows about LeFevre and be done with this."

"I'll do that. You just keep dressing like that." The rest would happen naturally. Unless she persisted in denying it.

"It worked, by the way."

She glanced at him impatiently. "What worked?"

"The dress." He gave her an up and down. "I'll take you

anywhere if it means I can keep looking at you." Except into the line of fire.

"I'm not having a sexual affair with you."

He thought twice about reminding her that they already were. "Then I'll just have to seduce you into more than that." Unable to believe he'd said that, he reasoned it was where this was headed, anyway. Why continue to fight it?

She stopped again, this time right in front of Rorey's yacht.

"Travis..."

He couldn't rationalize why he pushed for something he wasn't even sure he wanted himself. He didn't trust her not to reject him in her determination to ban men who reminded her of her father. What if she never accepted him for the man he was, with no ties to her father? His heart would be in danger of being broken, but he couldn't back down, either.

"Having sex with you was a mistake."

"Was it?" he challenged and immediately saw that she couldn't call it that with any conviction.

She humphed again and headed toward the stern of Rorey's boat. Travis climbed aboard ahead of her and turned to extend his hand. In those heels, she took it and he helped her aboard. He deliberately didn't move back so that she bumped against him.

She jerked back, her eyes afire with resentment. But underneath he knew he'd find passion. That addicting passion they'd created together. Right now he could walk away from her. Later...

Maybe she was right. Having sex again might be a mistake.

Rorey's yacht was about fifty feet longer than Harry and Meena's and worth about a million more. The blinds over the sliding glass doors leading to the salon were closed.

Travis knocked.

When no one answered, he tested the door. It was unlocked. Now he wished Raeleen wasn't so stubborn.

He opened the door and carefully stepped inside. All was silent, but the smell was potent. A bloated body lay on the salon floor. The man had been there awhile, but Travis recognized Rorey from the photos Odie had shown them.

"Uh." Raeleen covered her nose and mouth.

"I'd tell you to wait outside, but you won't."

She moved from behind him and saw the body that had been lying there for several days now. Travis covered her mouth before she screamed.

"We don't need to draw attention right now."

Her big, round, beautiful blue eyes stared up at him in horror.

"I don't want to be caught here by local police, okay?"

She nodded three times really fast.

"This is why you need to trust me when I tell you to wait somewhere."

She jerked her head back. "This is the first dead person I've ever seen."

"And hopefully the last…if you ever *listen* to me."

With Raeleen close behind him, Travis did a quick search of the rest of the yacht. As he'd anticipated, he found nothing that would reveal the murderer.

Back on the aft deck, he led her to the dock.

"Why hasn't anyone noticed him?" Raeleen asked, still disturbed.

"Must not have many friends here."

"Not even the marina noticed."

"He has a permanent slip. I'm sure they thought he wasn't even here."

"That poor man."

He was definitely innocent. Putting his hand on her back, he guided her to the steps leading off the yacht. Going ahead of her, jumping onto the dock, he reached for her. She leaned toward him and he lifted her by her trim waist and swung her gently onto the dock. She stood there looking up at him, calming now.

He took her hand.

"Harry and Meena's yacht is the other way."

"I want to look at you some more. You dressed that way for a reason, and now I want to accommodate you." He'd never spoken to a woman this way before. Was he so at ease with her that he felt he could say anything? Or did he feel he had nothing to lose?

"W-what? Travis, we just…"

"Come on. I want to have a look around the marina. See if anyone else is aware of Rorey's current state." A partial truth.

"I don't feel so good." She put her hand on her stomach.

"Keep moving."

"No. I really don't feel good."

"We'll get you a soda, then." He looked down at her shoes. "You won't be able to walk through the sand in those."

"I can take them off."

She did and he walked with her toward the beach. Vendors dotted the sea of blue-and-yellow umbrellas. Travis searched all of them, looking for anyone who stood out.

Sure enough, he spotted a woman dressed in jeans and a white blouse with a colorful scarf blowing in a slight breeze. Wearing a straw hat, her long brown hair hanging down, she leaned an elbow on the surface of an open marina bar and held a bottle of beer. The hat shaded her face, but he had a feeling she was watching them.

He stopped.

"What's wrong?"

"We've been spotted."

The woman abandoned her perch at the bar and started

toward them. She posed no threat to him in public. He'd be ready to draw his gun just in case.

"Who is that?" Raeleen asked.

"Let's find out." He waited for the woman to approach. She had to know he'd seen her. She seemed to be waiting for them...or someone. Waiting to see who came to find Rorey dead.

The woman stopped a few feet from them. "I'm sorry. I saw you board Rorey's boat and...and... Well, you aren't... You don't seem like..." She'd taken a chance approaching them. She knew Rorey was dead. Immediately he wondered why she hadn't notified local authorities. He could surmise only one reason.

The Portrait of Sarah.

"How do you know Rorey?" he asked.

Her lengthy hesitation convinced him she was reluctant to say. Why had him most curious.

"Who are you? Why did you come to see Rorey?"

"We're looking for whoever killed him," Raeleen answered, ignoring her question.

The woman studied them warily. "How do you know him?"

"We'd like to know the same from you," Travis countered.

"Rorey was an art dealer I frequently used," she finally relented. "I was aboard his yacht when three men arrived unannounced. They would have killed me, too, if I hadn't hidden."

That explained why she'd kept her distance and why Rorey's body was still on the yacht. She might have been afraid to notify authorities. "Come with us. We'll talk somewhere more private." He wanted to be somewhere he could control the situation without having to watch his surroundings. She may have been followed or her surveillance noticed.

Harry had been keeping vigil in the flybridge. When they drew nearer, he came down to the aft deck, Meena behind him, and led them all into the salon.

Raeleen passed Travis and turned to stand beside Meena and Harry near the open galley entrance.

After Travis introduced everyone, the woman told them her name.

"Jada Manoah." She wandered across the salon of the yacht, significantly less appointed than Rorey's, fingering the edge of a worn chair. "I collect art from all over world, mainly pieces with interesting history."

Just like LeFevre. "You were the private buyer Rorey found for Dietrich Artz?" Travis moved to keep facing her.

Turning her head, she nodded. "Yes. The day I came to pick Dietrich's painting up is the day Rorey was killed."

"How did you learn of *The Portrait of Sarah?*" Travis asked.

Jada wandered the salon again. "I've known about *The Portrait of Sarah* for years." Her gaze touched Harry and Meena's fish wall art without inflection. "Rorey was one of several brokers I use. He called me after Dietrich came to him. Dietrich's wife was sensitive to protecting her grandfather's name, so he asked Rorey to find a private buyer. I collect art like *The Portrait of Sarah*. I don't exploit it. To Dietrich, I was the kind of buyer he was looking for. But then—"

"Rorey was murdered by a black-market art dealer," Raeleen supplied.

"Yes." Jada looked at her. "Rorey told me about him."

"Lucian LeFevre?" Travis asked.

She nodded. "Lucian approached Rorey, but Rorey refused his offer. He found out about the painting after Rorey began searching for a buyer. In Dietrich's best interest, he chose me."

"Vivian was against selling the painting," Raeleen said. She'd arranged for her kidnapping to stop Deet.

"Rorey never told me that. He kept the owner a secret, at Dietrich's request. I only learned about him when Lucian came to kill Rorey."

"What did LeFevre say when he was aboard Rorey's yacht?" Travis asked.

Jada stopped her wandering and faced them all. "He wanted to know where Dietrich was. When Rorey couldn't tell him, one of his men shot him."

She was very refined, Travis observed. Definitely the artist type. He was good at reading people, and she was telling the truth.

Rorey had been killed after Vivian and her brother. And Rorey hadn't revealed Jada's identity. If he had, he agreed that LeFevre would have killed her. He'd eliminate anyone standing between him and *The Portrait of Sarah*.

There was something missing, though.

Jada may be an art collector, and she may be telling the truth, but there was something she wasn't telling them. He felt it. Stepping toward her, he stopped right in front of her to get a good look at her eyes. They never flinched.

"Manoah," he said. "It's Jewish, isn't it?"

One blink, then two rapid ones. "Yes. You're very astute, Mr. Todd."

He continued to watch her eyes, certain she well understood why.

"Don't you think it's strange that Deet didn't divorce Vivian sooner?"

Travis twisted to see Raeleen when she spoke, wondering why she'd asked the question.

"I mean, I was with him for a year," she continued, perplexed. "Why didn't he divorce her before then?"

What would she have done if he had? Moved to Anguilla? Travis stepped around to face her, his booted feet thudding on the polished floor. "Maybe he wasn't sure about you. You preferred a long-distance relationship."

She didn't seem to hear him, too deep into her thoughts to notice. "He must have stayed with her long enough to get the painting from her. That's why he didn't divorce her sooner."

Travis berated himself for letting his jealousy show. Harry noticed with a smirking grin.

"She probably hid it from him," Jada said.

"But then he found it," Meena added.

"And that's why we're all standing here right now," Harry concluded.

Travis turned to Jada again. "Not all of us." She had different reasons for being here right now.

Judging by the way her eyes blinked again, she knew damn well he was onto her.

"What do you mean, Travis?" Meena asked.

"I'm Sarah's great-granddaughter," Jada explained.

That loaded announcement plunged the salon into utter silence. Only Travis wasn't surprised. He'd already guessed that's who she was. His hunches were rarely wrong.

"You have the money to afford buying it back?"

Jada didn't appear to appreciate Meena's question. "I married well." She flashed her left hand, wiggling her fingers. "Divorced now."

Meena looked bashful. "Sorry."

Harry curled his arm around her waist and pulled her against him.

"Why pay to have what is rightfully yours, anyway?" Raeleen asked.

Jada turned to her. "My concern for the painting is the

same as Vivian's. The world doesn't need to know that my grandfather's wife was murdered by her Nazi art thief of a lover. And now people are dying to possess it. I'd rather no one discovered my identity. While I don't relish the danger of being killed for it, that painting means a lot to me. It belongs with me."

Travis agreed. She had conviction where the painting was concerned. He doubted she'd ever give up finding it and having it for her own.

What he wondered was how far she'd go to do that.

"I'll handle LeFevre."

"And the painting?"

She was asking if he'd give it to her. "Go back to your hotel and wait for my call. If you'll leave a number…"

"Do you know where it is?" Jada glanced at Raeleen, and Travis wondered why.

"We'll call you when we know something."

Jada's gaze shifted back to him and he thought she'd press him further. Instead, she gave him a business card and acquiesced.

When she left, Raeleen asked Travis, "Does she know Deet gave it to me?"

"Rorey could have told her."

"He must have," Harry joined in.

Raeleen looked at him. "Why not tell us, then?"

"LeFevre is the bigger concern right now," Travis said. "She probably thinks she has a better chance of getting it from us than him."

"I would," Meena said. "Black-market dealer as opposed to counterterror organization. It's an easy choice."

Maybe. Travis always reserved his conclusions until there were no missing pieces, and there was still something missing about Jada.

Chapter 13

"He's smarter than even I predicted."

In their opulent hotel room, Jada paced from the window to the sofa, where LeFevre sat listening to her debrief him on her meeting with Travis Todd.

"It went exactly the way we planned, darling." He stood and took hold of her hands, stopping her pacing. "Don't worry so much."

She couldn't believe how she'd come to care for him over the past few days. He seemed to genuinely care for her, too. They'd formed an alliance, an unexpected one. But a little voice in her head kept warning her not to trust him.

"I want you to have that painting, Lucian."

He lifted her hand and kissed the back of it softly. "And I want to have it for you, my love. Don't you think I know how much it means to you?"

They both had come to Anguilla for the painting, but Jada had conceded her claim to Lucian, assuring him that her greatest wish was for the painting to be removed from the Nazi hands that stole it from her ancestors. She'd tried to convince him that she was no match for him, while at the same time that she was enamored with his power. Flattery had gone a long way.

Now he'd professed he'd have it for her. And she could hear in his voice and see in his eyes that he meant it. Her heart welled with emotion she was afraid to name or unleash. "Lucian."

"You don't have to pretend anymore, Jada. I know the painting is what draws you to me."

That worried her no small amount. "Lucian, I…" Oh, dear God… Was she in trouble? She didn't know what to say. If he caught on to her true intentions…?

"When I seduced you, I was sure you'd back away. When you didn't…" Lust darkened his eyes with the memory.

Jada hadn't planned on having sex with him. Only the painting compelled her. He'd undressed her slowly, made her stand before him while he raved about her beauty and his fortune to have her.

It had taken every ounce of her willpower to stay in the hotel room with him. And once he'd entered her, her whole world had changed.

"Yes, that is a memory I will keep with me always," he said, sharing the intensity with her.

"I didn't expect it."

"Nor I. Your reasons for being with me are purely selfish, Jada, but I admire your determination."

"As it happens, I admire yours, too."

He moved closer, touching her face with his fingers. "Tell me what you'll do once I have the painting."

She searched his eyes and answered neutrally. "I don't know."

"You want the painting for yourself."

Running her hands up his chest, she looped her arms around his shoulders. "Yes. But I am content with you having it."

He read her eyes and she saw him draw the correct conclusion. If not for him, she'd take the painting. Maybe she'd still try.

"I was uncertain what to do with you once we finished this charade."

Jada waited, hoping she wouldn't have to resort to her emergency plan.

"But that night…"

"Yes. That night." And the next morning. Midday. And evening. Then he'd gone on his trip.

He was a good lover and she was addicted to that part of his anatomy—against her will, but addicted just the same.

"You are exactly the kind of woman I've been waiting for, Jada. Nothing will stop you from having what is yours. You are brave. Beautiful…"

"Lucian." He made her so hot talking that way. She pressed her body closer, wishing he'd kiss her.

"I'm going to give you your painting, my darling."

"Kiss me, Lucian."

"And then I think I'm going to have to marry you."

"Kiss me." His statement shocked her and made her crave him inside of her.

He did. And passion exploded. Oh, how she loved the way he ignited her blood.

"You will marry me."

She tipped her head back and he kissed her neck. "Lucian."

"Say you will."

"So soon…"

"I want the painting and so do you." His rasping breaths intertwined with his warm kisses.

"Yes." She met his searching tongue, so swept away with sexual anticipation that she'd tell him anything he wanted to hear.

After unfastening his slacks and letting them fall to the floor, he sat on the sofa. While he pushed his boxers down, she unbuttoned her jeans and removed them along with her underwear. Kicking off her sandals, she climbed onto the sofa and straddled him.

He held his erection for her, and she lowered herself onto it, already wet for him. She ground herself on him, feeling him long and hard inside her.

Grabbing her butt, he moved her faster.

"Jada," he almost hissed.

She leaned forward and kissed him reverently, her sweet, dark criminal. He was so bad, and she loved him.

Gripping the front of her blouse, he ripped it, only to encounter her bra. Unclasping the front hook, he freed her breasts with a satisfied sigh.

She kept grinding on him, close to reaching her prize. When he flicked his tongue on her nipples, she did. Lifting his hips, he began pounding her and she rode him until he joined her in their own creation of paradise.

Putting her hands on his face, she kissed him softly. "You make me the happiest woman alive."

"I'm going to make you even happier once I have the painting."

Kissing him a few more times, she sat up and looked down at him, fretting over how he'd do that. "What are we going to do about Travis Todd?"

"You forget we have something he doesn't."

"What's that, my fearless man?" She ran her hands up and then down his chest. Why she enjoyed doing that so much she had no idea. He wasn't muscular. It was what lay beneath the chest, what lay behind the windows of his brown eyes and past his thin lips.

"Habib."

Chapter 14

Αll that was left to do now was wait for Lucian LeFevre to make his presence known. Travis didn't think it would take long, and Raeleen agreed with him. She wished this was over and dreaded the inevitable confrontation.

All four of them were lounging on the flybridge, soaking up the sun. To anyone passing by, it appeared they were a pair of couples on vacation. Left unseen were the tension between her and Travis and the real purpose of their trip.

Travis lowered the binoculars again. He'd been watching Rorey's yacht. They'd arranged for someone at the marina to check on Rorey, and the local police were now processing the scene. The police investigation would remain behind theirs until they had LeFevre under control and the danger no longer existed for someone to be killed.

He walked past Raeleen, face toward her, eyes hidden behind his sunglasses. When he sat on the bench beside Harry, she felt him continue to stare. She stared back. They were all in swimsuits, and his abdomen was nearly making her forget they were in public.

I'll just have to seduce you into more than that....

What had he meant? Did he want more?

Travis's phone rang. Raeleen sat up straighter on her lounge chair as he reached to the built-in table beside the bench and put the phone to his ear.

"Habib." He stood from the bench, alert and ready.

Putting the phone on the fixed table at the end of the bench, he turned the speaker on.

Raeleen didn't have a good feeling about this. Why was Habib calling him again?

"Mr. Todd. I did not expect to talk to you again so soon."

"Why are you?"

"I have met with LeFevre once again. He came to my market to pick up his purchase. In the interim, he shared some more of his plans with me."

"He seems to share quite a bit." And travel a lot.

"He enjoys talking of this painting called *The Portrait of Sarah*. I do not understand it nor do I wish to. I am contacting you only to tell you that he is in Anguilla as we speak. He has discovered you are there."

"Thanks for the warning, but we expected that."

"I have no doubt of that. The diamonds he purchased from me. He is meeting with a man who will buy them. Tonight. I thought you would like to know."

"Here?" LeFevre was laundering money for his clients in Anguilla? Is that why he traveled to Monrovia? Out of convenience?

Habib told him what time and the location.

"When did he tell you?"

"When he came for the diamonds. He was not pleased to have to go out of his way because of the painting. He mentioned his business with the diamonds in passing, in his annoyance. LeFevre has always felt at ease in discussing things with me. I believe that is because I am not connected to any of his business transactions, or so he has assumed."

And Habib felt obligated to help Travis.

Travis met each of the other's gazes, staying the longest on Raeleen. She shook her head. This smelled of deception. LeFevre was using Habib.

Travis nodded. "You've been a big help, Habib. Thank you."

"There is no need to thank me."

Travis disconnected the call. "Harry, you stay here with Raeleen and Meena. I'll go intercept LeFevre."

Raeleen shot to her feet. "No!"

"It's the only solution," Harry said, essentially agreeing with him.

"Call Odie back and tell her to send more men."

Travis approached her. "There isn't enough time."

"Yes, there is. She could do it. She's the almighty Odie." Glancing self-consciously from him to Meena and Harry, Raeleen wondered if her worry stemmed from more than what was natural for any person facing such danger. And Travis was probably wondering the same.

"We only have an hour. If it's a setup, we can't all be in one place," Harry said.

In other words, someone had to protect the women. And Travis would push to keep her out of his way, out of harm's way.

"Travis doesn't work for TES because he's incompetent," Harry added.

Right then, Raeleen realized the only way Travis would learn is by failing. He'd walk into a trap and no one else could stop him. She could, however, get away from Harry and follow him. She'd take one of Travis's extra guns. If

Travis was too blind to see what he was doing, she'd save him herself.

He slid one of his hands around her waist and pulled her to him. "I do this for a living, many times alone. I'll be fine."

"Travis…" How could she make him understand?

"I'll come back." He moved his head and kissed her.

She didn't think he'd intended to—it was natural, automatic, and once it was done, he kissed her again.

That was the way it was with them. One touch and a fireball went rolling through both of them.

Raeleen watched Travis leave the yacht, feeling like a wife watching her husband go off to war. She would follow him as soon as he started down the dock if Harry wasn't standing guard.

"Inside."

She stepped back and Harry closed and locked the door. Pretending to go along with this cockamamy plan, she turned and walked from one end of the salon to the other, acutely aware of Harry's watchful eye. This was all because of Travis's fear of failing. He should have at least taken Harry with him. Raeleen didn't want to be worried about him, but she was.

Going into the galley, she opened the utensil drawer and reached far back to retrieve Travis's spare pistol she'd taken from his duffel bag right after the call from Habib. He and Harry had been busy talking contingency when she'd sneaked into his cabin. Meena had seen her go into the galley but she hadn't seen her slip the weapon from her jean shorts and put it into the drawer.

Hidden behind a pillar at the entrance of the galley, she tucked the gun once again into her shorts. Harry moved so that he could see her. She shut the drawer and walked back into the salon. He eyed her peculiarly but didn't say anything.

Now all she had to do was escape the yacht.

Footsteps on the aft deck made her go still.

"Is Travis back already?" Meena asked.

Harry picked up his gun from the table. "Too many footsteps. You two go back into the stateroom."

Meena started toward the cabin, reaching for Raeleen.

"I'll stay here." She had to get out of there and find Travis, but she couldn't leave Harry to fend for himself.

She slid out the pistol so Meena could see.

"Meena, go!" Harry roared.

She ran to the cabin.

A shadow passed in front of the sliding glass door. Then another. Raeleen took shelter behind the side of a built-in entertainment center, the hall to her right. Harry went to the door.

Glass shattered as someone threw a chair through the window. Harry ducked, covering his head to protect himself against flying glass. He ran to the side of the window.

Raeleen fired when she saw someone holding a gun. There were two of them. They disappeared from sight.

Harry left the salon after them and Raeleen followed.

Outside, she saw him peer around the corner of the deck that ran the length of the starboard side. He glanced back at her.

"Get inside!" he shouted.

One of the men fired toward the stern, dinging the corner and missing Harry. Peeking down the starboard side, he fired once and then ran toward the bow.

Going after him, Raeleen saw him jump up to the flybridge. There was another way into the yacht from there. Deciding to return to the stern and enter through the salon,

Raeleen poked her head around the corner first and then entered.

Meena's feral screech and the sound of fighting came from the stateroom. Grunts of pain followed kicks and punches.

Scared out of her mind, Raeleen made her way down the hall to the door of the cabin. She'd never done anything like this before. She knew how to use a gun because her father had taught her, but she'd never had to shoot at another person.

Harry kicked one of the men off his feet as the second man pivoted with Meena on his back. The man fighting Harry sprang to his feet and the other slammed Meena against the wall, dislodging her from her catlike hold.

Then he swung his gun to Harry and fired.

Raeleen fired at the same time.

Harry went down. Oh, no! He was shot!

Raeleen fired again, sending the men scattering. The one who'd shot Harry grabbed Meena and put his gun to her head.

"Drop it," he ordered.

Meena's eyes were big and round and her mouth parted as she breathed rapidly. "Harry!"

Raeleen dropped her gun.

The man let Meena go and she scrambled to Harry's side. The man's partner picked up Raeleen's gun and hauled her roughly into the stateroom, pushing her so that she fell onto the bed.

"Any one of you tries to come through this door, you're dead," the man who'd held Meena said. After picking up Harry's and Raeleen's guns, he and his partner left the stateroom.

They were being held captive. And Travis was in more danger than he realized.

Apprehension mushroomed in her, along with an urgency to escape and find him.

"Damn it!" Harry growled.

"Harry!" Meena knelt beside him, weeping and checking his wound.

He was bleeding pretty badly from his lower left side. If he didn't get medical attention soon, he might not make it.

Travis walked toward a palm-roofed shelter used for private parties, sensing something amiss. He'd had that feeling ever since he left the yacht. The shelter was far enough away from the resort to offer privacy. No one was on this stretch of the beach, and there were no parties scheduled tonight. The beach was dark and deserted.

Reaching the shelter, he approached the open doorway with stealthy silence, pistol ready and another in his boot.

Lantern-style lights hanging from the wood-framed ceiling revealed a small bar in the back and four tall, round tables in the front. At one of them, Habib Maalouf sat with a gun on the table.

Travis's mind spun to add everything up. All the while he berated himself for not seeing this coming. Although Habib's presence confused him, he'd always thought his help was out of place. Why had he turned to LeFevre? TES had saved him.

"Mr. Travis Todd," he said, not getting up. His fingers trailed along the gun handle.

"What are you doing here?" He stepped toward him, glancing back at the door. No one else entered.

Habib was alone.

For now.

He stopped at the table, greeted by Habib's shrewd but vengeful satisfaction.

"LeFevre invited me," he explained.

Too calm of an answer for Travis's comfort. LeFevre was one of his customers. Whose side was he on?

LeFevre's. But why?

He began to figure it out himself. "What happened after Farid Abi Salloum and his son were killed?" Travis asked.

The satisfaction left Habib's eyes in a flash. Anger replaced it. "What did your organization expect me to do? I was forced to engage in business with Salloum and his men. And then I was forced to engage in your organization's quest to kill what you Americans call terrorists. Who are the terrorists when you cause the same kind of destruction with your righteous brutality?"

"Habib...I don't understand. What happened? What went wrong?"

Habib slammed his palm down onto the dirty table. "Your organization has cost me more than I can bear. When Lucian LeFevre told me of the kidnapping of a renowned American colonel's daughter and showed me a photograph of the man who was sent to rescue her, I could not believe my fortune." He stood and walked around the table to stand before Travis. "At last I am able to avenge my wife."

"Your wife?"

"You killed her."

His wife had been killed? "I didn't kill your wife."

"Your organization killed her. *Colonel Roth* and his crusade against terrorism killed her. What you do not see is the fallout of your tyranny. Well, I intend to make you see it now."

Travis felt sympathy for his loss but none for his lack of objectivity. "Why haven't you come to us before this? We could have helped you."

"You could bring my wife back?" He leaned closer. "She is dead because of you."

"Habib, I was shot on that mission. I had nothing to do with it."

"You led Salloum's men to me. When your organization killed him, there was great rage against me."

"The man who killed Salloum didn't work for us. He was a mercenary."

"*You* led Salloum's men to me. And in retaliation for helping you, his men executed my wife. My only love in this life. The mother of my children. Do you know what it is like to have something so precious taken from you? To have what Allah has given you ripped away from your grasp?"

There would be no reasoning with him when he was so irrational. "I didn't kill your wife."

"Unfortunately, you are to become a message to Colonel Roth. An example. A lesson for how he operates in the future."

Travis cocked his pistol and put it against the middle of Habib's forehead.

Habib didn't flinch.

"Are you finished, Mr. Maalouf?" a French accented voice said.

Right now, Travis felt a lot like he had when he and Haley were being followed in Monrovia. He could also hear Raeleen say, *I told you so.* He feared failing with her in the line of fire, but she wasn't safe without him. Now she wasn't here and he had no way of protecting her.

"Yes," Habib finally answered.

"Good. Now let us be on with our business."

Travis lowered his gun and turned. Only Lucian LeFevre stood there. He didn't have to be told why neither Habib nor LeFevre needed a weapon.

They had Raeleen. Harry and Meena, too.

"You have twenty-four hours to bring me the painting," LeFevre said.

* * *

Meena tried to stop Harry from getting to his feet, but he pushed her aside with surprising strength, retrieving a knife from his boot.

At the other side of the bed, he lifted a small suitcase and opened it with one arm, holding his side with the other. He handed Raeleen a pistol and tucked another in his pants. LeFevre's henchmen hadn't thought to look in his luggage.

"Cover me," he said to her.

"I will."

When he put his back to the wall on one side, she stood to the other, aiming for the hall. He looked at her and she nodded. He pushed the door open so it drifted halfway. With a quick check, he saw one of the men at the end of the hall. He threw the knife and it stuck in the man's chest.

The second man stormed down the hall with a gun raised.

Raeleen aimed and then shut her eyes and fired. When she opened them, the man lay on the ground. Harry moved clumsily out into the hall. At the end, he leaned against the wall, having difficulty breathing.

"You should stay here." Raeleen turned to Meena. "Call for help."

Meena nodded.

"No!" Harry took hold of her arm to stop her, but his exertion cost him.

"Don't forget who my father is," she told him, easily escaping his grasp and leaping over the two bodies to get to the glass doors.

She might have deviated into a popular dining show, but she hadn't forgotten everything her father had taught her. What she had forgotten, she realized just then, was that he had spent a lot of time with her doing so. Those were good memories, peppered in with his long absences. Well into her early twenties, up until she'd graduated from college and began her television career. His absences had grown so tiresome. She'd grown tired of missing him, so she'd stopped fighting to see him. That's when the resentment had settled in.

All the way to the beach where Habib had told Travis to go, she thought of that.

Seeing two cars parked down the street from a beach resort, one of them with a woman inside, Raeleen drove her rented car past and saw Jada looking through the palm trees. She parked in front of the resort and hurried through the open lobby to the back. Passing the pool, she made her way to the beach.

When she saw the outbuilding Habib had described, she slowed, her tennis shoes sinking into the soft sand. There was no one here. She was too late.

She stopped, rising panic descending on her.

Why had Jada been waiting in the car? Just as she began to turn, she heard someone come up behind her. Jada. The woman swung a palm branch at her.

Raeleen blocked it and leaned almost horizontal to plant a kick against Jada's midsection. The woman went airborne for a second before landing on the sand with a grunt.

Drawing her gun, Raeleen pointed it down at Jada. "Where is Travis?"

Jada held her midsection and glared up at her. Then her face turned smug as another gun came against Raeleen's temple.

Climbing to her feet, Jada took the gun from her as Lucian LeFevre moved to stand beside her.

"It appears that I have underestimated the daughter of Colonel Roth." Then he glanced at Jada. "Are you all right?"

Her eyes warmed and she replied huskily, "Yes."

Seeing the exchange, Raeleen realized that Jada was helping him take the painting.

Where once she'd sympathized with the woman and would have helped her retrieve something stolen from her ancestors, now she vowed to do the opposite.

Leaving the outbuilding, Travis emerged from the trees after Habib, who headed for a car parked along the street just down from the resort. He didn't see where Lucian had gone. No one was in the car parked in front of Habib's, but Travis found it odd that they were both parked there and not in the resort parking lot. Was Lucian still here? After he took care of Habib, he'd find him next. The two of them must have assumed Travis had rushed off to get the painting to save Raeleen and his friends. They assumed wrong.

When Habib was about to open the car door, Travis made his move, using his hand to chop him on the back of his neck. Habib's head hit the car. Catching his slumping frame, Travis made sure no one noticed and dragged him into the trees. Lifting him, he carried Habib to the back of the outbuilding and leaned his limp body against the wall.

Travis would let Habib go back to Monrovia. He wasn't a threat. Grief had made him blame TES for his loss. But LeFevre wasn't going to be that lucky. He was an unscrupulous black-market thug and a killer who needed to be stopped. Not keeping a gun on Travis had been his first mistake. Giving him twenty-four hours had been his second. That was plenty of time to track him down and get back to Raeleen in time.

Hearing voices coming from the beach, Travis moved to the edge of the outbuilding. Spotting Raeleen standing in the shadows of meager light coming from the resort, LeFevre with a gun pointed at her and Jada beside him, he couldn't believe his eyes. What was she doing here? How had she escaped?

Jada must have seen her coming to the shelter, and she

and LeFevre had intercepted her. Not quite the way he'd planned this to go, but it would work.

Staying hidden in the trees, Travis followed the darkest shadows until he was positioned behind Jada and LeFevre. Then, just as he was about to make his move, Raeleen decided to start fighting. She chopped with her arm, dislodging the gun from Jada's hand and following up with a kick that sent her onto her backside. Simultaneous with the kick, she knocked LeFevre's wrist. She should have gone for him first. LeFevre used his foot to push her onto her backside.

"I don't need you anymore," Travis heard him say.

Already aiming for his head, Travis fired and LeFevre went down.

Jada screamed and crawled over to him while Raeleen stared in shock at Travis as he sprinted through the sand toward her.

Helping Raeleen to her feet, he waited for Jada to figure out that LeFevre was dead. Distraught, she looked up at him.

"You killed him."

"How many people has he killed?" Travis asked her.

She began crying harder, bowing her head. Travis didn't think she'd intended to get involved with a man like that.

"I'll go to the resort to get the police." Raeleen started to walk away when Travis stopped her.

She looked at him.

"Let's just go."

"But…" She looked down at Jada, whose crying subsided some as she lifted her head.

"She's done nothing more than get involved with the wrong man to try and get her ancestor's painting back."

"She set us up."

"She hasn't hurt anyone." He turned to Jada. "I'm giving the painting back to Deet. If you can talk him into selling it to you after all you've done, it's yours. Otherwise, you're getting what you deserve."

"It's my painting!" She scrambled to her feet. "Lucian was going to give it to me."

Putting his arm around Raeleen, Travis guided her up the beach toward the resort.

"You can't just leave!" Jada shouted.

"Watch us," Travis called over his shoulder.

Chapter 15

Just like the last time they were here, Raeleen had to wait for her flight home. Unlike the last time, she knew she was going home. Just like last time, she sat at the hotel bar. Unlike last time, there was no one watching, and Travis wasn't beside her.

Meena and a recovering Harry were on their yacht headed back to Florida. Raeleen had decided to fly home, and Travis had done the same. She had a feeling he'd done that to be with her, but now he was avoiding her. He'd gotten them two rooms and she hadn't seen him since check-in.

"I never noticed this restaurant had a patio."

Pure glee threatened to make her smile like a fool as she spun on her barstool to see Travis.

He twisted charmingly to indicate the double doors leading to a leafy oasis that had a view of the ocean and a setting sun.

"Me neither."

He extended his hand. "Last night on the island."

She gave him her hand, wondering what he intended. "Trying to get in my pants, soldier?"

Tugging her to her feet, he grinned. The way she'd said "soldier" had come out of nowhere. She felt nothing but warmth saying the word, and instead of making her tense, she let herself enjoy it as Travis led her to the patio. There, a waiter stood with a bottle of wine.

She sat and the waiter put a napkin on her lap.

"You are."

He gestured for the waiter to pour the wine.

"I already ate dinner."

"I only ordered wine."

She angled her head, trying to figure him out. Was he going for her or playing her because he didn't trust her anti-men-who-remind-her-of-her-father attitude? She still wasn't completely sure she wouldn't keep following that course, and she needed to be.

When the waiter left, Travis lifted his glass. Raeleen clinked hers with it and sipped with him. He set his down.

"You were right."

He was just full of mystery tonight. "About what?"

"I am afraid of failure. No one should have to die the way my sister did. No woman should have to die that way. I was afraid because I didn't want anyone else to lose their life to violence. But I'm not afraid anymore. You taught me that."

Had she? "Why are you telling me this?"

"I want tonight to be about us. In the morning, if you still feel the same, you can go back to your life and I'll have no hard feelings."

He was going for her. A thrill tingled through her. "Travis…"

"I know you're still unsure about a few things. I haven't

done a very good job of showing you how wrong you are about me."

"It's not you, it's—"

"You're afraid, too, Raeleen. You're afraid I won't be there for you. You're afraid any man won't be there for you."

"Travis—"

He held up his hand. "We have tonight. All I ask is that we spend it together. See how we really feel about each other. Then tomorrow you can decide if I'm as right about you as you were about me."

No pressure there. They were on Anguilla. Why not enjoy the last night here? She hadn't been able to enjoy the island at all since her kidnapping.

"All right."

He grinned. "You're in so much trouble."

She laughed with slight hesitation. When he leaned toward her to kiss her, she tensed. But only for a fraction of a second. One touch of his mouth and she fell into his invitation.

He slid her chair closer to his and they turned their heads to watch the sun slip beyond the horizon, the shimmering sea going dark.

She finished her wine with a warm glow lingering.

Turning his head toward her, he kissed her again. "Let's go somewhere more private."

Why not? She could enjoy him without any chaos in the way. Just a couple on vacation in Anguilla.

"Okay."

Telling the waiter to put the bill on his room, he led her by the hand out of the restaurant. In the elevator, he leaned against the opposite wall just looking at her. Her heart did acrobatics on her rib cage. Both of them were thinking about what they were about to do and questioning it. But not much. The real decisions wouldn't have to be made until after they returned to the States. She felt this between them. He distrusted her and she didn't trust herself. Two bad combinations. But not bad enough to stop either one of them.

Each step beat doubt into insignificance. She followed him into his room.

He put the key card down and she wandered to the window, a view of lights and a dark ocean glimmering beneath moonlight. She wasn't ordinarily a romantic person, but being with Travis changed that. She was glad the moon was shining tonight.

"Beats tree branches flying through the air."

She laughed softly at his reference to the storm they'd survived.

Standing behind her, he put his hands on her shoulders and ran them down her arms. Next, he put his face beside hers. She felt his warm breath just before he kissed her. So soft. She closed her eyes and arched her neck so that he could kiss her mouth. His hands roamed her body. Gentle. Slow.

She turned in his arms and kissed him again, in keeping with his slow and gentle touches. This could be the last time they were together.

"You have the softest hair."

Only then did she realize he had his fingers in it.

"I never thought I'd fall for a headstrong celebrity with blond hair."

"I never thought I'd fall for a soldier who always tells me what to do."

He laughed deeply.

As the meaning of what they'd both just said settled beyond the haze of passion, they met each other's eyes.

"Get undressed," he commanded.

And now she laughed. But she stepped back and did what he said, before his lustful eyes.

"At least you do what you're told in the bedroom."

Naked, she moved to him and planted her hands on his chest, giving him a push. "On the bed, soldier."

He lay on his back and she climbed onto him, straddling him. Letting her play for a while, he soon took control and rolled her onto her back, kissing her to soften the domination.

It crazed her with desire. Or something more. Something deeper that she didn't want to explore right then. She only immersed herself in the sensation of his mouth on hers, so full of meaning.

She moved her legs at the same time he began to seek her. They were so in sync. Raeleen took in the sight of him, his face, his dark blond hair, his mouth continually kissing hers.

When he slid into her, she felt more than the physical contact. She felt a celebration of whatever this was between them. She wouldn't, not now, maybe not ever, call it love. But it was worth celebrating.

She moved with him, slow and gripping, until he entwined his fingers with hers and dragged them up on the mattress. Then his smooth movements grew more intense. Harder. But slow. Ever so slow.

Raeleen suddenly lost her breath and all contact with reality. She called his name as she peaked and he gruffly responded with hers and shortly thereafter collapsed in completion on top of her, his hands still gripping hers.

Panic welled.

Raeleen struggled to quell it and managed to keep from running out of the room naked.

Travis rolled to lay beside her. He said nothing, and she sensed he struggled with the same problem.

The meaning this held had risen to heights neither could contend with at the moment. Too many uncertainties remained.

Waiting until he slept, not caring if he woke, Raeleen dressed and left. Special-ops man that he was, he must have been well aware of her escape. But the fact that he hadn't stopped her said enough.

Full of melancholy that was beginning to make her mad, Raeleen closed the last trash bag after cleaning up her apartment. She'd had to talk to the police when she returned, and she told them the whole story, leaving out any mention of Travis or her father and the secret hero organization called TES. She'd also lied and said *The Portrait of Sarah* was still missing. Travis had told her he'd give it to Deet, where Raeleen thought it belonged. The decision to sell to Jada was his to make.

The buzz of her intercom spared her from lamenting more over Travis and that last night they'd had together. She was still so torn over it.

"Yes?" she said into the intercom.

"Your father is here to see you."

Moments later, she opened her apartment door. "I can't remember.... Have you ever been here?"

Dressed in his decorated uniform, her father entered, a powerful presence. "None of that, Raeleen. It's long past the time we had this out."

She was too forlorn over Travis to fight him.

"Travis told me you left him behind in Anguilla."

"I didn't need his *protection* anymore." Even though her heart cried out for it now.

"He also told me why."

She stopped fiddling with a throw pillow on her couch to check his face for more detail.

"He reminds you of me?"

That explained his anger. She finished arranging her pillows the way she liked them.

Her father approached her, reaching to take her arm and prevent her from fiddling with anything else. She was forced to straighten and meet his eyes.

"I can tell you're unhappy."

She averted her eyes.

"Lucky for me, it isn't me you're unhappy with."

She returned her eyes to him, waiting for the politic-skirting colonel in him to push her.

"You can blame Odie's insight on everyone drawing the conclusion that you and Travis are meant for each other."

"Dad—"

He let go of her arm to hold up his hand. "I didn't come here to talk to you about that."

She knew why he'd come. She just wasn't sure she was ready to forgive him yet.

"I know you resent me for not spending more time with you when you were young," he said.

In that instant, she let go of the defenses she'd carried for so long. When she was young, having her father there every day wouldn't have been enough. She'd missed him when he was away, and that had compiled into anger against him.

"I've been selfish." She'd essentially realized it when she remembered all the long hours he'd spent training her in self-defense. "You have been there for me."

"I wanted to be there more. You grew up thinking I'd rather be working, and that wasn't true. I thought of you every day. Both you and your mother. The time I did have for you, I cherished. Those are my best memories. They're what made having to work long hours worthwhile."

She moved toward him, his declaration ringing true and warming her further. "They're my memories, too. I just forgot them over the years. But not anymore. I remember now."

"I promise I'll be there for you more."

She shook her head. "You don't have to."

"Yes, I do. Hearing you were missing nearly killed me. I kept thinking about how long it had been since I'd last seen you. And then when Travis brought you to Dad's..." Her stoic father lowered his head with the onslaught of tears. "I couldn't bear it if I lost you, Raeleen."

She rested her head on his chest as they hugged. "I'm sorry for being angry with you. I love you so much."

"I love you, too. More than anything. I'd do anything for you."

She leaned back to see his face. "I'd do anything for you."

He smiled softly and then moved back from their embrace, the colonel back in place again.

"Now that we have that cleared up, I wasn't completely honest before when I said Travis wasn't the reason I came here."

Hope and tension reared up in her.

"I told him about your show in Istanbul."

As soon as she'd arrived in New York she'd arranged to replace the canceled show with a new one...at the restaurant in Istanbul that Travis had mentioned.

"Dad!"

He chuckled. "Don't be surprised if he shows up. All I ask is that when he does, you remember that he isn't completely like me."

She knew that now. Raeleen had learned a valuable lesson in the days she'd spent with Travis. It wasn't about the amount of time someone spent with her, it was about the love she felt when they were together. Love that was made with that person.

Tears she rarely shed slid down her cheeks. "I was wrong about Travis. He's a good man. Just like you."

Her father headed for the door with a satisfied look in his eyes. There, he turned. "Your mother has been complaining she hasn't seen you."

"I'll come to D.C. on my way out of the country." She was going to be doing more of that. If her father was going to work at spending more time with her, she could meet him in the middle.

And she hoped Travis would meet her in Istanbul.

Chapter 16

Berk's Burger Café was near Istinye Park in Istanbul, on a side street filled with small restaurants and boutiques. The older architecture contrasted with Istinye's sleek sophistication, but Raeleen discovered she preferred the more ornate stone trim and rows of lights hanging over the entrances of many of the buildings. She'd just finished her show inside the weathered interior of Berk's and now stood with Berk, his wife and son, talking. Her cameraman had already gone to explore more of Istanbul. Landon was still recovering, so she'd been sent someone new.

The café had been everything Travis had claimed, and Berk and his family had been overjoyed with her offer to feature the restaurant on her show. She was sure it would give them just the boost they needed and her ratings would go up even more after it aired.

Glancing around the long and narrow café, she still didn't

see Travis. As with all the other times she'd looked for him, despondency plummeted in her core. He wasn't coming.

"You be sure and thank Mr. Todd for us," Berk said.

"I will if I see him," she answered forlornly. After the way she'd left him in Anguilla, she really couldn't blame him for not showing up.

"Ah, but you will." A big smile beamed on his dark-skinned face. "He is here."

Excitement and pure glee burst, perking her up. "H-here? Are you sure?"

"Yes. Yes. He came to see me just yesterday." He leaned in conspiratorially. "He asked me not to tell you until after the show."

What a sneak! "Where is he?"

Berk pointed to the exit. "Go and see."

Really? He was here? Outside? Waving goodbye, she stepped out onto the sidewalk and saw him. He sat, calm as could be, on a patio chair. Waiting. Her heart rejoiced.

"I'm feeling a little déjà vu." She walked over to his table and stopped, unable to subdue her smile. "The first time I saw you I was on travel for a show, too."

Wearing sunglasses, jeans and a short-sleeved green shirt, he was so sexy she couldn't subdue her infatuation. He stood and her breath caught. Seeing him reaffirmed how silly it had been to compare men she dated to her father. Travis compared to no man.

"Your father said he talked to you."

Not responding to her lightness, she realized he was uncertain about her, about how she viewed him.

"Yes. All that happened in Anguilla made me open my eyes. About you. About my perception of my father…all of it. You were right. I put conditions on the men I dated to avoid commitment. I was too afraid of feeling the way I felt growing up with a father who couldn't spend as much time as he wanted with me. That's the key. He wanted to spend more time with me, but the time he could spend with me was precious. I forgot about that. But I remember now."

"Good. You patched things up with him."

He still wasn't assured of her opinion of him.

"You think I still would expect you to quit your job with TES to be with me."

"Your father not being around a lot affected you significantly."

"Yes, but I love him and he loves me."

At last, he removed his sunglasses and she could see his blue-gold eyes. "You might not want to raise your own kids the same way."

"I'd teach them about love."

He stepped closer and his arm went around her waist. "I told you once that I'd be there for the woman I marry and the children we had together."

She flattened her hands on his big chest. "I remember."

"Do you trust me?"

"Yes." Did she ever! More than that, she loved him.

"Good, because I think I finally found a woman who'll stick around for me."

"You think?"

"Yeah, and it appears that my patience has paid off."

"But you aren't one-hundred percent sure?"

"Almost…but not quite."

She looped her arms all the way around his neck. "What will it take, soldier? I'll do anything."

His brow rose. "Anything?"

"For you, yeah."

"Marry me, then."

That was easy. "Just say when."

"How about right now?"

She leaned back a little. "Now?"

He indicated the street. A car waited there. A limo. And the driver was standing outside the back door, waiting.

Mouth dropping open, she stepped back from Travis and gaped at him.

"You didn't think I was going to let you get away again, did you?"

Raeleen started laughing. She'd left him in Anguilla and he'd used that as an excuse to speed up their marriage.

"Is the minister in the back of the limo?"

"No. He's waiting for us in an old church. And so are your parents." He took her hand and started walking to the limo.

Her parents were here? He'd planned everything and she couldn't be happier or more thrilled.

At the limo, she stopped and faced him. "What would you have done if I'd said no?"

He leaned closer, lips hovering over hers. "Taken you to my hotel room and kept you there until you said yes."

"What makes you so sure I would have?"

"This." He pressed his warm lips to hers.

"Yes," she murmured before he kissed her again.

* * * * *

The Secret Soldier

Special thanks goes to Dave Baker for letting me have my way in the opening scenes of this story.
Dave, those hours in front of your whiteboard were sure entertaining! You have an amazing brain and your knowledge of the military was invaluable to me.
Any mistakes are my own.

To everyone who supported me on my long journey to publication, your positive influence kept me going at my lowest moments. Everyone at DigitalGlobe—
there are too many to name you all. You know who you are. Gary Geissinger, don't worry, you won't end up in my novel. Neal Anderson and Walter Scott, any other bosses would have fired me for taking so much time off to write!
Natalie Ottobrino and Margie Lawson, your strength resonates with me. To my entire family, who put up with my many absences so I could write.
Dan, even though we aren't together anymore, you were an integral part of my success and will always be my friend.
Jackie, you are my favorite twin—
despite your poor taste in fiction. To Sandra Kerns and Annette Elton, for helping me make sure my characters didn't do anything too stupid. And to every other critique partner I have learned from along the way.

But the highest acknowledgment goes to my mother, Joan Morey, whose passing inspired me to follow my heart.

Chapter 1

"One more week in this hellhole."

Kneeling on the ground, Sabine O'Clery finished winding a water-level indicator reel from inside a borehole before looking up at her unhappy field partner. Samuel Barry scowled across the grayish-brown landscape of Afghanistan's Panjshir Valley. Sabine followed his gaze, a dry, hot breeze rustling the loose strands of hair that had escaped her ponytail. High, desolate mountains surrounded them under a clear blue sky, and yellow patches of grass covered the ground where they worked. She found immense satisfaction putting her hydrogeology degree to good use in places like this, but she couldn't argue with Samuel's sentiment.

"It's pretty here," she quipped.

Samuel grunted in disgust. "Yeah, if you like dirt and no amenities."

"Everyone needs clean drinking water," she said. She'd grown attached to some of the villagers, too.

Samuel grumbled as he put a portable reader on the ground next to the borehole. He was a big man who always talked about his wife.

"I can't wait to taste Lisandra's homemade orange juice," he said, as if on cue.

Sabine smiled. Would she ever find a man who made her feel like talking sweet nonsense about him? Ha! She wasn't going to hold her breath.

"She makes a killer crème brûlée, too."

"And her cheese soufflés?" she teased.

Samuel laughed. "My mouth is watering already." He looked at her. "Sorry. I just miss her."

"Really? I couldn't tell."

"Just wait 'til you get married. Then you'll know what it's like."

Marriage seemed so foreign to her. "Not everyone falls madly in love and lives happily ever after."

"Maybe not out here." He gestured to the dry landscape. The pages of the field book he held flapped with the movement, his thumb keeping the ones against the cover flat.

Maybe not ever. She didn't want to end up like her mother, loving a man who came around only when it suited him, always leaving for his next thrill. Nothing irritated her more than being treated like a thrill.

"You have to stop comparing every man to your dad," Samuel said.

She set the indicator reel aside and reached for the borehole reader, wishing she'd never mentioned her father to him. "I don't." Not *every* man.

He sent her an unconvinced frown from above the field book but didn't argue.

"I haven't seen him since he showed up at my college graduation and ruined what should have been my best accomplishment. Why would I compare anyone to him?"

Samuel raised a brow, telling her without words that the emotional response had just answered her own question.

Okay, so he was right. Her father epitomized the kind of man she never wanted to marry. She remembered the way she had felt when he'd shown up at her graduation. Unchecked hope that he'd come for the right reason flashed before a too-familiar self-doubt. Did he know about that B she got her freshman year? Never mind the honors. Maybe hydrogeology wasn't scientifically challenging enough. If she'd become the first female president of the United States, her father probably still wouldn't have been impressed.

So why waste any energy thinking of him at all? It wasn't supposed to bother her anymore. She'd overcome her insecurities and childish hopes the moment she left him standing in that college auditorium.

Connecting the reader to the piezometer inside the borehole harder than necessary, Sabine waited for the measurement to appear on the display. Samuel wrote the number down in his field book, eyeing her dubiously.

She'd never seen what real happiness looked like until she met her field partner. Maybe that's what had her thinking about her father so much lately. Happiness was not a word she'd learned from his example.

She straightened from the borehole. They were finished for the day.

"Let's go see if our supply helicopter brought us some cold beer." Samuel closed his field book.

"If Aden came with it, there'll be beer." As CEO of Envirotech and the one who had contracted them to do the groundwater analysis, Aden Archer always made room in the supply helicopter for good beer.

"He sure does come here a lot. Have you noticed that?"

"He doesn't come here that much."

"He doesn't need to be here at all."

She didn't think it was that unusual. "I saw him meet with one of the locals once. Maybe it's business related."

Samuel's brow creased as he looked at her. "Who'd he meet?"

She shrugged. "I didn't recognize him. All I saw was the back of his head."

It took him a moment to respond. "Don't you think that's a little weird? Why would he need to meet with any of the locals?"

"Who knows." Was Samuel as concerned as he seemed? Why? "He isn't hurting anyone."

Samuel looked at her a moment longer before he smiled, convincing her she'd misread him. "Especially if he brings beer. Come on, let's go." He started to walk toward the Jeep.

Sabine followed. She didn't feel like drinking beer. What she'd really like was a long, hot bath. With bubbles. And a good fantasy of a man who cherished her more than anything else in his life.

She breathed a laugh. Samuel's daydreaming was starting to rub off on her, apparently.

The sound of a vehicle made her stop and turn with a rush of alertness. No one ever came to see them out here. A pickup truck with the cab cut off bounced along the terrain. Several dark-skinned men were inside. Her heart slammed into a wild beat. They all held automatic weapons.

Samuel swore and dropped his field book before taking her hand to pull her ahead of him. She tripped as she started to run, her hand slipping free of his. Get to the Jeep. That was her only thought as she pumped her legs as hard as she could. But she could already see that the Jeep was too far away.

They weren't going to make it.

Oh, God, please no.

She heard Samuel's heavy footfalls behind her. Hard breathing. More swearing.

"Run faster!" he yelled.

She didn't have to be told. If they were caught…

She couldn't think it.

Gunfire exploded. Sabine screamed and scrambled to dodge the spitting dirt where bullets struck the ground. The truck skidded to a halt between them and the Jeep. More bullets sprayed at their feet, forcing them to stop running.

Several men jumped off the open truck, shouting in Farsi, "Don't move! Don't move!"

Samuel grabbed Sabine's arm and pulled her behind him. She wanted to keep running. Instinct urged her to get away. But they'd shoot her if she tried. Shaking, she peered around Samuel's big arm and watched in horror as rebels surrounded them.

After a stuffy flight from Washington, D.C., Cullen McQueen left Miami's sweltering heat and entered Executive Indemnity Corporation. A security guard behind a reception desk looked up and smiled.

"I'm here to see Noah Page," Cullen said. "He's expecting me."

"Your name?"

"Henrietta," Cullen answered.

The man nodded his understanding and stood. He led Cullen to a locked door and let him through. Cullen entered a sprawling office area surrounded by closed doors. He spotted a woman standing near one of them.

She smiled. "You can go right in, Mr.…."

"Thanks." He smiled back at her and went into the conference room. Only one person knew his name here, and he was going to keep it that way.

Noah Page stood with his arms behind his back, staring

out a panel of tinted windows on the far side of the room. He turned as Cullen shut the door. His face was lined and pale. Dark circles matched the grave worry in his blue eyes and his gray hair looked as if he'd run his fingers through it several times.

Cullen walked the length of the long conference room table and stopped before Noah, shaking his hand.

"Thank you for coming on such short notice," Noah said.

"You said it was urgent. Something about your daughter?"

Noah swallowed, a scared reflex. The notion of a man like Noah Page being scared piqued Cullen's curiosity. And a heap of foreboding.

"She's been kidnapped."

Cullen went still. "Do you know where she is?"

"Yes... Afghanistan. The Panjshir Valley."

That was in the mountains. The Hindu Kush. There weren't many worse places Noah's daughter could have been captured. "What's she doing there?"

"She's a contractor for Envirotech. She and another contractor were assessing groundwater conditions near one of the villages in the valley when they were abducted. I need you to get her out of there, Cullen. You're the only one I know who can do it."

Cullen laughed without humor. "You must have me confused with God."

"No." Noah sounded certain. "You know the terrain. You've done this kind of mission before. You do it all the time."

Not suicide missions, Cullen thought. He curbed his instinct to flat-out refuse Noah. "I know you're worried about your daughter, but you have to realize how difficult it will be to get her out of there. Not only is Afghanistan unstable, it's landlocked. You'd have to cross Indian and Pakistani ground defenses to get there." That didn't even begin to address U.S. forces inside the border.

"I've already met with the Minister of the Interior in Pakistan. He's agreed to clear you a flight plan into Afghanistan. There are regularly scheduled flights we can use as cover."

Cullen just stared at him.

"I've also procured two armed Mi-8 transport helicopters capable of flying high altitudes, one for backup and to carry extra fuel," Noah continued. "You'll have a DeHavilland Twin Otter equipped with a special jamming pod. It's been modified to fly long distances, too. I spared no expense on the equipment."

Rising tension tightened Cullen's jaw. He could not agree to this. But it was Noah asking.

"She's all I have left," Noah said in the silence, a pleading sound that didn't match the man. "I wouldn't ask if I had any other option." He leaned over the conference room table and pushed a newspaper toward Cullen.

Slowly, Cullen lowered his gaze. The page covering the kidnapping of two American contractors was exposed. Cullen had read about the kidnapping and seen it all over the news, but he'd never connected the name Sabine O'Clery with Noah Page. The media had stirred huge public interest in the female contractor who'd been taken by terrorists along with her partner, Samuel Barry.

He looked at the photo of Sabine. She smiled wide and had bright, green eyes dancing with life, red hair long and thick. She was a beautiful woman. He'd thought so the first time he'd seen the photo. He'd also thought with regret that she would probably be killed before anyone could do anything.

Cullen raised only his eyes to look at Noah. Why did it have to be Afghanistan?

"You're my only hope of seeing my daughter alive again," Noah said quietly, urgently. "I've made mistakes in my life, but this one will kill me if she dies over there. Before I have a chance to make things right with her."

Cullen wanted to groan out loud. How could he say no? To Noah. Any other man, he'd already have been walking out the door. But Noah...

He couldn't say no. He had to do it. He owed Noah too much.

"It's going to take time to plan," he heard himself say.

Noah closed his eyes, a sign that he recognized Cullen's indirect agreement. "How much time?"

"A week. Maybe less. I have to be careful." And wasn't that just the understatement of the year.

Noah nodded. "I know you'll do the best you can."

Even his best might not keep him alive, but he held that thought to himself. "What kind of intelligence do you have?" Cullen looked down at the table and saw a map and several satellite images.

"Before we talk strategy, there's something you need to understand about my daughter."

Cullen looked back at Noah and waited. What could possibly matter when her life was on the line?

"She despises me."

Cullen couldn't stop his brow from rising.

"She has for years," Noah continued. "Ever since she was old enough to think on her own."

"I'm sure she'll change her mind once she sets foot on American soil again, compliments of you."

Noah shook his head. "You don't understand. You can't tell her I sent you."

"What do you want me to—"

"If you tell her I sent you, she'll find her own way home

as soon as you get her out of Afghanistan. I know her. She won't stay with you."

"What am I supposed to say to her? I can't tell her who I am, either." What he did for his government privately had to stay private. No official could admit to asking him to do the things he did in the name of the United States. He couldn't risk telling Noah's daughter anything, especially knowing she was estranged from her father. And then there was the media hype to consider.

"Tell her whatever you want," Noah said. "Hell, lie to her if you have to. Just get her to me. I'll explain everything to her then."

What was that? Had she imagined the sound? Sabine felt every heartbeat in her chest as she lifted her head from where her aching body lay curled on a hard cement floor. She tried to see across the small cell that had been her prison for more than two weeks. Blackness stared back at her. None of this was real, was it? So much horror couldn't be real.

The rapid staccato of a man shouting something in Farsi convinced her well enough that she wasn't dreaming. She pushed herself to a sitting position, her body trembling from lack of water and food and, more than anything, from fear, as she scooted to the wall behind her, away from the door. Strands of her long, dirty red hair hung in front of her face, shivering with the tremors that rippled through her.

The door creaked open and one of her captors stepped in, holding a paraffin lamp. Beady eyes leered at her above an unkempt, hairy face. The others called him Asad. He wasn't their leader, but he frightened her nearly as much.

Glancing behind him, he closed the door. Sabine pressed her back harder against the cement wall as he approached, wishing it would miraculously give way and provide an escape.

Asad crouched close to her and put the lamp down beside him. He reached to touch her hair. Many of the other men seemed taken with the color, too.

Had Asad managed to slip away tonight? His presence this late and the look in his dark eyes said as much. Where was Isma'il? Would he stop him as he had all the other times?

She pulled away from Asad's hand and scrambled along the wall until the corner stopped her.

Anger brought Asad's brow crowding together. "Move when you are told," he said in Farsi.

If she lived, Sabine promised herself she'd never speak the language again and forget she'd ever studied it in college.

Standing, Asad stepped toward her and crouched in front of her again. She turned her face toward the wall and squeezed her eyes shut as he took strands of her hair between his fingers. "I will know this fire," he murmured, making her stomach churn.

"I'd rather die," she whispered in perfect Farsi, a soft hiss of defiance that belied her weakened state.

He let go of her hair but pulled back his hand for momentum and swung down to strike her face. Sabine grunted with the force of the blow, her head hitting the wall and one hand slapping the floor to stop her fall. She spit blood.

Voices outside the door of her cell made Asad pivot in his crouched position. He watched the door. When it began to open, he straightened.

"Isma'il is asking for you," a man said through the shadows.

Asad muttered an expletive and turned to look down at Sabine. Whatever he'd come to do to her tonight had once again been thwarted. She watched his anger flare with the snarl of his mouth. "The day will come when Isma'il will not interfere," he said. "And then you will die just as your friend did." With that, he picked up the lamp and turned to leave.

A shaky breath of relief whooshed out of her. Why was Isma'il protecting her? Terrorists would have no regard for a female captive. But who were they, if not terrorists? Were they holding her for ransom? Had they contacted Aden? Was he trying to save his contractors? Perhaps he'd lost some ground and that was why Samuel had been killed. She had no way of knowing. Her captors never spoke of their purpose in front of her and Samuel.

Samuel. She couldn't grasp that he was dead. They'd tortured and killed him. And they'd do the same to her. It was only a question of when.

Her soft, defeated sobs resonated against the cement walls that trapped her in this hellish place. She didn't want to die like this. Curling her body on the cement again, she stared through the darkness, trying to think of something to console her spirit. Fuel her strength.

Thoughts of her mother were too painful. She couldn't reconcile the difference between this place and the quiet innocence of Roaring Creek, Colorado, where her mother had raised her. Mae O'Clery was as much a best friend as she was a mother. When Mae told her this contracting job wasn't her calling, that she was doing it only to catch her father's attention, she should have listened. That arrowing insight had annoyed her at the time. But now, after being kidnapped and facing a horrific death, she could see the truth.

Unrelenting. That's how she had been when she'd gone after her college degree, and that's how she was in pursuing her career. Nothing had stopped her from proving to the world that she was…what? Tough? Smart? That she was worthy of envy and respect? She didn't like to admit that her relationship with her father had driven her to this moment, but it had. Amazing how his occasional visits to her mother had bled over into every aspect of her life. She wasn't good enough just the way she was. She had to try harder. Always harder.

A sound outside the door made her stiffen, lift her head. Had Isma'il sent for her? Was tonight her time to die?

Her heart beat so fast it made her sick. A hissing noise followed by a sort of zap sent a burst of light through spaces in the door frame.

Surely her mind was playing tricks on her. Wouldn't her captors use a key? Why was someone using strange explosives on the door?

The door swung open. A tall figure appeared. Silhouetted by meager light in the doorway, the man stood with an automatic weapon ready to fire. The folds of his black clothes and body armor encased a powerful body that was at least twice the size of any of her captors'. He turned first to his left, then scanned the room until he saw her.

Her heart felt like it skipped several beats as she watched him turn to look over his shoulder and make quick, firm gestures with his hand, holding the automatic rifle with the other. Slinging a strap over his shoulder, he hung the rifle against his back and approached.

Sabine wavered between elation and fear. Dare she hope this man had come to free her?

The tall man knelt in front of her, a small scope attached to his helmet and positioned in front of one eye. She guessed it was some sort of night-vision device. He was laden with other gear, too. A pistol strapped to his waist. Straps around his thighs from his parachute. A wide, dark backpack and several bulky pockets gave the appearance of size. Not that he was small; he had to be at least six-five and was no rail of a man.

"Are you injured?" he asked, putting his hand on her shoulder.

She jerked away from his touch, so conditioned to fear that the reaction was automatic.

He pulled his hand up as though in surrender. "I'm from the United States. I'm going to get you out of here. Do you understand?"

English. Her brain swirled in reverse and forward and sideways. He spoke *English*. And not just any English. He had a distinctive Western swagger to his vowels, strong and confident, marking him a wholly, one-hundred-percent, proud-to-be-American man. She couldn't let herself believe it, yet she felt her head nod twice.

"Where is Samuel Barry?" he asked.

Reminded of Samuel's death, the swell of tears renewed in her throat. "I...I'm the only one left."

The tall man's only reaction was the grim set of his mouth as he flipped another device down from his helmet.

"I've got the package. There's only one," he said into the small radio that arched in front of his mouth. "Have you found anything?"

"We're searching, sir," a voice said across the radio, barely audible. "So far nothing's turned up."

"Set the explosives and keep looking. Kill anything that moves."

"Roger that."

The tall man flipped the radio back against his helmet. There was nothing emotional about him. He was focused on his purpose, and right now that seemed to be getting her out of there.

"Can you stand?" he asked.

She didn't know and he didn't wait for an answer. He helped her to her feet with one arm around her back. She welcomed his strength as he supported her to the door. There, he leaned her against the wall beside the opening. She heard sounds outside. Something moving in the street.

Had her rescue been discovered?

"Don't move," the tall man said, his eye gleaming through the shadows, the other concealed behind the night-vision device.

Sabine didn't think she could move if she tried, she was so weak. Her legs were already trembling with the effort to keep her upright.

Pulling his weapon from his shoulder, the tall man peered outside. He had wide cheekbones and a prominent brow that gave his intense eyes a fearsome set. She didn't know how much time passed before she heard the sound of footfalls. The tall man made hand gestures through the open door, then shrugged his weapon back over his shoulder. He bent to lift Sabine, his arms under and behind her.

She looked over his shoulder as he carried her through the door of the small, six-by-six concrete cell that had been her home for so long. A crippling wave of remorse consumed her. She was leaving without Samuel. *His wife.* What would it do to her when she found out about her husband? Sabine squeezed her eyes shut to a grief that would stay with her always.

Outside the door the tall man joined two other men dressed like him. Aiming their weapons, the other men flanked the tall man as he carried her into the street. Two bodies were sprawled on the ground near the door of the concrete cell. She hoped one of them was Asad.

"Find anything?" the tall man asked.

"Negative."

"Detonate when we reach the Mi-8."

"With pleasure, sir."

The two other men swung their weapons on either side of the tall man as they moved across the street.

Shouts erupted behind them. The tall man ran faster while his partners turned and jogged backward, aiming their weapons and firing. Over the tall man's shoulder, she saw three figures drop in the distance, lifeless shadows in the night.

The tall man slowed his pace as he carried her through an alley. One of his partners moved ahead and the other fell back. They emerged onto another street. Bombed-out buildings and burned shells of vehicles echoed a violent tale of the past.

The woof, woof of a helicopter sounded in the distance. The bombed-out buildings thinned as they came to the outskirts of the deserted village where her captors had taken her and Samuel. Sabine could make out the dark shape of a helicopter just ahead of them.

One of the tall man's partners jumped into the helicopter. The tall man handed her over to him. He swooped her through a narrow door and inside the pod, and she found herself lowered onto a toboggan-like stretcher. The interior of the helicopter had no seats, but the exposed metal walls contained small, round windows. It was dim inside.

Sabine kept her gaze fixed on the tall man. He stood to one side of the opening as the helicopter lifted into the air. One of his partners knelt beside him. Both aimed their guns at the ground. The man kneeling depressed a remote of some sort. What she could see of the night sky lit up, and the sound of a giant explosion followed. Something pricked her arm.

Sabine looked up at the man kneeling beside her. In the light of the fire, she could see his brown hair and blue eyes. He smiled at her while he inserted the IV.

"You're goin' to be okay now," he said with a rich Southern drawl.

God bless America, she thought.

Gunshots made her grip the sides of the stretcher. Bullets sprayed the helicopter, and it dipped. It felt like something vital had been hit. Some of her captors must have survived and discovered her escape.

The man who'd inserted her IV scrambled to the cockpit.

"We're in big trouble if this thing goes down!" the pilot shouted, barely audible over the noise of the rotor.

The helicopter swayed and rattled amidst rounds of machine-gun fire.

"I can't go back there." Sabine struggled to raise her body. She crawled on her hands and knees toward the open door of the helicopter, heedless of the IV that ripped free of her arm and the sting of her raw shins, where her captors had beaten her the most. She searched for a weapon and spotted the pistol in the tall man's holster. When she reached for it, he put his hand around her wrist and stopped her.

"They're out of range now," he told her, one knee on the floor. "And you're not going back there."

Realizing the sound of gunfire had ceased, Sabine sagged at his words, falling flat onto her stomach with her forehead to the metal floor of the helicopter. Sobs came unbidden. They shook her shoulders and made her gasp for air. Relief. Gratitude. A cacophony of emotion too strong to subdue.

The tall man put his automatic rifle aside. She heard it settle on the floor of the helicopter. Sitting down, he reached for her. She let him pull her onto his lap, the promise of kindness from another human being too great to resist. Air from the opening at her back blew through her hair. She dug her fingers into the sturdy material of the tall man's body armor, resting her head on his shoulder until her tears quieted.

With a shuddering breath, Sabine inhaled the oily smell of the helicopter, the smell of freedom. Comfort she hadn't felt in weeks washed through her deprived soul. She wanted to stay close to the man who held her so warmly, his hand slowly moving over her back. He cradled her thighs with one arm, his hand pressed over her hip to hold her on his lap.

Sabine leaned back. Gray eyes fringed by thick, dark lashes looked down at her beneath the edge of his black helmet. He'd moved the night-vision device out of the way. There was sympathy in his eyes but something else, a hovering alertness, a readiness for combat. Her awareness of him grew. Those gray eyes.

His black hair sprouted from beneath the helmet, and she noticed for the first time that it hung low on the back of his neck. A few strands tickled the top of her hand. Lines bracketed each side of his mouth, his lips soft and full but unmoving. His jaw was broad and strong and covered with stubble.

"What's your name?" she asked, wanting to think of him as something other than a tall man.

"You can call me Rudy," he answered after a slight hesitation.

The sound of more gunfire made Sabine look through the door into the night sky. She spotted another helicopter firing at them. Rudy tossed her off his lap at the same instant bullets struck metal. She landed on her rear in a pile of gear and packs in the back of the helicopter. Rudy grabbed his weapon and fired alongside one of his teammates.

"What the—" The man beside Rudy was cut short when a bullet put a hole in his forehead. He fell forward, out of the helicopter. It happened quickly, but Sabine knew violence like this all too well. The helpless sorrow swimming through her was familiar, something that had clung to her through her captivity.

Rudy fired his weapon again. Explosions of answering gunfire throttled along with the roar of rotor and blades. Bullets struck the helicopter's interior, plugging holes in the stretcher where Sabine had lain. She covered her head and buried herself among the gear as much as she could, moaning. Exhaustion did nothing to dull the sickening fear that had been her constant companion for so long.

Then the flurry of gunfire died. Sabine lifted her head. Rudy crouched, ready for battle.

"Who the hell was that?" the Southern man asked from his seat in the cockpit.

The helicopter sputtered and lost elevation with a severe plunge.

The pilot cursed.

"What's our position?" Rudy demanded.

The pilot shouted back coordinates.

"Can you make it to the airstrip?"

"Maybe." The helicopter sputtered more. The pilot shook his head. "I don't know."

Sabine looked at Rudy. He glanced her way, and she saw his confusion. He hadn't expected to be attacked after lifting off the ground. The gunfire from the ground had been from what was left of her captors, but who had fired at them from the other helicopter?

"We're going down! We're going down!" the pilot yelled.

"No," Sabine breathed.

Rudy pushed away from the opening. Tossing his weapon aside, he landed on Sabine with the agility of a cat as the helicopter began to smoke and spin.

Chapter 2

Sabine screamed as the helicopter careened toward the ground. She could feel the pilot trying to keep the machine airborne. The roar was deafening. Debris flew through the pod. If it weren't for Rudy holding her, she'd have gone flying, too. But even he couldn't withstand the force of the crash. When they hit, she felt the jarring impact and knew her body had smashed against something hard, but she blacked out an instant later.

She regained consciousness to the smell of smoke and stillness. Flickers of fire alarmed her. She didn't know how long she'd been out. She didn't think it was longer than seconds or minutes.

Someone stirred beside her. She looked to see Rudy climb to his feet. He scanned the rest of the helicopter. The cockpit was barely visible through darkness and smoke and the tangle of metal.

"Comet!" Rudy shouted. "Blitz!"

There was no answer.

Sabine ignored the searing pain that sliced through her already bruised body and rose to her hands and knees. Rudy hefted a rucksack over his shoulder and stepped over scattered debris on his way to her. She grabbed his arm and used it as a tether to pull herself up. Instead of helping her walk out of the helicopter, Rudy bent and draped her over his big shoulder like a sack of dog food. She withheld groans of agony the pressure against her ribs caused.

Rudy hurried out of the helicopter. When he was far enough away, he lowered her to the ground. She sat on her rear—more like collapsed—and watched him drop the rucksack and jog back toward the helicopter for the other two.

An explosion flipped him onto his back. Sabine cringed and twisted away from the violent flames and rumbling blast. She rolled onto her side and covered her head as debris dropped from the air. A brief moment later, she pushed herself up by one hand and gaped at the inferno. Were the men still in there? They were, but she couldn't bring herself to face it. She crawled toward the helicopter, half sobbing, too numb to process everything all at once. She only knew she couldn't leave the men in that helicopter after they just saved her life.

She got as far as Rudy, who swung his arm out like an iron bar and stopped her. His face was stark with shock and maybe a few signs of grief. She didn't know him enough to read his emotions, but losing what must be his team had to be shattering.

Slowly, he turned his head. His eyes went from disbelieving to expressionless to angry before he eventually covered that, too. Gripping her arm just above her elbow, he hauled her to her feet, swinging the rucksack over his other shoulder. "We have to get out of here."

Sabine strained to see the burning helicopter. "Are we going to—"

"They're dead," he cut her off.

Tears pushed into her eyes. "Oh—my God... I'm so sorry."

He didn't respond, just pulled her along. With a will of iron that had seen her through two weeks of unimaginable suffering, she forced her tears away. She stumbled and fell against Rudy, nearly falling. Her legs wouldn't support her very much longer. She was amazed she could walk at all.

Rudy muttered a curse and hefted her over his shoulder again. She bit her lip against the stab of pain in her ribs. The glowing orb of the helicopter disappeared from view as Rudy walked. His strides grew monotonous. She had no concept of passing time.

When Rudy finally eased her from his shoulder, she groaned as she lay on the ground. Her entire body throbbed. She tried not to vent her discomfort with audible sounds. Rudy had enough to worry about. And she wanted him to get her out of there.

She saw him dig into his rucksack and pull out a hand-held radio. He lifted it to his mouth and depressed a button with his thumb.

"Dasher, this is Rudy. Do you read?"

The names he'd called his teammates penetrated her awareness. Comet. Blitz. Was that short for Blitzen? Now Dasher. Was Rudy short for Rudolph? Was that his code name?

"Dasher, come in." There was a short crackling noise followed by nothing.

Rudy wiped his forehead with the back of his hand.

The radio crackled. "Rudy, this is Dasher. I read you. What happened? Over." The radio crackled again.

"I'm going to set a flare. You have to get here before anyone else finds us. Over."

"I don't see any movement near the crash sight. I'll find you. Over."

"Hurry." Rudy tossed the radio into the rucksack and dug for something else. He stood when he found the flare and moved away from Sabine a few steps. He was efficient and fast with his hands as he lit the flare and sent it into the night sky.

Sabine watched the flare illuminate the landscape. She could see nothing that suggested anyone was after them, but she rubbed her arms anyway, afraid of the possibility, so afraid. She would not survive if she had to face more torture. Not after tasting freedom again.

Her gaze shifted to Rudy. He stood with his feet slightly parted, searching the landscape. Only then did she notice he held a pistol at his side.

The sound of a helicopter broke the silence. Rudy tipped his head back and closed his eyes. She felt his relief, and it sparked hope along with a fresh threat of tears. Were they really going to make it?

The helicopter neared. Soon it tossed up dirt as it landed and Rudy helped her to her feet, carrying the rucksack in his other hand. She leaned against him as they made their way to the helicopter, Rudy bearing most of her weight. He boosted her inside and she crawled into the pod. Leaning against the far side, she watched Rudy climb in as the helicopter lifted into the air.

He lay on his back and draped his arm over his forehead, his massive chest rising and falling from more than exertion. Sabine knew he was thinking of his men. Remorse overwhelmed her. It was so unfair.

She folded her arm over her ribs, wishing the pain would

ease. She closed her eyes to ride it through. Hearing movement, she opened her eyes and saw Rudy rolling to his hands and knees. He stood and crossed the small space of the helicopter.

Crouching before her, he asked, "How badly are you hurt?"

He must have noticed her holding her ribs. "I'll be all right." As long as she was away from those terrible men, she was fine.

Rudy pulled her arm away from her body. "Is anything broken?"

"I don't think so." She had her big-boned grandfather on her mother's side to thank for that. She'd never met her grandparents on her father's side. "Except maybe my ribs." Her injuries would fade. It was what she'd witnessed that would haunt her the rest of her life. The memory of Samuel.

She winced when he tested her ribs with his hands, unable to suppress a moan.

The furrow between his eyebrows deepened, and he pulled her T-shirt up to her breasts in a purely clinical maneuver. Only the tightening of his mouth revealed anything of his reaction to the expanse of bruises on her torso.

"Did your captors want anything specific?" he asked. "Did you hear any of them talk?"

"We never were told why we were being held," she breathed through the sharp throbs in her ribs.

Dropping her shirt, Rudy stood and moved away.

She watched him reach into the rucksack and pull out a canteen. Wordlessly, he handed it to her along with two pills. She studied him as she took the pills and popped them into her mouth. Next, she took the canteen and lifted it to her mouth with an unsteady hand. He seemed to notice and crouched in front of her again. His hand covered hers as he helped her hold the canteen. She met his eyes while she drank, the striking gray of them momentarily capturing her. He didn't have his helmet on anymore, and she realized she didn't remember when he'd removed it. He had thick, dark hair. Something about it struck her as odd. Didn't military men have close-cropped hair?

She wiped her mouth after she finished drinking, and he took the canteen from her.

"Who would want to keep you from leaving this place?" he asked.

The question gave her a jolt. Did he wonder if it could be someone other than her kidnappers? "I don't know."

"Someone must have. And it wasn't your captors."

She took a moment to absorb that. If not her captors, who would want her to die like that? Had they known she and Samuel were being held? And done nothing? Everything inside her rebelled against the idea. It was too awful.

"That helicopter wasn't in any of the images I saw," Rudy continued, his mouth a tight line of anger. "They knew we were coming." And that missing piece of information had cost him three good men.

Who would go to such lengths to see her and Samuel dead? She didn't have any enemies like that. Her father, but he had no reason to want her brutally killed. And if anyone had the means to orchestrate her rescue, it was he. She glanced at Rudy's longish hair.

"Who sent you here?" she asked more briskly than she intended. "Who are you?"

His anger disappeared behind a guarded mask. He unfolded his legs to stand. "I'm bringing you home. That's all you need to know."

"Was it my father?" she asked anyway.

"No." He turned away and went toward the cockpit of the helicopter, ending any further questioning.

* * *

Dust billowed into the air and the whine of engines drowned any other sound. Sabine hooked her arm over Rudy's shoulder as he carried her to a waiting plane. The airstrip was crude and deserted. The plane was painted white with a horizontal blue stripe and no other markings. Rudy climbed some steps and took her inside. There were no seats and darkness filled the row of windows. He put her down and she sat on the floor, leaning against another metal-sided wall.

Rudy turned to speak to Dasher, who was apparently an accomplished pilot, since not only had he flown the helicopter, but also he was going to fly this plane out of Afghanistan. For the first time in two weeks, she felt her shoulders sag in relief. Soon she'd be home.

Home. That seemed like a foreign place to her now, where everything was normal. She felt anything but normal. She didn't know the woman who'd survived what she had. How was she going to move on as though none of this had ever happened?

Samuel would never go home. He'd never see his wife again. The last conversation she'd had with him would stay with her always.

In the darkness of their cell, they'd talked well into the night. Sleep had been patchy and filled with nightmarish dreams. Like every other night.

Sabine had learned a lot about Samuel in the weeks they'd been held captive. He was steady and family oriented. He loved his wife to the depths of his soul and hated the time he had to be away from her; he wanted to build a house for her and the kids they'd planned to have. It was the reason he'd taken the contracting job.

Dasher headed for the cockpit. Once again, she was alone with the man who'd rescued her.

Rudy closed the door and the whine of the plane's engines increased. He sat at her feet on the floor, leaning against the adjacent wall that divided this compartment from the rear of the plane. With his eyes half-closed and his hands resting comfortably in his lap, he had an outward appearance of calm. Hovering alertness. Physical strength at rest but ready to move. And clever gray eyes. He was a dangerous man.

Her father wouldn't have sent any other kind.

Sabine didn't want to believe her father had sent Rudy. She didn't want to owe a man like Noah Page for something as precious as her life, especially after almost losing it because of him. All those years she'd wasted striving to prove she was worthy of his respect had gotten her nowhere. It made her sick to think she'd allowed him to influence her like that, to know that, at least on a subliminal level, she wanted his recognition.

She closed her eyes. No. Her father hadn't sent Rudy. This was a military operation. It had to be. Rudy didn't want to reveal his identity because of the nature of his covert operations and the press her rescue would shake up once word got out that she was on her way home.

Exhaustion overpowered her worry, and she lay on the floor. She woke briefly when they landed for a fuel stop, then again when she felt the plane begin its descent for another. Moments later the tires touched the ground.

The plane slowed until it stopped. Like the last time they'd refueled, the pilot left the plane while Rudy watched from the doorway.

"Where are we?" Sabine asked.

"An airstrip in Egypt," he said without looking at her.

Then his body went rigid as he peered through the door. Sabine pushed herself up to sit.

He looked at her over his shoulder. "Wait here." Then he leaped from the plane.

Sabine crawled to her feet. The crack of gunfire sent her heart skipping faster. Someone was shooting at them again. Who? More gunshots exploded.

She stumbled toward the doorway, searching the plane for a weapon on her way. Seeing Rudy's pistol sticking out of his pack, she slipped it free and leaned against the wall of the plane next to the door, breathing hard from exertion and fear. Peering outside, she spotted Rudy running back toward the plane, a man chasing him with a gun. In the distance, she could see a body lying on the dirt runway.

Forcing her fear down, Sabine lifted the pistol, aimed and fired. The man chasing Rudy dived for the ground, dirt spitting near his feet. Another man appeared in her view and fired at Rudy. She covered him as best she could, until he leaped into the plane, bumping her shoulder on his way. She stumbled as he slammed the door shut, then pounded it once with his fist.

Bullets hit the door. Sabine jumped back at the loud sound.

He turned and she saw the anger in his eyes before he hurried to the cockpit, his strides long and his feet thudding hard on the metal floor.

She followed, jumping again as bullets hit the plane once more. "Where's Dasher?"

"Dead." Rudy sat in the pilot's seat and worked controls, his face tight with fiery emotion. "They were waiting for us."

Again. How could it have happened again? Who didn't want her to escape her captors?

Sabine clumsily fell into the copilot's seat and fastened the shoulder harness. Darkness stared back at her through the window of the cockpit. The plane rolled down the dirt runway, picking up speed. The sound of bullets hitting metal faded. The plane lifted off the ground.

"Who keeps coming after us?" Who had fired at them in the helicopter, and who was firing at them now?

Rudy didn't answer, his face intense and focused on flying the plane. She let him for a while.

Looking out the window to her side, she saw only darkness. "Where are we going?"

"We have to get to Athens."

She turned her head toward him. "Do we have enough fuel?"

"Probably not," he said, still looking straight ahead and at the controls.

"But...don't we have to fly over the Mediterranean to get to Athens?"

"Yes. And we have to fly low."

Staring through the dark front window, she took several calming breaths. "We're going to die."

Rudy turned his head toward her, his eyes fierce with determination. "Not if I can help it."

As much as she'd have loved to fall into the warmth his energy stirred, Sabine gripped the armrests of her seat and remained tense.

He must have noticed because he said, "There are lots of islands off the coast of Greece. We'll find one and land there if we have to."

Did he actually think they'd find a lovely Greek island and have a nice little landing as if they'd planned it all along? She sat with tight, aching muscles for long, unbearable minutes. Each second felt like her last. At any moment the plane would roar down to the water and it would be over.

"We're getting close," Rudy said at last.

"Really?" She couldn't let herself believe it.

The plane gave her a jolt. The engines cut then roared to life. Cut. Roared.

Her heart thudded sickly in her chest. A lump of fear lodged in her throat.

They were running out of fuel!

"I think I see something," Rudy said.

Sabine strained to see through the night but saw nothing. Was he hallucinating in the face of death? The plane lost elevation as it sputtered along. She gripped the armrests tighter. They were going down. She didn't think she was lucky enough to survive two crashes in one day.

"Do you see it?" Rudy asked. He sounded excited.

She turned to look at him. How could he be enjoying this? He glanced at her and smiled, then jerked his head toward the front of the plane.

Sabine looked there and searched once again for something in the distance. She saw faint lights and panic spiraled out of control.

"We'll never make it!" It was too far.

"We'll make it," he assured her. "All we have to do now is find a place to set this thing down."

"Don't you mean crash it?"

The plane's engines cut and this time died altogether. Rudy guided the plane toward the lights. They were losing elevation fast. Lower. Lower. She could see the surface of the water now. Oh God, they were going to hit!

Instead, the plane whizzed by a rocky shoreline. The shape of a rooftop was next. One of the wings clipped the top of a tree. Rudy tilted the aircraft to one side to avoid another tree, then leveled it as a gently sloping hill appeared below them.

"This is as good as it's going to get."

Sabine squeezed her eyes shut and screamed as the plane struck the ground and bounced and rattled and shook. Her body jerked forward as Rudy worked to bring them to a stop. Loud thunks beneath the plane were the only clue to the kind of terrain they'd landed on. A tree branch smacked Sabine's side of the plane and cracked the front window. The plane slowed. Ahead, she saw the side of a mountain growing larger through the cracked window. The plane slowed to a safer speed but not enough to avoid impact. The crash threw her forward, but the shoulder harness held her body in place. Then she blacked out.

Moaning, she came to and looked around. Rudy was yanking off his harness. He scrambled out of his seat, crouched beside her and held her face in his hand, breathing fast as he inspected her.

"Are you all right?"

She nodded dizzily. "I think so."

He reached for her lap and unfastened her harness. "We have to get out of here and destroy this plane before anyone finds us."

Wasn't it already destroyed enough? She used his sturdy body as leverage and climbed to her feet. Wobbling, she leaned against the side of the plane and waited while he hurried to gather what gear they might need. After he threw a rucksack outside, he helped her through the door. She waited for him there while he set an explosive.

Hooking the rucksack over one arm, he took her hand. "Come on." He led her down the hill, away from the plane.

Sabine stumbled and gripped Rudy's T-shirt to steady herself. When he slowed to a stop, she fell against him.

He dropped the rucksack and put his arm around her. Pulling a black device from his pocket, he depressed a button. A violent explosion followed. Sabine watched as the burning plane lit up the night and gave her a glimpse of rocky peaks surrounding the hilly earth where they had landed.

"Can you walk?"

She looked up at him and nodded, not really all that

sure how long she could. But she didn't want him to have to carry her anymore.

Rudy led her the rest of the way down the hill. An hour later, they hiked over a steeper hill. Sabine thought of them as hills because they were nothing like the mountains she grew up in. Southwestern Colorado was filled with fourteen-thousand-foot giants that made these look like foothills.

Her limbs were trembling by the time they crested the peak. Rudy stopped. Sabine hooked her arm with his as she had several times along the way and leaned against him, breathing hard and closing her eyes even though she saw lights at the bottom of the slope that relieved her immensely.

"It's a village," he said, and she heard relief that matched hers and something else. Incredulity at their fortune.

"Where are we?" she asked.

"I don't know. One of the Greek islands."

She turned to study his profile, unable to comprehend how she'd come from a small concrete cell awaiting a horrific death to something as magnificent as a Greek island.

Rudy began walking again, taking her support with him. She collapsed to her hands and knees. A very strange sensation. She had no control over the movement of her legs. Virtually all her strength had abandoned her. Combined with her throbbing and stinging body, she was finished. Her head pounded like lightning strikes with each pulse of her heartbeat.

Rudy cursed. Two strides brought him back to her. He lifted her into his arms, rucksack hanging from one arm, and carried her down the slope. He found a footpath and followed it.

"Don't lie to me when I ask you a question."

She looked up at his rugged face. "I didn't lie."

"You said you could walk."

"I did walk."

He looked down at her beneath a scowling brow.

"You didn't ask how far. We've been walking a long time," she said.

He didn't respond but the scowl remained. Several minutes later they reached the main road going through the village. It was paved but it was the only one that was. No one moved in the street, but it was late at night.

A door opened in a building to their right. An older woman wearing a dark, embroidered dress spoke rapidly in a language Sabine didn't understand. She looked at Rudy when he answered fluently in the same tongue.

He stopped walking and spoke to the woman awhile longer. The woman pointed up the street and spoke again.

Moments later Rudy carried Sabine to a white mortar building with neat rows of square windows lining the first and second floors. At the door, he put her down but kept his arm around her waist for support. She leaned against him while he opened the door, her legs shaking. Inside, a small sitting room with a single light burning on a simple desk illuminated walls covered with row after row of ornately painted plates. Rudy stepped inside with her and closed the door behind them. A short, thin man with dark hair and missing front teeth yawned as he emerged from a dining area, slipping into a robe.

Rudy deposited Sabine onto a chair and spoke to the man, whose name seemed to be Alec. They exchanged words until Rudy finally nodded and handed over a few American bills. Alec handed him a key, and Rudy turned and approached her. She would have protested as he lifted her, but she was so exhausted she didn't think she'd make it three steps.

Their host watched but made no comment as Rudy climbed a narrow stairway. Down a hallway carpeted in a red mosaic pattern, Rudy stopped at a door and put her down on her feet. Her eyes felt heavy and she couldn't wait to lie down on a real bed. Rudy wrapped an arm around her waist and helped her walk inside. Two twin beds on top of a raised platform were covered in white blankets. The walls were adorned with hand-carved lutes and lyres, unique musical instruments that gave a charming clue to the culture of the people here. It was simple but clean and inviting.

Sabine looked to her right and spotted a bathroom. A small sound escaped her. A private bathroom. She tentatively stepped away from Rudy's sturdy support then stumbled toward it. Breathless, she leaned with her hands on the white pedestal sink and saw there was only a small shower. Standing would be a challenge, but she hadn't bathed in two weeks. The thought of a shower charged her with energy she didn't think she had. Determination to be clean fired through her.

Rudy peered into the bathroom, saw the shower with no tub and frowned. "Maybe we should just give you a sponge bath."

Sabine shook her head. "I want a shower."

He turned and met her gaze. Without arguing, he went back into the room and returned with some clothes.

"Leave the door open," he said, and left.

She looked down at the clothes he'd dropped on the floor, wondering where he'd gotten them. Just a white T-shirt, dark blue lounge pants and underwear, but it would be divine to get out of the clothes she'd been wearing for so long.

"You can sleep in this if you want."

Sabine took the bigger T-shirt he held, watching him go back into the room. He sat in a chair across from the bathroom where he could still see her.

Gripping the edge of the sink with one hand, she pushed the bathroom door with the other until it blocked his view of her, then undressed. She hoped her legs would hold her long enough to get clean. Rudy carrying her the rest of the way to the village had helped some, but what she really needed was rest. Turning on the faucet, she waited for the water to warm before she stepped inside.

Water showered over her head and caressed her battered body. Sabine closed her eyes and moaned. Standing, however, made her legs shake uncontrollably and water trickled into the open wounds on her shins, stinging her. She braced her hands against the shower wall but didn't think it would be enough to keep her upright. When she tried to turn in the shower, her knees gave and she collapsed. Sitting on her hip with her hands flat in front of her, she hung her head and let the water spray fall on her.

Hearing a curse, she looked up to find Rudy holding the shower curtain aside, his mouth in a hard line and his eyes fierce with something more than concern.

Chapter 3

Sabine's pulse jumped faster when Rudy stepped fully dressed into the shower. He leaned down and put his hands under her arms, lifting her easily. She didn't want to see in his eyes the purely instinctual male response to holding a naked woman, so she stood there staring at his broad chest, where her hands were spread.

Anchoring her around her waist, he reached for a small container of shampoo and put some on her head. Sabine wearily lifted her hands and began to wash her hair. Her breath came harder with the effort, but it felt so delicious she closed her eyes and let her head fall back a bit, bringing it more under the spray. She tried not to think about Rudy watching her.

His wet T-shirt heightened her awareness of her body against him. Hard muscle compressed her soft breasts. After she rinsed her hair, he reached behind her and retrieved a bar of soap. Readjusting his hold to support her with one of his powerful arms, he began to wash her back. It felt too good to stop him. She let her head fall to his wet T-shirt-covered chest.

"Turn around."

He sounded raspy. Sabine lifted her head and found her eyes trapped by his unreadable ones. She moved her legs but wouldn't have been able to turn on her own without falling. Now with her back against him, she took the bar of soap and moved it over her skin. She lost herself to the pleasure of feeling clean again. When she finished, she was shaking and short of breath.

Shutting off the water, Rudy lifted her dripping wet in his arms. Sabine pulled a towel from a rack above the toilet when he stopped there and held it to her body as he carried her out of the bathroom. In the other room, he sat in the chair and draped her legs over his. Sabine dried herself on his lap.

"Lean forward," he said, taking the towel from her.

She did and froze. Beneath her, a hard ridge told her just how much the shower had affected him. Seeming not to notice her sudden change, he wrapped her hair in the towel. Then he cradled her, stood and put her back onto the chair, by herself.

Slumping against the chair, she watched him go into the bathroom for the big T-shirt and return. His expression was stern as he gripped the shirt in his hands and pulled it over her towel-covered head. A couple of unceremonious yanks, and the top fell down over her body.

"Thank you," she murmured, glad to be covered again.

He said nothing in response and just lifted her and took her to one of the twin beds, where he'd already pulled the covers down. Before covering her with those, he opened the rucksack and pulled out a roll of bandages and a tube of ointment.

Propped by two fluffy pillows, she shut her eyes and bit

her lower lip to keep from crying out when the ointment touched the raw flesh of her shins. Her fingers gripped the sheet and blankets while he wrapped her legs. When he finished, her legs were throbbing so much her mind swam with pain and dizziness.

"I'm sorry," Rudy said.

She couldn't respond with more than a single nod.

He left her and went into the bathroom with the rucksack. When he returned, he was shirtless and in a pair of lounge pants. Sabine caught his profile as he passed the bed and couldn't look away from his broad back. Hard muscles tapered to a trim, fit waist. His butt was tight and perfectly shaped. She held her breath when he leaned over the table and retrieved a bottle of water. Opening it, he faced her and sat on one of the chairs with a long sigh. Lifting the bottle of water he held, he drained half its contents. Sabine forgot the stinging pain in her legs. Smooth skin and a light covering of hair followed the rippling muscles of his chest and abdomen. He sat with his knees spread and his big body slouched lazily in the chair. It gave her a shock to notice him like this, a man with overpowering masculinity that appealed to her on a level she had never experienced.

He lowered the bottle and she stared at his big hand. His other hand lay over the opposite arm of the chair. Those hands had touched her in the shower. Heat began to stir in her. She raised her eyes. He watched her. There was something erotic in his gaze. Leashed interest. Maybe even unwanted desire.

The first shiver of something other than fear raised bumps on her arms. She was alone with him on a Greek island. What would tomorrow be like, she wondered, waking to the Aegean Sea and this mysterious man who'd saved her life?

* * *

Cullen sipped a cup of strong Greek coffee and looked out across the turquoise waters of the Aegean Sea. Of all the places to crash-land a DeHavilland, this had to be the best. Under any other circumstances, he'd have enjoyed it. He'd known this rescue would be among the most dangerous he'd ever done, and he'd taken as few men as he could to avoid risking more lives than necessary, but no one should have died. That helicopter had been waiting for them. Anger simmered close to a boil inside him. Only someone close to Noah could have leaked their plans.

He'd give Noah every resource he had to find out who and why, and whoever was responsible would pay with their lives.

Hearing a sound, he glanced at the door of the room. He couldn't see her but knew Sabine had moved on the bed. She'd slept on and off for two days now. He'd decided to let her and had only disturbed her to make sure she drank water and ate and had clean bandages. Letting her sleep this long made him nervous, but it would be better if she could board a commercial plane without drawing too much attention. If he had to carry her, she'd attract attention.

"Hello up there," a woman called in Dorian Greek from below the balcony.

Cullen dropped his feet from the railing and leaned forward to see her better, sending her an answering smile. It was the same woman who'd told him where to find this pension and an available room to rent. Today she wore a white embroidered dress with gold coins draped around her neck. She was a nice enough lady, but she was way too curious about him and Sabine. All it would take was an awestruck villager like her to pick up the phone and talk to the press. The thought nearly made him break into a cold sweat. All he needed was the media to catch up to them.

The woman lifted a basket. "*Makarounes* for you and your lady."

He kept his smile in place as he straightened. "I'll come down."

He turned before she could respond and moved through the room, checking on Sabine before he left her still sleeping. He made his way to the lower level. The pension owner, Alec, looked up and smiled with a nod.

"Good morning," Cullen said in Greek, and Alec answered in kind.

The wrinkled woman stood outside the door of the pension and smiled when he appeared in the doorway. She extended the basket, its contents wrapped in a red cloth. He took it from her.

"Thank you," he said.

She nodded graciously. "You must bring your lady to my taverna when she is rested. We have fresh seafood every night, and it is very quiet." Her dark eyes held a secretive glint.

The notion of having a romantic dinner with Sabine tantalized him too much for his comfort. "We just might have to take you up on that," he said anyway.

"Alec told me about your crash, and that you were on your honeymoon. You come. Have dinner at my taverna." She told him where it was.

Cullen said nothing. She was just an old woman swept up by the intrigue of a plane crash and the couple who'd survived it. Alec had questioned Cullen on the crashed airplane, and Cullen had come up with the quickest explanation he could think of without revealing his and Sabine's identities. They'd come to Greece on their honeymoon and crashed before they'd reached Athens.

The woman waved and turned to go. Cullen squinted as

he leaned his head out the door and caught rays of sunlight, watching her walk down the narrow street.

He wasn't sure why being known as a newlywed bothered him. Maybe it was the shower, and Sabine's determination to see it done. The woman had grit. She also had a body made for his hands and eyes that beckoned with green fire. She flared an instinctual response in him. The degree of his interest made him nervous. He liked his relationships comfortable, not out of control. He didn't need that kind of intensity with a woman. His job gave him plenty of that. If he ever got married, it'd be to Mrs. Compatible and Good in Bed, not Mrs. Take My Heart and Twist It into a Pretzel of Agonizing Love. He'd seen what that could do to a man.

Back in the room, Sabine was as he'd left her, rumpled covers enveloping her, red hair tangled over the pillow. She looked very snug and content. He didn't want to explore the other "verys" he thought she was. *Knew* she was, now that he'd seen her naked.

Taking the basket out to the balcony, he set it on the table. At almost eleven, it was close to lunch.

An hour passed before he heard the sound of Sabine stirring inside the room again. He listened to the toilet flush, and moments later her bare feet trudged toward the balcony. He started to rise to help her but stopped when he saw that she was moving all right on her own, limping but all right. The T-shirt fell to just above her knees, exposing the bandages he'd wrapped around her tender shins. Her legs were skinny but spectacular. He bet they'd look even better once she healed and put on some weight. Just like the rest of her.

Cullen raised his gaze to her face as she looked across the Aegean Sea. Her mouth was slightly parted and her green eyes were the brightest he'd seen them since getting her out of Afghanistan. Their whites were healthy and the green color sparkled in the Mediterranean sunlight. The swelling on her lip had gone down, and the cut on her cheek was healing, though bruises still colored her skin and would for a while. She'd used the comb he'd bought in the village. Her hair was naturally curly, but it looked like soft, woven silk and fell to the top of her breasts. Even skinny, she was an extremely beautiful woman. All Irish with smooth, pale skin and striking features. Especially her eyes.

"Where are we?" she asked without looking at him.

He was glad she hadn't noticed his scrutiny. "A village called Olympos. The north end of Kárpathos. It's near Crete."

"Wow."

Cullen had experienced a similar reaction, despite his constant vigilance for someone with a camera or a gun.

He caught her furtive glance when she became aware of him watching her. She sat and reached for one of the bottles of water on the table, careful not to look at him. He had to agree it was strange being in a place like this with someone he'd just rescued. Especially at the cost of his team, the few that he'd dared bring on this mission.

The reminder of what he'd lost punched him again. Nothing had gone according to plan. Who had betrayed their mission and why? None of the men he'd hired were married, but the pilot and medic had parents Cullen would have to face when he returned to the States. He wasn't looking forward to that, especially since he was going to have to lie about where their sons had died.

Sabine's reaching for the basket diverted his attention. He welcomed it and watched her.

She glanced from the basket to him in question.

"Homemade pasta with cheese and onions. A local favorite."

"Mmm." She parted the cloth and lifted the ceramic bowl covered with a matching lid. Next came the bread.

"They make their own bread in outdoor ovens. You can smell it every once in a while." The appeal of this place had penetrated his vigil more than once. But then, he'd always liked Greece.

"Mmm," she murmured again, finding a plastic fork and starting to dig into the pasta.

It disturbed him how much he liked watching her. Her vibrancy. The look in her eyes, as if everything were new to her now.

When she sighed and put the bowl back into the basket, he knew she was full. She'd eaten less than half the *makarounes* and bread.

"How do you feel?"

She nodded, looking at the sea. "Better."

A moment passed with only the sound of waves washing ashore in the distance.

"I want to walk down to the ocean," she announced.

"Now?"

She nodded with a look of pure bliss on her face. How could he deny her after what she'd been through? "Are you sure you're up for that?" It wasn't far, but it would take a good hike to get there.

A smile spread on her face. The transformation hit him like a fist to the gut.

Then those green eyes so full of new life met his. "I want to walk on a beach. I really do."

Cullen struggled with the inclination to do anything she asked as long as she kept smiling like that. The feeling was a bit too strong for his liking. But a walk on the beach wouldn't hurt. "Okay. I went down there while you were asleep. There's a small beach down the hill from here." Secluded and easy to watch for anyone pointing a gun, too. He could plug them off the hillside if they tried to come after them. He ignored the fleeting thought that instead of going to the beach he should get a cab so they could leave the island that afternoon.

Sabine went into the bathroom to change. While she was in there, he stuffed a pistol good for a thousand yards in the waist of his jeans, letting his short-sleeved shirt hang over to conceal it. Then he waited for her at the door. She emerged in the dark blue lounge pants and long-sleeved white henley shirt he'd brought for her. The outfit would cover her bruises. He led her down the narrow stairs to the first floor of the pension. No one was in the sitting area of the entry.

Outside, Cullen watched Sabine for signs of fatigue. She started to breathe heavier as they walked down the street. At the footpath he'd discovered yesterday, he stopped.

"It's a steep descent."

"I'm fine," she said, dismissing him to gimp down the footpath on her own.

Impressed by her courage and spunk, Cullen followed. He caught himself looking at her butt as she moved down the hill and had to force his gaze elsewhere. Rocks and brush painted the hillside, ending where a sandy inlet sloped into the ocean. Gentle waves lapped the shore, the only sound to be heard other than their footsteps.

"Oh," Sabine breathed.

He stepped down the last of the incline, and his booted feet sank into fine, white sand. She was like a painting now. Hair sailing in a slight breeze, eyes full of appreciation that might not have been as profound had she not come so close to losing her life.

She sat on the sand and removed her hiking boots and socks. Then she rolled the hem of her lounge pants to the edge of her bandages, just above her ankles. Rising, she walked to the shore and went into the water, but only far enough to get her feet wet. That salt water would hurt her raw wounds like a thousand bee stings. Cullen removed his boots and rolled his pants up to follow her.

Waves splashed against rocks and crawled over the sand. Offshore, the water was so clear it looked like pool water, glittering, translucent cerulean fading to deep sea.

"Have you ever been to Greece before?" she asked.

"Many times," he answered. "But never here. I've been to Santorini and Athens."

"You speak the language like you're from here."

"My grandmother was born here." It caught him off guard how easily that came from his mouth, personal information he usually never divulged.

"You're Greek?" She gave him a survey, as though confirming it with her eyes.

"Partly. My mother married an Irishman. I had a knack for languages in college."

"What was your major in college?"

"Political science."

"What did you do after that?"

He just looked at her, knowing her questions were deliberate. He couldn't tell her much about himself, particularly what he did after college. Not when a media frenzy awaited her return. Public curiosity would leave his company—which didn't overtly exist and never could—too vulnerable.

"Did you join the military?" she asked.

"Something like that."

Her mouth pursed and she stopped strolling through the water. "What's your name? You can at least tell me that much."

He stopped, too, and faced her. "Rudy."

"That's a stupid name. Even for a code name. Tell me your real name?"

He wanted to, and that heightened his concern. "Sabine…"

Pivoting, she resumed her walk through the water, her steps not as smooth as before, frustration giving her verve even as she limped. But that only managed to intrigue him more.

He caught up with her, noticing the subtle jostle of her breasts.

"I'm sure you know everything about me," she said bitterly.

"I know your name is Sabine O'Clery and you're thirty-three years old. Not married, no kids. I know you're from Colorado and for some reason took the contractor job in Afghanistan." He knew more but now was not the time to tell her.

She glanced at him. "I speak Farsi. There was a need for people like me there. I liked the idea of contract work because it gave me an opportunity to make more money and see interesting places." She grunted her laugh. "At the time it seemed like a good idea." Her face grew haunted and she stopped walking, staring out to sea.

"I'm sorry." And he was, for putting that haunted look in her eyes.

Slowly, she turned and lifted her eyes. "How old are you?"

No harm in telling her that. "Thirty-five." When she continued to look at him with those brilliant green eyes, he added, "Not married. No kids."

"That sort of thing is hard for a man in your line of work, isn't it? Having a family, I mean."

He didn't reply, wondering if she was trying to pry more from him. He couldn't let her. He'd already said too much.

"How many of these missions do you do a year, anyway?"

Still, he didn't say anything.

"Who do you work for?"

That especially was off-limits.

Anger flared in her eyes. He marveled at the intensity and couldn't stop himself from looking down when she folded her arms in front of her.

"Is it my father?" She all but spat the last word.

"No."

Her eyes narrowed and he felt dissected as she searched for signs that he was lying. She wouldn't find any. He could pass any polygraph without flinching.

"Then it has to be the military."

He just looked at her. Let her assume he worked for the military. It wasn't completely a lie.

With a frustrated spin, she turned and limped to her boots.

He followed. "Do you have something against your father? Who is he?"

She sat on the sand and started to put on her socks, agitation showing in her movements. "I'm grateful you saved my life. And I'm sorry your teammates were killed."

The memory of his teammates kept him from pressing her for an answer. Instead, he sat beside her, studying her fiery profile. Whatever had estranged her from her father, it must have something to do with the secrets Noah had to keep. She definitely didn't like secrets. But he couldn't let that stop him from keeping some of his own from her. What he did through his company was so black not even his commander in the army reserves knew the truth. If the media got hold of that, it would destroy him.

Sighing, he looked out to sea. He and Sabine were way too curious of each other.

"You probably like not telling me your name," Sabine said without looking up from her boots.

He observed her for a moment, her words sinking in,

confirming what he'd already guessed. The curiosity that could mushroom into more if he wasn't careful.

"You don't need to know anything about me," he said as gently as he could. "As soon as I get you to London, you'll never see me again."

She stopped yanking the laces of her boots to look at him in surprise. "You're taking me to London? What happens when we get there?"

He didn't answer. Instead, he started to put on his boots.

Sabine grunted and jerked the laces of her second boot together.

Best thing would be if they could just get along until he got her to London. He didn't want her to bolt because he reminded her of Noah. "Why don't we forget how we got here and just enjoy the island? We might not ever get a chance to come to a place like this again. I say we find somewhere to have dinner tonight. Something local, with fresh seafood."

Deeper anger furrowed her brow. "What would we talk about, Mr. Thirty-Five, Not Married, No Kids?"

He supposed he should have expected her to react like that. And what was he thinking, suggesting they have dinner together?

"I told you I went to college," he said. "You know about my grandmother, too. That's a lot more than most people know."

"Am I supposed to be flattered?"

He had to get a grip on this. Fast. "Sabine, what I do for a living won't survive the kind of publicity your kidnapping is getting. Imagine what your rescue is going to do. As soon as you land in the United States, it's going to be a circus. I can't be seen with you after this. Can't you understand that?"

She didn't reply and struggled to her feet.

Cullen finished with his boots and followed her up the footpath. She was breathing hard climbing the steep slope.

Her grimaces and awkward steps told him her legs were hurting.

He started to reach for her.

She swatted his hands away and propelled herself faster up the hill, no doubt on sheer will, casting him a dagger look over her shoulder.

He almost chuckled. One thing was for sure—she was definitely getting better.

Sitting on one of the woven chairs on the balcony, Sabine wondered what had made her so angry earlier. If Rudy didn't want to tell her his name, he didn't have to. Right?

She could hear him moving in the room. The shower started to run. She tried not to picture him in there, but it was impossible after seeing him without a shirt. She didn't want to be attracted to a man who was just like her father.

She tapped the tabletop with her fingers. She wasn't sure what bothered her more—not knowing who'd sent him, or his secrecy. If her father had sent him, that made Rudy a mercenary. A ruthless killer with no loyalty to country or ideals. That notion wrestled with the honorable act of rescuing her, and a niggling inner voice taunted that she didn't know for sure her father's company was that disreputable. But Rudy was keeping things from her and doing it with ease. She hated that in men. Plus, he'd gotten a thrill crash-landing the plane. That in and of itself was a big enough warning sign. The man probably never enjoyed an idle moment.

The shower turned off. Sabine looked toward the room, unable to see him and upset that she wanted to. She heard the bathroom door open. Then Rudy appeared in the doorway in black jeans and a white short-sleeved dress shirt, gray-eyed and tall and dark and too gorgeous to be good for her.

"I'll be right back," he said.

He was probably going on another of his patrols. She nodded.

"Don't go anywhere and keep the door shut, okay?" he added.

"I'll wait here for you," she said. Why did that sound so intimate? Waiting for him. She was going to *wait* for him. And then what?

Her gaze collided with his for a long moment before he turned and left the room.

Sabine put her elbow on the table and propped her chin in her hand, looking over rooftops at the sea in the distance. The smell of baking bread reached her. She inhaled and welcomed the distraction. Below, the street bustled with activity. People riding or leading donkeys passed. Taxis drove by. She could hear the collective chatter from people sitting on a patio at a restaurant up the street.

She got lost in the pleasure of just experiencing the moment, listening to the sounds, smelling the smells, feeling the warm sun on her skin. Living. It lulled her into a doze. She leaned her head back and let the peace take her.

A while later, she had no idea how long, she heard the room door open and close. Rudy emerged onto the balcony and put a bag on the table in front of her.

Wariness mingled with delight. A present, but it was from him. "What's this?"

He seemed reluctant to answer. "For tonight. You can't wear what you have on."

A responding flutter tickled her before she could stop it. What was he doing? He didn't seem to know himself, the heat in his eyes at odds with his shift in weight from one foot to the other.

Flustered, Sabine turned to the bag and reached inside. She lifted a swath of soft white material, holding up the bodice of a dress. It was long sleeved with a scooped neckline. Standing, she faced Rudy. The flowing hem fell to her ankles and would cover her bandages.

"It's like I said earlier—we're here on this island, why not enjoy it?" He sounded defensive, as though he didn't want her to know he had other reasons for picking out this dress.

She smiled to cover the much more serious wave of pleasure that realization stirred. "If you're trying to get my mind off Afghanistan, you're doing a great job."

Chapter 4

All the while she showered and primped in front of the mirror, Sabine wondered if having dinner with Rudy was such a good idea. Granted, they had to eat, and this was Greece, but he'd made it clear she'd never see him again after he sent her on her way to the United States. Did she want to risk exploring something romantic with him? Because with all his secrets, he would be a risk. She'd dated a few men and slept with them, but this wasn't the same. Being with those men had felt comfortable. Being with Rudy set sparks on fire. Big difference.

She inhaled and blew out the air through pursed lips. As long as she kept Rudy's true purpose in mind, she'd be all right. He had rescued her. When he completed his mission, he'd go his way and she'd go hers. Dinner with him would be just that. Dinner. She'd go to taste the local fare, and tomorrow she'd be on her way home.

She left the bathroom and stopped. Rudy sat in a chair

by the bed, reading a brochure of some sort. He looked up and went still when he saw her. His gaze slowly devoured her as he rose to stand.

"Are you ready to go?" she asked, doing her best to hide how awkward she felt.

"I knew that dress would look beautiful on you," he said as though he hadn't heard her.

The compliment rushed through her in a warm wave. Just dinner, she told her heart. Stop letting nice arms and abs get in the way.

Seeming to catch himself, he went to the door and waited for her there. She reached the open threshold.

"By the way, we're on our honeymoon," he said.

She stopped abruptly, unable to keep her head from snapping over and up to look at his face.

"If anyone questions us, that's what you tell them," he explained. "For cover."

Embarrassed that she hadn't immediately caught on to that, she left the room, letting him follow down the hall and stairs. In the lobby, Alec looked up from a paper he was reading and smiled.

"I am happy to see you are feeling better, Mrs. Harvey," he said in accented English.

Sabine forced a smile. "Thank you. I do feel much better." She avoided any connection with Rudy's eyes as they left the pension. *Mrs. Harvey. Mrs.*

The sun was low in the sky as they made their way down the street. Rudy led her into an alley. It was so narrow that he had to move behind her to allow a man leading a donkey to pass. Through another alley, they dodged two more people with donkeys and emerged onto a street where a white building with tables outside came into view. Theodosia's, a sign read on the glass door.

Rudy opened the door for Sabine and she entered. The

interior was longer than it was wide, with windows along the back that had a view of a rocky shoreline. Dark wood tables with white tablecloths and miniature vases of white flowers filled the space between. The hum of conversation joined the clang of dishes, and the smell was divine. Sabine inhaled a full breath to savor it for a while.

Rudy leaned close. "It's called a *psarotavérna*. A taverna that serves fish."

"It smells like heaven."

"Welcome, welcome." The woman they'd first seen when they'd arrived in the village came forward, her wrinkled face smiling. She wore a red embroidered dress with gold chains hanging from her neck. Her hair was white and in a bun.

"This must be your lovely wife." The woman hooked her arm with Sabine's. "I am Theodosia," the woman said, leading them past tables of Greek-speaking patrons.

At a table in the corner, intimate and lit with a candle, Theodosia let go of Sabine, who sat and watched Rudy do the same across from her.

"Enjoy." Theodosia beamed.

Rudy said something in Greek that made her smile wider and laugh as she turned away.

"She's very friendly," Sabine commented.

Rudy scowled. "Too friendly. Maybe we should have gone somewhere else."

"We're the Harveys, remember?" She laughed a little, beginning to enjoy this.

He grunted and turned to the menu.

The tension on his face dimmed her playfulness. Did he regret bringing her here? Why had he taken the chance? She was afraid to guess. Why had she agreed to go with him? The answer sobered her. They were both too interested in each other.

A waitress arrived at their table and filled two glasses of water. "You ready, no?"

Rudy ordered. Sabine didn't understand a word he said, but when the waitress left the table, she assumed he'd ordered for both of them.

"What are we having?" she asked.

"Octopus pilaf."

He grinned at her questioning expression, all his tension evaporating.

"Never had it?" he asked.

She smiled and both felt and saw him notice. "No, but I love seafood."

"Me, too." He looked at her in a way that she shouldn't have liked, but oh, how she liked it. The heat and vitality of him warmed her.

One glass of wine arrived at the table. The waitress put it in front of her.

"Aren't you having any?" she asked Rudy when the waitress left.

He shook his head. "I don't drink."

The way he said it made her wonder. "Because your job requires it?"

"No. When you grow up with a drunk for a father, alcohol loses its appeal."

She lifted the glass of wine and sipped, thinking he had not meant to reveal so much feeling and not wanting to let on that she'd noticed. "Where is your father now?"

He met her gaze as she lowered the glass. At first, she didn't think he was going to answer, but it turned out there was too much emotion simmering in him.

"He lives in a low-income housing project with his crack-smoking girlfriend," he said, his tone laced with bitterness and sarcasm.

"Do you ever see him?" she asked, keeping her tone unassuming.

"No. I gave that up the day I left home, when I was sixteen."

"How do you know he has a girlfriend, then?"

"Every now and then I give in to the hope that he's changed and call."

Sabine met his gaze for a while. It hurt him to see his father like that. Had his upbringing motivated him to do what he did for a living? Maybe if he saved enough people, he could make up for not being able to save his father.

"My mother died when I was very young. He never got over it," Rudy added.

"He must have loved her very much."

"Too much. It's what destroyed him."

Sabine covered her inward response with another sip of wine. Maybe that's what had turned him into an adrenaline junky. He didn't want to end up like his father. What better way to accomplish that than always being on the go? Never home. Avoiding relationships that would make him feel too much.

She wondered if her father had had a similar experience that had turned him against commitment to a woman. When she realized she didn't know anything about his childhood, a spark of anger pushed the soft thought aside.

"Is that why you do what you do?" she asked a little harsher than she intended. "Do you feel safer when you conquer and control?"

"My father was a bad role model, and I was never close to him. Luckily, I had an uncle who cared what happened to me. He's the reason I do what I do."

His answer nipped her anger short. She hadn't expected him to reveal yet another detail about himself. Curiosity won over her defenses. "Your uncle is like a father to you?"

Pride and love softened his magnificent eyes. "He's an amazing man. Well liked by everyone, both in his hometown and in the military, even though he's retired. He taught me the importance of standing up for values. For country. For freedom. Fighting for what you believe in. Honor. Humanity. Integrity. All that. He retired a good man with a stellar reputation. I want that. I want to be able to look back on my life when I'm an old man and not feel like I could have done more."

"So your uncle was in the military." And so was he, if she understood his meaning. She didn't want to acknowledge it could be true, that he was nothing like her father. It would be too much of a risk, allowing herself to believe she could trust a man like him. Someone with secrets.

Instead of responding, his eyes went blank, the window to the man inside shut tight. Now that, she thought resentfully, was exactly like her father.

"Did my father hire you?" she asked.

"What kind of man would your father hire?" he answered with a question.

She let him get away with it. "Murderers. Men with no conscience."

"Is that how you think of your father?"

"It's what he is."

"A murderer."

She didn't reply.

"What does he do?"

"Don't you already know?"

He waited.

"He owns a private military company. He loves the thrill. The danger of going into a third-world country for the sole purpose of killing, teaching others to kill and pilfering the civilization while he's at it."

"You know an awful lot about him for someone who grew up fatherless."

Catching the meaning of his leading comment—that maybe she was exaggerating the truth out of spite—she said, "My mother told me about him when I asked."

"She told you he was a mercenary?"

"He was."

"Pilfering and killing."

She turned her head away, unable to deny emotion might be clouding her judgment.

"I know what it's like to grow up with a parent you feel doesn't love you," he said, bringing her gaze back to him. "So I suppose I can't blame you for the way you feel."

"I didn't grow up with my father around. My mother raised me. The great Noah Page came around often enough, but only for sex. My mother wanted more. He promised more every time, but in the end he always left. He was incapable of loving one woman, giving his whole heart to her. And the thrill of his job was always more important."

Rudy lifted his glass of water and drank, watching her over its rim.

"Does that sound familiar?" she taunted.

He lowered the glass of water. "Are you asking if I'm incapable of loving only one woman?"

He must know she wasn't, but she decided to play along. "Are you?"

"I don't know. I've never been in love."

"Do you want to be?"

His gaze intensified, not letting hers go and reaching deep into her, infusing her with the growing strength of their attraction. "She'd have to be one hell of a woman, Ms. Hydrogeologist Who Went to Afghanistan to Make More Money and See Interesting Places."

The sting of his reply ricocheted through her. His meaning was too clear. To all appearances, she went for thrills just like him and her father.

But until her kidnapping, she'd been living a lie. She'd been living to please others. And judging by Rudy's remark, he liked that she seemed to be a thrill chaser. Would he still hold her in such high esteem if he knew she wasn't that woman anymore? That Afghanistan had ripped her eyes open so she could finally see and accept the truth? She didn't know what she was going to do with her life now. She just had to find herself again, the part of her buried beneath years of identifying herself through achievements.

Upset, she turned her head and looked out the panel of windows along the rear of the taverna.

Rudy's hand slid over hers on the tabletop. Sabine looked down at his masculine hand covering hers.

"I'm sorry," he said.

She raised her eyes. "For what?"

"For putting that look in your eyes."

The gruff sound of his voice set off warnings in her head. If this night lasted too long, she wasn't sure she could resist wherever it led.

Rudy paid for their dinner, and the walk back to the pension was charged with unspoken tension.

Dim light from a paraffin lamp reflected on the knife blade. Then shiny metal grew bloody, spreading as if through soaked cotton. She closed her eyes. A man standing guard over her pummeled the butt of his rifle against her head.

"Open your eyes!" he shouted in the language she now detested.

She opened her eyes. The guard gripped her chin and jerked her head toward the wooden table where Samuel lay tied and writhing. She wailed and shut her eyes.

"Open your eyes!" the guard shouted louder.

She couldn't.

Samuel screamed in pain and she screamed with him. Another blow to her head made her dizzy. She opened her eyes.

The scene blurred. Mercy. But not for long. The monster was near.

She watched, terror a frenzy of incomprehensible energy, as a wiry man with short dark hair turned from his victim and faced her, a leer on his mouth and evil raging in his eyes....

Sabine sprang up in bed, staring through the darkness. The dream had been so vivid. She could see that room where Samuel had been tied. Heard his cries of agony all over again. She didn't want to remember, but the images hung in her conscience, awful and tearing. Bringing her knees up, she let her head fall there and cried. Once she started, she couldn't stop.

On the bed next to hers, Rudy stirred. He rose to stand and stepped over to her. Pulling the covers over her legs aside, he sat on the mattress and gently lifted her onto his lap. It was a smooth motion that accompanied the swell of desperate need pumping through her heart. She curled against him, shaken, disoriented. Lost. He offered her comfort and she took it.

She cried until she felt drained and empty. So empty. How was she going to find her way through the foreign landscape of her soul? How would she ever learn to live with the torture of her memory? She just wanted to forget.

"Do you want to talk about it?" Rudy asked, pulling her from the dregs of torment.

She shook her head, more of a roll against his hard muscled chest. It was too hideous to put into words. Unfathomable. That another human being could do what had been done to Samuel and what would have been done to her.

"You're going to have to at some point."

She raised her head to look at him. His eyes were mellow with caring, plain for her to see. Unguarded. She was seeing all of him right now. Such a gift, this willing exposure of his self. It loosened something inside her. She could forget the horror of her ordeal in his arms. Escape it. Why not let him do that for her?

Impulse made her lean closer, tilt her head. Her lips were a hair's width from his. Just a slight movement closed the distance. A feather touch. She tasted his warm breath. Sweet. Soft.

She moved back a fraction to look up into his eyes. Shadowed and darkly intense, they glowed in the meager light. She kissed him again, this time moving her lips over his to find the best fit. His arm went rigid around her back. She touched his lower lip with her tongue, then gently sucked where it had been, hoping he wouldn't withdraw. He made her feel so good. She needed to feel good again.

Rewarded by the sound of his quickening breaths, she slid her hands up his chest and around his neck. Now her breasts pressed against his hard body. She felt his hand on her thigh. The one on her back didn't move. She touched her lips to his again. His mouth answered hesitantly. She reveled in the intimate contact, the soft brush of their mouths, the gentle play. When he pulled away, she leaned her head back, closing her eyes to feeling.

Rudy kissed her neck, her jaw, the soft spot below her ear. His masculine rasps were erotic in the room. She moved her head and found his mouth again. A sound escaped her as she opened to him, wanting more than a chaste kiss. He reached deep with his tongue. Her injured lip protested against the force of his passion but wasn't enough to make her want to stop him.

His hand moved up her thigh, excruciatingly slow. When

he reached the hem of her underwear, he went inside and cupped bare flesh. Heat spread through her, sweet tingles radiating from her core to the ends of her limbs. Their breathing resounded like soft whispers in the room. She pulled away from his mouth to trail kisses down his throat. But she couldn't stay away from that mouth for long and returned for another long, searching kiss. He lifted up her T-shirt. She left his mouth only long enough for him to raise the shirt over her head and toss it aside. Her breasts touched his bare chest when she returned to kissing him.

"Mmm," he murmured, and Sabine knew he'd lost his remaining restraint.

The muscles of his stomach tightened as he rolled onto his hip, making her land with her rear on the mattress. She dropped her arms from his neck to touch his chest. He hooked the hem of her underwear and pulled the garment down her legs. Kneeling between her legs, careful of the bandaged area, he came down to her, gently, without putting weight on her ribs.

She stopped thinking about that when she felt his erection through his underwear. On his elbows, his fingers raked into her hair and he kissed her.

"Tell me your name," she said against his warm mouth.

"Rudy," he said, kissing her again.

"Please," she breathed. "I need…" He rubbed himself against her, and her mind blanked for a second.

Pushing the waistband of his underwear down, she cupped her hands over his butt. His hips moved again, harder this time, and she felt his erection, parting without entering. Her mind blanked again.

He took her open mouth and kissed her hard and deep, still moving against her. He sucked a spot on her neck then dragged his tongue down to her breast. Sabine thought her eyes would roll backward from the sensations firing through her.

"Tell me your real name," she barely managed to say. She had to know his name.

His mouth slid off her nipple and moved up her neck until he found her lips. Lifting his head, he looked down at her.

Passion mingled with hesitation.

"Tell me," she urged, lifting her head to kiss him reverently, a tender caress.

He kissed her back then looked down at her again. A long moment passed.

"Cullen."

"Cullen." She looked into his eyes and gave him another worshipful kiss. "Cullen. Cullen. Cullen." She met his mouth again. When she withdrew, she opened her eyes and found his.

"Make love to me, Cullen."

He kissed her. One soft taste after another, taking his time with it, heating her to mind-numbing rapture. He moved down, grazed her nipple with his tongue, then traced the edge of her bruises before kissing his way down to her stomach. He made her entire body sing with pleasure. Even her toes tingled.

Yes, this is exactly what she needed. To feel alive again. To forget.

Coming back up to her, he looked into her eyes while his hand went down her side, over the curve of her hip, down her leg. Shivers rocketed through her as his fingers caressed the tender flesh of her inner thigh, up, up, until they grazed her wetness. Her breath caught and for a moment she thought she would come apart right then.

"Mmm," he murmured darkly.

Sabine grabbed his wrist, unable to take any more. He met her eyes and seemed to understand. He rose to his knees and she watched him take off his underwear with jerky tugs, his smoldering gaze never leaving her.

He dropped his underwear off the side of the bed and stretched over her, propped by his hands to keep from coming in contact with her bruises. The hard ridge of him rubbed against her warmth. Sabine put her hands on his butt and urged him to do more. He pulled back and the tip of him found her and pushed inside. The delicious pressure of his never-ending length filled her. He groaned and withdrew to push into her again.

Sabine gripped his hard biceps. He stayed above her while he thrust back and forth, strumming unbearable sensation to a crescendo.

A powerful orgasm shook her. It went on and on, a gripping eruption that made her cry out. When the waves subsided, he drove into her with more force, sliding one arm under her waist, tipping her hips and renewing the sizzle. She met his feverish kisses and her moan was deep and raw as she clenched around him a second time. He sank hard into her a few more times before he made a gruff sound and he came down on his elbows, resting his head beside hers. Many moments passed as he lay there on top of her, still inside her but spent.

Peace settled over Sabine. The demons in her mind were far, far away. Where Cullen had pushed them. She was warm and safe and content. When he rolled onto his back, she sighed and curled against him, positioning herself so her ribs didn't hurt. No words were necessary. The peace was enough. Lulled, she slept.

Sabine woke to the sound of ocean waves and the smell of coffee. As she stretched, even her aches and pains didn't penetrate the lovely glow that greeted her.

Finding her big T-shirt, she pulled it over her head before heading toward the open balcony door. She could see Cullen's legs where he sat on one of the chairs. Warmth suffused her with the memory of what he'd done with her the night before. In the open doorway, she stopped. He turned his gaze from the ocean and looked up at her. She smiled.

"We need to leave in an hour."

Her smile vanished along with the lovely glow. Coldness swept into its place. Nothing remained of the gentle and caring man who'd held her and made love to her. He was the purposeful soldier he'd been when he found her in the Panjshir Valley. He was doing his job and she was part of it. Last night had been part of it. Or had it? Why was he so distant this morning? It crashed into her conscience that she already knew the answer.

Chiding herself for letting herself believe, even for a moment, that Cullen would change the course of his mission after one night, that it would mean enough for him to at least acknowledge what had happened, she turned without comment and went to get ready. What happened last night had been nothing more than a therapy session. With that first kiss, she'd asked him for an outlet to her despair and he'd given her one.

Dressing after a shower, Sabine entered the room and found him waiting by the door, rucksack at his feet. He watched her impassively as she approached. To her shame, she couldn't hold his gaze. She preceded him out the door and discovered he'd arranged for a car to come and get them. She sat on the opposite side of the backseat from him and stared out the window all the way to a small airport on the other side of the island.

She didn't know where he'd attained their passports and didn't care enough to ask. Asking would require that she speak to him, and she didn't feel like doing that.

They boarded a plane to Athens. Cullen let her board first

and she sat in the window seat. He made no attempt to talk to her. The few times she glanced at him, he was as emotionless as he'd been that morning. But he watched her. In an unnerving way she was beginning to hate.

In Athens, they had to wait for their flight to London. Sabine found a chair near their gate and occupied herself studying the crowd around them. Greek people were beautiful, which only depressed her further. Cullen was part Greek. He looked Greek.

He gave her a reprieve from his weighty presence and disappeared for a while. When he returned with two coffees, she took one of them.

He sat beside her. She ignored him but felt his frequent glances.

"You knew it would come to this," he said after a while.

Lowering her cup from the sip she'd just taken, she slid her gaze to him. "If you're worried about last night, don't be."

"Nothing would have happened if I'd have known you were expecting more from me."

She faced forward and resumed her people-watching to cover the gouge to her emotions. Hadn't she learned not to expect more from anyone? Every time she'd expected more from her father, she'd always been shot down. Cullen was no different. She reined in her building anger. "Well, I'm not, so you're off the hook."

"I can tell you're upset."

"I'm upset with myself, not you, so don't let it go to your head."

He grunted a short laugh. "You were the one who kissed me."

"You kissed me back."

She heard him sigh, a frustrated sound. "But if I'd have known you were expecting more, I would have stopped."

She hated how he repeated that. "I wasn't. I was just... I wasn't thinking, that's all."

"Me, neither," he said.

She caught his gaze and held it. Had he been as swept away as she? Is that what had made him so distant? She fought the desire to cling to that rationale. It was such a familiar instinct, so like how she'd felt growing up, after each time her father came home, then left her mother broken when he inevitably left.

An announcement came to board their plane. Cullen stood and Sabine followed him onto the plane. He stuffed his rucksack in the upper compartment and sat next to her. She propped her elbow on the armrest and stared out the window. Moments later the plane raced down the runway and they were airborne. It wouldn't be long now. Soon she'd be in London. She'd never see him again.

She tried not to notice how close his thigh was to hers, or his hand on the armrest. The same hand that had touched her so intimately last night. His nearness suffocated her. She could even smell him. It was disconcerting, how her heart had become so tangled with him in such a short period of time.

The plane landed in London and taxied toward the gate. A lump formed in her throat. She didn't even know the man beside her. She knew only his first name and precious few details about him. How could she have feelings for him? It was her ordeal. She was emotional and vulnerable. Any man would have done the trick.

But she knew that wasn't true. Not just any man would have done what Cullen had done for her.

He said nothing as he walked with her through the London airport. When they reached the main terminal and the doors leading to passenger pickup, he slowed, taking her hand to stop her.

Reluctantly, she faced him. He wasn't going any farther with her. She would walk one way and he would walk the other. Her nerves began to fray.

He pulled her toward him. She flattened one hand on his chest as he curved his fingers around the back of her neck.

"I don't regret what happened," he said gruffly.

The sound of his voice, what he said and the hungry heat in his eyes washed through her. Finally there was the emotion he'd hidden from her all morning. One night together hadn't satisfied him any more than it had her.

His head came down. She felt the featherlight touch of his lips on hers. The same fire that had pulsed between them last night flared to life again. He released her hand and slid his to her lower back. She curled her freed hand over his biceps. Angling his head, he kissed her deeper. Harder. She answered with everything she had in her heart. People moved behind her. The sound of voices and people shuffling by were dim in comparison with the riot of sensation clamoring inside her.

Long seconds later, Cullen lifted his head. She shared a silent moment with him, looking deep into his eyes. Then she touched his face, running her fingers along his jaw and lips. She hadn't imagined the poignancy of last night. He'd felt it, too.

He took her hand in his, kissed it, then lowered it to her side. Letting go, he stepped back.

"There'll be a black Mercedes SUV parked outside. Waiting for you."

Reality intruded. Waiting? She stiffened. "Who?"

"You'll recognize him."

Dread washed through her in one awful wave. If it was her father waiting outside, then Cullen worked for him. Nothing she'd begun to believe about him was true. She stepped backward, watching a kind of resignation creep into his eyes. He had expected this moment to come. Of course she'd suspected her father might have sent him, but finding it true was far more painful. Cullen *was* a mercenary. She'd slept with a mercenary.

She turned and walked with a limp toward the door. There, she couldn't stop herself from one last look. People walked to and fro, taking no notice of him where he still stood near a cement column that concealed him from most angles except behind and in front of him. Hands at his sides, messy dark hair, eyes shadowy and hard, he looked tall and formidable.

She'd never see him again. Part of her screamed not to leave. Pretend he wasn't the kind of man she feared and that it wasn't her father waiting outside this door. If she could just stay in Cullen's arms. Go back to Kárpathos. Keep kissing him and never surface into reality...

But that was impossible. Sabine had no place in Cullen's life. He'd deliberately kept details of her rescue from her, knowing she would not have agreed to go with him to London. Not with her father waiting here. Not knowing her father had arranged everything. Cullen. Her rescue. Everything.

Numbly, she pushed the door open. She stayed in the doorway, frozen by the sight ahead of her. A man stood near the rear passenger door of a Mercedes SUV. It was shiny and black, with windows so dark she couldn't see inside. Her heart turned to ice as she stared at her father.

Noah Page stood with his hands clasped behind him, dark sunglasses hiding the blue eyes that had so bewitched her mother. His dark hair had grayed, and he'd gained a few more wrinkles since she last saw him, but his tall frame was still fit. A requirement of his profession.

Beside him another man leaned against the front fender

of the SUV. The open lapels of his jacket revealed the strap of a harness, telling her he was armed.

She looked once again at her father. She hadn't seen him since the day she graduated from college. He hadn't been invited and must have known she'd resent his presence. Yet he'd come, as though years of neglect and empty promises could be forgotten by such a feeble gesture of interest in her life.

And now he was here, picking her up after one of his henchmen had rescued her. A mercenary on her father's payroll. Cullen, who'd made love to her last night like no other. Cullen, who epitomized the worst kind of man for her. A man who lied to ensure he'd get her here.

She wondered what she would have done had he told her the truth. Maybe she'd known the truth all along. Just hadn't allowed herself to believe it.

Oh, God. Sabine's hand tightened on the door handle. Ever since Cullen had held her in the helicopter, something about him had reached her heart. His heroism. His strength. Everything good in a man…everything she dreamed a man should be.

Still holding the door open, heart racing with a riot of conflicting emotions, Sabine looked behind her. The spot where Cullen had stood was empty.

Chapter 5

Nothing could have prepared Sabine for the welcome home that awaited her in Denver. She could see the throng that had gathered behind a short concrete barrier as her father's business jet came to a halt in front of the jetCenter at Centennial Airport.

"My God," she murmured, staring in awe at the crowd of well-wishers.

"Damn her," Noah cursed from the leather seat beside her. "No one would have known about our arrival if it weren't for her."

Knowing the "her" he referred to was her mother, Sabine turned from the window to glare at him. He'd tried several times on their way to strike up a congenial conversation. More than once she'd caught herself wanting to rejoice that he was showing an interest in her at all, that perhaps she'd finally achieved the ultimate reward and won his respect. But his effort to assume the role of father came too late, and she resented him for having the gall to use her rescue as a means to get close.

"So sorry you're in a bind, Father," she said, moving her gaze back to the scene outside the window. So many people. She had no idea what she would say. Did she have to say anything?

Her father stood and extended his hand. "Come on."

Ignoring his offer of help, she pulled her own weight from the seat and forced him to step back as she made her way to the exit.

Her heart jackhammered as she emerged from the jet. A roar of cheers erupted. Sabine smiled and waved, nervous and happy and confused. She didn't feel deserving of such a grand welcome. All she'd done was survive something terrible.

Her mother materialized from the crowd, running toward the jet. Sabine laughed and cried at the same time as she stepped down the remaining stairs, using the rail for support.

Nothing had ever looked so good as her mother coming toward her with open arms. Mae O'Clery smiled with tears streaming down her face. An active woman of fifty, Mae had retained her shape and kept her hair shoulder-length and dyed red to hide the gray. Sabine limped toward her. Air whooshed out of her when she found herself encased in her mother's arms. The cheers grew louder and clicks from cameras went off everywhere.

"My baby girl." Her mother's pet name for her had always annoyed Sabine because she used it so often. But now it was like music. Sabine cried harder.

"You don't know how happy I am to see you," her mother croaked.

"I think I do," Sabine said. "About as happy as I am to see you."

They laughed through tears.

"Oh." Mae leaned back and touched Sabine's face with both hands, her green eyes moist with tears. "Welcome home, darling."

Her mother's smile faded when her gaze shifted. Sabine watched her wipe her tear-streaked face. Turning, she saw her father standing close, his eyes fixed on Mae with a look of longing.

All the old resentment and uncertainties boiled up, the worry that her mother's love for him would once again blind her into another brief reunion. Then it would be only a matter of time before her father got restless. He'd leave like he always did. And the agony would play its course inside her mother.

"Thank you," Mae said to Noah.

A soft smile formed on his lips, changing his expression to one of affection. "You know I would have done anything to bring her back to you."

"Sabine."

The sound of her name interrupted the animosity building toward her father. She turned and saw Aden Archer come to a stop beside her mother, wearing sunglasses, a hesitant smile flickering on his mouth. His thinning brown hair waved in a slight breeze. He leaned his wiry, average-height frame forward and hugged her.

Sabine felt awkward hugging him back. It seemed so stiff. So forced.

When he moved back, she wanted to take his sunglasses off to see if there was anything telling in his eyes. And there were so many questions she wanted to ask.

"I'm so glad you made it home," he said, and sounded deeply sincere. "I wish I could have done something. If it wasn't for your father…"

"I know." She didn't want to say more, to feel so beholden to her father.

"The papers are saying no one knows why you and Samuel were taken."

She nodded slowly. "That's true." Would she ever be able to hear Samuel's name without feeling a wave of grief? His body had been found along a village road near where they had worked, her father had told her on the way back to the States. It had been left there as a message, but of what, and by whom?

"You couldn't tell the authorities anything that might help?" Aden's question jarred her from her thoughts. "No leads? Nothing?"

Still thinking of Samuel, she answered more aggressively than she intended. "No. Believe me, if I knew anything, I'd tell them all I could."

He nodded. She wondered if he was as guarded as he seemed. Was he hiding remorse, or something else she couldn't read?

"We should go, Sabine." Her father cupped her elbow and began to lead her away.

Aden stood watching her, a half smile emerging on his mouth. It gave her an eerie chill. She couldn't explain why.

When she couldn't crane her neck to watch him any longer, she faced forward and spotted a dark car waiting. Mae caught up to her and Noah and slipped her arm under Sabine's.

The renewed roar of cheers was deafening. Cameras went off like firecrackers. Security personnel kept the crowd behind the concrete barrier.

"I'm afraid I caused quite a stir," Mae said with a giddy laugh. "I couldn't stop telling people you were coming home today. I'm afraid word got around. I'm sorry."

"Don't worry, Mom."

Noah walked beside Sabine toward the waiting car. If

so many people hadn't been watching, she'd have cringed away from his hand on her back.

"Will you tell us about your rescue, Miss O'Clery?" someone shouted.

Sabine saw a young male reporter with determined brown eyes standing behind the barrier.

"Is he the one who got you out of Afghanistan?" another reporter asked.

Sabine saw a woman with short blond hair holding up a newspaper on the other side of the concrete barrier. Trying to hide her swell of foreboding, she stepped away from her parents and took the newspaper from the blonde. A security guard moved between them, but Sabine was barely aware of his protective gesture. She stared in shock at the picture on the front page of that morning's *Washington Daily,* a nationally recognized newspaper.

Big and bold, the headline read Rescued Contractor Welcomed Home.

Below that, Sabine stood in Cullen's arms, and he was kissing her like a man who'd already tasted more than her mouth. That kiss was hot and deep and full of emotion. A heartfelt goodbye. With his back to the camera, most of his face was concealed, but his lips and jaw were in clear profile. Part of one closed eye was visible through a few strands of hair. With the concrete pillar on one side and a wall on the other, there weren't many angles a camera could capture him from where he stood. Even someone who knew Cullen would have a hard time recognizing him in this photo.

Her eyes lifted. Cameras went off with a flurry.

Sabine could see the blonde around the security guard's shoulder. The woman smiled a knowing smile, then wrote furiously on her small notebook.

Sabine turned and resumed her trek to the car. Shouted questions trailed after her.

"Where is he now, Miss O'Clery? Why isn't he with you?"

"Was that a farewell kiss instead of a welcome home?"

"It's been rumored your rescue was funded by a private source. Would that be your father?"

"Is the man in that photo one of the men who got you out of Afghanistan? Does he work for your father?"

"Is it true your rescue plane crashed on a Greek island, Miss O'Clery?"

Sabine stopped in her tracks and gaped at the reporter who'd asked the last question. A tall, slender woman with dark hair and observant blue eyes stood with a ready pen. How had she learned that? Had someone recognized her in Kárpathos? Or had someone close to the mission talked?

The woman smiled. "Were you alone with your rescuer there?"

Her mother tugged her arm and she moved toward the car.

"We have no comment," Noah said. "Surely you understand my daughter needs rest."

Sabine looked back at the throng one last time. Cameras pinged and clicked.

"Get inside, baby girl."

Sabine did as her mother said. Mae followed and Noah shut the door. Tinted windows hid them from view.

Noah lowered himself into the passenger seat, and the driver, doing his best to appear unaffected by all the ruckus, maneuvered the car away from the crowd.

Noah twisted around to send Sabine an ominous look. "You left a few important details out, I see." He pointed at the copy of the *Washington Daily* in Sabine's lap. "What the hell is *that?*"

Sabine looked down at the picture, at Cullen's closed eyes, the line of his jaw and those full lips pressed to hers in a hungry kiss. She felt it all over again. The warm breath from his nose. His tongue reaching as desperately as hers. A tingle coursed through her just as it had then.

Oh, God, it was worse than she thought. How could it matter so much? They hadn't been together long enough.

"This could be damaging for him, you know. Doesn't that mean anything to you?"

"I didn't call the press, so stop blaming me." She jabbed the paper with her forefinger, venting her frustration, wishing she could turn off the emotions the photo wrung from her. "This isn't my fault!"

Beside her, her mother sucked an audible lungful of air. "So it's true?"

Feeling blood creep into her face, Sabine looked at her mother.

Mae's eyes widened. Then she looked crestfallen. "You were alone with the man Noah hired to rescue you...on a Greek island?"

"We..." Sabine faltered to hang on to her willpower and swallowed hard. Had her father only *hired* Cullen to rescue her? Who *was* he? She struggled with the hope that generated. What if he wasn't a mercenary?

Stop, she told her inner voice. He still had chosen to let her go, to never see her again.

"What happened?" her mother pressed.

In the rearview mirror, Sabine caught the driver's riveted glance.

"We...had trouble flying out of Afghanistan," she found the aplomb to say.

"The rescue helicopter was shot down, and they had to fly on low fuel to Athens," her father took over for her. "The plane crashed on Kárpathos. They were there for three days but only because Sabine wasn't well enough to travel commercially."

Sabine stared at her father. "When did Cullen tell you all that?"

Her father looked taken aback. "He *told* you his name?"

Fighting a flush with the memory of when he'd told her, Sabine stammered, "O-only his first name."

Noah cursed a line of swear words, glancing down at the photo with disgust. She couldn't tell whether it was aimed at her or Cullen.

Her mother gripped her hand and looked meaningfully into her eyes. "Did something happen between the two of you while you were on the island?"

Sabine pulled her hand away, sent her father a wary glance, saw his tightly held anger, then turned to look out the window.

"Oh, Mother Mary," Mae wailed. "Something did!"

"She's alive, damn it. Who else could have gotten her out of there?" Noah's fist pounded the dash. "I wouldn't have sent him if I hadn't known he was capable of pulling it off!"

"Are you going to see him again?" her mother asked on the heels of her father's outburst.

"No," Sabine answered shortly. Too shortly.

"Oh, baby girl..."

"The publicity will kill him," Noah said.

"She's coming home to Roaring Creek. Eventually the public interest will fade," Mae said shakily.

Noah ran his hand down his face, a clear indication of his agitation, and turned to look at Sabine. "Will you do that? Will you stay with your mother until the publicity dies down?"

Nothing appealed to her more than moving back to Roaring Creek. She belonged there. Never should have left. Maybe the woman underneath the pride-driven achievements would blossom again. All the As in physics and chemistry and calculus, all the daredevil contracting jobs, even the recognition as a distinguished hydrogeologist—none of that mattered in Roaring Creek. It was easy to agree with her father this one time.

She nodded.

"All right. Good. If anyone asks about the man in the photo, just tell them he was someone you knew from London but you ended your relationship because of your ordeal."

"I don't know if that'll wash." Mae tapped the newspaper with her finger. "Look at that. Neither one of them looks ready to give each other up."

Sabine did not want to see that picture ever again. "Don't worry, Mom. I'm never going to see him again and I'm okay with that." She looked at her father. "Trust me. I'm more than okay with that."

Cullen didn't straighten in the leather chair as Noah Page leaned over the conference room table and dropped a copy of the *Washington Daily* in front of him. It was a day old.

"What the hell is the matter with you?"

Looking at the front-page photo, reading the headline, Cullen had to cover his alarm.

"*Current Events* wants to interview my daughter on national television. What do you suppose they'll want to talk about?"

Cullen's mind raced. Where had the photographer been? It must have been a tourist or someone passing through the airport who recognized Sabine. The media couldn't have known they'd be there. Noah hadn't told a soul and neither had he. Not when someone close to the mission had leaked information about the rescue.

But how had he missed someone shooting pictures of him? Details in the photo came into sharper focus and he got his answer. Kissing Sabine had sapped his usual awareness. All he'd felt and thought while his tongue was in her mouth was how much he wished he'd spent more time with her in Kárpathos.

He raised his eyes. With his hands braced on the gleaming mahogany table, Noah's brow creased above his nose like the face of a hawk while he waited for some kind of reaction from Cullen.

Cullen hid it from him. He was too thrown by how easily Sabine had distracted him. In Kárpathos, when she'd kissed him, he'd been taken off guard by the strength of his passion. Kissing her in London had brought it all back. He couldn't, wouldn't, make the stretch and call it love, but sex with her had been equal to nothing he'd ever experienced. How was he supposed to explain that to Noah, a man who'd trusted him to save his daughter's life? A man he owed, at the very least, respect.

He looked down at the photograph again. Sabine's face had taken the brunt of the camera's lens, but it was where their lips joined that snared his attention. He could feel what it did to him. Even now. It could be the very thing that destroyed him.

If his commander learned of his mission, there would be no way to explain himself. If his contacts in the government learned of it… He swore inside his head. They were few but went all the way up to a senator. He had to protect them all. No matter what happened to him personally.

"Has anyone recognized me?" he finally asked.

"Not that I'm aware."

Cullen let go of his held breath. Maybe he'd gotten lucky and no one had seen enough detail to make a connection. The photographer hadn't been able to get a clear shot of him. At least he'd been careful about where he chose to part ways with Sabine. Good thing he was never going to see her again. Being with her consumed him to an unnerving degree.

"It's not like you to risk your career this way," Noah said.

Cullen kept his hearty agreement to himself. To think how close he'd come to losing himself in her....

"Judging from the looks of that picture, I can hardly believe you're the same man I sent to rescue my daughter."

Hearing the leashed anger in Noah's voice, Cullen knew what really bothered him. "Nothing happened that she didn't want, Mr. Page."

Noah lifted one of his hands from the table and pointed a finger in front of Cullen's face. "Don't 'Mr. Page' me. This is my *daughter* we're talking about. I asked you to get her out of Afghanistan, not screw her on a Greek island!"

Cullen looked unflinchingly into Noah's raging eyes. "I wouldn't have touched her if I didn't think it was mutual."

"She might have been vulnerable from being held captive by terrorists," Noah said caustically. "Did you ever think of that?"

Cullen pressed his mouth tight, unable to argue. Noah's daughter was a beautiful woman, and that beauty had muddled his brain. He wasn't accustomed to that kind of weakness.

Once Sabine started kissing him, he'd been lost in her. All thoughts of resisting had fled right along with the consequences. His career had no room for a woman like her. She needed a man who could invest the time to devote himself wholly and completely to her. He'd gleaned enough from her relationship with her father to know that much. Cullen didn't want that kind of love.

"Was she upset about never seeing you again?" Noah sounded like a worried father and made Cullen feel like a teenager in trouble for corrupting his little girl.

He faltered for words. Sabine had been upset, but not because she didn't understand the situation between them. Noah saw his hesitation, and his expression tightened with renewed rage.

"She knew I wouldn't be able to see her once we returned to the States," Cullen said quickly. But inside he wondered if she had. Before they'd made love, had she known? Even so, he doubted she'd considered the consequences until the next morning. He sure as hell hadn't.

Noah straightened and turned his back, moving to the window at one end of the conference room, where sunlight streamed through tinted glass and a view of the Miami skyline sprawled. "You shouldn't have let it happen."

Cullen lowered his gaze to the newspaper on the conference room table, studying the photograph that was sure to stir imaginations everywhere. He didn't think he could have resisted her even if he'd tried harder. The strength of it crept from nowhere and threatened to smother him.

"I'm sorry, Noah. If I hurt her, I never meant to."

Noah moved back toward the conference room table, stopping opposite from where Cullen sat.

"I owe you my life. The last thing I want to do is dishonor you or your daughter."

The rest of Noah's anger left his eyes. "You don't owe me your life. I'm more grateful to you for bringing Sabine home than you can possibly imagine."

Cullen pushed his chair back and stood, tucking his hands into the pockets of his white cotton shorts.

"What are you going to do about that?" Noah gestured to the newspaper on the table.

Knowing Noah was referring to the media, Cullen answered with his only option. "Wait until the curiosity dies down."

Noah smiled wryly. "That might take a while. Reporters are romanticizing Sabine's rescue to the hilt. It's on every channel. Everyone's wondering who the big, tall, dark-haired man is in the photo. It's you they're curious about, Cullen. More than her."

Cullen slid his hands from his pockets and lifted the newspaper to skim the article. Noah was right. In all, the article and photograph did a fine job of stirring interest in the identity of Sabine's rescuer. Sighing, he rubbed his eyes and ran his hand down his face. Kissing Sabine in the middle of an airport had to be one of the stupidest things he'd ever done.

"Well, look on the bright side," Noah said. "Even if you wanted to see her again, she wouldn't have anything to do with you anymore."

He lowered his hand. "Why not?"

"You're lower than dirt by association," Noah said, trying to sound flippant but failing.

"To you?"

"She thinks I'm a mercenary who prefers traveling the world spreading mayhem to settling down with her mother. Since I hired you to rescue her, she'll pin the same label on you."

"Mercenary."

Noah nodded.

Memories of dinner with Sabine made him chuckle.

"You find that amusing?"

"She's got fire in her, that's for sure."

Noah nodded again, looking rueful. "Got her mother's temper."

Cullen rolled the newspaper up and held it in his hand at his side. "Is that why she despises you? She thinks you're a merc?" He already knew but wanted to hear Noah's side of it.

"I was, at one time in my life. Now I just hire them."

Noah ran a private military company, but its purpose was security. Executives and foreign dignitaries hired his services, as did corporations with assets in foreign countries that needed guarding and natives who needed protection against rebel groups. For Noah, humanity came first on every mission. Sabine was wrong about him.

"You never lost sight of what was right," Cullen said.

"That's not what Sabine thinks."

"Sabine has never gotten over growing up without a father around."

"If I could have been around, I would have. I swear it."

"You don't have to convince me." Cullen smiled a little.

"She doesn't understand why I had to stay away, after years of trying to make it work with Mae."

"Why couldn't you?"

Noah turned his back, a clear attempt to hide his emotion. "I wasn't ready to give up my profession for Mae, and she wasn't willing to leave her hometown. At the time, I didn't think small-town life was for me."

"Isn't asking a man to give up his career a bit much?"

Noah faced him again. "Not if the career is controversial and keeps him from the woman he loves."

Cullen saw the genuine emotion in Noah's eyes and felt a flash of contrition. It was too close to what he'd done with Sabine—acted on concern for his career and left behind anything that might have sparked in Kárpathos. Or had it been more than that? Waking up after making love to her had knocked him off balance. The way he'd felt. He'd wanted nothing more than to get rid of her, to cut short the uneasy sensation crawling up his spine that she was like no other woman he'd met. He could fall into deep love with her. And deep love he did not do. Deep love wasn't for him. Not ever.

"It may be too late for Mae and me, but I want to make things right with my daughter," Noah said. "I want to know her and have a good relationship with her. You've given me a chance to do that, Cullen."

But not without a price. He'd lost four good men saving Sabine, and it never should have happened. No matter how many times he went over it in his head, he saw nothing he could have done differently. His plan had been solid. Nothing in the intelligence indicated they were dealing with anything other than terrorists. How could he have predicted that someone other than the kidnappers wouldn't want Sabine to make it out of there alive?

He'd have to work in the background to avoid the press, but he'd help Noah find those responsible. He wouldn't rest until he had retribution for his team.

As though reading his thoughts, Noah walked over to the center of the table and leaned over to press a button on the phone. The speaker came on and a woman answered.

"Yes, Mr. Page?"

"Bring me the al Hasan file."

"Have you found something?" Cullen asked, wondering if it would support his suspicions.

Noah didn't answer. Seconds later the conference room door opened and Noah's assistant entered the room. The slender brunette eyed Cullen up and down. Noah took the file from her.

"Thanks, Cindy."

Cindy smiled at Cullen with a smoky look. Cullen didn't encourage her. He turned his attention to Noah, and the woman left the conference room, closing the door behind her.

Noah handed him the file. He took it and put the newspaper on the table to free both hands. Opening the folder, he found a picture of Isma'il al Hasan, the leader of the group who'd kidnapped Sabine and Samuel. He flipped through other pages containing background information.

"I've confirmed he was killed in the explosion you and your team set," Noah said.

That came as good news to Cullen, for Sabine's sake. And Samuel's.

"He was a rebel who came from a wealthy family that has ties to al Qaeda," Noah went on as Cullen read. "He had the means to have a helicopter in the abandoned village where Sabine and Samuel were taken. He could have had it there all along as a precautionary measure."

Cullen shook his head. "It didn't show up in the satellite images. And that doesn't explain why someone was waiting for us in Egypt. Isma'il kidnapped your daughter, but he didn't do it for terrorism."

Noah sighed with frustration. "I've searched every angle. Why would Isma'il kidnap two American contractors for any other reason? He had confirmed ties to al Qaeda."

"Isma'il couldn't have known about the rescue mission. None of his men were expecting us. It wasn't until we were in flight with Sabine that things started to go wrong. Someone was waiting for us outside the village with the helicopter…like they didn't want Isma'il and his men to know they were there any more than we did. And mercenaries were waiting for us in Egypt like somebody hired them for the job. Whatever reason Sabine and Samuel were kidnapped, that same somebody wanted them dead."

"You think the men who attacked you knew about the kidnapping? Knew where Samuel and my daughter were being held and that Isma'il would kill them?"

Cullen said nothing, just let the plausibility of his assessment sink into Noah's mind.

"What you're suggesting is unthinkable! Who would do that? Sabine doesn't know why she was kidnapped. She couldn't tell authorities anything. She isn't a threat to anyone."

"Maybe whoever tried to stop her rescue didn't know that, or didn't want to take the chance that she did." But they must have had a reason to think she was, or might be, a threat. "Isma'il could have told them anything."

"Except he didn't."

"And now he's dead."

Noah ran his hand over his face, blowing out another long sigh.

"Sabine's kidnapping was all over the news," Cullen went on. "Her rescue is even more of a splash. What would happen if the truth got out? Who would it expose? Why did Isma'il kidnap the contractors to begin with, and why would someone want him to kill them?"

Noah stared at Cullen, his expression tight as he absorbed it all.

"Find the person who leaked the mission details, Noah. Then you'll find whoever did this." He paused. "My secretary is prepared to help in any way you need her." Odelia Frank wasn't just any secretary. The woman was amazing.

"No one in this organization would betray me like that."

"There's no other way it could have gotten out."

"The only person other than me and the operatives on your team who had access to that kind of information is Cindy, and I never told her where Sabine was, or your refueling locations."

"Could she have overheard you sometime? Maybe she or someone else stole the information without your knowledge."

"Why would she do that? Cindy is young, and she's not very bright."

Cullen didn't expect to solve everything right now. "Your daughter is in danger until you find that person, Noah. Nobody goes to that much trouble to try and kill someone if they don't have a reason to feel threatened. You can't assume it's over just because she's in the United States now." He put the file down onto the conference room table. "If I were you, I'd start with taking a harder look at Aden Archer and his company."

"Aden has been nothing but distraught over all this."

"It doesn't have to be him. It could be anyone working on that contracting job or anyone close to it."

"Sabine was there to assess groundwater conditions."

"A perfect cover for some other nefarious activity. Do you want to risk your daughter's life again?"

Without hesitation, Noah shook his head. "I'll dig deeper. I'll find who leaked the information. I just wish I had more to go on."

Gnawing dread churned inside Cullen. He was in danger of involving himself in this situation more than he could afford. This could destroy a career he'd worked years to develop. Did he want to throw it all away for a woman? No. No matter how great the urge was to go to Sabine, he had to stay away. No one could learn the truth about his company, however noble its purpose, and he had to protect the men he served. Men who could not admit to having anything to do with the creation of such a company.

"Maybe you should send someone to Roaring Creek to keep an eye on her," he said. The best he could do was make sure Sabine was safe. "The press has done a good job of convincing everyone she doesn't know why she was kidnapped, and the publicity might have scared whoever tried to kill her away for a while, but that could all change. What if Sabine gets too curious or remembers something she didn't think was significant before?"

"Don't worry. I already have someone on her. She'll be watched until we get to the bottom of this."

Wondering if the man Noah had assigned to Sabine was competent enough, wanting to ask but refusing to let himself, Cullen picked up the newspaper from the table. The photo drew him in, brought him back to the moment and convinced him he hadn't imagined the way it felt with her. He didn't feel comfortable leaving her safety up to Noah.

Or any other man, for that matter. Noah's men had experience guarding people and assets in foreign countries from rebels and other extremists. But would they know what to do with a more sophisticated foe?

He tucked the paper under his arm. "I'll have Odie call you."

Noah nodded. "I'll let you know if anything comes up."

Cullen moved toward the conference room door. The choice had been made. He'd made it when he left Sabine in London. No looking back.

Chapter 6

The media were really starting to annoy her. Sabine lifted a fondue set out of a box. In the four weeks since her return, they'd hounded her for information every chance they'd gotten. While she was no longer a headline, every now and again she'd catch a snippet about her, along with a photo. Her father's opening an office in Denver only kept the intrigue alive. He'd told the press he was doing it to be closer to his daughter. The gesture threatened to soften her defenses, something she'd done one too many times as a child—trusted her hope when she should have known better.

All she wanted to do was live a simple life here in Roaring Creek. Put Afghanistan behind her, forget her father's involvement in her rescue and his apparent change of heart. Cullen, too, though there hadn't been any sign of his leaving her mind. At least she had the bookstore to occupy her.

As soon as she'd arrived back in town, she'd seen this old two-story building for sale and known exactly what she wanted to do. Books, and not the scientific kind, were a piece of her she'd abandoned on her way to proving her worthiness through achievements. She didn't need to keep grabbing bulls by the horns. She could open a bookstore downstairs and live a simple life above it in this two-bedroom apartment. Just the thought alone gave her a boost of elation.

"Are you sure you're ready for this? It's only been a month."

Sabine turned to see her mother put a stack of plates into the kitchen cupboard, her shoulder-length red hair up in a clip.

"I can't live with you the rest of my life, Mom."

Mae reached for a stack of bowls and put them in the cupboard, with her green eyes glancing Sabine's way. "I wouldn't mind if you did. But maybe you should have at least stayed awhile longer. You know, until you were sure."

"I'm as sure as I'm going to get." Sabine put her fondue set in the cupboard above the refrigerator and stepped down from the stool. She moved to a box on the table. "You can't protect me from everything." Opening the box, she reached inside for a glass and began to unwrap it from the packing paper.

"Charlotte and Camille are close by anyway," her mother rationalized. Charlotte and Camille were twins who ran the local bakery. "If you need them, their house is just down the street."

"So are Elwin and Cloe and Buddy. I'll be all right, Mom. Like you said, there are people close by. I live in town."

"I don't like thinking of you all alone when you can't sleep."

Reminded of the dream she'd had the night before, Sabine stared at the wineglass she was about to put away. It was the same dream she'd had in Kárpathos. Details seeped into her conscience even as she tried to ward them off. The knife. Samuel. Isma'il. The face of the beast.

"Do you want to talk about it?" Mae asked.

Sabine shook her head. "It's just a bad dream."

"Maybe if you tell me about it, they won't wake you anymore."

Sabine held the wineglass tighter as the same sick feeling churned in her. In the dream, the beast turned to face her. It always started with the back of his head. There was something familiar about it. She went still.

"Sabine?" She barely heard her mother.

That was it! The beast turning…its face morphed into a man's. Someone recognizable. Sabine's heart raced.

Isma'il.

She saw him clearly for the first time. How his cold, beady eyes blazed a hateful gaze into hers. How his head turned to face Samuel, presenting the back of his head to her while he resumed the torture that had eventually killed her field partner. She couldn't go there. Couldn't remember that. It was too horrible. But another time came to her, when Isma'il walked away after one of his brutal beatings. The back of his head again.

The back of his head.

A chill spread through her skin. She'd seen it before. Her heart raced faster. No. No. It couldn't be.

"Sabine? Are you all right?" Her mother started to approach.

Too overwhelmed with the horror of her realization, Sabine didn't answer. She'd seen the back of Isma'il's head before her abduction. Aden had met him in the village where she and Samuel were working. She remembered telling Samuel about it. And he'd thought it was odd. Had he known something?

Aden had met with Isma'il.

The glass she still held slipped from her hand and shattered on the cream-colored tile floor.

Her mother gasped, watching Sabine with confused and deeply concerned eyes.

Sabine put her hand on the kitchen countertop to support herself. She was dizzy with the realization that Aden had met with the man who'd killed Samuel.

Or had he?

Was she certain Isma'il was the man Aden had met? Or were her dreams out of proportion with reality?

You couldn't tell authorities anything that might help? The question Aden had asked when she'd first arrived home in Denver echoed in her mind. Was he relieved she hadn't known why she'd been kidnapped?

"Sabine, tell me what's wrong." Her mother's voice penetrated her shock.

Sabine lifted her hand to her forehead, hearing her own breathing and feeling her rapid pulse going helter-skelter. She shook her head. "I-I'm all right." She knelt to clean up the broken glass.

Her mother knelt with her, doing a poor job of covering her sob. But Sabine couldn't summon the wherewithal to reassure her any further. She was too overwrought.

What if her dream was not so far from the truth? What if Aden had known Isma'il? Someone had gone to great lengths to try to stop her rescue. Someone other than Isma'il and his men. Had Aden wanted her and Samuel to die?

Prickles of dismay made Sabine even more sick to her stomach. Bile rose in her throat, and in the next instant she knew she was going to throw up. Rushing to the bathroom, she fell light-headed to her knees before the toilet. If Aden had known the man who'd slaughtered Samuel, had he known the reason for their abduction? Could he have prevented it?

Sabine had dry heaves above the toilet. *Samuel.* Oh, God.

Their kidnapping couldn't have had anything to do with Aden's dealings with Isma'il. It was too horrible to imagine. Yet, the helicopter that had come after them, and the attack in Egypt, made it plausible. Aden wouldn't want anyone to know his connection to Isma'il.

With a pale, trembling hand over her mouth, Sabine slumped onto her rear and leaned against the wall. She still felt so ill that it made her weak. She closed her eyes and struggled to make sense of it.

"Are you pregnant?"

Sabine opened her eyes like a spring had triggered them and froze, staring up at her mother. Mae stood in the doorway of the bathroom, anxiousness tight in her brow. The consequences had mattered very little after the first time she'd kissed Cullen. She'd reached out to him after her dream, but something stronger had led to the intimacy they'd shared.

"No," she answered her mother stiffly. "It isn't that." It couldn't be, thank God. Having a baby would be the cruelest irony, following in her mother's footsteps and raising a child on her own. At least she didn't have to worry about that. At least that much about her and Cullen was different than her mother's relationship with Noah.

"Then what just happened here?"

Sabine didn't want to worry her mother if her suspicions were wrong. So she had a terrible dream… That wasn't unusual given what she'd survived. She had to be sure before she started pointing her finger at Aden.

"I was just thinking about Samuel," she said, her mind still reeling.

How could she confirm it was Isma'il whom Aden had met in the village? She'd never mentioned to the authorities that she'd seen Aden with a local villager. Nothing in the press revealed she knew anything about the reason for her abduction. She shouldn't pose a threat to anyone. But what if Samuel had known something? It would have been so like him to protect her by not telling her anything. And Aden might have assumed she knew just as much as Samuel.

Sabine drove into Denver, worrying if she was doing the right thing. She wasn't comfortable going straight to Aden. What if her dream had nothing to do with reality? It could be a by-product of her trauma. Maybe Samuel's wife could tell her something. Maybe he'd said something to her about Aden. Anything that might give Sabine a clue, confirm or dispel what the dream suggested.

She had to stop for directions at a gas station, but finally she made her way to Lisandra's house on Cathay Street, a middle-class subdivision of Aurora, Colorado. The brick-and-beige-colored tri-level had mature landscaping and a big lot. Sabine parked in the driveway, glancing around her as she walked to the front door. Ringing the doorbell, she waited. Lisandra might not even be home. Sabine hadn't called first.

But the door swung open and Lisandra stood still, staring at Sabine, obviously recognizing her from media pictures. Her thick, dark hair was up in a messy clip, and her dark eyes looked weary and lost.

"I'm sorry to stop by without calling you," Sabine said.

Lisandra opened the door wider. "Come in."

Sabine stepped inside, seeing a kitchen with hickory floors to her left, and a railing overlooking a spacious living room to her right.

"I'm sorry about Samuel," Sabine said, facing Lisandra. "He talked about you all the time."

Lisandra lowered her head. Her mouth pressed tight, as though struggling with emotion. After a moment she lifted her head again. "You didn't have to come here and tell me that."

"Actually, there's another reason I'm here." She hesitated, uncertain about how much to tell her. Not much, that's for sure. She didn't want to put the woman in any danger. "Samuel said something just before we were kidnapped. I wondered if… I wondered… Well, it may be nothing but I need to be sure." She faltered for words.

"What is it? What did he say? Please, tell me."

"He seemed to think Aden's visits to the valley were odd. Did he ever say anything to you?"

"What would Aden's visits to the site have to do with your kidnapping?"

"Maybe nothing. Samuel just thought it was odd, and I wondered if he had said anything to you. Maybe in one of his letters? Even if you didn't think anything of it at the time."

Disappointment dulled Lisandra's eyes. "No. He never mentioned anything about Aden, on the phone or in any of his letters. Why? Do you think Aden knows something?"

Sabine sighed with her own disappointment. "I don't know. I may be reaching."

"No," Lisandra quickly disagreed, touching Sabine's forearm as though in emphasis. "If there's anything that will help bring Samuel's killers to justice, I'm glad to know you'll try."

Sabine nodded and didn't know what else to say.

"Envirotech did send a package to me," Lisandra said, dropping her hand.

Sabine straightened as her alertness sharpened.

"It came last week. It's with his belongings from…over there." Her eyes took on a drawn look and her lower lip trembled. "I haven't been able to open it yet, but maybe you'll find something that will help you."

"Does Aden know it was sent?"

"I don't know. His name wasn't on the return address. It was from one of the other contractors."

Would Aden have checked the contents first? Maybe he never had a chance. Maybe he hadn't known the contractor had mailed it. Could she be so lucky…?

Lisandra led her past a wall and up some stairs on the other side. At the first room, she stepped aside. "There's a box in the closet."

Sabine sensed the woman's tension. Without commenting or showing any notice, she went to the closet and started to root through the contents of the box.

Other than clothes and other personal items, she found his backpack. She lifted that out and unzipped the opening. Reaching inside, she pulled out an empty water bottle, a change of clothes, an old granola bar and finally an orange field book. Samuel's field book. He'd had it with him the day they were abducted. The contractor Lisandra mentioned must have been the one to find it and put it with Samuel's things.

She opened the front cover. Three pictures fell to the floor. She knelt and picked them up, staring with foreboding at the first. Two men she didn't recognize stood inside a narrow, badly disintegrating building with hats hanging along one side. It looked like a hat shop in a filthy bazaar somewhere. She didn't know where, only that it was somewhere in the Middle East. The second picture showed the men shaking hands. The third showed them walking toward the back of the hat shop.

Tucking the pictures back in the field book, she leafed through the pages to make sure Samuel hadn't written anything other than field notes. He hadn't.

She had no way of identifying the men in the photos, and the only person she knew who could she didn't want to see.

* * *

Sabine left Lisandra's with Samuel's field book, managing to avoid telling her about the photos. Outside, she noticed someone open the driver's door of a white minivan. A spark of apprehension sent her pulse flying. But then the man lifted a camera and started shooting pictures. In an instant, she knew that stopping for directions at the gas station had cost her this. Now Aden would know she'd come to see Lisandra. Would he wonder why?

She tried to hide the field book but feared it was already too late.

"Excuse me, Ms. O'Clery!" the reporter shouted, hurrying toward her. "Whose house is this?"

Sabine reached her Jeep and climbed in.

"Did you meet your rescuer here?"

She turned a glare on the reporter and shut the Jeep door.

Revving the engine, she squealed the tires racing away. The reporter didn't try to follow. A few minutes later, she drove onto Wilcox Street in Castle Rock, just off I-25, and found the brick building her father had rented. Parking, she noticed a dark green Civic in front of the building, one she'd seen parked outside her bookstore more than once, or one like it. No, it was the same one. It had a dented front left bumper and fender and a cracked windshield. She hesitated before walking toward the darkly tinted glass windows and doors of Noah's new office.

Noah opened the door before she got there, his face tense with lines of frustration. "Where have you been?" he demanded.

She entered the building, not liking the fatherly concern she heard in his voice. The sound of remodeling under way echoed, banged and buzzed. A man with pitted skin and dark eyes leaned idly against a wall ahead of her. She tried to remember if she'd ever seen him before but couldn't.

She turned to her father. "Who is that?"

"He's supposed to keep an eye on you."

Sabine couldn't believe it. "You have someone watching me?" A *mercenary* was watching her.

"You weren't supposed to leave Roaring Creek. You said you wouldn't. He lost you on the way here. You don't know how worried I've been." Noah turned an accusatory glance on the man.

The man raised his hands in protest. "It's a long drive from Roaring Creek to Denver."

"Why didn't you tell me?" Sabine rounded on Noah.

"It's for your own good."

"My own…" She narrowed her eyes as she began to piece things together. "Why do you have someone watching me? Do you know something?"

"No, I—"

"You know something and didn't tell me." Aggravated, she growled low in her throat. "Oh, that is so like you."

"I don't know anything."

"Then why are you having me followed?"

"Where did you go?" her father demanded again, ignoring her temper.

"Tell me why you feel I need protection first."

Noah signed in resignation. "You're as stubborn as your mother." He paused before he relented. "I still don't know who tried to stop your rescue."

"But no one's come after me here in the States. Why do you think anyone would?"

"The media have done us a favor in that regard. It's obvious you don't know why you were kidnapped."

"Then I don't need a bodyguard."

"I disagree. Until I know who's behind your kidnapping, that's how it's going to be, Sabine."

She pointed her finger at him. "Don't you talk to me like that. I'm not your daughter."

"You are my daughter, and whether you like it or not, I'm going to protect you."

She narrowed her eyes at him again but held her tongue and lowered her hand.

He looked down at the field book. "What's that you're holding? Where did you go just now?"

She looked down at the book, then back up at her father. She had no choice other than to trust him with this. "I went to see Lisandra Barry. Envirotech sent her Samuel's things. I found this among them." She handed him the field book.

He took it from her and turned. She followed him into a conference room, glancing at the man with pitted skin on her way. He stayed behind, a silent watcher. Her bodyguard. It frightened her to know her father thought she needed one.

Inside the conference room, Noah closed the door and faced her. He opened the cover and found the photos, taking his time looking at each one. At last, he raised his head.

"Do you know who these men are?"

She shook her head. "That's why I came here." The only reason.

He looked down at the top photo in his hand. "I've been to this bazaar before."

"In the photo?" Then she realized. Of course, in his active days as a mercenary, he'd been there.

"It's the Khyber Bazaar, not far from the Afghanistan border in Pakistan."

"What does it mean?"

"I don't know. Maybe nothing. But as soon as I know something, I'll tell you. I promise."

He was going to tell her? Noah? She was taken aback. And she believed him, which made her uneasy. It sneaked past her defenses and warmed her.

"You told me you'd stay in Roaring Creek," he said, repeating his earlier comment.

"I…"

"I need you to stay there, Sabine. No more driving alone down the mountain and into the city where anything can happen to you."

He seemed genuinely concerned. She wanted to tell him about her dream, but she stopped herself. It was too easy to fall into old patterns and trust him with her heart. The dream disturbed her too much. She wasn't comfortable with him seeing that much of her emotions.

"What do you know about Aden?" she asked instead.

"Archer? Why are you asking?"

"He might know something about the kidnapping. Samuel and I were his contractors."

He studied her face and she could see his question. Why was she asking? She appreciated that he didn't press her. "So far, he's clean. Don't go near him, Sabine. You leave that to us. You stay in Roaring Creek, do you understand?"

"Us?"

He hesitated. "Me and the others working to find the people who tried to stop your rescue."

Cullen? Was he still involved? She didn't welcome the surge of warmth that thought gave her. She decided not to ask her father. The last thing she needed was to start wondering if Cullen cared more than she thought.

"I don't want you digging any deeper into this, Sabine. If Aden was involved in your kidnapping, I don't want him to have a reason to get nervous."

She looked down at the field book. It might be too late for that. But she nodded to her father.

Late the next afternoon, Sabine was about to leave for the supermarket when a buzzer sounded, indicating that someone was at her back door. Going down the stairs and into the office behind what would soon be her bookstore, she peered through the peephole and saw Aden.

The shock of it gave her a jolt. What was he doing here? It was too much of a coincidence after the blurb of her visit to Samuel's wife. But if she didn't answer the door, she might lose an opportunity to learn something. Besides, her father had found nothing incriminating against him. And she had her very own mercenary for a bodyguard.

Too curious not to, she opened the door.

Aden smiled without showing any teeth, his narrow face framed by thin, straight, dark hair. "Sabine."

"Hello, Aden."

"I came by to see how you were doing. I hope you don't mind."

She shook her head. Instead of letting him inside, she stepped out onto the back stairs and left the door open. "I'm fine. You could have just called instead of driving all this way."

"I had to see for myself." His brown gaze took a quick look over her before meeting her eyes again. "You look great."

"Thank you," she said. Was he telling the truth, or did he have another reason for coming here?

"Things seem to keep popping up in the news about you," he commented.

"Everyone loves a happy ending." She smiled cheekily, while inside her heart flew. Why was he bringing that up?

"Was it a happy ending for you?"

"I'm alive."

"No, I mean about that man in the *Washington Daily* photo."

She knew what he meant. "Oh." She didn't know what else to say.

"They keep waiting to catch you with him," he said.

"I suppose the London airport photo is to blame for that."

"No supposing about it." Aden grinned.

In other words, the photo revealed an intriguing amount of passion between her and her mysterious rescuer. She hid her discomfort. She could still feel that kiss whenever she saw that picture.

"Did you meet him at Lisandra Barry's like the article speculates?"

She breathed a single laugh to cover her anxiety. He was leading up to something. "No."

"Why did you go there, then?"

"I haven't seen Lisandra since I came home. I wanted to pay my respects."

Was that doubt she saw cross his eyes? "The photo showed you holding a field book," he said. "Was it Samuel's?"

She hesitated. "You noticed I was holding his field book?"

"Why did you take it with you?"

"Why do you want to know?"

His smile was too wily. "Someone tried to stop your rescue. I'm as interested as your father in finding out why."

She didn't believe him. "You talked to my father?"

"He came to ask me some questions."

"Really?" She tried to sound surprised. "Why did he question you?"

"Do you have the field book?" he asked instead of answering.

Cold apprehension rushed her. Did he know about the photos? How? He must not have been able to find them before they were shipped to Lisandra, and now he suspected they were hidden in the field book.

"You're awfully persistent over something as benign as a field book," she hedged.

He didn't say anything, just looked at her with steady, unflinching eyes.

They were playing cat and mouse, and she had to let him know she wasn't planning on being the mouse. "I saw you meet with one of the locals in the village where we were working," she said, hoping it wasn't a mistake. "Maybe that has more to do with why you're here than Samuel's field book."

He stared at her for several more seconds. "Who did you see me meet?"

"I was going to ask you that very same thing, Aden."

His eyes narrowed. "Be careful, Sabine. This goes deeper than just me."

Chills sprinkled down her arms. Her pulse quickened. He may as well have admitted his involvement outright.

"Aden, if you know something…"

A sound to her left made her turn with him. The man from the dark green Civic emerged from around the corner of her building, walking with a slow, long stride, watching Aden.

"Is everything all right here?" he asked.

"Fine," she said, eyeing Aden.

"I was just leaving," he said, meeting her look. "If I could have done something to help you over there, I would have, Sabine. Remember that."

What did he mean? Was he trying to tell her he was a victim like her?

Or had he met with Isma'il and played a hand in her and Samuel's kidnapping, one he now wished he could withdraw?

The next morning, Sabine parked in the grocery store lot. As she locked her car, her mind still raced with everything Aden had said, and what he hadn't. Her bodyguard had questioned her about Aden's visit and said he'd relay the information to Noah. She hadn't told him about her dream, though. What would it gain? Noah had already questioned Aden, and Aden wasn't talking.

"Ms. O'Clery?"

Turning, Sabine saw a tall, slender woman with short dark hair approach from the direction she'd just come.

"Rhea Graham with *Current Events*."

A sinking feeling tumbled through her middle. She didn't move to take the woman's outreached hand.

"We've been trying to reach you by phone," Rhea said. "I'm sorry to sneak up on you like this, but you really gave us no other alternative."

Facing the reporter fully, Sabine cocked her head at the woman's audacity.

"Have you given some more thought to doing an interview with us?" Rhea asked.

"I don't need to. I'm not doing an interview. Not with anyone. I'm sorry, you've wasted your time coming here." She started toward the grocery store entrance.

The reporter kept up with her. "How important is it to you to keep your rescuer's identity a secret, Ms. O'Clery?"

Sabine's steps slowed and she glanced at the woman.

"Someone close to your father knew things about your rescue no one else could," Rhea said. "It's how we learned of your crash landing in Greece. With a little more digging, it won't be long before we have a name."

Sabine stopped altogether and faced the woman again. How much had her contact told her? It couldn't have been too much, or it would have been all over the news by now. "My father isn't that careless in his line of work."

"Are you sure about that? I thought you were estranged from him."

True. She had no way of knowing whom her father employed, much less about those he'd entrusted with information concerning her rescue. But even if he'd made a mistake, Cullen wouldn't have. "You're bluffing."

"Are you willing to take that chance?" In Sabine's silence, she added, "This contact says she has a phone number. We're working on convincing her to give it to us. She claims the number can be traced to the man your father hired to rescue you."

"Her?"

The reporter smiled. "It's your story we want, Ms. O'Clery. The more people who are curious about your rescuer, the more our ratings go up. The man in the *Washington Daily* photo can stay a mystery as long as the public stays interested…as long as you want him to stay a mystery."

"You can't trace his number. He wouldn't have used a traceable line." Cullen wasn't a stupid man. Then again, there was a picture of him kissing her in the London airport.

The reporter smiled. "Maybe not. But if we keep looking, eventually something will turn up. A tiny clue that leads to a slightly bigger one that leads to something else." She raised her brow with a sly look. "He can't hide forever."

Sabine felt her pulse throb and tried to conceal her growing need for more air. "You're saying that if I agree to this interview, you won't try to expose the man who saved my life."

"That's exactly what I'm saying. But only if he stays away from you. If we see him with you, the deal is off."

"You won't." If she'd learned anything from her father, it was that a man like Cullen would have no problem staying away.

"Then you'll do it?"

"How do I know you'll keep your word? And what about other reporters?"

"No one other than me knows about the contact who's close to your father."

"Tell me who she is."

"Do you agree to do the interview?"

"I'll talk about the rescue, but I refuse to talk in detail about my captivity. Or the men who rescued me."

"Agreed."

"Now tell me the name of your contact."

Chapter 7

"Isn't your girlfriend going to be on *Current Events* this morning?"

Cullen sent Penny a withering glance from the kitchen, where he was helping Luc pack for yet another fishing trip. Both of them had been making comments like that ever since he'd arrived to wait out the Sabine O'Clery media frenzy. "She's not my girlfriend." And she better not have agreed to appear on national television.

From the chair at the end of the table, his uncle's eyes lifted from his tackle box and Cullen could read his silent skepticism.

Something had happened between him and Sabine in Kárpathos and his uncle knew it. It didn't help that his uncle had seen the newspaper he'd taken from Noah's conference room. Cullen had taken it on impulse. He'd been surprised by how much the photo revealed. More than a kiss between a man and a woman, it showed how invested they were in each other. How invested he'd been. Maybe still was.

The television went from a commercial to the *Current Events* show. A blonde anchorwoman started talking.

"A little more than a month ago, Sabine O'Clery was rescued from her captors by a group of men working independently from the U.S. government…."

Cullen rose to his feet as the anchorwoman continued. What the hell was she doing? He raged inside. Why had she agreed to appear on *Current Events?* She was going to ruin him yet!

"She and one other contractor were assessing groundwater conditions in the Panjshir Valley when they were abducted and taken to an abandoned village. Little is known about the group who captured the contractors, but their leader, a man by the name of Isma'il al Hasan, is believed to have ties to al Qaeda. One of the contractors was killed during captivity, but Sabine O'Clery was miraculously spared." The short-haired, mid-thirties anchorwoman turned to Sabine. "Ms. O'Clery, can you tell us what happened the day you were captured?"

The camera moved to Sabine. In a black pantsuit with a white blouse under a stylish jacket, she glowed with health. Cullen couldn't help noticing other things, too. Though she sat on a sofa and her clothes covered her well, he could tell she'd gained weight. Her face was fuller, her curly red hair shinier. She was even more striking than he remembered. Her green eyes stood out with the dark lines of her lashes, and her lips were glossy and full of color.

Cullen realized he'd tuned out what she was saying as the anchorwoman asked her about her job and what she was doing in Afghanistan. He was that absorbed in seeing her again. The sight of her fed his starved eyes. He didn't know what to do with such a foreign inundation of feeling. She threw him off center. And a gnawing desire mushroomed in him to find her, be with her again.

"What happened to the other contractor? Why were you the one who survived?"

Cullen watched her face as the question was asked, saw how her eyes grew blank with memory. Why had she agreed to this interview? She must have had a reason. Was she doing it to spite her father? Him? To gain popularity? Money? What?

"I—I don't know why...." He saw her swallow. Her eyes lowered.

"It must have been terrible."

Sabine didn't respond to what Cullen thought was a lame attempt to get her to talk. After a few seconds the anchorwoman gave up and tried a new approach.

"Did you see what happened to the other contractor?"

Cullen tensed with the question.

"I'm sorry, I can't talk about it. I just can't." She shook her head and he knew she was struggling with her emotions. Her hands were gripped tightly in her lap.

"Was he tortured?"

Sabine moved her eyes to look at the anchorwoman. The slight quiver of her hair told Cullen she was starting to tremble. He wanted to reach through the television and choke the anchorwoman for asking such a difficult question. Obviously, she had seen what happened to the other contractor, and it had been horrific.

Sabine turned from the anchorwoman and looked into the camera that was focused on her. For an instant Cullen felt as though she were looking right at him, and it arrowed straight into his heart.

"Can you tell us what happened to Samuel? Samuel Barry."

A photo of Samuel smiling with his wife appeared on the screen.

Tears visibly pooled in Sabine's eyes. Cullen's hand curled into a fist, and he realized he'd moved closer to the television, oblivious to Penny and Luc.

"I'm sorry," the anchorwoman said. "I know this must be hard for you."

He watched Sabine fight for control of her crumbling emotions. "I can't…talk about that. You agreed not to…" A tear slid down her cheek.

"I understand. How about you tell us what happened when you were rescued, then?"

Sabine took the tissue the anchorwoman extended to her. Her eyes had that haunted, faraway look of someone who'd seen horrors no one else could imagine. Or ever wanted to.

"Who was it that organized the mission?" the anchorwoman asked.

Sabine stared at some point in the studio and answered absently, "I don't know."

"If it wasn't the U.S. military, then who was it?"

Sabine's head turned slowly toward the anchorwoman. "I wouldn't know anything about how my rescue was planned."

"Your father owns a company called Executive Indemnity Corporation, with headquarters in Miami. There have been reports on some of their activities. Your father's company is a private military company, isn't that right?"

Sabine didn't comment.

"Was it your father who organized your rescue?" the anchorwoman asked.

"My father abandoned me before I was born."

"So you're saying it wasn't your father who organized your rescue?"

"No, I'm saying my father hasn't been a part of my life. Ever."

"But he must care about you or he wouldn't have helped to free you from your captors."

Sabine said nothing, but Cullen could see she was torn, as though she wanted her father to care about her but didn't want to believe or couldn't bring herself to believe he did. Even though he'd arranged her rescue.

"Did your father hire the man in the *Washington Daily* photo? Does he know the man shown in that picture?"

"I don't know who rescued me." A true enough statement, Cullen thought with a pang of regret.

The anchorwoman smiled too shrewdly for his comfort. "What happened that day, Sabine? How were you rescued?"

Sabine sighed and cleared her throat, sitting rigidly in the chair. "A soldier broke down the door and told me he was from the United States and that he was going to get me out of there."

"A soldier? So he's U.S. military?"

"That's what I thought. I—I mean, that's what I assumed. He never said who he was."

"Is he the man in the photo from the *Washington Daily?*"

The stirrings of anger appeared in Sabine's eyes. "The man who rescued me was part of a team of several other men. I was flown to an airstrip, where a plane was waiting to fly me to London."

A very brief explanation of what had actually occurred. Cullen was impressed. She'd also avoided answering the woman's question.

"Your helicopter crashed before you made it out of Afghanistan, isn't that correct?"

Sabine wondered if that piece of information had gotten out along with the plane crash.

"Yes, but another one arrived shortly after and took us to an airstrip."

"Where was the airstrip?"

"I don't know. I wasn't aware of much except the fact that I was getting out of Afghanistan."

"What happened once you were on the plane?"

"I was flown to London."

"Didn't the plane crash?"

Sabine didn't answer the anchorwoman. He could see she knew as well as he where this line of questioning was going. Hadn't she considered this possibility when she'd agreed to appear on national television?

"We have it from a reliable source that your plane crashed on a Greek island."

Sabine's anger fired hotter in her eyes. She pinned the anchorwoman with a warning stare. "One of the men on the team was forced to crash-land the plane. We didn't know where we were at the time. We knew we were on an island somewhere in the Mediterranean, but it wasn't until we walked to a nearby village that we knew it was Kárpathos."

Cullen cringed at her use of the word *we* after referring to "one of the men."

"When you say, 'we,' do you mean you and the man in the *Washington Daily* photo?"

Sabine blinked twice but didn't lose her cool. "No," she lied.

"Why did both the helicopter and the plane crash?"

"The plane didn't really crash. It was more of a rough landing."

"But what caused both the helicopter and the plane to go down?"

"The helicopter was shot down during the rescue."

"And the plane?"

"I'm not sure, exactly."

"Do you think it's possible terrorists held you captive and tried to kill you when you escaped?"

"Yes, that's possible."

"Could it have been anyone else?"

A brief pause. "I don't see how." Cullen saw the doubt in her eyes and wondered if anyone else could. Her vague answers were enough to raise curiosity.

"It's ironic that you were forced to land where you did. What was it like to find yourself in the middle of paradise after surviving such a terrible ordeal?"

Cullen felt like cursing loudly.

"We were very lucky to make it to an island. We could have crashed into the sea."

"Very lucky, indeed." The anchorwoman nodded, her accompanying smile knowing. She let a second or two pass. "We spoke with one of the villagers in Kárpathos, where the destroyed plane was discovered." Cullen inwardly grimaced, knowing his predicament was about to get much, much worse. "A woman who recognized you from this photograph—" she held the cover of *Washington Daily* up into the camera's view "—told us she saw a man carry you through the village to a local pension. She described you as newlyweds whose private plane had crashed on the island. She said you were alone with this man and didn't leave your hotel room for two full days, and when you did finally leave it, the two of you walked down to a secluded beach, where you spent more time alone together. She invited you to her taverna, which she said you accepted and shared a romantic dinner. Octopus, I believe, is what she said you both ate that night."

Sabine's green eyes were wide with shock, and her face flushed a telling shade of red. She stared at the anchorwoman with her lips slightly parted, no doubt to accommodate for the rapid breaths he could see she was taking. She might as well admit defeat now. Every inch of her body communicated without words that everything the anchorwoman said was true. Damn her. Didn't she know the media would focus on all the speculation surrounding the plane crash?

Cullen closed his eyes and pinched the bridge of his nose, wanting to groan.

There was a poignant silence on the television, and he was certain millions of Americans were riveted by this new turn of events.

"Was the man you were with one of your rescuers? The man in the *Washington Daily* photo?"

Cullen looked over his fingers at the television and Sabine's flushed face.

"I can't…comment on that."

The anchorwoman smiled. "Did you have an affair with him?"

"I'm sorry, I—"

"Are you still?"

"No!"

Cullen ran his hand down his face with a rough sigh. She was killing him.

His uncle grunted a derisive laugh. "You might as well kiss that company of yours goodbye, son."

Sabine parted a section of the wooden blinds on her living room window and saw the white minivan still parked down the street. It was after 10:00 p.m. The throng of reporters that had swarmed her bookstore after her appearance on *Current Events* had dwindled to this single man. Minivan Man, she was going to start calling him. He was an annoying, persistent little fellow, waiting like a dog frothing at the mouth for a chance to catch her with her secret lover.

Disgusted, she let the blinds go and carried her glass of iced tea toward the stairs. After the *Current Events* broadcast, the news had buzzed with curiosity over Cullen's identity and romanticized what had mushroomed into their torrid affair on a Greek island. The hype disturbed her, mostly because it made her think about Kárpathos—and Cullen—too much.

She stepped down the narrow stairway and emerged into the bookstore office. Flipping on lights as she went, she entered the main area of the bookstore. She passed a section of tall empty shelves where boxes of books were scattered and put her glass of iced tea on the checkout counter near the front of the store.

The books she'd ordered had arrived earlier that day but she'd waited for the cover of night to begin unpacking them. She'd dipped into her 401(k) to buy a collection of general fiction, literary fiction, nonfiction, children's books and touristy books about the region to stock her shelves. The front corner of the bookstore was under renovation and would be a coffee counter with a few quaint round tables near the front windows. Maybe she'd plant flowers in pots on the sidewalk in front of the building this summer.

A noise in the back of the store made her go still. Holding three hardcover books in her hand, she looked toward her office. Rows of shelves formed a hallway that was slightly offset from the office entrance, so she couldn't see it from where she was. Was someone in there?

Her heart started to beat faster. She put the books down and stood. Moving to the checkout counter, she pulled out the 9 mm pistol she kept on the shelf under the register. Buddy from the liquor store had taught her how to use it after she'd come home from Afghanistan. Inserting a loaded clip, she moved out from behind the counter and headed for her office, holding the pistol with both hands and pointing it ahead of her. The hallway of shelves allowed her to keep out of view of the doorway leading to the office.

The sound of the back door opening made her jump into the space between the last two shelves near her office door.

She closed her eyes and willed herself to have courage. Someone had broken into her bookstore. Blood drained from her head and she fought the rise of an all-too-familiar fear.

Footsteps shuffled. It sounded like more than one person. One grunt accompanied another. She leaned around the corner of the shelf. Two men crossed the doorway, locked in a fighting struggle. Both held a gun and both gripped the other's arm to prevent either from taking aim. She recognized her bodyguard, the smaller of the two. The bigger man tripped him and he fell.

She had to do something. Gun raised, she emerged from the row of shelves and hurried to the office door. Peering around the frame, she saw the bigger man standing over her bodyguard, aiming his weapon. A file cabinet blocked most of his body from her. He was going to shoot the man on the floor.

"No!" Sabine shouted and fired her pistol.

But the big man fired, too, one silenced shot that hit her bodyguard. She could tell because he groaned and rolled onto his side. She saw only his chest and head, but it was enough to know he struggled to reach his gun, which was too far away.

Sabine didn't have time to help him. The big man—tall, lean, with dark hair and eyes—swung his weapon toward her. She pivoted and ran from the office, ducking behind the first row of empty shelves, hearing a bullet hit wood. She fired her gun through the space of a shelf, forcing the man to stay behind the wall of the office. Her gun wasn't muffled and the explosions rang her ears. She ran to the end of the row and moved up the next one, crouching low, trying to see through the mesh of shelving.

Hearing the sound of slow footfalls on her wood floor, fear cauterized her. That awful fear. She moved along the shelf. The man appeared around the edge of the row. She fired again. He jumped behind the shelf. She turned to run, heard him chase her. Before she made it to the end of the row, he tripped her from behind. She went down on her hands and knees, the gun skittering from her grasp and bouncing off the wall just ahead of her. Rolling to her rear, she kicked her leg up and connected with the big man's hand. His gun went sailing over the top of the shelf to her left and fell to the floor on the other side.

The man unbuckled his belt and whipped it free of his black jeans. Sabine rolled back onto her hands and knees and scrambled toward her gun. She would not fall prey to anyone ever again. She'd kill this man without a second thought!

The tether of her hair stopped her. The man yanked her back toward him. Her scalp stung where he pulled. He looped the belt around her neck and released her hair. Sabine clawed at the belt as it tightened on her throat, furious with herself for allowing this to happen.

Choking for air, and getting little, she reached for something, anything that would provide her a weapon. Her pistol still lay a few feet away, too far for her to reach. A box she'd opened but hadn't begun to empty yet was right next to her. She reached inside for a hardback Webster's dictionary and aimed the corner at her assailant's head. With a hard wallop, she hit something that made him grunt and loosen his hold. She yanked the belt from her throat, gagging and gasping as she crawled for her gun. She stretched her arm. Her fingers curled around the handle. Rolling onto her back, she started firing.

The man scrambled to escape the explosion of bullets. She emptied her gun.

He ran into her office. She followed but only when she heard her bodyguard fire his gun. A shout and the big man's stumble told her he was hit, but he managed to run out the back door before her bodyguard could finish him off.

Reclining on a hammock in his uncle's backyard, Cullen rested his head on one folded arm, his other hand on his stomach. He chewed on a straw left over from the chocolate milk Penny had given him while he occupied himself watching white puffy clouds pass over the branches of a cottonwood tree. All this peace and quiet gave him entirely too much time to think. And all he thought about was Sabine.

Maybe he should take a trip somewhere. An exotic beach resort or something similar. The only thing stopping him was his fear that he'd be recognized. He could just go home, too, but what was there that wasn't here? A big city, for one, and he didn't think that was a good place to lay low. A suburb of Washington, D.C., was nothing like the wide open spaces of Montana.

On the patio, Luc sat on his lawn chair watching a fishing show. Cullen liked fishing but enough was enough. Once a year was enough. Every day was nauseating.

As though hearing his thoughts, Luc turned the channel. Cullen felt bad for thinking bad of his uncle's favorite pastime. Luc was getting older and couldn't keep up the pace he'd once kept in the military.

Luc stopped surfing at a news program.

"Authorities are speculating whether the man who attacked O'Clery in her Roaring Creek bookstore was responding to her recent interview on *Current Events*."

Cullen lifted his head, instantly focused on the television. His stomach muscles tightened as he rose halfway between sitting and reclining. A picture of Sabine disappeared from the screen, and the news program went to commercial.

Cullen swung his feet over the hammock and stood, shards of fear shooting through him. "What happened?"

He stepped onto the patio, where his uncle had a television mounted below the eave of his house. "What happened to her?" He knew he sounded frantic. He felt frantic. And he was not accustomed to that.

Luc glanced up at him, then quickly surfed until he found another news channel. A video of Sabine being helped out of a storefront ripped through him. That haunted look was back in her eyes. She held a hand to her throat, but it didn't hide the red and chafed skin there. Something dark and uncontrollable expanded in him. He tried to steady his breathing.

"Sabine O'Clery, the woman rescued more than a month ago from Afghanistan, narrowly escaped with her life late last night after two men broke into her Roaring Creek bookstore. One man, who reportedly tried to help her, was shot and taken to a nearby hospital. Doctors say he'll recover, and guards posted at his room are refusing to let anyone but police question him. O'Clery said she and the injured man fired at her assailant, but he managed to get away. Local authorities are searching for the suspect and aren't releasing the identity of the man hospitalized during the attack."

The screen showed a picture of Noah in one corner. "Noah Page, O'Clery's estranged father, is founder and CEO of the private military company rumored to have arranged her rescue from Afghanistan, where she was held prisoner for more than two weeks. Page denies any ties to the man hospitalized during the latest attempt on her life. Roaring Creek authorities aren't commenting whether the attempt on O'Clery's life is related to her kidnapping in Afghanistan...."

Cullen let go of a vicious curse.

"Some quack tried to off her?" Luc asked, incredulous.

Someone had nearly succeeded in killing Sabine. Noah had told him about her visit to Samuel's wife and the photos she'd found. He'd worried about Aden showing up at her bookstore, too. Now there was no doubt; Aden knew about the photos. But was Sabine's finding them enough reason to kill her? He and Noah were missing something. What did Aden have to hide, and who were the men in those photos?

Cullen stormed through the house and went to the guest room, where he found his cell phone. Punching numbers with trembling fingers, he waited until Noah answered.

"What happened?" he said flatly.

"Cullen?"

"Someone tried to kill Sabine."

"I know. I've been trying to reach you but your phone was off. Cullen—"

He couldn't get a grip on the feelings swarming him. It was such a foreign sensation. "What have you learned about the chopper that fired at us? Has Odie been in touch with you?"

"Your resources are helping, Cullen. It's just going to take some time."

Cullen dug his fingers through his hair and stopped trying to hide his unease. He swore and it came from the depths of his soul. He was sick with worry.

"Don't do anything rash," Noah warned.

Cullen pinched the bridge of his nose, fighting a too-powerful urge to go to Sabine. To see for himself that she was all right and to keep her that way. All the years he'd worked to get where he was, and he was willing to throw it all away for a woman? He didn't understand what was happening to him.

"I'll send more men," Noah said. "I'll send twenty if I have to. Cullen, you aren't responsible for this. *Stay away from her.*"

Cullen moved across the guest room and didn't reply for several seconds. When he spoke, he feared it was from his heart and nothing else.

"Don't send anyone, do you understand? I'll be there by tomorrow night."

He disconnected the call and stood staring out the window of the guest room. What was he *thinking?* If the media was thick around Sabine before, they'd be like ticks on a dog's ass by now.

He paced the room. Ran his fingers through his hair once again. Sighed hard. Going to Sabine right now was suicide for his career, both with the reserves and his company.

He leaned with his hands against the wall beside the window and shut his eyes, breathing faster than normal. How could he ignore the attempt on her life? How could he go on as though he'd never gone to Afghanistan to free her? As though he'd never made love to her? He couldn't, that's how.

No matter what it cost him in the end, no matter how he felt about this unreasonable drive to risk everything for her, he couldn't stand by and watch the news to find out what happened next.

He had to do something.

Three days after her attack, Sabine folded a towel and stacked it with the rest on the kitchen table. It was late for doing laundry, but she'd had the dream again and had given up on getting any more sleep for the night.

What sounded like floorboards creaking downstairs made her go still. She listened for a while. The washer had finished its cycle but she hadn't loaded the dryer yet, so the apartment was quiet. Another creak sent her pulse leaping. Someone was in her bookstore. *Again.*

Turning, she lifted the handset of the telephone in her kitchen. No dial tone. Her breathing quickened and she fought that too-familiar fear. Yesterday, she'd practiced for several hours with Buddy, shooting her pistol. If the man who'd attacked her had returned, this time she wouldn't miss.

Putting the phone down, she went to her bedroom for the gun, stepping lightly. She slid in a clip and made sure the gun was ready to fire. With a deep breath to bolster her nerve, she left her room and moved carefully to the door leading to the lower level. The hardwood floor was cold on her feet. Pausing at the door, she heard only silence on the lower level, which only made her more nervous. Silence could be more terrifying than any sound. She didn't like the memory of that.

Turning off the kitchen light, she slowly turned the doorknob. Opening the door a crack, she looked down the narrow stairs. No one was there. She opened the door a fraction wider, not making a sound, aiming the pistol down the stairs.

Assured she was alone and out of sight for now, Sabine stepped down the stairs on tiptoe, avoiding the areas she knew would creak. At the bottom, she stopped to listen. No sound. Not one.

Around the wall, in the moonlight, she spotted a man standing near the back door of her bookstore. He was dressed all in black, and it frightened her to see he also wore a black mask over his head. He was taller than the man who'd attacked her. Bigger, too. At the moment he was pointing a big gun with a silencer through a narrow opening of the door, his back to her as he appeared to be watching for something outside.

She stepped softly toward him. Holding her pistol with both hands, she stopped and aimed for his head. At this distance, she wouldn't miss if she fired.

He seemed to sense her presence then. His head turned slightly and he went very still.

"Don't shoot," he said without looking at her.

His voice flustered her. There was something familiar about it. He raised his hands and slowly turned.

All she saw of him beneath his cover of black was the

glitter of his eyes. They were light in color but she couldn't tell what shade. He was very tall. As tall as…

"Drop the gun," she said, without finishing the thought, afraid it would distract her too much.

He didn't move, which gave her time to notice more about him. His tactical canvas pants with cargo pockets fit close to his hips and legs without being tight. His shirt was made of the same durable material but molded to his muscular upper body and still managed to appear flexible.

She adjusted the aim of her gun. "Drop it. Now. Or I'll pull this trigger."

She watched him blink before he slowly lowered the gun to the floor, bending, then straightening.

"Don't shoot," he said again, standing with his hands spread wide so she could see they were empty.

That voice…

He took a step toward her, sending her heart skittering. "Don't move!" A tremble shook her hands.

"Sabine—"

That rasp… She knew that voice.

He knew her name.

While she struggled with what this information meant, he sprang into action. He moved so fast she didn't see what he'd actually done until she felt a sting on her wrists and her pistol went flying. The same instant she realized she was no longer armed, she felt her feet swept out from under her and found herself on her butt. Dazed, she watched as the man crouched for his weapon smooth as a cat.

"Stay here," he said, then ran out the door.

"What—" Sabine gave herself a mental shake and jumped to her feet.

Grabbing her pistol, she ran through the door after him. She stopped and looked left and right, seeing nothing through the darkness. A sound brought her head whipping back to her left. She ran with her gun pointed to the ground, holding it with both hands. She ignored her cold feet and bare arms as she reached the corner of the building. Leaning forward, she peered around the corner. There was only a field to the west of her bookstore, which was located on the west edge of town, but a streetlight to the south illuminated the man dressed in black chasing another figure into the street.

Sabine ran after them. What was happening? Why were two men sneaking around her bookstore in the middle of the night—*again?*

She watched the man in black catch the second figure, a lean man who was not as tall. Tripped by quick and agile feet, the shorter man fell in the street. Before he could regain his balance, the man in black struck him with his gun. The shorter man went limp.

Was he dead?

The man in black hefted the shorter man up and over his shoulder then turned to look back. Sabine felt goose bumps from more than cold raise the flesh on her arms. But instead of coming toward her, he walked the opposite direction across the street.

He might as well have been carrying a sack of grain for all the trouble it took him to step up the curb and open the front door of the vacant building across the street…directly across from her bookstore and apartment. He left the front door open as he disappeared inside, as though beckoning her to follow.

Wary of the familiarity she felt toward him, she did. Somewhere in the depths of her mind she knew who he was. But the implications of his being here, in Roaring Creek, with an unconscious man in a vacant building, were too much for her to accept all at once.

Shivering from cold and apprehension, she put her hand

against the door frame and tried to see through the darkness inside the building. A light snapped on, illuminating a stairway leading to a lower level, a basement.

She didn't want to go down there, but curiosity moved her feet for her. She paused halfway when she heard the clatter of something metal. Taking several deep breaths, she stepped the rest of the way down the stairs.

The basement was small. A single bulb lit the open space, deep shadows swallowing the far wall. A modern furnace looked out of place surrounded by the old wood-and-stone frame of the house. The man in black stood with his arms at his sides, pistol hanging from his right hand. Sabine felt him looking at her through the twin holes of his mask.

Next to him, the figure from the street was on his knees, and his hands were tied by a chain that slung him from a pipe running across the ceiling, the metal clatter she'd heard. It was the man who'd attacked her in her bookstore. She stared at the man in black. How had he known? A riot of emotions warred in her, resistance against what a deeper part of her already knew.

Sliding his pistol into the waist of his black pants, the man in black moved toward her. His head barely fit under the low ceiling. His power lurked in the play of sinewy muscles beneath his dark covering, in the sheer size of him, long thighs, big shoulders and arms. She would have taken an instinctive step back if she hadn't been so frozen with disbelief.

The closer he came, the clearer she saw his eyes. When he stopped before her, she could no longer cling to doubt. Those eyes had looked into hers with naked, intimate heat.

When he reached to pull off the mask, she stopped breathing. Black hair fell in disarray around his head, and the full impact of his gray eyes was just as intense as she remembered, but tinged with a familiar energy. Focused and ready for combat. His gaze lowered down the front of her, unhurried, remembering, as she was. Dressed only in her thin white cotton top and matching pajama pants, she felt stripped by that look.

"Cullen," she whispered.

He lifted one gloved hand and traced the bruise on her neck. The trail of his finger left a tingle on her skin. She stood still while he told her without words what had drawn him here. His gaze shifted and met hers, burning hotter with the promise of vengeance.

She stepped back, out of his reach, not at all trusting herself with the way he made her feel. Her gaze passed over the man secured by the chain and then around the dark basement.

"We have to call the sheriff." She started to turn.

Cullen took hold of her arm just above her elbow and pulled her back to face him. "No sheriff."

She curled her hand over his biceps, meaning to push him away. Instead fiery awareness of the iron-hard muscle shot through her.

"That's the second time that man tried to attack me," she spat. "We have to report it."

"No police. No reporters. I don't want anyone knowing I'm here."

"Then why did you come? I don't need your help any-more."

His eyes indicated the bruises on her neck. "Go home, Sabine. You don't have to worry about anyone hurting you again. I'll make sure you're safe from now on."

"Go *home?*" She tugged her arm and he let her go. "And what? Forget you're here? That you have a man tied by a *chain* in the basement of what I thought was a *vacant building* that happens to be *right across the street from my bookstore?*" She couldn't help looking at Cullen's body again, so huge and ominous dressed in black. Disturbed by the warming reaction the sight gave her, she turned and climbed the stairs.

On the first level, she stood in the middle of the empty room, uncertain what to do. The house didn't appear lived-in. Something caught her eye. Near the windowsill on an upside-down cardboard box, silhouetted by the streetlight, was a pair of binoculars. She went there, staring at the binoculars a moment before looking out the window. Her bookstore was in clear view.

A sound made Sabine turn. Cullen stood at the top of the basement stairs, gun still tucked into the black pants, watching her. Next to him, stairs led to a second level. She engaged the safety on her pistol and headed there. Climbing the stairs, she heard him follow.

Straight ahead at the top of the stairs, a hall led to three dark rooms. Sabine's hand trailed along the round ball at the end of the railing as she stepped into a room to her right. An unmade and otherwise unadorned mattress was the only piece of furniture other than a card table, where a black briefcase was open. A cord trailed from the briefcase to a plug in the wall. Inside the briefcase was a small monitor surrounded by other electronics. The monitor blinked a red "Camera 2" along with an unobtrusive beeping sound.

Cullen had been spying on her.

"It's infrared."

She turned to see him standing at the top of the stairs.

"For motion detection," he added.

She barely heard him. He'd come for her. He'd come, despite the risk of exposure. Why? A warm rush of hope threatened her resolve to keep him out of her heart.

He moved toward her, those eyes glowing with answering heat. "It isn't over, Sabine."

It took her a few seconds to realize he wasn't referring to the two of them. Just when she was beginning to feel strong again, he had to show up and knock her off balance. He was like one of her misguided achievements. She'd have to sacrifice too much of herself to have him, even for a little while.

"Did my father send you?" she asked.

He stopped too close. "No."

"I don't believe you."

"He didn't want me to come."

His eyes lowered and she felt his gaze like a physical touch, lingering on her chest. Then all that energy captured her with an unspoken message. She couldn't look away. Her pulse warmed with the shift of his gaze into hers. She flinched when he touched her hand, but his fingers only took hold of the gun. Letting him have it, she rubbed her arms and watched him tuck it in the back of his pants.

"I'll take you home."

From downstairs, the sound of something clanging to the floor ended the argument. Cullen ran down the stairs and Sabine followed. She heard glass shattering. At the bottom of the basement steps, she saw Cullen standing with his gun aimed out the basement window. It was broken, and the man who'd been hanging by the chain was gone.

Chapter 8

"While you're wearing the stain off my wood floor, I'll be downstairs stocking my shelves." Holding a fresh container of sun tea in one hand and a small cooler of ice in the other, she waited for Cullen to stop pacing in the middle of the living room to look at her. He'd seen her safely home in the wee hours of morning, just before Minivan Man arrived for his shift. Early. Now Cullen was trapped here, although he'd cracked a smile at her name for the reporter.

He didn't respond, but his impatience etched stern lines on his face. It was almost comical. "You don't do well with nothing to keep you occupied, do you?"

His brow put a deeper crease above his nose.

Smiling, she opened the door leading to the stairs and quipped, "I'll send you a bill for the floor."

Stepping onto the first stair, she closed the door on his slightly less brooding face. Downstairs, the blinds were open in her bookstore. The sun was shining this morning, and there wasn't a cloud in the sky. It perked up her mood. She put the jug of tea on the checkout counter. She'd keep the Closed sign up and front door locked just in case Minivan Man decided to try to corner her.

Finding a plastic cup on one of the shelves behind the checkout counter, she put ice in it and filled it with tea. The sound of boots thudding a slow tread made her look toward the row of shelves that blocked her view of the office. Cullen appeared in one of the aisles. She'd known he wouldn't be able to stay upstairs with nothing to do. Pulling out another cup, she poured him a glass of tea. He stopped and lifted it from the counter when she finished.

"Thanks."

Sipping, he eyed the windows at the front of the store and started to go there.

"I want the blinds open," she warned him.

He didn't stop.

"I like the sunlight," she raised her voice.

He reached for the string hanging from the blinds nearest the door, heedless of the demand in her tone. Pulling, he lowered the blinds over the window.

"Leave the damn blinds open!"

Paying her no heed, he moved to the second set and shut them, plunging the bookstore into gloomy light.

Pursing her lips tightly with the rise of temper, she left her tea on the counter and stomped to the front of the store. She jerked the first blinds open. When she reached for the second one, his fingers slid around her wrist and stopped her. His touch along with his nearness kept her from yanking away.

"We'll leave one open," he compromised.

She watched his lips form the raspy words, disarming the rest of her temper. Those gray eyes held hers with heat that he tried to subdue with a slow blink, telling her he also felt the chemistry mixing between them. Slipping her wrist free, she went to a box of unpacked books and struggled to regain composure.

Cullen followed, setting his cup of tea on a table between two Victorian chairs in front of a gas fireplace. She tried to convince herself this was no big deal. So her rescuer was here in her bookstore. Did she have to fall all over him? No. Did she want to? No.

Yeah, right. She sneaked a look at his tall, cut body.

"I was surprised when I heard you were opening a bookstore," he said without looking at her. He was opening another box of books.

"Why?"

"You decided to give up your career?"

She stilled in the act of pulling some biographies from a box. "I didn't give up."

"I meant," he amended, "not many people could come back from what you went through and start their own business."

She straightened from the box and began slipping biographies on a shelf. "You're in Roaring Creek, Cullen. Don't act like I've invested in a franchise."

He moved closer to her and put some books on the shelf. "It doesn't have to be a franchise."

She let go of the last biography and slid her gaze to him. "Doesn't it?"

"I only wondered why a bookstore."

"I gave up an exciting hydrogeology career to open a boring old bookstore in a little mountain town. Do you think that's taking a step backward?"

"No. I think you took that job in Afghanistan to prove something to your father."

She flinched at his accurate assessment.

He half grinned. "It doesn't take much to see it, Sabine. When he was young, he was never around, used your mother, had a thing for thrills. It made you feel unwanted."

Swallowing, she faced the biographies. "That isn't important to me anymore."

"Your father's changed since then."

Grunting her cynicism, Sabine bent to the box of books, a jerky, awkward movement. Why did what he say bother her so much? It wasn't important to her what her father thought or felt. And she was living for herself now, not anyone else. This bookstore proved it.

Cullen opened another box. Her first glance turned into another. It was the one that contained some of her Pulitzer prize winners. Her favorites. And his hands were on them. Trying to ignore what that did to her, she put more biographies on the shelf.

"They go on the shelf by author name," she said.

"I've been in bookstores before," he answered.

She couldn't resist a sassy remark. "For what? G.I. Joe books?"

He laughed once and not very loud.

"Playboy?" She placed another biography on the shelf, sending him a slanted look as he carried a few books to the shelf beside her.

"The last time I bought one of those I was sixteen years old and nervous about a date with the first girl I ever slept with." His voice was deadpan, but she knew he was only playing along with her.

"Did it help?" she teased, even though she was actually curious.

He put a few books on the top shelf, calm as could be. "You ought to know."

She slid another book into place. "You weren't that good."

"That's not what I heard."

She looked at him and saw his lopsided grin in profile. "I didn't make any noise."

"The fact you don't remember says it all."

What had she done? Moaned? She didn't think she'd cried out…then she did remember…she had.

"Don't make fun of that. It isn't funny." She slid the last biography onto the shelf and didn't move her hand from the spine. Just stared at it while her heart filled with feelings she did not want.

"I know," he murmured. "I'm sorry."

He stacked the shelf with a few more books. After a moment, she joined him.

"You've got some good books in here," he said, holding up a book by John Kennedy Toole between them.

"How would you know?"

"I read this one." He glanced up at the shelf. "I've read a lot of these."

"*You* read *A Confederacy of Dunces?*" She put her hands on the edge of a shelf level with her face and she stared at him.

"Twice." He smiled, continuing to stack the shelf.

She didn't know what to say around her surprise. And that smile was disarming.

"I like the author's view of people and society."

"He hated them."

"He understood their idiosyncrasies. Too well. It's a shame he committed suicide," he said.

Her curiosity got the better of her. "What other books have you read?"

Lowering his hands, he shrugged and turned in two little steps to face her. "A little of everything. The classics. Action or adventure. Thrillers. I like nonfiction, too."

"For a knuckle dragger you sure are well-read."

A chuckle rumbled from him. "I started reading a lot when I was in college."

"When did you have time to read?"

"I made time. I like to read."

It seemed so unlike him. "What happened that you ended up working as a mercenary?"

"I'm not a mercenary."

"How do you know my father, then? Why did he hire you?"

His expression closed and she knew they'd reached an area he couldn't, or wouldn't, talk about. Disappointed, angry for being disappointed, because that meant she actually cared, she went to a box and got a few more books, jamming them into place on a shelf.

"Your father and I are just friends," he said.

"All his friends have secret lives. It makes perfect sense."

"Would you rather the whole town knew I was here and destroy everything I've worked for?"

Finished with the books, she folded her arms and cocked her head. "If it would help me get rid of you, sure. But somehow I don't think that's what would happen."

"You probably like it that I'm trapped in this bookstore."

"I didn't invite you here."

He stared at her a long time, unable or unwilling to argue. It was enough to tell her what had driven him to come to Roaring Creek. She straightened her head as memory rushed forward, taking her back to the pension, to the way he'd held her while she cried, the way he'd gradually responded to her kisses. His gentleness. His skin against hers.

As if sharing the memory, his eyes began to smolder with hunger. Undercurrents fired between them. She itched to pull him against her.

"I didn't need an invitation," he said. His raspy voice

touched a place in her that hadn't been touched since Kárpathos.

She struggled against the temptation to let down her
guard. "You make it sound as if that night in Greece meant
something."

"Didn't it?"

Oh, it was getting warm in here. Her hands tightened on
her arms where they were folded. "I thought guys like you
didn't get tangled in long relationships."

"Is that what you want? A relationship?"

"Have you ever had a relationship with a woman?"

He half laughed. "Of course."

"What qualifies as a relationship to you? A one-night
stand?"

"No. One that lasts at least a few months."

That she hadn't expected. "When's the last time you had
one of those?"

"In college."

"You're thirty-five. Don't you ever want to get married?"

"Maybe. Someday."

Maybe. But it wasn't important enough to make him
worry much. Kárpathos hadn't been important enough. It
had been important enough to make him want to protect her,
but not enough for a real relationship. That hurt. Annoyed
by her reaction, not wanting to start having fantasies of him
in a relationship with her, she resumed stacking the shelf.

"What about you?"

She didn't turn to look at him. "We're finished with this
conversation."

"It's only fair that you answer the same questions you
asked me…and I answered."

The mischievous glint in his eyes said he was enjoying this.

"All right, what do you want to know?" she asked.

He braced his hand on the shelf, leaning closer, eyes glowing. "When's the last time you had a relationship?"

"Last year."

"How long did it last? Who was he?" He didn't seem so mischievous now. He looked...jealous. No, it couldn't be that.

But she smiled and said, "Almost a year. He was another geologist."

"Did you love him?"

"I liked him. A lot."

"Why did it end between you?"

"I realized I didn't love him."

He took his time responding. "Do you ever want to get married?"

"Of course."

"When?"

"When I fall in love."

The bookstore grew uncomfortably quiet. Cullen looked as if she'd said something frightening...and she felt she had.

A knock interrupted them. Sabine was grateful for it and started to go answer the back door. Cullen stopped her with his hand on her upper arm. She followed to where she could see into the office and watched him ask who it was.

"Noah," the voice answered.

Realizing she wasn't disappointed to learn he was here, Sabine gritted her teeth.

Cullen let Noah inside with a wary glance at Sabine. She looked like a tightly wound spring, the reaction to seeing her father compounded by her earlier mention of love. The way she'd said it kept ringing through his head. He was still fighting a cold sweat. Love? With Sabine, there'd be nothing comfortable about it. He'd lose himself in her. The very thing that had destroyed his father.

He caught the way Sabine watched Noah as he came farther into the office. She seemed wary and stiff, but the animosity he'd seen in her before was missing. Maybe she was starting to see that Noah wasn't the dishonorable man she'd once perceived.

"Did you find something?" she asked her father.

He nodded grimly. "More about Isma'il." He looked at Cullen. "I think his reason for kidnapping Sabine and Samuel had something to do with emeralds."

"What makes you think that?" Cullen asked. Finally, they were getting somewhere.

"When we found some villagers to question, none of them could identify the men in the pictures, but they were able to confirm Isma'il took over an emerald mine by force and was paying someone to fly gems to a dealer in Peshawar, Pakistan."

"You think Isma'il was smuggling gems into Peshawar? How is that linked to Sabine's kidnapping?"

"Someone must have crossed him. I'm guessing that someone is one or both of the men in that photo. And Aden might have known them." He looked at Sabine. "Did you know about the emerald mines when you were working there?"

Slowly, as if struggling to absorb it all, she nodded. "Everyone did. But we were there to assess groundwater conditions, not the potential mineral resources of the area."

"So no one had any reason to suspect Aden may have been working with Isma'il? Samuel never said anything?"

At Noah's question, Sabine's eyes took on that haunted look. She shook her head. "Nothing significant."

"He must have known what Aden was up to. And if he hadn't been kidnapped, Aden might have tried to kill him anyway." Noah looked at Cullen. "One of the villagers my men questioned was a friend of Isma'il's. He said Isma'il met Aden on a regular basis. They were doing business together."

Sabine made a choked sound and that haunted look intensified.

"I'm sorry, Sabine," Noah said to her. "I know this is hard for you."

She shook her head unsteadily. "No…I'm all right."

Cullen didn't believe that. She was terribly upset. While he could understand that, he had a feeling something more bothered her.

"Did your captors ever say anything about the emerald mines?" Noah asked. "Did they bring up Aden's name at all?"

She didn't seem to hear the question, just stared at some point between him and Noah.

"Sabine?"

Her eyes moved to look at Noah.

He repeated his question, and Cullen wondered what had her so spooked.

"No," she finally said.

Noah's mouth pressed in a grim line as he looked from Sabine to Cullen. "The only other person who can tell us anything about Aden is missing."

"Who?"

"My secretary. She's been gone for a few days now. I'm sorry, Cullen. You were right. I had Cindy's house searched and found copies of handwritten notes about your mission in an envelope addressed to her. If Aden was working with Isma'il, he could have persuaded her to give him the information and then threatened her to keep quiet."

Cullen's jaw tensed and his fists tightened with the thought of the men who'd lost their lives because of Noah's secretary. "How did you know it was her?"

"A reporter coerced Sabine to do the *Current Events* interview by agreeing not to expose her rescuer. Aden must have decided his mole talking to the press was too much of a risk, even with his threats."

Cullen didn't miss the revelation that Sabine had done the interview to protect him. It reached into his heart and warmed him. "So he makes her disappear before anyone can talk to her."

"And tries to kill Sabine in case she pieces together something damaging about her kidnapping."

"There has to be more," Sabine said. "Aden is afraid of more than being linked to my kidnapping."

"I'd have to agree," Noah said. "And those men in that photo might tell us what that is."

"Odie is working on that," Cullen said.

Noah nodded. "I'll let you know when I find out more." He started toward the door, stopping when he reached it to look back at Sabine. "Mae is cooking dinner tomorrow night. Will you be there?"

That snapped Sabine to attention. She straightened. "She didn't tell me."

"She asked me to let you know." He looked at his daughter with a silent message in his eyes. He was trying to make inroads with her.

Sabine's eyes hardened, her defenses building again.

"What time should we be there?" Cullen asked, earning a narrow-eyed glare from Sabine.

Noah looked relieved. "Six o'clock." With one more hopeful glance at Sabine, he left. The office door closed behind him, leaving Cullen alone with her.

"You didn't have to do that," she said, marching back into the bookstore.

Following, he deliberately ignored her mood. "There's something you aren't telling me about Aden."

She stopped, folding her arms in a defiant stance. He

moved in front of her, unable to help noticing how her arms plumped her breasts.

"Yeah? Well, how does it feel?" she asked.

He'd take a little sass from her, considering what she'd learned today. "Do you know something that will help us end this?"

She put one leg forward, hips cocked. "Tell me your last name."

"McQueen."

Silence. He knew he'd just surprised her with his quick reply. Actually, he'd surprised himself.

"Are you lying?" she finally asked.

Fearing his heart was going to overrule his better judgment this time, he answered anyway. "No. My name is Cullen McQueen. I have a house in Virginia. My uncle lives in Montana. He owns a ranch there. That's where I was before I came here."

Her fingers relaxed where they curved over her arms, and her eyes softened. "Not married. No kids," she said in an intimate whisper.

She transported him back to Kárpathos, when they'd said the same words to each other. Except this time the meaning went so much deeper. Last time she'd said it to mock him. Now it told him she felt he was giving her more of him. Not keeping so many secrets. It was a dangerous path for him to follow. In more ways than one.

"Not married. No kids," he said in return.

Her eyes softened further, and he let himself fall into her gaze for a while.

"I saw Aden meet with a man just before we were kidnapped," she said, that haunted look returning, growing stronger with each passing second. "I saw only the back of the man's head."

Cullen waited for her to continue.

"I keep having dreams of a monster who does terrible things. In the dream, I see the back of the monster's head. When he turns, his face becomes Isma'il's."

It supported what Noah had just told them. "I'm sorry, Sabine." If there was a way he could take away the pain that must cause her, he would.

"I didn't want it to be true," she said.

Anguish gave her voice a quiver. But she held herself together. It couldn't be easy knowing the man she'd watched kill Samuel was friendly with her employer, that her employer had known all along the reason they were kidnapped, that it could have been prevented. Maybe Sabine even thought she could have done something, had she only known whom Aden had met the day she'd seen him.

He moved toward her, pulling her against him and holding her while she struggled to keep from crying. She put her hands on his chest and he felt her sag against him, welcoming the offer of comfort. The last time he'd done this it had led to more. He tried to steel himself against the memory, but it circled his senses, luring him into its spell.

When her breathing slowed and tiny shudders of emotion died, she flexed her fingers. She was growing more aware of him, like he was of her, soft and molded against him. She leaned her head back and he looked down at her.

The desire to kiss her swarmed over him. Her gaze fell to his mouth. He felt the heat inside him kick up a few degrees. Her eyes met his, coherency returning, then going round with alarm. She pushed his chest and stepped back.

He couldn't help looking at her. At the faded jeans that showcased long thighs, at the plain but feminine white T-shirt that did the same and more to her breasts. Her small waist. Long red hair. Green eyes. He felt starved of her.

"I-I'm going to…to go upstairs…for a while," she stammered.

He watched her hurry from the bookstore, glad that at least she still had a hold of her senses.

Chapter 9

Steam from boiling potatoes on her mother's stove fogged Sabine's view of Cullen. He sat on one of Mae's plaid green chairs in the living room, surrounded by refurbished antiques and a river-rock fireplace. Cabin architecture and her mother's decorative charm made for warm atmosphere. Warmer with Cullen in the midst.

In a black long-sleeved T-shirt that flattered his chest and arms, he made it hard for her to concentrate. Ever since he'd held her the day before, things felt awkward between them. The way he looked at her. The way he noticed her looking at him. Something had shifted between them, and it tested her resolve.

Noah sat on the couch beside him. Cullen's gaze moved and caught hers. There it was again. That spark. She felt the heat sweep through her. Noah was still talking, but she didn't think Cullen was listening. Maybe she shouldn't have worn this little black dress.

"Are you mad at me?"

Sabine almost jumped when her mother came back into the kitchen. She'd just finished setting the rugged pine table adjacent to the living room.

"No," she said, trying to figure out why she'd asked.

"I didn't want to force this dinner on you, but Noah wanted it so much…." Her mother let the sentence silently end.

Noah had tried to strike up a conversation with her twice thus far, but she'd found a way to avoid him both times. He'd finally given up and gone to sit in the living room with Cullen.

"He can be persuasive when he wants to get his way," Sabine said, defenses pricking her.

"I agreed with him. It's time to put the past behind you, baby girl."

"That's a little hard after thirty-three years. I don't know the man and I have no desire to."

"I don't think you really believe that. He's your father."

"Biologically."

"Sabine, he's changed since he was younger. And I'm afraid I'm as much to blame as him for the way you perceive him."

She watched her mother pour iced tea into four glasses. "He was never here. What am I missing?"

Mae put the pitcher of iced tea down and looked at Sabine. "I refused to marry him because he was a mercenary who didn't want to live in Roaring Creek."

"You were right."

"No, I wasn't. Not completely. Deep down, he was always a good man."

What had softened her mother toward Noah? Sabine wasn't comfortable giving him the same consideration.

Disconcerted, she looked to where her father sat with

Cullen. Cullen saw her and those hungry gray eyes drew her attention. She wished she could see the detail of them, their energy, the way she was beginning to learn their subtleties. Heat flickered and spread into a wildfire before she could stop it.

"Wow," her mother said. "He looks like he's ready to drag you back to your bookstore."

Not expecting her to notice so much, Sabine remained cautiously silent.

"Maybe I was wrong about the two of you," Mae went on. "When I saw that picture in the paper, I was so afraid you were going to fall in love with the wrong man just like I did."

Okay, it was time to take the focus off her and Cullen. "You don't seem to think Noah is wrong for you."

"There's a lot you don't understand, Sabine. I loved your father for a lot of years, but it's too late for us."

"Too late?"

Mae hesitated. She held Sabine's gaze. "I met someone after you left for Afghanistan."

"You *met* someone?"

"He's a rancher who moved here a few months ago."

Sabine struggled to wrap her mind around her mother being interested in someone other than Noah.

"Is it so hard to believe?" her mother asked, teasing.

"No. I'm happy for you."

"For the wrong reason."

"No, I—"

Mae handed her two glasses of iced tea. "Put those on the table. We're ready to eat."

All right. She'd try to give her father a chance. But only for her mother. Taking all four glasses to the table, she avoided looking at Cullen as he and Noah sat at the table. Sitting beside her mother, too aware of Cullen across from her, she glanced at Noah. He gave her a hesitant smile. She struggled with that old hope and avoided looking at both men. Only the sound of silverware against dishes filled the open room of the cabin.

Sabine picked at her food.

"You're doing a fine job with that bookstore," Noah commented, breaking the awkward silence. "Cullen said you were going to sell coffee, too."

She couldn't just turn off all the resentment she felt. Did he expect her to? She looked down at her plate and didn't respond.

When she looked up, it was to Cullen's softening eyes. No longer laced with desire, they silently encouraged her. He wanted her to forgive her father.

"Sabine was never the quitting kind," Mae said, adding to the small talk.

"We're having nice weather for this late in the fall, too," Sabine couldn't stop herself from saying. She couldn't pretend she wasn't still hurt by her father's desertion.

Noah met her smart remark with resignation. Long moments passed while he studied her, seeming to struggle with what to say.

"Sabine…" he began. She almost took pity on him. Finally, he gave up and just said, "You don't know what it did to me to almost lose you."

The honesty she heard in his tone and saw in his eyes grated against her defenses. She hadn't expected him to get so deep so quickly. "You're right. I don't know. Because I know nothing about you."

"What do you want to know? Ask me anything." More sincerity.

"You'll tell me?"

"Yes."

"Anything I ask?"

"Yes."

"All right. Why did you ask Cullen to rescue me?" Let's see how far he'd go with that one. She sent him a smug look.

Noah frowned his aggravation. Clearly, he knew where this was headed—somewhere Cullen couldn't, or wouldn't, want to go.

"It's okay," Cullen said. "I'll tell her."

Those gray eyes touched her, reaching past her surprise with purpose and certainty.

"Noah saved my life," he said, his voice warming her, the essence of him in it, strong and steady, full of honor and integrity. This was the man who'd rescued her, who'd held her in that helicopter and again in the pension on a little Greek island.

"You did it because you felt you owed him?" she had to force herself to ask.

"I was on a mission in Liberia. There were rebels rising against the government. They were part of a coup to overthrow the country's leader. My team was sent to take out a separate group of terrorists hiding there. What we didn't know was the Liberian government had hired Noah to send men to help fight the rebels. We were in a bad location, outnumbered and trapped by the rebels. Noah sent his team in to help us. If it hadn't been for that, everyone on my team, including me, wouldn't have made it."

She looked at her father. "So you cashed in on a favor?"

"Cullen is the only man I know who could do a mission like that," Noah said. "I wouldn't have asked if I'd had any other choice. And because Cullen is a man of honor, he agreed."

The fact that he chose that particular word knocked Sabine off balance. In everything Cullen did, honor drove him. But that honor didn't include her. Not beyond her rescue. How could she feel so much for a man who so resembled the kind she'd vowed never to love?

Love?

Panic billowed inside her. Where had that come from?

She found Cullen's eyes, saw the vitality that was becoming so familiar to her, a strength of character so few men possessed. It pushed her further off her axis.

"Do you work for Noah?" she asked, needing him to say it, to confirm it. "At all? Have you ever?"

"No."

"Who do you work for, then?"

He just looked at her.

"He can't tell you, Sabine. It's better you don't know, anyway."

She didn't acknowledge her father when he spoke, just held Cullen's gaze. "You lied to me when I asked you if my father sent you."

"I knew you were estranged from him."

"So you'd do anything, say anything, to get me to London, is that it?"

"To bring Noah's daughter to him alive? Yes, I would have done anything, said anything, to accomplish that."

The passion in his voice stopped her. Told her just how much his mission had mattered to him. More than she ever would. It crushed her. She felt the first sign of tears burning in her eyes and willed them away. No way could she cry now.

"All I can tell you is I'm a reservist," he said, a small crumb to placate what must be written all over her face. What a fool she'd been, falling for him like a lovesick teenager.

"What's your full-time job?" she asked, tossing it at him.

Defeat weighed the energy in his eyes. He couldn't tell her. She already knew he wouldn't.

Secrets were going to hurt her again. Just as they always had. Secrets had kept her from knowing the father she'd always longed to know, and secrets would keep her from knowing Cullen. What really stung was she wanted to know him. More than any other man she'd ever met. But nothing would move him to let her.

Putting her napkin onto the table, unable to take any more, she pushed her chair back and stood. "I want to go home now."

Now more than ever she understood why her defenses were so sharp. It was a layer of protection, something Afghanistan had stripped away, leaving bare the girl who yearned for a man to love her regardless of her achievements. The achievements were only a pretense. The girl underneath was real. Cullen had seen that girl after rescuing her. But it hadn't been enough. Like always, it was never enough.

After a stiff farewell to Noah and her mother, Sabine clutched her coat to her as Cullen drove down the mountain. She felt exposed. More unwanted than ever.

The truck stopped and Sabine saw that he'd parked behind his building. She opened the truck door and stepped down. The gravel seemed harder to navigate in high heels now that she didn't have her verve. All she wanted to do was go home and be alone. Anywhere as long as it was away from Cullen.

Heavier footfalls warned her he followed. She closed her eyes and leaned her head back, coming to a stop. There was no way she could outrun him in these shoes. Lord, how she didn't want to confront him right now.

"Sabine." He touched her arm with his hand as he came around to face her. She opened her eyes as he said, "I'm sorry."

Coldness gave her strength. She stepped back, out of his reach. "You're sorry."

"Yes."

Though his eyes revealed the truth behind the statement, she remained indifferent. "About what, Cullen? About who you are?"

"No."

"What, then?"

"You don't know what it would cost me."

"To trust me?"

"I trust you. I just... You don't understand." He averted his gaze.

She bristled that he was so adamant about protecting his career. "You risk your life doing what you do. And for what? To be like *Noah Page?*" It went deeper than that, but right now she wanted to lash out at him.

"I'm nothing like Noah."

"That's not what I see. I see a man who holds his secrets dearer than the people around him. Noah does that. He did it to my mother. And me."

"Sabine." He moved closer and put his hands just above her elbows.

She saw the first sign of deeper emotion creep into his eyes. Though she braced herself, the heat of him seeped through her resolve. She took another step back, once again out of his reach. "I want you to leave Roaring Creek."

"I can't do that."

The way he said it told her he meant it. Despair swirled inside her. How much longer would her resistance to him last? How much longer before he broke her heart? She started walking toward the side of his building. Before she reached the street, he stopped her, pulling her around to face him.

"This isn't over yet," he said. "Someone is still trying to kill you."

"For you and me it's over. I don't need you to fight my

battles for me." She pulled her arm free, stepped away and turned to walk briskly into the street. Didn't he see that she had to preserve herself? She needed a man who'd be there for her no matter what. She could not compromise on that. And Cullen was not that man.

His hand curled over her upper arm and forced her to slow. A tug made her fight for balance. She came against him in the middle of the street.

"I'm not leaving," he said gruffly.

"You've repaid your debt to my father. Go home. Go anywhere but near me."

"Damn it, Sabine." His hands slid up her arms and came to rest on the balls of her shoulders.

She put her hands on his chest. Feeling the hard muscle underneath, a flash of desperation rocked her. "Please, Cullen, don't make this harder than it already is." Emotion broke in her voice, all the desire she felt for him coming out, and the fear that she wouldn't be able to fight it much longer. She wanted to shut her eyes to the anguish in his.

"I can't," he said with equal emotion. "I can't leave you like this."

She did close her eyes then, overwhelmed by feelings more powerful than her will. His hands slid to her waist and he moved closer. She pressed her body against his, seeking to envelop herself in the invisible bond keeping them together.

He let his forehead rest against hers, and she stared up at his eyes, blurred so close to her own. She heard his breathing and realized she was breathless, too. He kissed her. Once. Twice. She wrapped her arms around his neck. He slid his hand to the small of her back and pulled her firmer to him. With his other hand, he cupped her head and kissed her deeper. From there this thing between them erupted. She strained to get more of him. He strained back. But it wasn't enough. She tipped her head back as his mouth planted wet, fevered kisses down her neck.

He lifted his head. Sabine opened her eyes to the ravaging hunger in his and knew she was falling hopelessly in love with him.

"Cullen," she breathed, wishing the thought had never come.

Hearing a sound, she felt him go still. He looked down the street. She followed his cooling gaze. A man stood twenty feet from them…holding a camera. He was snapping pictures of them. Cullen was facing the lens dead-on.

Cullen swore, pushing her away.

He stormed toward the reporter, who lowered his camera, then turned and ran. Minivan Man. At his minivan, he leaped inside, slammed the door and then the lock. Cullen tried to open the minivan's door, but it didn't budge. The reporter revved the engine, and the minivan rolled down the street toward Sabine. She turned as it passed by her.

Glancing at Cullen, she saw that he hadn't moved from where he stood in the street. It was hard for her to pity him when she had no idea what he was afraid the press would reveal about him. Knowing there was nothing she could say or do to make a difference, she walked toward her bookstore. Inside, she made her way upstairs, leaving the doors unlocked.

Several moments later she heard Cullen follow. The door to her apartment opened and she waited for his rage. But it never came. Instead of anger, she saw disbelief.

Closing the door behind him, he moved into her living room, where he sat on her sofa and bent forward to put his face in his hands.

Sabine relented and took pity on him. "You should leave town. Tonight. Now."

He didn't move.

"There will be more reporters by morning," she said.

"It won't matter," he answered, dropping his hands. "The damage is done."

"But—"

"It will only be a matter of time now."

Hearing the note of hopelessness in his tone, she lowered her eyes. She resented his secrets but she never meant to cause him pain. "I'm sorry."

She raised her eyes in time to see his gaze take in the bodice of her black dress, then travel lower before coming back to her face, his disgust with himself plain for her to see. It arrowed into the deepest regions of her heart.

Turning before he saw something she didn't want him to, she left him alone and went to her bedroom. She took her time changing into lounge pants and a matching shirt. Hearing him talk on the phone, she reluctantly went back to the main room.

"I'm sorry to call so late," he was saying as she came to a stop near the kitchen table. "I'm all right—" Whoever was on the other end of the connection must have cut him off. "Just listen, Odie. A Commander Birch will probably be calling sometime tomorrow. When he does, I need you to give him a number where he can reach me." He gave the person named Odie Sabine's phone number.

After a pause he said, "You'll know when you watch the news in the morning." Another pause. "Just give him the number. And if anyone asks you about SCS, tell them you have no comment." Sabine couldn't tell if the person named Odie was talking.

When he disconnected, he turned and saw Sabine standing there. She felt uncomfortable, as though she'd pried into his personal affairs. Then she caught herself putting his feelings ahead of her own. If the media exposed him, it wasn't her fault. Besides, she wanted to know what they'd have to say and it was the only way she'd find out. Cullen wouldn't tell her.

Since early that morning, Cullen had been watching the news, waiting for the break to come when someone figured out who he was. He found meager satisfaction that they weren't having an easy time of it. What really gnawed at him, though, was how the mystery heightened public fascination over his alleged romance with Sabine.

A sound made him look toward the hall. Sabine appeared, dressed in jeans and a white turtleneck sweater. The fact that the sight of her still stirred his desire annoyed him to no end. He knew what was underneath that sweater and inside those jeans. It was the candy that made him careless enough to send his entire life into chaos.

She moved farther into the room. Sweet candy. Irresistible sugar to his senses. His temper simmered hotter—at himself, not her. For letting her get to him the way she did.

He watched her fold her arms as she moved closer to the television. She looked tentative and he wondered if she was curious of what the news would reveal about him. When she saw there was a commercial playing, she turned and went into the kitchen.

He listened to her pour a cup of coffee from the pot he'd just brewed. Moments later a local newsbreak began. Sabine came into the living room, sending him a wary but stoic glance.

Pretty soon she'd know everything. He wasn't sure how he felt about that. Angry with himself, for sure. Disconcerted. Maybe even a little nervous.

"Little is known about the man who rescued Sabine O'Clery from what appears to be terrorists in Afghanistan," the anchorwoman began, "but one thing is clear—he's resurfaced in Roaring Creek, Colorado, O'Clery's remote mountain hometown."

A picture of Cullen looking right at the camera appeared on the screen.

"Aside from photographs and O'Clery's claim he's from the United States, her rescuer's identity remains a closely guarded secret. Sources from the U.S. military continue to deny any involvement in O'Clery's rescue, and her father insists the man shown in this photo doesn't work for his private military firm, credited with arranging the mission.

"So who is this man who saved Sabine O'Clery's life?" The anchorwoman smiled. "Nobody seems to know."

Another photo appeared, this one of Cullen and Sabine kissing in the middle of the street.

"But whoever he is, the romance that started on a Greek island hasn't cooled. Is it love? And the question on everyone's mind—has O'Clery's rescuer resurfaced in response to her recent attack? George, can you tell us more?"

A live view of the reporter who'd photographed Cullen appeared on the screen.

"I saw Sabine O'Clery's rescuer come out from behind that building." The camera moved to show the building where Cullen had stayed. "Which is right across the street from O'Clery's bookstore." The camera returned to Minivan Man. "It isn't confirmed yet, but we think he's living there."

Cullen stood and went to the window to peer outside. He spotted Minivan Man in front of a camera and wanted to clamp his hands around the reporter's scrawny neck.

"As soon as he realized I was taking pictures of him, he came after me. I ran to my vehicle and barely had time to close and lock my door before he reached me. For a while there I thought he was going to tear the door off to get at me." The man laughed as though in awe and shook his head. "Wouldn't want to mess with that fellow. Not only was he mad, he looked like he could take down a tree with his bare hands. More than capable of rescuing a woman from a country like Afghanistan...."

Cullen smirked through the window.

Sabine's telephone rang. He spun in time to see her go to answer it. He strode toward the telephone. When she lifted the handset, he took it from her.

"Yeah."

"I'm looking at your face on television."

Cullen closed his eyes. It was the call he'd been dreading yet desperately hoping would never come. Tyler Birch. His army commander. Cullen gripped the phone tighter.

"Tell me you aren't the man who rescued Sabine O'Clery in Afghanistan. Tell me I'm mistaken."

Cullen didn't say anything. He opened his eyes and found himself looking at Sabine. He resented the sympathy he saw.

He didn't waste time or words. "You're not mistaken."

Birch cursed vividly three times. "What the hell is the matter with you? Does your duty mean nothing to you?"

"It means everything to me."

"Your actions don't show me that."

Arguing would only make this worse. Cullen said nothing.

"You've embarrassed me," Birch said. "And you've embarrassed the army. How do you expect us to answer questions from the press? One of our own carried out a mission in an unstable country without our knowledge. How do you think that makes us look?"

"I rescued a civilian."

"Yeah, and I'd like to know how. Where did you find the resources?"

Cullen couldn't answer that. Telling Birch his company was only a guise for something much bigger would jeopardize key people in the government who could not be exposed. If he had any hope of salvaging anything of his career, he had to play this very carefully. He hated the prospect of losing his position with the army, but if he had to, he would.

"Can't tell me, huh?" Birch said, anger growing in his tone. "Who's in on it with you? More of our own?" Birch laughed without humor. "That company of yours always did make me wonder. What are you hiding, McQueen?"

"I never intended to put you in a compromising position," he said, unable to say more.

A long silence carried over the line. "When I found out it was you kissing Sabine O'Clery at the London airport, I couldn't believe it. I thought the man in that photo looked familiar, but I didn't think you were stupid enough to do something like that."

Cullen felt himself go numb as he continued to look at Sabine. "I saved her life, sir."

"Don't you 'sir' me. What do you want? A medal?"

"She would have been killed if I hadn't done it."

"That doesn't change a thing. You went in there on your own, without army authorization. If you were more than a reservist, I'd court martial you."

"I didn't do anything wrong."

"Did you kill anyone while you were over there?"

Cullen didn't answer, because he had.

"If you did, you did plenty wrong. Those kills weren't sanctioned, McQueen. Some people will see that as murder."

Cullen turned his back to Sabine to hide his crumbling hope.

"You crossed the line. I'm going to initiate administrative action to have you discharged from the army."

Defeat made him drop his head. This could end everything he'd worked for, and there was nothing he could do to stop it. "I'm asking you to reconsider."

"There's nothing to reconsider. I've made my decision. You're finished, McQueen."

Birch disconnected before Cullen could protest.

He stood holding the phone to his ear awhile longer, unable to believe this happened. His commander didn't have to initiate administrative action against him. Birch couldn't court martial him as a reservist, but he did have a choice over whether or not to take administrative action. And he had made that choice. Cullen's Black Ops went deeper than even Birch knew, and that came as too much of a blow to his pride.

Hanging the handset back on its base, Cullen was glad his back was turned and Sabine couldn't see the depth of his angst. Losing his company was one thing, but losing his reputation with the army was unthinkable. There was no honor in a dismissal like the one Birch threatened. No integrity. How could he look back on this when he was an old man and not have regrets?

He turned then. Sabine stood with her arms folded protectively in front of her, her beautiful green eyes round and wide with concern and sympathy.

Letting her kiss him that first time had started all this. If he would have just stopped it, if he hadn't made love to her, maybe he wouldn't have felt compelled to come to her after hearing about her attack. And if he hadn't made love to her, he wouldn't have been caught kissing her in the middle of the street. He was so angry for losing control of his self-discipline. He should have known better. He should have seen this coming and stopped it.

Chapter 10

Another breaking news report sounded from the television. The corner of the screen filled with the face shot of Cullen.

He moved into the living room as the anchorwoman summarized what she'd said in previous reports. Then she started into the new information that must have been gathered through the morning. "Margaret Schlepp, a neighbor of Luc and Penny McQueen, has confirmed the identity of the man who rescued Sabine O'Clery from Afghanistan. Cullen McQueen is a reservist with the U.S. Army Special Operations Command in Fort Bragg, North Carolina, and he's anything but ordinary. His uncle, Luc McQueen, a well-respected retired army commander, has declined to comment on the heroic efforts of his nephew, but his neighbor had plenty to say." The screen showed an old woman standing on her front porch.

"I always thought it was strange the way they talked so proud of Luc's nephew when all they said he did was run

a security temp agency somewhere in Virginia," Margaret
Schlepp said, squinting under the Montana sun and showing
missing front teeth. "SCS or something like that."

The woman had no idea of the damage she'd just done,
Cullen thought, his spirits sinking to a new low. The name
of his company was on the news. It was all over now. They
knew who he was.

"The more we learn about this man, the better it gets,"
the anchorwoman quipped, smiling.

Sickened, he watched the screen fill with a view of his
company in Alexandria, Virginia. The camera zoomed in
on SCS's redbrick exterior and darkly tinted windows.

"With no advertisements describing its operation, no
phone listings or evidence of a customer base, SCS appears
to be much more than a simple temp agency. In fact, that
seems to be the cover that hides its true purpose. Workers
from neighboring businesses say they aren't familiar with
the company or its founder and sole owner, Cullen Mc-
Queen. Few reported seeing employees enter and exit the
building and couldn't identify McQueen as one of them.
The SCS Agency is so secretive that it was difficult learning
what the acronym stood for. Security Consulting Services
sounds like a temp agency, but it's much more than that."

A video of Cullen's secretary waving away a cameraman
and a reporter who followed her toward the entrance to SCS
played on the television.

"Ms. Frank," a reporter called, "did your employer orchestrate the rescue mission that saved Sabine O'Clery's
life?"

"No comment," Odelia answered harshly as she marched
away.

"Did O'Clery's father hire your company to rescue her?"

Odelia opened the front door of SCS and disappeared
inside.

The screen showed the anchorwoman again. "Odelia Frank might seem like an ordinary secretary to someone who walks through the bulletproof doors of SCS, but her background dispels any doubt as to the character of the company. Former J-3 Operations captain with the Joint Chiefs of Staff, Ms. Frank still holds her Top Secret security clearance and is an expert markswoman. This from an interview with her ex-husband." The screen went to a picture of a man sitting lazily on his living room couch, gloating as he revealed his ex-wife's expertise. A few minutes later, the screen switched back to a smiling anchorwoman. "With a secretary like that, there's little doubt the SCS Agency is capable of carrying out a rescue mission. We'll update you as we get more."

The anchorwoman turned to her coanchor, still smiling. "It seems Ms. O'Clery has caught herself quite a man."

"Yes, it does, Mary," the newsman beside her said. Then the man led the broadcast into the weather.

The telephone rang again. Sabine went to answer it on the third ring. When she hung up, Cullen knew it was a reporter calling. They had her phone number now.

He moved to the front window and watched the chaos building in front of Sabine's bookstore. The sight increased the weight of his situation. He was beginning to understand how his father had felt when his life had begun to crumble.

The telephone rang yet again.

Sabine answered and he heard the strain in her voice.

"I know. We just saw it." There was silence while she listened. "A reporter caught us when we got home after dinner last night." Pause. "Yes." Pause. "No." Pause. "I don't know." A longer pause. "All right."

Sabine hung up. "My father wants us to come to my mother's house. He said he can secure us from the media here. He can help us."

Realizing he did need help, probably for the first time in his life, Cullen sighed as he continued to look down at the growing throng in front of Sabine's bookstore. His career with the army appeared to be over. His company could lose the covert government support it needed to exist. He couldn't imagine what his life was going to be like without the things he'd worked so hard to achieve. Lost in all this was the impact such a company had on the fight against terrorism. American dignity. Freedom. Humanity. Everything that mattered most to him.

"All we need to do is get there."

Cullen turned. Holding a duffel bag in one hand and the keys to her Jeep in the other, she looked wary of him.

Walking toward her, he reached for the keys in her hand. "I'll drive."

She gave him the keys.

Downstairs, Cullen swung the back door open and marched outside. Three reporters were on him in an instant.

"Mr. McQueen, can you tell us why you're here?"

"Do you suspect Sabine's attack is related to her kidnapping in Afghanistan?"

"Do you have any plans to marry the woman you rescued?"

Cameras pinged and snapped all around him. He grabbed the nearest one and yanked it to the ground, shattering it into pieces.

"Hey, you're going to pay for that!"

He leaned over the cameraman. "Make me."

"Cullen." Sabine's fingers curled over his biceps. "Let' go."

The cameraman's eyes were wide and he stepped back. Cullen sent each of the others a threatening glance before he moved out of Sabine's reach and climbed behind the wheel of the Jeep. When she closed the door on her side, he sprayed gravel driving away.

Sabine moved to the dining room window of her mother's cabin. Through the large pane of glass, clouds painted the sky a gloomy gray, matching her mood. Last night the news had flourished with images of Cullen destroying the reporter's camera, followed by his menacing "Make me" comment. Rather than painting him as a dangerous character who operated outside the law, they embellished the he-man quality of his reaction, making references to his size and fearlessness. It was all so ridiculous, particularly in light of the fact that they were crucifying a man's livelihood.

She never thought she'd be happy her father had access to men who could keep the reporters at bay. But this morning a helicopter had landed in the clearing near her mother's cabin and six men had filed out. They were now camped at the end of the driveway. Mercenaries were guarding them, and she was glad about that. Who would have thought?

Turning her head, she spotted Cullen sitting in a plaid living room chair, his body slouched against the back, eyes hard and looking right at her. She could almost hear his thoughts beaming across the room at her. If only he hadn't been stranded with her on a Greek island. If only he hadn't made love with her. If only he hadn't kissed her in London.

If only, if only.

Her father sat on the couch. He'd just finished talking on a radio with one of his men down at the end of the driveway. Her mother waited in the kitchen for another kettle of water to boil for tea. They were all waiting for Cullen's secretary to call.

Sighing, impatient and feeling trapped, Sabine moved to the couch and sat beside her father. He looked at her in surprise as he clipped his phone to his belt. From the chair, Cullen brooded.

He looked lazy slouched the way he was, legs spread, arms on the rests. Only his eyes moved, but she could feel the energy from them. His cell phone rang. He answered it as he stood, tall and big in dark blue jeans and a white button-up shirt. Sabine listened to him go into the sunroom next to the dining area.

"It's worse than I thought," her father said from beside her.

She turned to look at him, wondering what he meant. "Excuse me?"

"You and Cullen."

Realizing he'd been sitting there taking mental notes of her and Cullen's behavior, Sabine felt her guard go up. "It's a little soon for a father-daughter talk." She couldn't even imagine them having one.

"I've seen the way he looks at you," he said anyway. "I'm not a blind man. He's on his way to making the same mistake I made with your mother."

She really didn't want to have this conversation with him. But she said, "He blames me for what's happening."

"He doesn't blame you. He's angry with himself for allowing it to happen in the first place. I just hope he comes to his senses before it's too late."

Sabine studied her father's profile and grew uncomfortable. Did he think Cullen felt that much for her? "Is he going to lose his company because of me?"

He turned to see her. "Whatever happens, it isn't your fault."

"Is he going to lose it?" she persisted.

"Maybe. He could also lose his position with the army."

She'd only caught Cullen's side of the conversation when

he'd gotten the call from his commander. "But he rescued me. I would have been slaughtered if it hadn't been for him."

"Unfortunately, that won't matter. Cullen is a weapon. The army can't afford to have a guy with his background running rogue missions in unstable countries like Afghanistan. It's a huge political risk."

Sabine was beginning to understand the magnitude of what Cullen had risked to free her. "It isn't fair."

"It might seem that way now."

She angled her head in question.

"Cullen needs to decide what he wants out of life. Is it Special Ops and casual relationships, or is it more than that? This whole thing is going to force him to make up his mind. I just hope he makes the right decision."

"He'll never give up his career."

"Losing his company the way it's structured won't take that away from him. Neither will losing his position with the army. He might have to start over with a new company, maybe change his business strategy. Instead of dangerous clandestine missions, he can move over to infrastructure security. He can teach governments and big businesses how to protect themselves against terror attacks. Or he could move into an intelligence role rather than an operative one and send other men just like him on the secret missions. He can do that from anywhere. He might travel a lot, but he could live wherever he wants."

"What kind of company is he losing?"

Noah chuckled. "Even I don't know that."

She searched his eyes to see if he was telling the truth.

"Cullen works through the government, Sabine. You don't have to question his integrity. But it would be infinitely more damaging to him if the identities of his contacts were revealed. That's why he couldn't risk saying anything to you. He has other people to protect. Think of the media surrounding your rescue."

Her heart splintered under the weight of warmth. Not only was her father talking to her without reservation, but also he was revealing things about Cullen that confirmed what she'd known from the first time he'd held her.

"How do you know all that?"

"I don't know much. I only know how the system works. And I know Cullen. He'll sacrifice what he has with the army reserves to protect the people who make his company possible."

And that was the very thing that would drive him away from her. Losing something like that. His honor along with it. She turned to stare at the fireplace. "Roaring Creek isn't enough of an adrenaline rush for him."

"It wasn't for me, either," Noah said from beside her. "But now I'm an old man and I know what a stupid mistake it was believing that."

"I just spoke with my secretary," another voice interrupted.

Sabine looked up to her right, where Cullen stood at the end of the couch. His face was dark with anger. How much had he heard of her conversation with Noah?

"Odie was able to ID the men in the photo from Samuel's field book." He looked directly at Sabine through a heavy pause. "One is Casey Lowe, a supply helicopter pilot Aden hired. The other is a Polish gems dealer who frequently buys smuggled emeralds in Peshawar and sells them to a Colombian miner, who passes them off as his."

Sabine stood and approached Cullen. "Then what are we still doing here? We have to go see Aden, and this time make him tell the truth."

Cullen put his hands on her arms, stopping her from passing him. "I'll take care of Aden. You'll stay where I think you'll be safest."

She sent him a warning look he wouldn't miss. If he thought he could just tuck her away somewhere... "And where might that be?"

"With me."

After boldly landing the helicopter in a hotel parking lot in south Denver, Noah's pilot waited for Sabine and Cullen to get far enough away before lifting off and flying back toward the mountains. Cullen carried his rucksack and her duffel bag and, beneath stares from everyone who saw the helicopter land and take off, led her to a bus stop not far from there. On the bus, Cullen forced her into the window seat of the first row. The whispers began. A young woman in her early twenties moved up the aisle and extended a notebook to Sabine.

"Can I have your autograph?"

Sabine smiled at her and took the pen she offered along with the notebook. She scrawled her name, then handed it back. The young woman didn't take them from her.

"Can I have yours, too?" she asked, looking at Cullen with unbridled awe.

Cullen took the notebook and pen from Sabine and thrust it toward the young woman without signing. She timidly took it from him and turned away. Sabine signed two more autographs but no one else asked Cullen for his. The look on his face was enough of a warning.

Cullen pulled her out of the seat at the next stop. They walked down 14th Street in downtown Denver and stopped close to the performing arts center. He was looking at a tall building to his left.

"Why are we here?" she asked, since he wasn't going to volunteer the information.

"Aden lives in that building. Brooks Tower."

She looked at the building, the upper floors visible from here. "Are we going to see him now?"

"Not yet."

Cullen took her hand and tugged her across the street. A doorman opened the door of Hotel Teatro, and Sabine found herself inside an old luxury hotel. Straight ahead, the lobby stretched to two elevators. Through a wide doorway to the left, Cullen led her to the front desk. He paid for a room, ignoring the attendant's curious looks at both of them. The man said nothing and gave them a card key.

Sabine stepped into the elevator ahead of Cullen, the door closing on a view of two bellmen's smiling faces. Following Cullen out of the elevator, she stopped with him at a room door. She entered ahead of him, pausing in the narrow hallway to admire the spacious bathroom with large square tiles and a rain-style showerhead. Moving the rest of the way down the hall, she emerged into the bedroom. To her right, a dark wood desk separated an armoire and entertainment center. The room wasn't big, but it was elegant. To her left, a single bed was centered on the opposite wall. King-size—but there was only one bed.

She sent an accusatory look at Cullen. He ignored her, dropping his rucksack on the bed and removing a pair of binoculars.

"There's only one bed," she said.

He went to the window with the binoculars. "It was all they had left on this side of the building." He drew the heavy curtains open and lifted the binoculars.

"We aren't sharing a bed," she said.

"I'm not sleeping on the floor."

Her heart skittered faster. "Well, neither am I."

He lowered the binoculars and twisted to look at her. "Then we'll sleep on the same bed."

Despite her trepidation, a responding flutter tickled her. Needing a diversion, she kicked off her shoes and opened the entertainment center doors to turn on the television.

For the next three hours Cullen studied Brooks Tower, spying on what she had to assume was Aden's condo. Sabine found a movie to pass the time and was halfway through a second when he finally put the binoculars down and looked to where she leaned against the pillows on the bed. She lost interest in the movie. He seemed more relaxed now.

"Are you hungry?" he asked.

For you, she thought.

His eyes began to smolder in response to what he must see in her expression.

"Yes," she said.

She watched him control his rising interest. "I know a good seafood place near here."

"Good idea." She climbed off the bed. They needed to get out of this hotel room.

A short walk to Larimer Street brought them to Del Mar Crab House. Sabine followed Cullen down wide stairs. A smiling hostess—who didn't recognize them—seated them at a table near the bar. It wasn't very crowded at almost nine-thirty. Sabine looked around at the tables. A family of four sat at a table two down from them, and a couple sat across the aisle. There were two people sitting at the bar and three other tables occupied by small groups of people.

Sabine took in the brick walls with pictures. The restaurant was open and rectangular, like so many of the older buildings in downtown Denver. It smelled like seafood. Facing forward again, she noticed a candle in a glass container, glowing between her and Cullen. He watched her as he sipped his water. Being watched by him was an erotic experience. She leaned back and enjoyed the slow burn that took over his eyes. But only for a moment. Where would this lead if she allowed it to continue? With no small effort, she reined in the pleasure of his sultry appreciation.

"Be careful. Roaring Creek might start to look appealing to you," she teased.

"It already does."

He had to mean something other than what she'd like to think. "You'd climb the walls with nothing to do."

"I can think of one thing I'd like to do."

She half laughed, too nervous to trust him. "What? Fish?"

He didn't answer, not verbally anyway. His eyes said it all.

A spark of awareness rushed through her. She struggled to cover it. "If only you were a permanent resident."

That worked to cool his ardor well enough. She felt him withdraw. It also reminded her that he didn't belong in Roaring Creek. She pretended to look around the restaurant, willing the sting of his subtle rejection down to a manageable level. His reaction proved he was the wrong man for her. How much more did she need to keep her distance? If only it were that easy.

The sound of a news program filtered into her musings. She turned to a television above the bar.

"More information has surfaced about the man who daringly rescued Sabine O'Clery from her captors in Afghanistan," the newswoman said, a big smile bursting onto her face. "This hero is one to remember. Although the army has repeatedly denied any claim McQueen was once a Delta Force soldier, fellow Ranger Anthony Timmons says otherwise."

The screen switched to a ruthlessly short-haired black man. "It was years ago, but he was my platoon leader. I remember him because he was a scary dude. Big and serious and good at everything he did. Got promoted to captain about the time he applied for Special Forces. Lost track of him after that. He just sort of, you know...disappeared."

"Disappeared?" the reporter interviewing him repeated.

"Yeah. Nobody knew where he went or what he was doing. I kept sayin' he joined Delta, but nobody'd believe me." He laughed. "Now he shows up on the news and people aren't in such a hurry to call me a liar. I didn't know he joined the reserves, but it makes sense, since he runs his own Ops company now."

"You know it's an Ops company? Do you mean Special Operations?" the reporter asked.

The camera changed to a view of both men. "I don't know it for fact, but with McQueen's background it don't take much of a stretch. That company is probably blacker than anybody will ever know...."

The interview ended and the newswoman's beaming face filled the screen again.

That's when the murmurs gathered momentum around them. The woman sitting with a man across the aisle from them said, "Oh my God, it's them. They're *here!*"

"Mommy, look," came from another table.

Watching Cullen's reaction, Sabine's heart broke for him. His livelihood was crumbling and there was nothing she could say or do to stop it. When she realized she wanted to, feelings warred inside her. How could she have ever thought of him as a mercenary? She could barely think of her father that way anymore. The truth frightened her because it tore down defenses when she needed them most.

Cullen stood, dropping several bills onto the table. "Let's go."

Sabine didn't protest. Nearly every eye in the restaurant was lasered on them.

Jogging to keep up with him, she braced herself for his stormy mood. His boots thudded on the sidewalk with each of his long strides. He didn't look at her once on the short walk back to their hotel. There, the doorman smiled and opened the door for them. She was grateful that he didn't say anything, if he'd recognized them. They rode the elevator alone.

It dinged on their floor and the doors slid open. Cullen preceded her into the hall. At the door to their room, he opened it and went in before her, going to stand in front of the window. Across the street and in the distance, the Brooks Tower loomed.

She felt so bad for him. "Cullen—"

"I'd rather not talk right now, Sabine," he interrupted, without turning.

Recognizing his need to be alone, she went into the bathroom to take a long shower. Knowing the truth about him had stripped away her defenses. Whatever his company did outside the army reserves, it was for the right cause. He was a hero through and through. How could she find the strength to stop feeling so much for him? She wanted him now more than ever. If only she believed she could have him. If only she believed he'd want her the same way.

Chapter 11

Cullen unfolded his body and stood up from the chair, irritated with his inability to ignore Sabine. She looked sweet and sexy in her nightgown as she warily made her way to the bed, smelling fresh from her shower. He picked up his ringing cell phone from the desk.

"Yeah."

"What are you doing to yourself, Cullen?" Odelia Frank said.

She must have seen the news and all it had revealed.

"Lining myself up for a career change," he joked with a bitter bite to his tone. "Did I forget to mention that? I'm sorry."

"You're going to lose everything over this. You do know that, don't you?"

"I had a feeling."

"What are you going to do?"

"They're hanging me by my balls, Odie. What do you expect me to do?"

All he heard was Odelia's breathing for a moment. "I don't understand you, Cullen. It's so unlike you to allow something like this to happen."

Cullen twisted his body to look at the reason he was in this situation. Sabine lay in bed, her eyes open and watching him, so beautiful that it gave his heart a warm pulse. "I'll just have to find a way to fix it."

There was a long silence on the line. "Since you're still in denial, let me spell it out for you. Without anonymity, SCS is finished. Like the bottom of a dry martini. All right? You can't run a company like this one as a celebrity."

The sourness in his stomach started an ache. Odelia was right. He couldn't run the kind of covert missions he ran and expect them to stay that way with the media following him everywhere. Even years from now, he'd risk the possibility of someone recognizing him at the wrong time. The senator, the two generals at the Pentagon and the colonel at U.S. Army Special Operations Command who made his company possible would all turn their backs without so much as a see-you-later. Contacting Cullen would be too risky. Even if he were able to protect their identities, he'd have no guarantee any of them would be willing to step forward and support a new company.

"What are you going to do?" Odelia asked again.

He couldn't imagine a life without the army or his company. Complete disconnection from Special Forces.

"I don't know. But don't worry, I'll make sure you're taken care of no matter what happens. You've been a critical part of the team, Odie. I wouldn't leave you out in the street."

"Don't get wishy-washy with me, Cullen. I can take care of myself."

He smiled a little, looking at Sabine again. Her thick red

hair was spread out on the pillow, and her green eyes still watched him. Holding the blankets up to her chin, sexy as all get-out. Despite everything, he still wanted her. More than before, probably.

Sabine propped herself up on her elbows while she listened to his side of the conversation, her breasts perky and free beneath the nightgown.

"Just a couple more things and you can get back to ruining your life with your future bride," Odie said.

"She's not my—"

"I got copies of Aden's bank statements," she said, cutting him off. "There were some peculiar, regular cash deposits."

"Yeah? What do you make of it?"

"The transactions aren't large enough to make it worth his while smuggling emeralds on his own, but maybe he was helping Isma'il in some way. Like providing the use of a mule."

"Lowe?"

"None other. He could have flown the gems into Peshawar for Aden, who could have paid him to make the trips. He always withdrew a lot of cash before his trips to Afghanistan."

"Except Lowe got greedy and stole a pricey bundle of emeralds for himself."

"Aden had to be in on it. And neither of them thought Isma'il would kidnap Samuel and Sabine, which explains why there was no communication from Isma'il. At least, not overtly. But he must have gotten a message to Aden."

"Who ignored it."

"Of course. They don't care about the contractors. Samuel was onto them. Sabine is with Samuel, so they assume she knows as much as he does."

"Or that Isma'il revealed his reason for kidnapping them

during their captivity. To demand Aden give him back the emeralds."

"Either way."

"So Aden and Lowe wanted Isma'il to kill them."

Sabine's eyes drooped with sadness with his comment. He wished he could spare her this.

"And when you rescued Sabine, Lowe was ready with low-budget mercs."

"Compliments of Noah's secretary."

"Right."

"There has to be more. Nobody in the States is after Aden or Lowe. There's no evidence Aden got his share of the money from the emeralds, either. What are they so afraid of?"

"I'm working on that."

"You're an amazing woman, Odie. Have I told you how much I love you?"

"You're full of it, McQueen. Why do I put up with your ass?"

Cullen chuckled, catching the way Sabine watched him now. She was wary of the way he talked to Odie. "Because I put up with yours." He winked at Sabine.

Odie laughed while Sabine's lips curved with the hint of a smile. "At least you haven't lost your sense of humor."

"Ha, ha, ha."

"One more thing."

"Yeah?"

"Noah's secretary was killed in a car accident. Car went off the side of a mountain. There was a blurb on the news. Maybe you missed it."

"Car accident, huh?" He had missed the news on that. He'd been too wrapped up in his own downward-spiraling world.

"That's what they said."

"Call me when you find Lowe. I'd like to meet the man." He already knew where to find Aden, and now he couldn't wait for the encounter.

"You got it."

He ended the call and sat on the edge of the bed to remove his shoes.

"Who was that?" Sabine asked from behind him.

"My secretary."

"Oh," she exaggerated the word. "The J-3 captain, expert markswoman secretary."

He stood and faced her, liking the way she looked lying there all soft and warm. "She's good at her job. I'd trust her with anything. Including my life."

"So would I, as long as I don't have to fight her for you."

Heat dropped low in his abdomen. Was she doing that on purpose? Flirting with him again, like she had at the restaurant? He looked at her while he removed his clothes down to his underwear. The way she watched, the way her gaze roved over his body and then stayed on his face, moved him in a way that should scare him. Instead, he crawled onto the bed, caging her on his hands and knees. Her eyes widened as he took in her face.

"You don't have to fight anyone for me," he said.

She blinked once. Her lips parted slightly and her breasts elevated with a deeper breath. He bent his elbows to bring his mouth closer to hers, staring into her eyes while an inner struggle took place in his head. If he kissed her, he might not be able to stop. If he didn't stop, what then?

He'd lose himself in her. He'd fall in love with her. And not a comfortable love. With her it would be intense. Deep. Life altering.

The cold shock of fear swept him. He jerked back from her mouth. Then rolled onto his back and stared at the ceiling.

* * *

A sound woke Sabine. Opening her eyes to a dimly lit room, she remembered where she was. The light came from the bathroom down the hall, but movement in the room made her lift her head. She blinked the sleep from her eyes, some of her hair falling in front of one eye as she spotted Cullen standing at the foot of the bed. Glancing at the clock, she saw only two hours had passed since they'd gone to bed.

She brushed the hair out of her face as she watched him load his pistol with a metallic click, anxiety bringing her fully awake. Dressed all in black, he looked much as he had the night she'd found him in her bookstore, which did something hot to her insides. The only thing missing was a mask.

Where was he going at such an hour, and what was he planning to do?

His eyes raised. Combat mode again.

Though the news report yesterday had painted him nothing less than an American hero, he looked dangerous right now.

"Where are you going?" she asked.

He shoved the gun in a holster against his left rib cage without answering.

Pushing the covers back, she crawled to the edge of the bed and sat on her folded legs. He picked up a hooded sweatshirt that zipped up the front and shrugged into it. When he zipped it halfway up his chest to cover his gun, he looked almost normal. Except for his height and general menacing appearance in black.

"I want you to wait here," he said.

He started to turn, but she rose up onto her knees and stopped him by gripping his sweatshirt.

Facing her, letting her pull him closer, his lower legs came against the mattress and his gray eyes found hers.

"What if something happens to you?" Realizing she

sounded like a worried lover, she lowered her eyes. What was the matter with her? He knew what he was doing. He got her out of Afghanistan. What made her think he couldn't handle downtown Denver?

He bent his head until she was forced to look at him. His eyes were soft above an unsmiling face. His gaze moved to her nightgown. She could feel him warming further, which disconcerted her because it warmed her, too. How close he'd come to kissing her enveloped her.

"Don't worry about me."

Trying to get a grip on herself, she released his sweat-shirt. But she couldn't resist touching him, so she flattened her hands on his black top between the partially open zipper of the sweatshirt. As his chest muscles flexed underneath, heat flowed more freely in her.

"What are you going to do?" she asked.

He didn't answer. Instead he raised his hand and slid his fingers into her hair and around the back of her head. She stared up at him, into the burn of his eyes. His mouth came down. Pressed hard against hers. His other hand slid over her rear for a kneading caress that pulled her against him while he kissed her long and deep.

Too soon, he withdrew and stepped back. "Don't try to follow me."

At the threshold of the hallway, he looked back at her. "There's a gun on the nightstand. It's loaded. Use it if anyone other than me comes into this room. Don't open the door for anyone."

The door shut with a solid thud, and Sabine collapsed onto her back on the bed. She stretched her body, arms above her head, humming with desire, wishing he was back in the room. On top of her. Inside her.

Sabine was sick of looking out the window at Brooks Tower. Every once in a while, a car passed on the street below. Lights glimmered from buildings. She bit her thumbnail. What was taking him so long? What was he doing? She didn't like imagining him hurting Aden, but she suspected that's where he'd gone.

The sound of the door opening gave her a jolt. She scrambled for the gun on the nightstand and aimed it at the hallway. Heavy footfalls drew closer on the tile floor. Cullen's dark shape emerged, sending her heart skipping with more than relief. She lowered the gun and put it on the table beside the chair.

Cullen dropped a small duffel bag he hadn't had with him when he left and shrugged out of his sweatshirt. He unfastened his gun harness and put it on the desk. It sounded heavy. He moved toward her, his biceps and shoulders pronounced in the formfitting black top, his eyes on her like an urgent touch.

He stopped before her. "He told me everything."

"He stole emeralds with Lowe?" Somehow knowing it was true changed the way she felt. It was no longer speculation. Aden and Lowe had stolen emeralds, and that was why she and Samuel were kidnapped.

"Aden never wanted you and Samuel to get hurt. But he was most concerned about you. He warned Isma'il if anyone touched you, the gems would never be returned."

Was that why Samuel had been killed and not her? "But he never intended to give them back."

Cullen shook his head, his eyes still radiating warm intensity, with concern for how she'd take this news. "Lowe made that impossible. It was Lowe who put mercs in the helicopter that fired at us, and it was Lowe who had more waiting for us in Egypt. He forced Aden to use Envirotech's resources to make it all happen. He also knew Aden could keep him informed about the mission. Aden persuaded Noah's secretary to give him information because he had no other choice."

"But I thought… I thought Aden didn't want anyone hurt. Why did he help Lowe try to kill me? Why did he feel he was forced to do it?"

"Isma'il had a friend in Afghanistan's Ministry of Justice. Turns out that friend made some noise about wanting whoever stole three million in emeralds to pay for their crime. Aden was contracted by the U.S. government to help with the groundwater analyses in the Panjshir Valley. There was a Status-of-Forces Agreement in place, but it didn't protect nonmilitary personnel if a crime was committed. Aden and Lowe are both civilians. If the Ministry of Justice learns they were the ones who stole the gems, Isma'il's friend could demand their extradition to face trial and the United States would have to comply."

"Because of the agreement."

"Yes."

Facing trial in Afghanistan as an American was a horror not unlike the one she'd survived. Aden and Lowe had plenty of incentive to make sure that never happened. Even if smuggling emeralds wasn't a capital offense in Afghanistan, the punishment could be severe.

"So when I start digging, Aden gets nervous and goes along with Lowe to kill me."

"Lowe saw the photo of you holding Samuel's field book. They looked for it near the borehole but never found it. Aden searched Samuel's things, but the field book wasn't there. He must have just missed the contractor who found it, and that contractor must have put it in the shipping box right after Aden searched it. Lowe sees you have it and hires an affordable gun to kill you. Aden is too afraid to interfere. He doesn't like the way Lowe operates, but he also doesn't want to face trial in Afghanistan. With all the press surrounding you, they had even more reason to worry about exposure. It wouldn't take much for Isma'il's friend to hear about who planned your kidnapping and why."

Was she supposed to sympathize with Aden? She found herself wishing they both had been caught. It was what they deserved. Because of them, Samuel had died a terrible death. It made her so angry. Aden may not have wanted anyone to get hurt, but people *had* gotten hurt. People had *died* because he'd helped Lowe do what he couldn't.

"Is he dead?" she asked.

"Who?"

"Aden. Did you kill him?" She knew she was being unreasonable, but the injustice of Samuel's death brought it out in her. For the first time since her abduction, she wanted to imagine someone being tortured. She wanted Aden and Lowe to suffer the way Samuel had.

"I didn't lay a hand on him," Cullen said in a gentle voice. And it reached through her angry emotions, showing her he understood her so well. He knew it was grief over Samuel that made her lash out like this. "I didn't have to. He wanted to tell me everything. I think he was glad to finally get it off his chest. It was almost as if he expected me to show up, to give him a reason to come clean. He never wanted Lowe to kill you, but neither did he want to face trial in Afghanistan, and Lowe threatened to turn him over to Isma'il's friend if he didn't help him."

She moved around him. At the table where she'd left the pistol, she picked it up. She handled the gun for a while, wondering if she had the nerve to go across the street and shoot Aden herself. Cullen put his hand around her wrist, stilling her.

"Killing him won't bring Samuel back," he said.

Slowly she looked up, struggling with a riot of emotions churning inside her. "Why didn't you kill him? Why didn't you kill a man who just stood aside and allowed a good man to be slowly and brutally tortured to death and others to die trying to save me?"

"He's not the one who deserves to die, Sabine."

But someone else was—she silently finished his unspoken thought. And he intended to hunt that man down. She nodded her understanding, satisfied that justice would be served. Samuel's death would be avenged.

Cullen moved to where he'd left the duffel bag. When he returned to stand in front of her, he handed it to her.

"What is this?"

"Open it."

She put it on the end of the bed and unzipped the top. Inside were several bundles of cash. Aden's share of the emeralds.

"Do whatever you want with it," Cullen said. "Burn it. Keep it. Do something Samuel would have liked with it. It doesn't matter. It's your decision."

She stared into the bag for a long time, but she already knew what she was going to do. She was going to give it to Lisandra. It wouldn't make anything right, but Samuel would have wanted to take care of his wife.

Late the next morning, Cullen put his finger to his lips when he opened the door to the room-service attendant. The graying dark-haired woman smiled and nodded. She eyed him as she carried a tray into the room. He wore only his jeans. Was she looking at his bare chest, or did she recognize him? He knew it was the latter when she saw Sabine sprawled sleeping on the king-size bed and her smile turned impish. Covered to her chin and curled on her side, Sabine looked rumpled and content beside the spot he'd vacated.

Setting the tray of fruit, omelets, toast and orange juice on the counter between the armoire and entertainment center, the woman faced Cullen with covert but obvious glances toward the bed. As though on cue, Sabine rolled onto her back with a moan. She sounded sexy as hell.

Clearing his throat, Cullen opened his wallet.

"You don't have to worry," the woman said. "No one will know you're here."

He paused in the act of pulling out two twenties to cover breakfast and a tip.

"The entire staff has strict orders not to say a word to anyone." She winked and looked at Sabine again, who had folded her arms over her head to enhance her appearance of a woman who was sleeping off a night of hot sex.

Cullen grinned and replaced the twenties with a hundred.

The woman thanked him profusely as she left.

Taking the tray to the end of the bed, he stopped and stared down at Sabine. Two things she loved since coming home from Afghanistan were food and sleep. He adored that about her. He had no idea why.

She made another sleepy sound as her eyes fluttered open and found him. It was all he could do to keep himself from crawling on top of her. She made it worse by rising onto her elbows, the blankets falling from her breasts and the strap of her nightgown slipping off one smooth shoulder.

"Good morning," he said.

She smiled sleepily up at him. "Same to you."

Did she know what she was doing to him? Cullen moved on his knees toward her. Sabine sat straighter, crossing and folding her legs as he placed the tray in front of her. He stretched onto his side beside her, bracing himself up by his elbow. He was very close to that bare shoulder.

Sabine lifted the carnation that someone had placed inside a small glass of water and brought it to her nose. Watching her smell the flower kept his interest stirred.

Lowering the flower, she turned her head toward him. He looked at her mouth.

"What are we going to do?" she asked, twirling the carnation in her fingers.

He could think of something, but that's not what she was asking. She wondered what they would do about Aden and his pilot. Taking the carnation from her fingers, he lifted it to her lips and used it to brush their soft fullness. "You're not doing anything."

Her lips parted and he saw the quickening of her pulse in her neck. Heard it in her breath. Then she wrapped her fingers around his. He let her take the carnation from him.

"Are you going to find Lowe?" she asked.

There went the mood. But it was just as well. He didn't want to give her false hope there was any kind of future for them. She couldn't do casual and he couldn't give her more. "Yes."

"And then what?"

He didn't answer, which for Sabine was the same as answering her question. She was getting to know him too well.

"You're going to kill him, aren't you."

He could see in her eyes that she didn't like the idea. Last night she was ready for blood, but today she was back to herself. While he couldn't blame her after what she'd endured in Afghanistan, it spurred his annoyance. Casey Lowe would kill her without a second thought. Sabine might think she could defend herself, but Cullen knew better.

"Lowe isn't going to get another chance to come after you, Sabine. I won't let him."

She didn't say anything, but he could tell he hadn't swayed her.

"I can't always be around to protect you."

That ignited green fire in her eyes. "No, you'll run away to your next mission and I'll be just an afterthought." She stabbed the carnation back into the glass of water and slid her legs over the side of the bed to stand. "God, I should have seen this a long time ago."

What did she mean, *run away?* He watched her stomp toward the bathroom, then propelled himself up off the bed to go after her.

"What do you want me to do? Let him get away with it?"

"No." She started to close the door.

He slapped a hand on it to stop her. "What do you want me to do?"

She met his eyes with the fiery energy of hers. "Can't you think of anything other than your missions? What's so frightening about having feelings for someone?"

"What?" Where had all this come from?

She moved forward, pressing her hands on his chest and giving him a shove. Perplexed, he let her back him against the wall.

"What are you so afraid of?" she whispered.

"I'm not afraid." He wished he knew what had her so riled.

She raised up onto her toes. Eyes alive with energy, she pressed her mouth to his. The shock of it stilled him. An instant later, it inflamed him.

He wrapped his arms around her, pulling her higher and tighter to him. Her tongue slid against his. He angled his head and took her deeper, cupping the back of her head with his hand. He felt every inch of her beautiful body against his.

All he'd have to do is turn and put her back against the wall, lift her nightgown and push his underwear down and he could assuage this maddening lust that wouldn't leave him alone. He could drive it out of his system. He started to do just that when she withdrew. She stepped back and he had no choice but to let her slip out of his arms.

"Do you want me?" she asked.

"Yes," he rasped.

"And then what?"

Realizing this was a continuation of their original dialogue, he scowled at her.

"You run off to your next mission," she said, answering her own question.

Because he was afraid. He got it now. He understood what she meant. He was afraid of the *then what*. Though it irritated him to be accused of that, he couldn't argue her point.

His cell phone started to ring, and he was glad to go answer it. He flicked on the television while he lifted his cell to his ear.

"You aren't going to believe this," Odie said.

He barely heard her. A breaking news report showed the front entrance of Brooks Tower, where police and emergency vehicles, lights flashing, were parked. A newswoman was in the middle of a sentence.

"…are no leads and no witnesses have come forth."

"Lowe is in Denver," Odie continued.

"Really." He said it sarcastically.

When Sabine got out of the shower, she realized she'd left her clothes in the other room. Wrapping a towel around her instead of putting the nightgown back on, she left the bathroom. It wouldn't take long to find something to wear. Just a minute or two. She tried not to think of Cullen's reaction to seeing her in only a towel, and ignored the lurking thought that maybe deep down she wanted him to see her like this. Her time in the shower had done little to cool what kissing him had brewed.

She emerged from the hall. Cullen held a pistol, pushing a clip into place. He wore jeans and nothing else. Those gray eyes lifted and saw her, then lowered to take a startled journey over the towel and everything it didn't cover. A fraction of a second later, heat wiped out any surprise.

She stopped halfway to her bag, her hand tightening on the towel as a flutter blossomed inside her. He stood as still as she did, his bare chest smooth over hard muscle, bent arms globing his biceps, holding the gun in his big hands. He reminded her of the way he was when he'd rescued her. Clearly her brain was muddled if she found the way he held a gun sexy.

He turned the safety on as she moved forward and came to a stop before him.

"Did something happen?" she asked.

"Lowe killed Aden after I left him last night."

That worked to dim the invisible chemistry flying between them. "How do you know?"

"Odie told me. And it was on the news."

"How did Lowe know you went to see Aden?"

"He must have seen me."

"Wouldn't you have noticed that?"

His mouth hitched up higher on one side. "I appreciate your confidence in me, but he's probably watching us from a building. I'm guessing The Curtis hotel. I'm waiting for a room number."

"How did Lowe know where to find us?" she asked.

"He didn't. But he knew we'd come to see Aden."

She looked toward the window where the drapes were drawn aside, not liking the idea of being watched. "Odie can get that room number for you?"

"If she can't, I will."

She turned back to him, wondering how long they'd be stuck in this room, alone. "What are we going to do?"

He paused. "Wait for Odie to call."

His hesitation and the warming embers in his gaze left

her no doubt he was thinking the same as her. They were alone, with nothing to do but wait.

He looked down where the towel left the tops of her breasts bare. She wished she hadn't kissed him. More than helping her make a point, it fueled an already smoking passion.

This morning he'd turned a carnation into a sex toy. The last tether of control was a weak one. She felt it hover between them. Felt him want to finish what she'd started. She held the towel with both hands, as though it would keep her from letting him.

Without moving his eyes away from her, he leaned to his side to put the gun on the only table in the room. His muscled chest flexed and relaxed as he straightened, biceps pressing against his sides. He moved toward her and didn't stop until he stood close. She felt her forearms brush his skin. A lovely shiver raced through her.

Lifting his hand, he slid his fingers into her wet hair at the back of her neck. She couldn't breathe as his head came closer.

"I can't stop this anymore," he said, soft and raspy.

The words melted through her, so mirroring the way she felt. He kissed her. She shuddered with need and strained to take more of him. Angling his head, he opened his mouth over hers. She gave him all of her.

He curved his arm around her waist, drawing her fully against him. She let go of the towel to put her hands on him, loving the contour of muscle as she ran them up his body to bring her arms around his neck. The tickle of his hair on her skin, the warm force of his mouth on hers, his tongue making love with hers, the smell of him, it all wrapped around her senses and obliterated everything else. He gripped the towel behind her and pulled. She heard it fall to the floor. Her bare breasts pressed against him.

He lifted her and she folded her legs around him, kissing his mouth. This was so much more intense than in Kárpathos.

"I want you too much," he said against her kisses, stepping toward the bed.

The words sent emotion soaring in her heart. She kissed him, a way of answering without saying out loud the truth of what she felt. He took over the kiss, slanting his mouth over hers, meeting her passion and urging her for more.

Her back came against the mattress. She watched him straighten and jerk at the button and zipper of his jeans, push them down his legs and kick them aside. All the while he looked at her, hungry anticipation ablaze.

He crawled over rumpled blankets and sheets until he was on top of her. The feel of his body on hers amplified her yearning to have him inside her. He lowered himself onto his elbows, his face close above hers, eyes beaming a growing message of love. Oh, to believe and trust what she saw....

"Cullen," she said, sighing his name before his mouth came down to hers. She wanted to say more but held back.

He kissed her with all the force of his passion. And she met it with her own, telling him that way.

"Too much." He sounded breathless. She exulted in his confession, knowing he felt something deep, that it matched what she felt.

Trailing his lips from her mouth, he kissed her chin, her neck. His hands slid from her shoulders to her breasts. He kissed his way down, took a nipple into his mouth, then the other. His hands sank into the wet strands of her hair on the pillow. His breathing warmed her skin as he planted gentle, wet kisses along the slope of her breast, her ribs, her stomach. Then he reversed the journey, a silent reverence of unspoken love.

He moved up from her stomach and held himself over

her. Those strong arms bent to bring his mouth to hers. She craved kissing him. Running her hands over his warm skin, she caressed the hardness of his muscled chest and abdomen, sliding around his trim waist to his smooth back. She kissed his cheek and chin, finding her way back to his mouth, sharing the salty taste with him.

He lifted away with a coarse breath and found her eyes with his. She died a tiny death as he slid into her. He pulled back for another wet, tight slide. She sought his mouth and he gave her another soul-moving kiss, pushing deep.

A shiver of building heat made her whisper his name again. It drew a ragged exhale from him. He kissed her hard and quick before he drove into her with more urgency. An insatiable ache gave way to spectacular sensation that spread everywhere in her body. Sabine heard her own guttural yell.

Cullen collapsed on top of her, his head resting beside hers. She trailed her hands down his back, letting them lie on his waist while they both caught their breaths, never more at peace. Certain for the first time that no matter where this led, no matter what happened between them, she would never have any regrets.

Chapter 12

Sometime during the night Sabine woke to Cullen stirring. She moaned, remembering the afternoon they'd shared, most of it right here on this bed. Realizing he wasn't in bed with her anymore, she lifted her head and blinked her vision clear. Through the darkness she watched him shove his pistol into the holster strapped to him. He was dressed in black again. Alarm jarred her fully awake.

She sat up on the bed. "Cullen?"

He looked at her in that way of his. The soldier going out for a kill.

"Where are you going?" Of course, she already knew. But after what had transpired between them, she didn't want him to go anywhere. What if something happened to him? What if he was killed?

"Stay here, Sabine," he said, his eyes willing her to heed him.

"Don't go," she said.

He turned and moved toward the hall.

"Cullen." She couldn't stay here imagining him killing a man. Methodically. Intentionally. Choosing that over her. His mission. This is what he did. No. Her heart wrenched with a painful lurch.

"Please." If he left without acknowledging the way she felt, he'd lose her. She wouldn't compromise herself after this. It was time to take action where he was concerned. He either had to show her how much she meant to him or let her go.

Stopping at the threshold of the hall, he put his hand on the wall and turned his head to look at her. Seconds passed and then he dropped his hand, turning to face her.

"Sabine..."

"Don't go, Cullen." She shook her head. "Not tonight."

Even as he sighed, his eyes softened. Then warmed as he took in the sight of her naked above the blankets. He strode slowly to the side of the bed. Leaning over, he braced his hands on the mattress and brought his face close to hers.

"I have to do this," he said. "Odie called. I know where to find Lowe now. I have to go before I lose the chance."

She curled her fingers around the strap of his holster. "Don't, Cullen. If I matter to you at all, don't go."

His mouth formed a hard line with the pitch of his brow. "What do you want me to do? Let him live so he can come after you again?"

"This has nothing to do with Lowe. This has to do with you and me."

Cullen lifted his hand and cupped the side of her face. "I have to end it, Sabine."

She put her hand over his. "Not like this." Didn't he see? He would have sneaked out into the night without telling her where he was going. When he was on a mission, he tried too hard to shut her out of his mind. Well, this time she wouldn't let him. She wanted him to acknowledge his feelings for her—and hers for him. Just once.

As he stared at her, she could see him beginning to waver.

"Don't leave." She turned her face to kiss his palm. "Don't leave me."

A heavy breath sighed out of him, and he knelt on the bed beside her. Taking her face in both hands, he kissed her. Sabine felt his heart in the way he moved his mouth over hers.

Stretching out beside her, he pulled her close and did as she asked. He stayed.

She slept. Content and warm. In the morning she woke to something hard digging into her ribs. She opened her eyes. Her hand rested on the rough material of Cullen's black top. The hard object was his gun. Raising her head, she saw that his eyes were still closed. His arm was around her, his hand over her hip. Her leg was between his.

He stayed.

Sabine studied his face while the meaning of that soaked through her, drenching her heart with love. His long dark lashes lay beneath his eyes and stubble colored his skin. His lips were soft with sleep.

She'd asked him to stay and he had. He'd chosen her over his mission.

She moved up and pressed her lips to his. Breath from his nose warmed her skin. His arm around her tightened. She rolled on top of him to avoid his gun. Straddling his hips, she smiled at the heat that grew in his sleepy eyes as he woke.

Leaning over, she kissed him. His hand came to the back of her head and held her there. She pulled back and crawled down his body. She kissed his stomach through his clothes then boldly kissed the hard bulge in his pants, taking her time there, dragging her tongue over the material that blocked her from him. She raised her eyes and saw that he'd lifted his head off the pillow to watch her. His features were fierce with desire.

She smiled at him and climbed off the bed.

"Where are you going?" he asked gruffly.

She laughed lightly. "I want to go shopping."

He sat up on the bed, quick as a big cat, and took her wrist. "Later."

Hooking her with his arm, he pulled her onto her back and rolled on top of her. He rose up on his knees and shrugged out of his gun holster. It thudded on the floor.

Sabine reached up and grabbed the black material of his shirt, pulling him down to her. He kissed her, smoothing her hair back from her face.

"See what you do to me," he rasped.

"Yes." She smiled against his mouth.

He chuckled, deeply and manly, vibrating against her stomach and chest. His laughter faded as he shifted his hips, the black material of his pants brushing against her bareness. She reached between their bodies and tugged at the button. It loosened while she looked up at him, into gray eyes full of an emotion she knew he wasn't ready to name. His breath rushed out and he took over the task, yanking his pants down over his hips. He kissed her and found her at the same time, every hard inch shoving into her wetness.

Sabine ran her hands over the black material of his shirt, reveling in the feel of hard muscle underneath. She continued over his shoulders and down to his chest. All the while he moved inside her, hard but slow. She closed her teeth over the muscle of his forearm through the material of his shirt as an incredible celebration of love burst between them.

Sabine walked beside Cullen on their way to dinner, worried by his mood. He seemed disturbed. While emotion burgeoned inside her, pushing to come out in words she longed to say, a wall seemed to be growing inside him. He'd chosen her over his mission, but he wasn't ready to call what they made together love. They'd spent the morning in bed and the afternoon shopping. No mention of Casey Lowe had been made, though Cullen carried his gun with him, hidden in his boot.

Passing the Paramount Cafe, Sabine heard '80s music and stopped to listen. People sat on a patio, in front of the old stone architecture of what once was the Paramount Theatre.

Cullen took her hand and led her to a table, and they ordered a light dinner. The old charm of the building relaxed her. After their dishes were cleared away and Cullen paid, he pushed back his chair and stood. Extending his hand, he said, "Let's go back to the hotel."

She knew what he'd do once he got there. Prepare to find Lowe. She couldn't explain her disappointment. Maybe somewhere deep inside she knew once he killed Lowe, his mission would be over, and so would they. Even after what they shared.

"I need to find a bathroom first," she said. The hotel was a long walk, and she didn't think she could wait.

He let her go. Down a hallway of terrazzo tile, she found a bathroom and went inside. She relieved herself, then bent over the sink after washing her hands to splash cool water on her face. Shutting off the water, she dried her face and hands and left the bathroom.

As soon as she entered the dim hall, she saw a flash of metal before something hard slammed against her head. Then everything went black.

Cullen stood near the edge of the patio where several people talked and laughed over dinner. The feelings swimming around in him made him edgy. He was so lost in Sabine he wondered if he'd ever be able to think coherently again. The media had destroyed his company and may have cost him his career with the army. His life was in chaos. Yet, all he could think about was her.

How had he come to feel so much for her? He didn't want to love her. Or was it too late?

Cullen felt the shock of the thought ripple through him. Did he love her? The intensity of their lovemaking said a lot to that end. Panic rushed him. No. He didn't love her. Not like that. He couldn't. He checked his watch as he paced in front of the building. What was taking her so long?

Suddenly, he froze. Jerking his head toward the building, he looked at the door Sabine had entered.

"No." He ran inside.

He searched for her but couldn't find her in the crowd. He hurried down a hall that was disturbingly dim and pushed the door to the women's restroom open. All the stalls were empty. No one was in the bathroom.

His heart slammed in his chest and his breathing grew erratic.

Back in the hall, he looked for another exit and found a door. Pushing through, he found himself in an alley. It was empty of people.

"Oh, God," he panted, running the opposite direction of 16th Street until he emerged in a parking lot.

Where had Lowe taken her? Cullen could only guess. He'd been so besotted with her, so caught up with the way she made him feel that he'd forgotten the danger.

Pulling his gun from his boot, his hands trembled as he flipped off the safety. This was like no other mission he'd experienced. He was scared. Really scared. Sabine…

What if she was already dead? He felt sick with the possibility. Lowe had no reason to wait to kill her.

"I can't lose her." His mind became a kaleidoscope of

dread. If she died, it would kill him. Never before had he felt closer to knowing the agony that had destroyed his father.

Think.

The money. Maybe Lowe wouldn't kill her until he got Aden's share of the money. He clung to that thought as he ran to The Curtis. A car screeched around the corner behind him. When it passed, he spotted the driver. Blond hair.

Cullen started looking for a car to use.

Sabine drifted out of unconsciousness and opened her eyes to darkness. The sound of tires over a dirt road told her she was in a car. In the trunk of a car, suffocating and eerily familiar. Instantly she was back in Afghanistan. In her dark cell. Alone. Waiting to die.

Her heart pounded so hard she felt her pulse in her ears. Her frightened breaths surrounded her. Fear overwhelmed her, an otherworldly vapor that threatened to choke the strength out of her.

She squeezed her eyes shut. *Stop,* she ordered herself. *Stop it!* Fear would be her only adversary if she allowed it. She had a choice whether to give in to fear or not.

Opening her eyes, she tried to see around her. It was too dark. She felt with her hands for some kind of weapon. There was nothing in the trunk.

The car came to a halt. Her heart raced faster. It was okay if it raced. She needed it to race. It was the fear she had to control.

Sabine adjusted her legs and mentally prepared herself to attack as soon as the trunk opened. The engine turned off and she listened to the car door open and close. Footsteps grew closer. A key slid into the lock. Turned. The trunk began to open.

Sabine pushed upward with her back, sending the trunk springing the rest of the way open. Lowe raised the gun.

She registered his blond hair and glacial-blue eyes before she rammed her palm against his big nose. She recognized him from Samuel's picture.

Lowe stumbled back, holding his nose. Sabine jumped out of the trunk and ran. In the distance, cars moved along a busy street. Between that and her, an old farmhouse with dark windows stood perched on the bed of a truck, ready to be moved.

Lowe's gun exploded. He missed. She heard the bullet strike the ground far off its mark. She made it around to the other side of the truck before more bullets pinged against metal and wood. Peering around the back of the truck, she watched Lowe tread toward her. Looking up at the farmhouse on top of the truck, she spotted an open window. Climbing up onto the flatbed, seeing Lowe raise his gun and take aim, she hurried to pull herself over the windowsill.

She jerked as a bullet splintered the trim to her left, but she fell inside the house unharmed. Scrambling to her feet, she ran through a badly run-down bedroom, down a hall and into the front of the house. The front door was open a crack, but Lowe hadn't come inside yet. She heard something in the rear of the house. Her heart beat as fast as bird wings. She tried to quiet her breathing and looked for something to use as a weapon.

Cullen drove the Sebring he'd stolen onto a deserted road that connected to a busier one that led to Tower Road and Denver International Airport. By some miracle he'd managed to keep Lowe's car in sight. He'd gotten lucky, catching up to him after stealing the car.

Lowe had parked his car near an old farmhouse supported on the back of a truck. The trunk of the car was open, but there was no sign of Lowe. No sign of Sabine, either.

Cullen had to fight the dread electrifying his senses, force himself to remember he was trained for this.

Getting out of the Sebring, he ran toward Lowe's car. He searched his surroundings. Bare, flat ground. The house on a truck. Nothing moved. Lowe must have taken her into the farmhouse.

Holding his gun ready, he peered into the trunk. It was empty. Closing his eyes briefly, breathing through the light-headedness of relief that he hadn't found Sabine's body there, he moved toward the house.

Stay focused. Find Sabine. Kill Lowe.

At the front of the truck, behind the cab, he climbed onto the house's covered porch. The door was open a crack, and he could hear the sound of a struggle. He pushed the door open, aiming his weapon inside, wishing he had night-vision gear. Stepping inside, he moved to the end of the entry wall and carefully peered around it. In a badly maintained kitchen, Sabine swung a piece of floorboard trim at Lowe. Lowe blocked it and knocked it from her hands. It fell to the floor with a clatter. Cullen stepped into the open the same instant Lowe saw him. Instantly Lowe hooked his arm around Sabine's neck, hauling her against him and putting a pistol to her head. Sabine clawed at the arm that held her, her eyes seeing Cullen and staying on him with a silent plea.

Cullen's breath stopped and his heart felt near to doing the same. *Stay focused.*

He aimed for Lowe's head.

"Drop the gun or she's dead," Lowe said.

"Let her go."

Lowe shook his head, his eyes filling with anger. "I've about had it with you. Drop it now or I'll kill her."

Don't hesitate, Cullen told himself. *Shoot.* He wouldn't miss. He never missed. Not at this range.

"He wanted you to follow us here, Cullen," Sabine said.

Lowe gave her a jerk and tightened his hold. "Quiet!" To Cullen he repeated, "Drop the gun."

Sabine's warning dropped inside him. Lowe planned to lure him here to kill them both. Perhaps he thought he could eliminate everyone who could expose him to Isma'il's friend. He met Sabine's eyes. She nodded once, a subtle reassurance. Even frightened, her eyes beamed her will. She trusted him.

He returned his attention to his aim. It hadn't moved. Sabine closed her eyes and dropped her weight. Lowe started to adjust his hold on her. Cullen fired three times in rapid succession.

Lowe's body crumpled to the floor, his head hitting a dirty white cabinet door, lolling until it went still, a stream of blood trailing from three holes in his forehead. The gun thudded to rest a few feet from his hand.

Sabine crawled backward until she came against Cullen's calves. Flipping the safety on his gun, he stuffed it in his boot and bent to slip his arms under hers, pulling her to her feet. She turned and threw her arms around him. He held her, burying his face in her hair, smelling her, feeling her tremble despite her bravery. He closed his eyes to the sensation of her alive in his arms. Safe. Once and for all.

"You're safe now," he said, swallowing because his heart was still pounding from the fear that had ripped through him.

He felt her relax against him. Her breathing slowed.

"I thought I lost you," he confessed, because it was so overwhelmingly true.

She leaned back, eyes red and face moist from tears. He watched his meaning take hold in her eyes. "You didn't."

"Yeah, but I thought I did, I was so…so…" Afraid. It appalled him to know what losing her could do to him. Shred his soul. Incapacitate him. Reduce him to a shaking mess of a man.

"You didn't lose me," she insisted.

He never wanted to feel like this again.

Chapter 13

Watching the landscape pass by the window of Cullen's rental car, Sabine's head pounded and it felt as if there was a heavy fog in her head. She had a slight concussion from being struck on the head by Lowe. But that was easy to ignore with Cullen's silence on the ride home from Denver.

They'd had to stay and talk to the police. They were probably only free to go because of Cullen's connections. It had still taken a few hours. She was tired...but mostly because of Cullen.

Did he think she hadn't noticed how his fear had driven him to withdraw? He had a glimpse of what it would feel like to lose her, so now he'd remove himself from the possibility of it ever happening again. Maybe he didn't want her to know how his fear had weakened him. Maybe it made him feel like less of a man to know he was capable of feeling so much for another person. Part of her took heart that he did, in fact, feel that much for her, but mostly she was disappointed. And mad.

She knew what was going to happen as soon as they arrived at her bookstore. He was going to leave.

Ironic, that she'd placed so much significance on his choosing her over his mission when that had never been the thing that would keep them apart. Watching his father ruin his life to alcoholism over a woman had made an irreversible imprint in his subconscious. It seemed they had that in common, although she was closer to resolving things with her father than he with his. The thought caught her unguarded. Was she ready to forgive her father? Maybe not quite, but in time she might. He wasn't the way she remembered, and in her heart she knew he was sincere in his desire to know her.

Cullen drove to a stop behind her bookstore, and her nerves turned her stomach. This was it. Time for goodbye. She resigned herself to letting Cullen go. It was all or nothing for her. She wanted all of him or nothing.

He left the car running and neither of them moved for a while. They'd escaped the media for now. Not even Minivan Man was here yet.

Finally, Sabine opened the car door and got out, hearing him do the same. At the foot of the stairs leading to her office door, she faced him. He came to a stop before her, and all she could do was look at his face. She couldn't imagine never seeing him again.

Those gray eyes found hers and they stared at each other. She felt his struggle, the difficulty he was having saying goodbye. So she put her hands on his chest and rose onto the balls of her feet. She pressed her lips to his. His hands went to her waist.

"Sabine..."

She stopped him by moving her hand to place a finger

over his mouth. That mouth she loved kissing so much. "Don't," she said. Finding his eyes with hers, those gray eyes that were always so full of strength and vitality, she told him silently of her love. "Do what you need to do, Cullen. Don't worry about me. I'm where I belong." She forced herself to smile, seeing his wary look. "If it weren't for you, I wouldn't be here right now. I wouldn't be looking forward to opening my bookstore and living a quiet life in a town I love. I'm safe and I have you to thank for that. I've got my bookstore and I'm going to be happy." Someday, she thought.

He closed his eyes and rested his forehead against hers. "I'm so sorry."

"I'm not," she whispered. And she wasn't. This wasn't the same as her parents. Sabine wouldn't let Cullen keep reappearing in her life if he chose to turn away from his feelings. She also would never regret believing they had a chance, because it was true. They had a chance. Cullen was just blowing it.

A moment passed. Two. Then he stepped back.

Sabine willed the sadness that numbed her to a manageable level. He was leaving. Turning his back on her, on what he felt for her, and what she felt for him. The risk to his heart was too great for him.

This was the way it had to be. He had to go and she had to let him. She didn't want a man whose heart wasn't totally hers. He had to be sure of his choices. And she couldn't help him decide.

"Goodbye, Cullen," she said, feeling tears brim her eyes. She turned so he wouldn't see them and climbed the stairs, opening her back door.

"Sabine…"

She closed the door and leaned her forehead against it. This was it. Cullen was out of her life.

She heard the rental car drive away.

Oh, God. It tore her from the inside out to hear him leave. Despite her best efforts, more tears filled her eyes and a few spilled free.

Cullen sat at his desk with his fingers in his hair, leaning over a pad of paper full of his scribbles. His attempt at starting over with a new business strategy.

The phone rang. At least the number still hadn't gotten out to the press, so he knew it wasn't a reporter.

"McQueen." There was no point in hiding his identity.

"You have very powerful friends."

The shock of surprise rendered him mute for a second. "Commander Birch."

"As much as I hate to admit it, I have to agree with Colonel Roth."

Hope singed his nerves. Roth had gone to see his commander?

"I'm not stupid, McQueen. I know there's more to that company of yours than the press is going on about. I knew you were good, but I never would have guessed you were that good."

"I'm sure you didn't call just to tell me that." If Birch was trying to pry information out of him, it wasn't going to work. He was still willing to sacrifice the army reserves to protect those who helped make a company like SCS possible.

"Colonel Roth explained to me how valuable you were to the Special Forces community. He also explained he wasn't going to allow a discharge. The only kind of action I can take…is no action at all."

Cullen leaned back in his chair, exultation and relief and gratitude so great it thrilled him for a few seconds.

"So you're still a part of this group," Birch continued. "Your reserve status remains what it was. However, I do recommend you work in intelligence from now on, rather than Ops. But as Colonel Roth put it in no uncertain terms, the choice is yours."

"Done. I'll move over to intelligence."

Birch's silence told him he'd gained back a little ground with his commander.

"For what it's worth, I'm sorry I had to go behind your back."

"I don't ever want to hear you mention this again, McQueen. If you have to run a private company, make sure it stays private from now on. Is that clear?"

"Yes, sir." In his head he roared another *yes!* And ended the call.

He hadn't lost his position with the army. And from the looks of it, he had backing for a new company.

Sabine's face pushed his elation down. Reporters still hung around the building, hoping to get him to talk about her. But his answer was always the same.

Sorry, no comment.

Did you go somewhere to be alone with her?

Sorry, no comment.

Why was someone trying to kill her? Are Aden Archer's and Casey Lowe's deaths related to her kidnapping?

Sorry, no comment.

Are you two still having an affair? Did she call things off or did you?

No comment, no comment.

Are you going to marry her?

That one always tripped him up.

All he had to do was recall how he'd felt after discovering Sabine missing, and it drove away any doubt he harbored over leaving her. He truly, absolutely, never wanted to feel like that again. He'd self-destruct.

It should be so clear to him. Get his company back on its

feet. Move on. He could regroup. Start over. All he needed was a new plan.

"You look like hell."

Cullen slid his hand from his hair and looked up at Odie. She looked smart in her oval, black-rimmed glasses and dull gray suit with her long, thick black hair piled in a sexy mess on top of her head—deceptive cover for the strength that lay beneath the shell of a powerful woman.

"Thanks. Glad to see you, too."

She humphed and moved into the office. "When are you going to admit defeat and get on with your life?"

"Right now. I'm going to sell the building and start another company somewhere else. Hire a few more operatives."

"In Roaring Creek?" Her dark eyes slanted at him skeptically.

Odie wasn't stupid and he resented her audacity. "I don't know where."

With a roll of her hips, she planted her rear on his desk, right on top of the documents he'd been studying. "Look at yourself, Cullen." She used her forefinger to flick his uncombed hair. "When's the last time you showered?"

"This morning," he said, meeting her indomitable gaze.

"You didn't go home last night."

"Oh, yeah." He nodded, caught in the lie. "Yesterday morning, then."

Every time he went home, he was suffocated by the emptiness that surrounded him. He couldn't believe he'd lived like that for so long. So alone and in such a sterile environment. He didn't even have any pictures of his family anywhere. Not that he wanted any of his dad.

"You're pathetic. You know that, don't you?"

"Just say what's on your mind, Odie." He leaned back in his chair and waited.

She didn't waste a beat. "It's painfully obvious you love her."

"No, I don't." He refused to believe it.

He didn't want to love a woman that much. It was precisely what he'd struggled to avoid all these years. That kind of love. The kind his father felt for his mother. The deepest kind. The kind a man could never walk away from. Even if death forced it upon him.

Odie's eyes narrowed in a shrewd study of him, then relaxed as she came to a conclusion. "You're running scared."

He felt his brow shoot low. "Now wait just a minute—"

"You're *afraid* to love her."

"I am not."

"You're scared to death, McQueen." She laughed with her realization. "That is so priceless. *You.* Afraid of a little ole thing like love."

Lifting her weight off the desk, she stood. "You know what? I'm going to do you a favor." She walked toward his office door with all the brass of a woman who could bring politicians to their knees.

What was she up to? When Odelia Frank started to use her brain, frightening things happened.

"What are you going to do." It wasn't a question. He'd seen her like this before. When she took down the barriers standing in her way of ferreting out terrorists.

"First—" she turned in the doorway "—I'm going to put a For Sale sign up." She turned her back and headed for the front door. "Then I'm going to give you a little...*push.*"

He looked out the window and inwardly kicked himself for not predicting this. A reporter sat in his car, a tan Malibu.

Cullen stood up from his chair so fast that it crashed to the floor. By the time he made it to the front door of SCS, Odie had a handwritten sign taped there and was sauntering toward the reporter.

Cullen shoved the door wider and approached. His steps slowed when he heard her talking.

"It's true he went somewhere to be alone with Sabine O'Clery," she was saying. "They stayed at Hotel Teatro in downtown Denver. Just the two of them...for days. They couldn't get enough of each other."

He hissed an expletive.

"Are they still having an affair?" The reporter wrote with a frenzy on his little notepad while the cameraman at his side filmed Odie's smug face.

"Oh, yeah. Things are steamier than ever between them. He just needs to tie up a few loose ends before he goes back to Roaring Creek."

"So, he's in love with her?"

Odie glanced at him with a wicked smile. "Why don't you ask *him* that."

The camera moved to Cullen and he froze on the sidewalk a few feet away.

The reporter and cameraman bustled closer to him.

"Are you in love with Sabine O'Clery, Mr. McQueen?" the reporter asked.

Envisioning millions of Americans watching this on the next newscast, the only face that really stood out was Sabine's. If he answered no, what would that say to her? If he answered yes, what would that mean for him?

The reporter smiled.

Cullen swallowed the dry lump in his throat.

Beside him, Odie smothered a giggle. She was enjoying the sight of his squirming on national television, that was for sure.

"Are you in love with the woman you rescued from Afghanistan, Mr. McQueen?"

All of a sudden it was so clear to him. Odie was right. He was scared and he'd run from something for the first time in his life. But running from Sabine wasn't going to save him the way his career had from the grief and anger he'd felt watching his father dwindle away and give up on everything. Cullen didn't want to run anymore. He wanted to take his greatest risk yet and go back to Sabine.

He looked right into the camera and said, "Yes."

"Yes."

Sabine's knees stopped supporting her. She plopped down onto her mother's couch, staring at the television with a slack jaw. Cullen had just said the word.

Yes.

He loved her. He looked terrified, but he *loved her.*

A smile flickered and died with her disbelief.

"Are you going to marry her?" the reporter asked.

Sabine watched Cullen say, "Yes. If she'll have me." And her heart melted all over itself. He sounded so certain. She put her hand over her gaping mouth.

"Oh, my Lord, *listen* to him," Mae said from behind her, incredulous. She sat down beside Sabine and together they watched Cullen pledge his love to Sabine O'Clery, the woman he'd rescued from Afghanistan.

"Did you fall in love when you were in Greece?"

Cullen looked dazed. "I didn't realize how much I love her until now."

"Now?"

"Yes. Now. Just a few minutes ago. Right now."

The reporter chuckled, clearly amused. "What about her? Does she feel the same about you?"

Cullen turned toward the camera. Sabine felt his unease. He didn't like the publicity but he was using the camera to communicate with her. The realization made her weak with love for him.

"That's exactly what I plan to find out," he said, turning.

* * *

Much later that day, Roaring Creek was teeming with media. Sabine paced inside her mother's cabin, biting her fingernails until there was nothing left.

She knew Cullen was in town, because a breaking news update showed him entering the building across from her bookstore, a fact the media exploited with relish.

"You should go down there," Mae said from beside her. "This town will never be able to rest until you tell him you love him."

Sabine looked at her mother, nervous and excited at the same time.

"Go," her mother urged. "He's expecting you." Stepping closer, she handed Sabine the keys to the Jeep and gave her a push toward the door.

Knowing there was no arguing with her, Sabine left and drove into town. The throng of media sent her heart skipping anew. It looked different on television. Much more intimidating in person.

She parked behind her bookstore and wormed her way through the crowd of people asking questions, all with big smiles on their faces, loving the hype of her romance with the man who'd saved her life. It would take too long to explain it was more than that to her. She'd fallen in love with more than a hero.

Locking the door, she went to the front of her bookstore and opened the blinds. Cullen stood outside his building, squinting his eyes in the sunlight, made brighter by the reflection off the fresh layer of snow that had fallen. The sight of him sent a wave of anticipation through her.

He stepped off the sidewalk and strode across the street. His long, powerful legs moved with heavy grace in a pair of faded blue jeans. His arms swung at his sides, corded muscle beneath the soft material of his black henley. His black hair waved in a slight breeze. He looked good. All man walking toward her. An American hero. And he was all hers.

Reporters scurried like cockroaches from the back of her bookstore to the front. They swarmed around Cullen, shoving microphones in front of his face. His sure strides never faltered. He looked straight ahead, a man on a mission. She couldn't hear the reporters' questions, but the sound of their voices traveled through the window.

Unlocking the front door, she pulled it open and felt a rush seeing him standing, flesh and bone, in front of her. His eyes were intense and began to smolder. Clicks from the cameras went off behind him.

She stepped back as he entered. He closed the door without taking his gaze off her.

"How are you?" Cullen asked, love in his eyes and voice.

She smiled in answer. "Fine."

"Yeah?" he said.

"Yeah." Were they really having this ridiculous conversation while a horde of reporters waited outside to learn whether Sabine was going to marry him or not?

"I'm sorry I left you the way I did," he said.

A reporter shot their picture through the glass.

"Are you going to move in across the street?" she asked.

He nodded and shifted on his feet, rolling from his heels to his toes. "For now."

His nervousness was uncharacteristic but endearing. They were getting close to The Question. "What are you going to do? I mean, for a living?"

"I thought I'd open a mountaineering shop."

"Across the street?"

"Yeah."

She wasn't fooled. "That would give you good cover." He could never remove himself from Special Ops completely. It was in his blood. "I mean, when all the publicity dies down."

He glanced back at the window to another camera-clicking flurry. When he faced forward, a slight grin creased the side of his mouth. "You think it'll die down?"

She laughed softly and he stepped closer. With one arm, he hooked her waist and pulled her against him. She didn't have to look to know the cameras were going wild on the other side of the window. She put her hands on his chest.

"Might as well make it worth their while," he said.

"Yeah?"

"Yeah." His husky voice made her heart pound faster.

He closed the space between their lips. She couldn't hear the camera pings but knew they were going off outside the window. Her ears were humming too much from the impassioned rate of her heartbeat.

He lifted his head and looked down at her.

"Let's go upstairs," she said.

"Does that mean you're going to marry me?"

"I'll marry you a thousand times."

He grinned wider than before. "Really? A thousand?"

"Ten thousand."

"In that case, wait here."

Stepping back, he turned to the door. Swinging it open, the click and ping of cameras went off again.

"She said yes!" he shouted, and the crowd cheered.

* * * * *

COMING NEXT MONTH from Harlequin®
Romantic Suspense
AVAILABLE AUGUST 21, 2012

#1719 THE COP'S MISSING CHILD
Karen Whiddon

Cop Mac Riordan thinks he's found the woman who might have stolen his baby. But will she also steal his heart?

#1720 COLTON DESTINY
The Coltons of Eden Falls
Justine Davis

When kidnappings of innocent young women bring FBI agent Emma Colton home, she never intends to end up longing for Caleb Troyer and his peaceful Amish life.

#1721 SURGEON SHEIK'S RESCUE
Sahara Kings
Loreth Anne White

A dark, scarred sheik hiding in a haunted monastery is brought to life by a feisty young reporter come to expose him.

#1722 HIDING HIS WITNESS
C.J. Miller

On the run from a dangerous criminal, Carey Smith witnesses an attempted murder. But she can't run from the handsome detective determined to keep her safe.

REQUEST YOUR FREE BOOKS!
2 FREE NOVELS PLUS 2 FREE GIFTS!

ROMANTIC

SUSPENSE

Sparked by Danger, Fueled by Passion.

YES! Please send me 2 FREE Harlequin® Romantic Suspense novels and my 2 FREE gifts (gifts are worth about $10). After receiving them, if I don't wish to receive any more books, I can return the shipping statement marked "cancel." If I don't cancel, I will receive 4 brand-new novels every month and be billed just $4.49 per book in the U.S. or $5.24 per book in Canada. That's a saving of at least 14% off the cover price! It's quite a bargain! Shipping and handling is just 50¢ per book in the U.S. and 75¢ per book in Canada.* I understand that accepting the 2 free books and gifts places me under no obligation to buy anything. I can always return a shipment and cancel at any time. Even if I never buy another book, the two free books and gifts are mine to keep forever.

240/340 HDN FEFR

Name	(PLEASE PRINT)	
Address		Apt. #
City	State/Prov.	Zip/Postal Code

Signature (if under 18, a parent or guardian must sign)

Mail to the **Reader Service:**

IN U.S.A.: P.O. Box 1867, Buffalo, NY 14240-1867
IN CANADA: P.O. Box 609, Fort Erie, Ontario L2A 5X3

Not valid for current subscribers to Harlequin Romantic Suspense books.

Want to try two free books from another line?
Call 1-800-873-8635 or visit www.ReaderService.com.

* Terms and prices subject to change without notice. Prices do not include applicable taxes. Sales tax applicable in N.Y. Canadian residents will be charged applicable taxes. Offer not valid in Quebec. This offer is limited to one order per household. All orders subject to credit approval. Credit or debit balances in a customer's account(s) may be offset by any other outstanding balance owed by or to the customer. Please allow 4 to 6 weeks for delivery. Offer available while quantities last.

Your Privacy—The Reader Service is committed to protecting your privacy. Our Privacy Policy is available online at www.ReaderService.com or upon request from the Reader Service.

We make a portion of our mailing list available to reputable third parties that offer products we believe may interest you. If you prefer that we not exchange your name with third parties, or if you wish to clarify or modify your communication preferences, please visit us at www.ReaderService.com/consumerchoice or write to us at Reader Service Preference Service, P.O. Box 9062, Buffalo, NY 14269. Include your complete name and address.

HRS11B

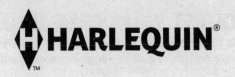

*In the newest continuity series from Harlequin®
Romantic Suspense, the worlds of the Coltons and their
Amish neighbors collide—with dramatic results.*

*Take a sneak peek at the first book, COLTON DESTINY
by Justine Davis, available September 2012.*

"**I**'m here to try and find your sister."

"I know this. But don't assume this will automatically ensure trust from all of us."

He was antagonizing her. Purposely.

Caleb realized it with a little jolt. While it was difficult for anyone in the community to turn to outsiders for help, they had all reluctantly agreed this was beyond their scope and that they would cooperate.

Including—in fact, especially—him.

"Then I will find these girls without your help," she said, sounding fierce.

Caleb appreciated her determination. He *wanted* that kind of determination in the search for Hannah. He attempted a fresh start.

"It is difficult for us—"

"What's difficult for me is to understand why anyone wouldn't pull out all the stops to save a child whose life could be in danger."

Caleb wasn't used to being interrupted. Annie would never have dreamed of it. But this woman was clearly nothing like his sweet, retiring Annie. She was sharp, forceful and very intense.

"I grew up just a couple of miles from here," she said. "And I always had the idea the Amish loved their kids just as we did."

"Of course we do."

"And yet you'll throw roadblocks in the way of the people best equipped to find your missing children?"

Caleb studied her for a long, silent moment. "You are very angry," he said.

"Of course I am."

"Anger is an...unproductive emotion."

She stared at him in turn then. "Oh, it can be very productive. Perhaps you could use a little."

"It is not our way."

"Is it your way to stand here and argue with me when your sister is among the missing?"

Caleb gave himself an internal shake. Despite her abrasiveness—well, when compared to Annie, anyway—he could not argue with her last point. And he wasn't at all sure why he'd found himself sparring with this woman. She was an Englishwoman, and what they said or did mattered nothing to him.

Except it had to matter now. For Hannah's sake.

*Don't miss any of the books in this exciting
new miniseries from Harlequin® Romantic Suspense,
starting in September 2012 and running
through December 2012.*